•••Tripletrap

Also by William H. Hallahan

The Dead of Winter

The Ross Forgery

The Search for Joseph Tully

Catch Me: Kill Me

Keeper of the Children

The Trade

The Monk

Foxcatcher

•••Tripletrap

William H. Hallahan

William Morrow and Company, Inc.
New York

●●●
You could always get
free cheese in a mousetrap.

—Brooklyn proverb

Copyright © 1989 by William H. Hallahan

Library of Congress Cataloging-in-Publication Data

Hallahan, William H.
    Tripletrap / William H. Hallahan.
       p.   cm.
    ISBN 0-688-08902-X
    I. Title. II. Title: Triple trap.
    PS3558.A378T75   1989
    813'.54—dc 19   88-36443
                                                                    CIP

Printed in the United States of America

First Edition

1 2 3 4 5 6 7 8 9 10

BOOK DESIGN BY WILLIAM McCARTHY

●●●Part One

••• Chapter 1

A t two-thirty that afternoon, as instructed, Charlie Brewer entered the maximum security screening theater of the Mally Center on Fourth Street, a few blocks north of the Library of Congress. It was empty.

He sat down in one of the theater seats and waited.

A few moments later, a colonel holding a small clipboard entered through a side door and walked up the aisle to Brewer's seat. He looked closely at the number on the plastic visitor's badge clipped to Brewer's lapel. Then he looked at a notation on the small clipboard. Then looked once more at the visitor's badge.

He cleared his throat and read a statement from the clipboard. "Everything you see and hear in this room is to be kept in the strictest confidence. The document you are about to receive is to be read in this room only and is to be returned to me at the end of this screening. Its contents are not to be revealed to anyone. May I proceed?"

Brewer nodded patiently.

The colonel handed him a sheaf of papers, 8½ by 14. "This is the script for the slide presentation you are about to see. Attached to it are several other documents which I will refer to in my presentation. I have been instructed to disclose to you the contents of a secret report given on December twelfth to the Technology Export Control Committee of the National Security Council. As you can see from the title page, the subject of this talk is the 'Unauthorized Acquisition of U.S. Technology by the Soviet Union.' It is for your eyes and ears alone. Please sign here."

When Brewer signed his name, the colonel walked to the podium, lowered the lights, and turned on a slide projector.

On the screen appeared a photograph of a submarine.

Colonel: "This is the new Soviet submarine Typhoon. Naval experts consider it to be the deadliest weapon ever conceived by the mind of man. It can dive deeper and run faster than any other submarine on earth. It is believed to be capable of outrunning our fastest torpedoes. It can settle on the bottom of the ocean for months on end, absolutely soundless, beyond reach of even our most sensitive detecting devices. It is equipped to fire over two hundred warheads at Western military targets and cities. It is a product of technological and engineering skills largely stolen from the United States. From stem to stern, if you removed the thousands of Western—mainly American—components and research developments, it would sink like a stone.

Slide: MiG-25 Foxbat.

Colonel: "This is the MiG-25 Foxbat. With an airspeed of 1,625 knots, it is one of the fastest—perhaps *the* fastest—military aircraft in the world. Reportedly, it has exceeded three times the speed of sound. From nose to tail it contains thousands of parts invented by, made in, and stolen from the U.S. It could almost literally be stamped Made in the USA."

The colonel pointed to the next slide on the screen. It showed Soviet troops raising a flag over the parapet of the Reichstag building in Berlin in May of 1945. Below them and beyond could be seen the ruins of the smashed city.

Colonel: "Berlin fell in May of 1945, and that ended World War Two in Europe. The armies of the Soviet Union seized vast areas of eastern Europe, most of which it still holds by main force today. It was one of the biggest land grabs in history."

Slide: The ruins of Leningrad.

Colonel: "Despite its seizure of many captive nations, the post-war Russian nation lay in ruins. Its industrial infrastructure was crippled. Its technology—what was left of it—was more than fifty years behind the United States."

Slide: Photographs of FBI arresting Soviet spy Dropov.

Colonel: "For more than forty years since then, to make up for critical gaps in its own technological establishment, the Soviet Union has been conducting an unremitting campaign to acquire American military technology by any and all means—legal, illegal, covert."

Slide: Customs authorities examining a truck at a border checkpoint.

Colonel: "During this forty-year period, the Soviet lag in technological development has become much greater—so enormous, in fact, the Soviet military installation now has had to resort to massive illegal acquisition of Western technology on a scale never before seen in history. Only in this way has it been able to maintain parity with the West. In fact, in a number of critical areas, as was just indicated, stolen U.S. technology has given the Soviets a dangerous advantage over the West."

Slide: Aerial view of Zeleenograd.

Colonel: "This is the Soviet's secret city of Zeleenograd. It is so important to the Russians, they have put land mines around the entire area, barbed wire and watch towers around the perimeter of the city, into which only the most carefully screened workers are admitted. To a greater extent than ever before, the Soviet government now rigorously pursues a formal, elaborate program for the illegal acquisition of Western technology. Much of its stolen technological apparatus is located in this city. That program is an official and vital element in the development and production of the military weapons and military systems of that country."

Slide: Photograph of Yuri Andropov.

Colonel: "It was Yuri Andropov himself, former head of the KGB and later Premier of the USSR, who formed Directorate T, a special division of the KGB, created specifically and solely for the purpose of stealing U.S. technology. He stocked the operation with some of the finest technological minds in Russia."

Slide: Photograph of Directorate T headquarters.

Colonel: "Directorate T has its own huge office complex just outside Moscow. In addition it maintains its own offices in Soviet compounds throughout the world. As we talk here, some twenty-two thousand Soviet intelligence people in Directorate T are busy illegally acquiring that technology from locations all over the world. Although it routinely gathers information on technological developments in the West, particularly the U.S.—much of it published in business and trade journals—the great

bulk of it is acquired by relentless spying. Please note I under-
line twenty-two thousand personnel in just Moscow alone."

Slide: Photograph of Kaline, convicted Soviet spy.

Colonel: "Hundreds of Soviet nationals have been caught
spying on Western countries. In addition, countless Western nationals have been suborned into spying for the Soviets. The Soviets regard spying and the acquisition of Western secrets as an
extension of its dedicated warfare against the West."

Slide: *Aviation Age* magazine.

Colonel: "The contents of *Aviation Age* magazine alone are
deemed so important by the Soviets, each copy is transmitted
page by page by electronic scanner to Moscow, where Soviet
technical specialists translate every word of it—including the ad-
vertising—for immediate dissemination. And *Aviation Age* is
just one of thousands of U.S. publications the Soviets study."

Slide: A pile of U.S. technical magazines.

Colonel: "Summaries of Western publications are provided
to Soviet designers of military weaponry. When these military
specialists are apprised of an important new piece of Western
equipment or design, they submit a written requisition for it directly to Directorate T of the KGB. Directorate T in turn determines whether to try to purchase the requisitioned item through
illegal front companies or to hijack and smuggle it. Due to more
stringent enforcement of Western export laws recently, theft is
now more the norm."

Slide: Pages of parts listings.

Colonel: "The devastating results of the Soviets' illegal acquisition of Western technology are everywhere evident. Ap-
pended to your document is a partial listing of some parts and
equipment acquired by them in just the last few years. As you
can see, it is more than twenty pages long. Much of this equipment is so important to the Soviet military program, they have
killed to get it."

Slide: Photomicrodensitometer.

Colonel: "As an illustration of how the Soviet system
works—this is an American photomicrodensitometer. It is a crit-
ically important piece of equipment in military photography.
The KGB illegally purchased one through two dummy companies. While it was in transit to Moscow, authorities in Austria

impounded it. Undaunted, the KGB front company, two months later, purchased another. This one was stopped at New York's Kennedy Airport."

Slide: Heidelberg Airport.

Colonel: "Since clandestine purchase had failed, the Soviets turned to theft. A photomicrodensitometer legally shipped to NATO was stolen from this loading platform in Heidelberg in West Germany . . ."

Slide: Lebedev Institute in Moscow.

Colonel: ". . . and smuggled through East Germany, and then flown here—the Lebedev Institute in Moscow. At this moment it is performing vital military analyses of streak camera photography of Western installations."

Slide: VAX 11–782.

Colonel: "Another example: this is the highly sophisticated American VAX 11–782 supermicrocomputer manufactured by Digital Equipment Corporation. The VAX 11–782 has a number of critical military applications. In West Germany two years ago authorities boarded a Polish jet transport just minutes before takeoff and seized this VAX 11–782 with all its peripherals, destined for Moscow. Yet fifty other VAXs have already disappeared behind the Iron Curtain.

"Needless to say, without these fifty U.S. supermicrocomputers, plus an unknown number of IBM mainframes, Russia's military capability would be significantly diminished—perhaps even crippled."

Slide: Customs officers standing beside a seismograph and a laser unit.

Colonel: "This advanced laser system and this very sensitive seismograph which can be used to detect nuclear detonations were seized by American authorities, yet many others have already been acquired by the Russians."

Slide: Two sonar buoys.

Colonel: "The item on the left is a Soviet sonar buoy. It was found floating in the ocean near our submarine base in Washington State, gathering critical information on the activities of U.S. Trident missile submarines. As you can see, it is an exact copy of a U.S. sonar buoy on the right."

Slide: Processing machine.

Colonel: "And it was made on this machinery acquired illegally from U.S. sources."

Slide: Several Soviet aircraft.

Colonel: "An Air Force analysis reveals an even more devastating story, including the aforementioned Soviet MiG-25 Foxbat. U.S. parts and components are performing vital roles on almost all Soviet tactical aircraft—everything from the Su-24 Fencer to the MiG-25 Frogfoot and the MiG-29 Fulcrum, and all the aircraft between MiG-23 Flogger and MiG-25 Foxbat."

Slide: Charts of Soviet military aircraft.

Colonel: "Copies of these charts are in your document. The charts indicate speed, radius, armament and wingspan, firepower, and equipment of Soviet aircraft."

Slide: Another chart.

Colonel: "The numbers on the left are aircraft production figures for Soviet bombers, fighters/fighter bombers, transports, ASW, helicopters, and even utility/trainer craft. Matching them on the right are current production figures for comparable NATO aircraft. Please note the items printed in red—these are vitally important pieces of equipment on Russian aircraft illegally acquired from Western technology. The full list is attached to your script. As you can see, it runs for pages."

Slide: Airborne view of MiG-31 Foxhound.

Colonel: "This Soviet MiG-31 Foxhound interceptor now has a technology that the Soviets struggled for years to get: a true look-down/shoot-down radar system. The entire system was stolen from the U.S. As a result, when the F-14 Navy TomCat confronts the MiG-31 Foxhound, it is facing an enemy with the identical advanced American radar system, thereby canceling an enormous advantage that had cost the U.S. vast sums of money and years of unremitting research."

Slide: MiG-21 Fishbed L.

Colonel: "This MiG-21 Fishbed, with a speed of over twelve hundred knots, carries four air-to-air missiles—the AA-2 Atoll. The Atoll is an exact copy of our own Sidewinder missile."

Slide: Soviet aircraft flying in formation.

Colonel: "Without illegally acquired Western technology, it is clear, the Soviet air capability would be that of a third-class power. Much of its air force would not be able to fly."

Slide: A child's self-teaching computer unit.

Colonel: "Soviet depredations extend to even the smallest items. In the early years the Soviets were able to acquire microchips from children's toys in stores all over the world."

Slide: An array of microchips.

Colonel: "Later, Soviet military programs required large quantities of U.S. microchips. These were obtained direct from manufacturing sources in the U.S. through dummy companies."

Slide: Microchip machine.

Colonel: "Recently, they have been acquiring the manufacturing capability needed to produce microprocessors inside Russia. To date they have obtained a few American machines which they have copied through reverse engineering. The really advanced machinery has so far eluded them. Getting it is high on their list of priorities."

Slide: Wooden crates at an Italian customs station.

Colonel: "Twice recently the Soviets had tried to smuggle some of this advanced chip-making equipment into Russia— through Italy to the Tyrol, across the border into Austria at the Brenner Pass, all with ostensibly legal papers. And twice Italian authorities had impounded the equipment."

Slide: Photograph of chip-making machine.

Colonel: "It is believed that a third and more determined acquisition effort by the Russians is imminent."

Slide: Photograph of Export Control offices.

Colonel: "The Export Control System of the Department of Commerce has been assigned the job of stopping these illegal Soviet acquisitions. Recently aided by efforts from many other branches of government, it has made heroic efforts to stop these depredations, but with very little success."

Slide: Directories and handbooks of matériel and parts.

Colonel: "The Contraband List of the Export Control System of the Department of Commerce consists of some three hundred thousand items. The entire staff of the Department's division is composed of less than one hundred people. They are opposed by the twenty-two thousand Soviets in Directorate T in Moscow plus uncounted thousands around the world who are busy night and day finding, acquiring, and shipping material to Moscow."

Slide: Military research laboratory.

Colonel: "The consequences of this Soviet policy are quite clear. Organized widespread theft has saved the Soviet Union billions upon billions of research dollars, years of research time, and all the agony of testing, retesting, and redesigning."

Slide: Military equipment in May Day parade, Moscow.

Colonel: "Russia lets the West do all the creative conceptualizing, the developmental programs, and the perfecting and fine tuning of the technology and the manufacturing process, then it steps in and steals the perfected new item."

Slide: Soviet soldier with SAM missile unit.

Colonel: "It acquires new technology almost as soon as the West does . . . technology it would otherwise be unable to match with its own limited capabilities. In addition to the billions it saves on research, the Soviets also save many more billions of dollars in manufacturing capabilities they do not have to invest in."

Slide: Computer mainframe manufacturing activity.

Colonel: "In effect, the Soviet Union is using the formidable defense budget of the United States and the highly sophisticated manufacturing capability of American industry to build their own high-tech military installation."

Slide: Soviet troops on parade in Moscow.

Colonel: "It is estimated that the Soviet Union has saved over one hundred billion dollars by stealing Western technology. Those billions it has saved in advanced high-tech weaponry are then used to build its conventional weapons arsenal and its huge standing army—and also to develop its space program, including its highly secret Star Wars project. In all these categories, especially in Star Wars, it is getting technology it cannot develop itself."

Slide: Air-to-air missile fired by jet fighter.

Colonel: "Worst of all, the Soviets are forcing the U.S. to spend additional tens of billions of dollars to build defenses against its own weapons—defenses that the Russians quickly acquire. The Russians have succeeded in pitting the United States against the United States."

Slide: Reprise of Soviet submarine.

Colonel: "Clearly, this policy of technological theft has enabled it to surpass the West in many military categories."

Slide: Russian missile launchers.

Colonel: "More important, it has helped raise Russian military capability from that of a third-rate conventional power to a first class high-tech military machine."

Slide: Space satellite firing a laser beam at another satellite.

Colonel: "If continued unchecked, the Russian policy can ultimately give it an unbridgeable lead in Star Wars technology. This, it envisions, will enable it to conquer the world without firing a shot."

The colonel put down his script. "Are there any questions?"

"Yes," Brewer replied. "Who authorized you to show this to me. And why?"

"I cannot answer either one of those questions," the colonel answered.

••• Chapter 2

The winter was terrible that year.

Leningrad recorded the lowest temperatures in its history, and even the southern part of England had a series of two-foot snowfalls. In the eastern United States the bitter cold and the deep snow drove all the water birds to the seashore, and there, in spite of organized feeding efforts by the authorities, many birds starved and froze. In the cities soot-blackened mounds of snow lay until April.

It was a winter people talked about for years afterward. Some never forgot it.

In Munich late that night the two American agents, Sauer and Court, sat wearily drinking beer while studying several large road maps on the tavern table before them. It had been a long day.

"They must be sending it to Vienna," Court insisted. "See what they're doing? Look." He tapped his fingers on the maps. "They flew part of the contraband from the U.S. through London. Right? And part through Belgium here at Brussels. Okay? And part—most of it—they flew into Germany, here and here. So okay. Now they've got it all together—what do they do? They're moving it like checkers through Germany from here to here to here, always moving southeast toward the Austrian border. Right? And here, all the way at the other end of Austria—right next to the Czech border and the Hungarian border—is Vienna. A dime'll get you a dollar that's where they're moving the stuff to."

Sauer looked skeptical. "There's no guessing where they're going to move it next, Court. 'Kay? We've been following trucks

up and down every road in Germany. They could move it back
up here through East Germany into Berlin. They could move it
across the border into Czechoslovakia, here through Germany
or here through Austria. Or here through Austria to Hungary.
See what I'm saying? There're just too many goddamn options.
We're playing a shell game with some real wiseasses. And
there's just the two of us against them. 'Kay?"

"Then I'm going to say it again," Court said. "We should
blow the whistle right here in Munich. They almost slipped the
stuff past us once already, in Stuttgart. And if they ever split the
load up again and send it in different directions, we'll really be
in the soup. All this high-tech stuff would end up in Russia, and
that would be a disaster. You're trying to have your cake and
your penny both, Sauer."

Sauer nodded soberly. "It's all or nothing," he said with
weary determination. "'Kay?"

All day they had followed that truck with its load of smuggled contraband up and down German roadways, until the
driver finally pulled into the freight depot outside Munich. Sauer
was sick of the cat and mouse game.

"Listen," Court said, pressing his point, "if we lose this load,
our names would be mud back in the pickle factory."

"My name," Sauer said. "I'm responsible for this operation."

"So? Take my advice. Let's impound the stuff right now.
Tonight. Before they repaper it again. We'll be home for Christmas."

"Our orders are to track this shipment to the end," Sauer
said, "then grab everyone and roll it up all the way back to
Kansas City and L.A. If we stop it now, we're just going to get
the small fry. And if we call in help, we're going to look like we
couldn't handle it. See what I'm saying?" He poked Court on
the arm. "Come on, Court. We got a chance to make ourselves
look good. God knows we both need Brownie points. I say
chance it. These bastards haven't given us a mickey so far.
'Kay?"

"Then at least let's grab their man in L.A.," Court replied.
"He's folding his tent and he'll be out of there in the next day or
two. We've got enough federal raps on him to make him sing

like a turkey. If we grab him now, he can cop a plea and give us the names of the others."

"If we grab him, that'll tip our hands," Sauer said. "These guys over here will run for the woods, and we'll end up with some small fry in L.A. who doesn't know who any of these people are."

Court tried once more. "Look how many times they've re-papered this stuff," he insisted. "In Brussels the papers said the stuff was heating units. In Stuttgart they labeled it plumbing supplies. Next it'll be Christ knows what all. Have you counted how many trucking terminals and airports we've been through?"

"Let's get some sleep," Sauer said. "That truck is going to pull out at six-fifteen in the morning."

"Okay. I said my piece." Court yawned and stretched. "Just one more thing. We should at least level with Hardy."

"Level with him. If he had any idea what was going on, he'd have us back in Washington before breakfast."

"Well, he is the case officer, Sauer. You can't lie to him."

"He is the worst case officer in the world. In the universe. 'Kay?"

"Sooner or later we have to tell him. We could both get busted in the ranks for withholding information from him."

"Do you want to be the one who tells him?"

"No," Court said. "No, I don't. But those rosy reports you've been filing don't square with what's really going on, and if he finds out, you know exactly what he's going to do."

"I'll worry about that tomorrow," Sauer said. "Let's get some sleep."

Court followed him to the front door, yawning. "When was the last time we were home? It's been weeks. Since before Kansas City. I've been wearing this suit for so long, it just jumps on me in the morning like a trained monkey."

"My granddaughter will be three months old tomorrow," Sauer said sadly. "And I've only seen her twice. With a little bit of luck we'll both be home for Christmas."

"When you miss a Christmas away from home," Court said, "you never make it up."

"I never knew Germany could be this cold."

"Neither did Germany," Court said. "The deskman says it's

the coldest winter here in fifty years." Court pushed the road maps into his parka pocket. "Where to tomorrow, do you figure?" he asked.

"There," Sauer said, pointing east. "Across the Austrian border. My guess is they're going to ship the whole load to Salzburg tomorrow. See what I'm saying?"

Court nodded. "Okay. And where do you think we're going to spend Christmas? In Vienna? Or Moscow?"

On the way back to their hotel Sauer drove past the truck depot. The long tractor and trailer rig was still where it had been parked at eight P.M., alongside the terminal in a row with other rigs. Behind them was a high wall of plowed snow.

"Eleven o'clock and all's well," Sauer said.

"And at six A.M.," Court said with his eyes half shut, "we're going to start following that goddamn thing again. All day tomorrow. And the day after that and the day after that. Forever. We've died and gone to hell and this is our punishment until judgment day."

"Six-fifteen," Sauer corrected him.

The driver of the truck sat by the potted plants in the tiled hallway of his hotel, waiting for the phone call. It was eleven-thirty P.M., and he'd been waiting patiently for more than a half hour. He had already watched the cleaning girl scrub the tiled floor, then dry-mop it, then dust every single leaf on the potted plant, then wax them.

"Cleanliness is next to godliness," he said with a smirk.

She smiled back at him. "Then I've already washed my way to heaven twice," she said.

He watched her carry her cleaning things up to a frosted-glass door. "You didn't wash the roots of the plants," he said. "We could wash them together."

She turned and looked at the driver—the hanks of oily hair and the bad teeth. Her silence was her answer as she pushed the door shut. The whole hotel smelled of strong soap.

The phone rang a few moments later.

"Hello," the driver said. "This is Ruskin."

"Good," the mystery voice said. "How did it go today?"

"Well," Ruskin said. "I led them up and down the roads, and finally stopped at eight here in Munich. This is getting us nowhere. Why don't we split the load up into a dozen packages and send them in different directions? They'll never be able to follow all that."

"If we alarm them, they'll impound the goods," the mystery voice said. "We have to finesse them. Make the shipment disappear so that they have no idea where it went. We don't want them to know that we know they are following us. So tell you what we will do, Ruskin. You will leave an hour before schedule time."

"Five A.M.? Tomorrow?"

"Yes. Five A.M. tomorrow. Sleep well. I will send you more money. Before you go to sleep, make sure the two of them are tucked in bed for the night."

"You can be sure of that," Ruskin said. "They are as tired as I am."

Before going to bed, Ruskin walked back through the snow to the terminal with a flashlight and looked at his rig. He yanked the hoses and peered at the tires and checked the locks and hoped that nothing would be frozen in the morning. Then he walked by the hotel of the two American agents, saw their car parked in the parking area, and walked back to his own hotel. He was shivering when he got back.

Ruskin got into bed with a sigh, wishing that the little cleaning girl would come into his room and wax his plant for him.

Sauer got out of bed and put on the light.

"What's the matter?" Court asked, raising his head from the pillow.

"Something's up," Sauer said. "I can feel it."

"What are you going to do?"

"Sleep in the car," Sauer said. "I'm going to keep my eye on that load. I'll see you in the morning."

Sauer put his clothes on over his pajamas, zipped into his heavy parka, and went out to the car. He drove several blocks through the streets to the truck terminal and picked a parking spot with a clear view of the truck with the contraband.

It was the coldest night he could remember, and his breath

came in long steamy plumes. There was a frost halo around the moon, and sitting in the midst of the frozen, snow-covered terrain, he could imagine the cry of a wolf. Sauer shivered. How he hated winter.

He got a heavily insulated sleeping bag from the trunk of his car, got into the backseat and zipped himself into it, parka and all. He took a long pull on a pocket flask of brandy and composed himself, half reclining, half sitting, and soon dozed off.

Sauer was awakened by the sound of scraping.

It was still dark. A heavy mist had settled over the city, covering his windows with frost that completely blocked his view. Through the frosted panes even the streetlights were little more than a glow and a blur. He cranked down the window, feeling bitterly cold air tumble into the car. Inside the terminal compound he could see the truck driver scraping the ice off his windshield. Sauer looked at his watch. It was just before five A.M.

Sauer zipped out of his sleeping bag and clambered into the front seat. As he searched for the window scraper, he heard the truck motor start. He cranked down the window and looked again.

The driver stepped down from the cab, and guided by a flashlight, was taking a inspection walk around his rig. Sauer started the car, backed around the intersection, then turned and drove back to the hotel with his head out of the open window in order to see where he was going.

"Quick, quick, quick!" he said to Court as he rushed into their room. "Up up! The son of a bitch is pulling out an hour early." He yanked Court from the bed, and seizing the man's clothes, pushed them into his arms. "Dress in the car. Come on, come on." He threw everything in sight into the suitcases and led the way, bumping down the steps to the front. The defroster had melted two small holes in the frost on the windshield.

"I told you something was up," Sauer declared.

"Good God, it's cold," Court said, trying to get his pants on.

Sauer raced through the heavy mist back to the truck terminal. Even in the thick fog it was obvious that the truck was gone.

"Holy Good John," Sauer said. "How could he have moved that fast?" He took the road that led to the autobahn.

"Slow down!" Court cried. "You can't see ten feet in front of you. Slow down!"

Sauer stopped the car abruptly and turned off the engine as he cranked down the window.

"What are you doing?" Court asked.

"Listening for the sound of his engine," Sauer answered. He started the car again and drove with more caution through the mist toward the autobahn, then he made a U-turn and headed back toward the terminal. "He couldn't have gotten that far ahead of me," he said. "He must have gone in a different direction. Hot damn! If that bastard got away from us, we're ruined."

Court clicked his tongue and said nothing.

Sauer drove around in the mist, which was so thick that at times he couldn't find the intersections.

"Do you know where the hell you are?" Court asked. "Slow down. You're going to get us killed."

Sauer cranked down his window again, listening. "Bastard! He left an hour early. I should never have come back to get you. I thought I had time. Hot damn!" Sauer sat there, baffled, in a rage and panting heavily. "Now what?" he demanded of himself. "Now what?"

Abruptly he spun the wheel and drove off. "Court. Get that road map out. There's a back road to the border that parallels the autobahn. You know the one I mean? We were looking at it. Remember? Find it and guide me to it. It has to be this way."

Court, with one leg in his trousers and his lap full of clothes, looked at the map under the overhead light. "Okay. You're coming to a fork ahead. Take the left hand and follow it until we get to the next town."

"Do you remember the license number of the truck?" Sauer demanded.

"It's burned in my memory," Court said. "It's 484951. I'll give you five hundred dollars for a cup of coffee." He tried to pull his trousers on.

Sauer, with a furious grimace, had his head pressed forward over the steering wheel, trying to see through the rolling fog.

Periodically it would clear and he would speed up, only to plunge into another rolling embankment of fog.

"Give it a break," Court said. "Slow it down. You've lost him."

"No!" Sauer said. "I'll find him. I'll bet you anything he's going on the side road to the Austrian border."

"Okay, okay," Court said. "Just slow down before you hit something."

Sauer abruptly slammed on the brakes. He was inches away from the rear end of a truck. Its license plate loomed in the middle of their windshield.

"They don't make them any luckier than you, Sauer," Court said. "There it is—484951."

Chapter 3

A t the German-Austrian border the freezing
mist of morning had been blown to flinders
by a sudden rising wind that promised more
snow. The customs station parking lot was crowded with cars,
many of them with ski racks. People had formed lines at the
currency exchange windows inside, and there was a backup of
cars going through the passport check on both sides of the
border. Snapping the flags on their poles, the steady breeze
made the officials walk stiffly, hunched inside their greatcoats.

The truck had joined a long line of parked trucks waiting for
clearance, leaving the driver in his cab with nothing to do but
fold his arms and shut his eyes.

Sauer and Court sat in their car in the parking lot, waiting
for the truck to clear customs. Sauer looked at the backup of
traffic at the passport check stations and at the long line of
trucks. "This is abnormal," he said to Court. "They're looking
for something."

"Let's hope it's not our guy," Court said. "That's all we'd
need."

At last a customs official with a fluttering clipboard came
striding down the line, one hand holding his cap on his head
against the stiff breeze. He took the driver's papers and studied
them. The driver stood with his hands in his trouser pockets,
shivering. Two other customs men went over his rig, pointing
and talking to each other. The hoses, the brakes, the coupling,
the locks and seals on the doors. They held a mirror under the
cab chassis to study the underside. They even climbed up and
carefully examined the interior of the cab.

Finally, after the customs man had handed him his papers
and went on to the next truck, the driver rolled through the

border check with Sauer and Court not far behind him. Salzburg
was just down the road.

The trucker offloaded his cargo at a freight depot near the
Salzburg airport and drove back toward Germany. Before he
reached there, another trucker, Wolf, received a phone call with
new shipping instructions.

"Did you receive the money?" the voice asked.

"I did, sir." Wolf listened attentively, as usual, bemused by
the faint accent in the voice. He was never able to identify that
accent. Indeed he was never quite sure it was an accent. "What
can I do for you?"

"Ruskin has dropped off the cargo in the terminal near the
Salzburg airport. You know the place?"

"Yes. Of course," Wolf said.

"This is what I want you to do. Bring your rig to that terminal and pick up the cargo. You'll have the papers shortly by
messenger. Understand?"

"Yes."

"You leave the Salzburg terminal and drive to Neumarkt—
you know the route. You will probably be followed by a car with
German license plates. Don't pay any attention to it. At Neumarkt you pull into the terminal there and drive around the
back, where you can't be seen from the road. Muller's truck will
be there waiting for you—you know who I mean, his truck is
identical to yours. You switch license plates with him and let him
leave. The car with the German license plates will see Muller's
truck with your license plates and think it's your truck and follow it. It will drive toward Graz. You understand? When it is
well gone, you leave and drive to Linz on the autobahn. You
understand? The car with the German license plate will follow
the other truck for two or three days, long enough for you to get
that cargo into Vienna, and I'll take it from there. Later on,
arrange to meet with Muller and swap license plates again. Do
you understand?"

"I do." Wolf wondered if it was a faint Russian accent he
was hearing.

"I will call you at the usual hotel in Linz with more instruc-

tions. I'll probably want you to stay overnight and drive to
Vienna the next morning. Understood?"

"Yes. Understood." Wolf smiled. The voice's money was
very nice, and there was never anything quite illegal about the
jobs.

For two days the freight, still marked Plumbing Supplies, sat
there inside the Salzburg truck terminal. In a room in a small
inn that looked out on the terminal, Sauer and Court took turns
with binoculars watching through the lace curtains. They dozed
on the beds, read magazines, and paced up and down. But
mostly they watched the trucks that came and went until late at
night.

"I'm not going to let that happen again," Sauer said.

"What happen again?" Court asked.

"That truck nearly got away from us in the fog in Munich.
I'm getting a directional beeper unit and I'm sticking it into the
cargo. See what I'm saying? From now on that goddamn cargo is
going to bleat like a lamb wherever it goes."

"How you going to plant it?"

"I'll figure a way."

"Sounds like you're belling the cat."

"You'll see." Sauer made a phone call. "'Kay," he said to
Court. "The unit will be delivered here late tomorrow."

"What if they move the cargo before then?" Court asked.

"Then we'll have to do without it."

Court said nothing for a moment. He sniffed. Then he
asked, "How are you going to put it in the cargo?"

"When we get it, we're going to take it over to the depot and
put it in one of the cartons. 'Kay?"

"Sure." Court sniffed, then clicked his tongue again.
"You're the boss."

At two-thirty in the afternoon Court lowered his binoculars.
"They're moving it," he said to Sauer. "The whole load."

Sauer stepped from the bed to the window and looked out.

"Looks like local talent," Court said.

"Yeah," Sauer said with a sigh. "They're going to repaper it
again. Hot damn."

They followed the truck at a safe distance through the out-
skirts of Salzburg to a side road. The truck drove into a large old
brick barn and shut the doors. Sauer and Court, familiar with
the procedure, waited.

"What do you think they'll paper it as this time?" Sauer
asked. "Cuckoo clocks from the Black Forest?"

"Computerized skis," Court said.

Sauer folded his arms and slumped in his seat. "Wake me up
when spring comes," he said.

The truck emerged from the garage, drove back to the terminal, and offloaded the cargo once more.

"That beeper better get here soon," Court said. "We don't
know any of the new waybill numbers, manifests, or whatnot.
We'll never be able to impound that stuff without them."

Sauer scratched his cheek thoughtfully. "Where the hell can
that beeper be?" he asked.

Court paced. Then he picked up a photograph of a baby beside Sauer's wallet.

"What's her name again?"

"Who?"

"Your granddaughter. I forgot her name."

"Rosemary."

"Oh yeah. Rosemary."

"I gave her that name."

"You told me," Court said.

"This is one Christmas I don't want to miss."

"You'll miss more than Christmas if you get caught with that
beeper inside that terminal," Court said.

The package arrived by special messenger after four, when it
was almost dark. They sat in the car while Sauer fiddled with the
reception unit, turning the dial, adjusting the earphones, and
attaching the outside antenna to the right rear window then
cranking it shut. He worried about getting a draft on the back of
his neck.

"Looks great," Court said impatiently.

"There's still a gap between the window and the top. Air can
get through there."

"We'll seal it with masking tape," Court said. "Let's get this over with."

Sauer studied the transmitting unit thoughtfully. It looked like a long nail.

"So," Court said. "Belling the cat. Now how?"

"We push this into a carton then we cover the head with masking tape.

"We?" Court asked.

"Okay," Sauer said. "Me."

They walked over to the depot. Court, whose German was excellent, went in to engage the nightman in a discussion of freight rates to Paris. Through the windows he watched Sauer pass along the loading platform to the cargo area and disappear inside.

The nightman stood before his thick volumes of freight rates, the pages crinkled and bent and darkly marked with thumbprints. Then, laboriously with a freshly sharpened pencil, he calculated the freight rate through two different routings and noted them down on a pad. Sauer was still not back. Court asked for rates from Salzburg to Nice. The nightman patiently worked it out. Sauer still was not back.

Abruptly the freight office was filled with light from headlamps as a truck pulled up. When the driver came in, Court stood with the papers the nightman had given him, pretending to study the rates thoughtfully. Where was Sauer?

The nightman and the driver, talking in loud voices, walked into the cargo area. As Court stood there, Sauer appeared from the other side of the building and tapped on the window. Court met him outside.

"Where the hell were you?" Court asked.

"I had a hell of a time finding the cargo. It had all new papers on it."

"That truck is here to pick up a lot of cargo, including our load," Court said. "He's leaving first thing in the morning."

"We're ready," Sauer said. "This time we sleep in our clothes, with our bags in the car, ready to go at a moment's notice. See what I'm saying?"

The truck left the terminal at six A.M. the next morning. Sauer listened to the beeping with his earphones.

"Perfect," he said. "Loud and clear."

"How long does that beeper send a signal?"

"Couple of days. Until the battery runs down." He pitched the earphones onto the backseat. "Don't ask, Court."

"What?"

"You're going to ask me what we do when the batteries run down."

"The thought did cross my mind," Court said.

The truck took the road north and drove to the town of Neumarkt. And there it pulled into a truck terminal and drove around the back. Sauer and Court waited in their car out on the roadway.

"Maybe it's unloading the stuff," Court said.

"Nah," Sauer said. "Here it comes again. It didn't have time."

The truck pulled out on the roadway and headed south. Sauer checked the license-plate number. "That's it," he said. Court waited a few moments then turned and followed the truck.

They drove a few miles when Court said, "Shouldn't you check the beeper?"

"What for?" Sauer said. "That's the right truck."

Court made a face at him.

"Come on, Court, loosen up." Irritably, Sauer reached into the backseat and picked up the earphones. "Humh," he said, twisting the dial. He turned and looked at the antenna outside the back window. "What the hell's wrong with this damned thing?" He tried it again, fiddling with the dial, checking the connection through the cigarette lighter.

"Quick!" he said. "Turn around. They pulled a switch on us. Turn around, I said!"

Court slowed down. "You're the boss."

Sauer twisted the dials and checked his connections and the antenna again. "Hot damn! Now what? Now what? Oh, those dirty bastards."

"What are you going to do now?" Court demanded.

"I don't know!" He turned and looked through the back window. Distantly he could just see the truck follow a curve and disappear. "If we screwed this up, we've lost everything."

"We," Court murmured to himself. He sped back up the road to Neumarkt to the terminal.

"Drive around the back," Sauer said.

There were no trucks behind the terminal building.

"Drive back out," Sauer said. "And head for the autobahn to Vienna. 'Kay?"

Court drove fast along the road to the autobahn while Sauer turned the dial on the beeper unit. It was silent.

"I can't believe it," Sauer said. "They slipped us a mickey and we fell for it."

Court shrugged and said nothing. The beeper remained silent. Sauer sat with his fists clenched and head bowed.

"Maybe we ought to go back and catch up with the truck," Court said. "Maybe the beeper's busted."

They drove another mile.

"What do you want to do?" Court asked.

"Shit. I don't know," Sauer answered. "We've blown it now."

"We," Court said in a low voice again.

The beeper emitted a faint whistle for less than a second. Sauer listened and turned the dial. There was nothing.

"Court," he said. "Go back to that crossroads we just passed."

Court made a U-turn and drove back. The beeper made no sound.

"Take that right-hand road there," Sauer ordered.

Court turned right and sped down the road. They came upon a string of slow-moving cars. Court blew his horn and passed them on a curve.

"Jesus God on the cross," Sauer said.

"Sorry about that," Court replied.

The beeper whistled briefly once.

"Faster," Sauer said. Court picked up speed. The beeper whistled once more, a little stronger signal. Then the beeper emitted a longer signal.

"Dead ahead," Sauer said. The signal grew stronger. "We're getting closer."

"You picked it up?" Court asked.

"Yes. It's ahead of us."

"Hallelujah," Court said. Ahead of them now they could see the truck.

"It's a twin to the other truck," Sauer said.

"Be damned," Court said. "No one can be as lucky as you are, Sauer."

"Lucky! Me! Court, you have to be kidding. I'm the king of bad luck."

"What do you call this?"

"Instinct."

They got within five cars of the truck, the beeper so loud that Sauer had to turn the volume down. The cargo they had followed from Kansas City was bleating like a lamb in the trailer ahead of them.

Chapter 4

C ourt cleared his voice. "I think it's time to stop crapping around, Sauer. They almost got away from us this time. If I hadn't told you to check the beeper, we'd still be following that other truck to God knows where. Let's impound the whole load now before we lose everything."

Sauer squirmed uncomfortably. "Damn," he said. Then he sighed. "Listen, Court, what you say makes sense. 'Kay? We probably should shut these people down, but then we end up right where we were before Kansas City. All these weeks, all this effort, and we go back to the pickle factory with an empty net. That's not for me. I have to come back a winner. I have to start putting some big points on the board or it's all over for me. See what I'm saying? I'll be just another spear carrier in *Aida*. This is my last chance. See what I'm saying? So if you want, I'll get the desk to put you on a plane home and I'll take it from here. 'Kay?"

Court shrugged. "In for a penny, in for a pound," he said. "I'll see the hand out."

"'Kay."

"One thing, though," Court said. "How about making a counterfeit load? We can pack the cartons with rocks and send the sensitive stuff back to the States in a special jet. Just recovering the stuff will make us look good."

"How?" Sauer demanded. "How are we going to get the stuff without them knowing it? They're watching that load like hawks."

"Then if they see us, we at least get the stuff back and we can chase them next time. They end up with the bloody nose, not us. All those weeks, all that effort, all the money they laid out for the stuff, all those freight costs, all that labor lost. We can say we won this round, and nobody will disagree."

"No. I want to go home a real winner. I want to bring their scalps back on my belt. They're not invincible. We outfoxed them with the beeper. If I'd kept the damned phones on my head, it would have been as easy as shit through a goose." Sauer looked at Court. "Sooner or later they're going to make a mistake. We're getting closer to Vienna every minute now, and they're running out of maneuvering room. With each mile, we're pushing them further into the corner. If I were them, I'd abandon the whole load somewhere. Tell me the truth, Court— in this cat and mouse game since Kansas City, who would you rather be, us or them?"

"The truth?" Court asked.

"The truth," Sauer replied.

"Them."

The truck drove east toward Vienna. It stopped at the freight depot in the city of Linz, behind the main post office, by the railroad station. And there in a small railway hotel the driver took a room for the night.

"Show's over for today," Sauer said.

That night at eleven-thirty the driver received a phone call in his hotel.

"Well," the voice said. "I have just learned that they didn't follow Muller's truck as we expected. It isn't possible that they followed you, is it?"

"They did," Wolf said. "All the way."

"Ah!" There was a long silence. "Tell you what," the voice said at last. "There's a place in Linz that sells all kinds of electronic equipment."

"It's late. Everything is closed."

"I know. I will make some phone calls. I want the proprietor to go over your cargo. There must be some sort of radio transmitter in there somewhere. After he's through, you are to drive on to Vienna."

"What if he finds a transmitter?"

"I don't know yet. Just leave it in place and drive on to Vienna tomorrow."

The truck left Linz the next morning shortly after eight o'clock and headed east on the autobahn toward Vienna. By nine a wet snow was falling and traffic had slowed. Court and Sauer looked out at the snow-filled world through flogging windshield wipers and patiently crawled through the miles into Vienna a short distance behind the truck. Sauer sat, arms folded, with the reassuring beep in his ears.

"Did you really sleep all night with those earphones on?" Court asked.

"I don't care if it makes me deaf," he said. "I'll never take the phones off again. Trouble is, the signal is getting weaker."

"Great. We're back to square one," Court said. "If we lose him now, we're really lost."

"Stay close to him, Court," Sauer said. "I think the showdown is coming up. In Vienna."

"I think we need to pull the Austrian authorities in on this one," Court volunteered.

"Never," Sauer said. "We do this alone."

"Maybe you ought to think about it first," Court said.

Vienna shivered.

It was late December, and the Tyrolean Alps of western Austria were reporting excellent pre-Christmas skiing conditions on a snow base of more than two feet. Skiers from all over Europe in their designer ski outfits and equipment had thronged to Innsbruck and Salzburg; the serious skiers skived down the slopes of Arlberg, even in the lower mountains of Kitzbühel and Kammergut. Rooms throughout the Tyrol were going at premium rates, and there were lines at most restaurants.

Innkeepers smiled at the weather forecast: another six inches of powdered snow expected during the night.

But in Vienna, at the eastern end of Austria, the cold brought no pleasure. A wandering wind crept down the abandoned promenade of Karntner Strasse, past the stacked sidewalk chairs and tables of summer, whining at the wooden cathedral doors of Stephansdom and driving Christmas shoppers indoors. Occasionally, under grim gray skies, a rogue snowflake sailed across the promenade.

In the coffeehouses the Viennese sipped warming coffee with their tortes, chafed their hands, and read their newspapers. Some, drawing close to the fireplace, talked of spring.

In spite of the cold, the cleaning staff in the Staatsoper Opera House on Opern Ring Road busily buffed brass handrails and glass door panes in preparation for the night's opera performance of *Die Fledermaus,* while not far away, the Vienna Boys Choir was making final arrangements for its Christmas season performances at the Chapel of the Hofburg; and nearby, in the Spanish Riding School in the Hofburg Palace, the tack and trappings of the Lippizaner horses were being polished to a high gleam for an evening of equestrian perfection.

Gogol arrived in Vienna on the flight from Zurich in the afternoon and immediately went to the café on Karntner Strasse.

Arnoski was patiently waiting for him, drinking coffee and reading a newspaper. He watched Gogol approach and felt the familiar anger rise in his throat. Such ostentation—diamond rings, gold watches, that expensively-fed figure, deliberately corpulent—as though he were trying to occupy more space—expensive custom-made clothing, even the beard. And those arrogant blue eyes. Gogol had made greed into an art.

"Well?" Arnoski asked expectantly.

"We still have some problems," Gogol said. "Two American agents."

"The same ones?"

"Yes," Gogol said. "The same."

"Then it's an impasse," Arnoski said.

"It's a standoff," Gogol said. "We didn't elude them, but they didn't impound the merchandise."

"Of course they didn't impound it," Arnoski said. "They want to follow it to you."

"I think they came close to impounding it several times," Gogol said. He made a show of pulling a cigar from a leather cigar case, then with a gold trimmer cut the cigar end off. He put the snippet of wrapper leaf on Arnoski's saucer. "If we had split it up in Germany as you wished, I'm sure they would have moved." He puffed a cloud of cigar smoke. "Will you smoke a cigar? No? They're the finest in the world."

"Those two men are exceedingly dangerous," Arnoski said. "They can break up our smuggling network."

"My smuggling network, Arnoski. Mine. Not ours."

Arnoski gave an irritated little shrug. "They want to break it up," he said.

Gogol studied the tip of his cigar thoughtfully. "It took me months of planning and coordination to assemble that matériel."

"Well, where is it now, I would like to know?"

"A few kilometers from here," Gogol said.

"Here? In Vienna?"

"Yes," Gogol answered. "Just across the canal. In the public warehouse." Gogol watched Arnoski's face. "Surrounded by American and Austrian authorities."

"Austrian!" Arnoski collapsed his newspaper angrily. "They summoned the Austrians?"

"Yes. Much to my surprise. I never thought they would do it. Now it's around-the-clock surveillance."

Arnoski folded his arms angrily. "You've put us in a corner now, Gogol," he said.

"Marten," Gogol said. "Remember? My name is Eric Marten."

Arnoski flapped an annoyed hand. "We've lost it. The whole thing."

"I don't think so," Gogol said.

"No? How do you expect to get it out of there?"

Gogol shrugged in silence.

"The committee is going to be very upset when I report this," Arnoski said.

"Are they?" Gogol said irritably. "They're very good at being upset."

"It's months late. And now it's boxed up in a warehouse here in Vienna, surrounded by the Americans and the Austrians waiting for you to come and get it so they can arrest you. That puts it a very long way from Moscow."

"The committee tried four times to get that same matériel," Gogol said. "Four times. And it failed four times. And lost an enormous amount of money doing it. And now the committee is upset with me?"

"You were told to get the matériel at any cost. You were told to kill the two agents in Germany. You were told to split the cargo up and ship it piecemeal to Moscow through a half-dozen different ports of entry. You have disobeyed every single order, and you've lost weeks of time, lost a fortune in rubles, and now you've lost the matériel itself. I would think the committee feels justified in being upset, Gogol."

"Marten," Gogol corrected him again. "My name is Eric Marten. Remember? It's the name on my passport. I am a Swiss businessman named Eric Marten."

Arnoski looked at Gogol with a furious face. "If I were you, Marten, I would be worried about my future as a Swiss businessman."

Gogol laid his head back and chuckled.

"I will tell you," Arnoski continued, "if you don't get that matériel out of that warehouse and into Moscow, your career is finished—as Marten and as Gogol both." Arnoski reached for his overcoat.

"Really? Do you think I've failed?" Gogol chuckled again.

"Of course you've failed!" Arnoski replied. "And your arrogance is infuriating. There is no possible way in the world you can get that shipment out of that warehouse."

"Then just watch."

"Watch?" Arnoski answered. "There's nothing to watch. I return to Moscow in the morning. I give you seven days to get that shipment over the border. A week, Gogol. If you don't, you're going to end up in a clerk's cubby in Moscow." Arnoski flung aside the newspaper and left, buttoning up his heavy overcoat. Outside, the wind stole his hat, and he lost all his strutting dignity chasing it down Karntner Strasse.

Gogol laughed as he watched through the café window. But the smile soon died. He had no way in the world of getting that matériel out of that warehouse. He was cornered.

Perhaps Arnoski would get his way. Emil Gogol sat in the coffeehouse on the famous Karntner Strasse in Vienna in the most expensive clothes money could buy and stared at a clerk's cubby in Moscow.

Across the Donau Canal just off Prater Strasse, Sauer and Court and Austrian customs agents kept watch over the premises of the old warehouse. Sitting in cars, standing in doorways, concealed inside the unheated warehouse, freezing around the clock, the watchers waiting impatiently while the seventeen cartons and crates sat there. And sat there. Their patience was being tested severely by the biting cold, and they now murmured their discontent to each other. After five days of surveillance, they knew something was amiss.

Inside the warehouse, maddeningly, in sullen winter light, the equipment sat untouched in the midst of the busy terminal, stenciled and labeled with a false waybill. Instructions: hold for pickup.

So far the addressee had failed to claim it.

"I was right," Sauer said to Court over breakfast in the hotel. "They've abandoned it. We should never have called in the Austrians."

"Maybe." Court made a skeptical face. "They've fooled us before. If they walk away from it, then we still have it and we win. We didn't get the masterminds behind it, but better luck next time."

"I should never have listened to you." Sauer threw down his napkin and walked away.

"Sorry about that," Court called after him. He reached for another roll.

It was cold. So cold. The duty seemed interminable, and there was no way of knowing when it would end. Then, on the snowy afternoon of the sixth day, the break came.

That day had begun like all the rest, with a biting cold wind under depressing gray skies, and the threat of snow. Austrian customs men were in their positions behind shaded windows, in several parked vans and inside the warehouse.

The men shivered and yawned and smoked and murmured to each other as the hours passed.

At one o'clock snow began to fall thickly. At three in the

afternoon an envelope arrived at the Kaiserin Elisabeth Hotel just off Karntner Strasse, addressed to "The American agent Sauer."

He ripped it open with his forefinger and pulled out a single sheet of plain white paper with one word written on it. Folded in the paper was a Russian ruble note.

"What's that word mean?" he asked the deskman.

The deskman shrugged at it then looked at the other deskman.

"It's Russian," the second deskman said.

"What does it say?"

"Cpaceeba," said the deskman.

"What does it mean?" Sauer asked patiently.

"Thanks," the deskman said. "In Russian, it means thanks."

Sauer looked from the single word on the paper to the ruble note. Thanks for what?

Austrian customs men with Sauer and Court entered the warehouse in force. There they found nothing amiss: the seventeen cartons and crates were intact, sitting in the middle of the floor exactly where they had been placed six days before. Bewildered officials milled about.

Sauer touched a carton. It moved at the push of his fingertip. He picked it up. It was empty. He pushed another: empty.

"Zeleenograd," he said aloud. And they all understood. Zeleenograd, the Soviet's secret city of high-tech activities, ringed about with mine fields. The equipment was undoubtedly already in Zeleenograd on military duty against the capitalists who had made it.

Angrily, with flailing arms and legs, Sauer waded into the shipment. The neatly labeled empty containers fled in all directions from his attack.

The Austrian agents tried to hide their smiles. Several turned away in laughter.

Cpaceeba.

In the Hotel Kaiserin Elisabeth, Sauer and Court packed their bags and descended to the lobby to wait for a taxi to the airport.

"Christ," Sauer said. "It's cold." His face was gaunt and he looked old beyond his years.

Court asked, "How much longer can the Russians go on doing this—I mean, getting the technology they need by stealing it from their enemy?"

Sauer shrugged. "How much longer are we going to let them get away with it?"

Court shrugged. "I don't know. How can we stop them? They're pretty good at it."

The taxi arrived and the bellhop wheeled their baggage through the front door.

"Christ," Sauer said. "I'm ruined. I was outsmarted. I lost the whole goddamn payload and I got bupkis in return. The Russians got critical technology—it's worse than a military defeat—and I got egg on all our faces. It's the end of me."

"You did what you could," Court said.

"No, Court," Sauer said. "I knew exactly what I was doing. I put everything on one roll of the dice and lost. I won the booby prize—a desk job."

"One thing," Court said. "We'll be home for Christmas."

••• Part Two

Chapter 5

S auer stepped out of the car and looked up and down the dark parking plaza. The freezing breeze was going right through his coat. Beyond the bare trees he could see the lighted dome of the Jefferson monument; behind him was the skyline of Washington.

"Where is this guy?" he asked.

Court cranked down the car window. "What are you standing out there for?"

"So he'll see us."

"He'll see the car," Court said. "You think he's blind?"

"Then why the hell is he so late?" Sauer got back into the car, shivering. "My God, it's cold."

"Maybe you need a heavier coat."

"It's not the coat. 'Kay? It's sixteen months in Panama station. Thin blood."

"Thin blood? You've been back for four months."

"Takes longer than that. 'Kay?" Sauer held his hands down to the warm air of the heater. "I'm still shivering from Vienna. I've never been so cold in my life."

Court watched him. "Easy does it, Sauer."

"Easy does it? Easy did it. This Vienna thing screwed both of us and you know it."

"Without prejudice, they said, Sauer."

"If you believe that, then I've got a nice bridge in Brooklyn I'd like to sell you. 'Kay?" Sauer watched a snowflake fall into the light of a streetlamp. "Snow," he said. "Eight goddamn inches day after tomorrow. I wish I were back in Panama."

They sat in the car with the motor running and waited. At twelve-thirty Sauer squirmed irritably.

"What's the story on this guy?" he asked. "What'd you say his name is?"

"You said you didn't want to know anything about him."

"He's half an hour late, and now I changed my mind. 'Kay? What's his name."

"Brewer. His name is Brewer."

"Where have I heard that name before?" Sauer asked.

Court took a three-folded sheet of paper from his overcoat pocket and snapped on the dashboard light. "I have to tell you, Sauer. I got this information in strictest confidence from Borden himself. So don't tip your hand."

"Okay, okay. Tell me about him." Sauer watched Court read from the paper.

"You may have heard of him because of Bobby McCall. The first thing I have to tell you is this is the guy that took the fall for Bobby McCall."

"The one that was framed? The prison rap?"

"That's it. He hasn't been out very long, and Borden says he's feeling very pissed off—especially about the way Washington failed to help him get out. So go easy. Or you'll have your hands full in a hell of a hurry."

"He's not the only one feeling pissed off."

"Sauer. Listen to me. Borden says this guy is a dangerous piece of work if you get him started."

"What else? What's his background?"

"Okay. According to Borden's notes, this Brewer is a specialist in computer technology. In artificial intelligence, whatever that is. He's an expert on Russian smuggling—especially, it says here, in high-tech arms smuggling."

Sauer shivered. "Christ, all I want to do is go home." He unscrewed the cap from a flask and swallowed a mouthful. "You?"

"No, thanks." Court shook his head. Then he yawned. "I'm still feeling that jet lag."

Sauer looked up and down the dark parkway. A lifetime of checking the shadows. Across the Potomac he could see the Washington Monument, a glowing lighthouse in the bitter night.

"How are we ever going to live down those empty cartons?" he murmured.

"Come on, Sauer. We did our jobs. Blame it on the Austrians."

"Who's going to believe that? They busted their humps for us. This thing made the Austrian government look as bad as we do."

"So okay, then," Court said. "We're not all alone on this one. The Reds fooled us and the Austrians both."

"It's easy for you to say that, Court. You don't look so bad. You just followed orders. But I was the one in charge. It's my ass that was on the line." Sauer looked out at the shadowy shrubs blowing in the sharp breeze. "It was a goddamn disaster. First, those Russian smugglers make us look like two assholes. Then some grandstander named Brewer comes swooping in—and when he finds them, he'll get all the glory. And you and I end up in the clown suits."

"Come on, Sauer. It's not that bad."

"You heard them. What did they say? They think those Russian smugglers are geniuses. They said those guys could steal eggs from under sitting hens. They said they could steal a hot stove with bare hands. They say its going to take a genius to catch them. Is that us? No. It's some guy named Brewer. If the smugglers are geniuses and Brewer's a genius, then we're two hairy assholes. If you think that helps our careers, then you need a white cane and a seeing-eye dog. 'Kay?"

Court shrugged indifferently then held the paper down to the dashboard light again. "I can't figure out who this Brewer's with. He's been on loan to everybody—a real alphabet souper. CIA. NIA. NSA. ICIG. DDB. ACU over at State. Everyone borrows him. Guy lives out of a suitcase."

"When you're hot you're hot," Sauer said in a low voice.

"Ha?"

"Nothing." Sauer pointed at the white piece of paper. "What's his G.S. rating?"

"He outranks both of us by a big number. And he'll be even higher when he gets McCall's job."

"He's up for McCall's job?"

"Yeah. A real plum. He'll be Borden's boss."

"What else does it say?"

"Here. You read it."

Sauer took the sheet then held it down to the dashboard light. "Christ. He's been all over the map. This thing doesn't say who he's with now."

"That's what I just said," Court replied. "Anyway, it doesn't matter. It's a shit detail."

Sauer looked thoughtfully at Court then snapped off the light. "Well, ain't that tough old beans? This Brewer can step in and make a hero of himself finding those smugglers. Then when the medal's pinned on him all nice and neat, he steps into one of the cushiest jobs in Washington. Poor Brewer."

They sat waiting in the darkness and the silence.

"What a goddamn mess this has made of my life," Sauer said.

In his memory, Sauer's career stretched back like footprints wandering in a desert, searching for an oasis. He scanned the terrain in vain for his last victory. He looked back on a dozen failures—personal battlefields littered with wreckage and salted with defeat and now capped by the ultimate disaster in Vienna. He no longer dreamed of seeing the exultant face of victory. His wounds could no longer be soothed by the licking lie.

"Listen, Sauer," Court said softly. "Borden told me some stories about this Brewer. So I'm warning you again. Don't mess with him or you'll really have your hands full."

"Mess with him? All I want to do is put my life back together again."

"Still and all, you're pretty pissed off. So don't tangle with him. Hear?"

The bitter breeze off the Potomac pushed against the car, trying to get inside.

At quarter to one a car came slowly down the curving drive and pulled up behind them. The headlights went out.

"Okay," Court said. "We've got a lot riding on this. So let me do all the talking. And remember what I said. Don't mess with him. Nice nice nice."

A man walked up to their car. He curled himself inside the backseat and pulled the door shut.

"You were supposed to be here after midnight," Sauer said.

"Are you Sauer or Court?"

"He's Court," Sauer said.

Brewer nodded. "Who's idea was it to meet here?"

"Are you giving grades, Brewer?" Sauer demanded.

"You still haven't asked me who I am or shown me any I.D. How do you know I'm Brewer?"

"Let's skip the crap," Sauer said. "We have business to conduct."

"Easy does it, Sauer," Court said. He turned and reached out a hand. "Court's the name."

"Okay," Brewer said, taking Court's hand. "What's up?"

"We need you to help us find some guys. It should be right down your alley."

"Go on."

"Smugglers. Russian. High-tech arms smugglers."

"Got any names?"

"We don't know," Court said. "In fact, we don't much at all. We don't even know what they look like. All we know is they're very good at smuggling. They just pulled off a major job in Vienna."

"Were you two on the case?"

"From the beginning," Court said. "Since Kansas City."

"Is that all you can tell me?" Brewer asked.

Sauer turned an angry face and looked at Brewer fully for the first time. Even in the poor light he felt the presence of the man: the head thrust forward from the shoulders, the short neck, the large square teeth and muscular jaw, the skeptical eyes. In the backseat Brewer was as impassive as a pile of rocks.

"Listen, Brewer," he said. "You're here because you're supposed to be good at finding people. 'Kay? And that's what we need you to do—find some people. And, no, that's not all we can tell you. 'Kay?"

Brewer asked, "Who was in charge of the Vienna detail?"

"He was," Court answered. "The Russians really pushed our face into the pie."

"I see. Bad luck." Brewer looked at Sauer's sullen profile. "Why me?"

"Because," Court said quietly, "your background fits it. If you can do this, we'll give you all the information we have and all the help we can."

"We want to catch the bastards ourselves," Sauer said.

"That figures," Brewer said.

"You have to get on this right away, Brewer," Sauer said. "It's red hot."

Brewer shook his head. "You've called the wrong man. I'm not available. I've got another assignment coming up."

"The McCall job?" Court asked. "We were hoping you could help us with this even after you start that job."

Brewer grunted thoughtfully.

"This one's off the books, Brewer," Sauer said.

"Off the books?" Brewer looked at the two faces. "It gets worse and worse. Off the books."

"Look, Brewer," Sauer exclaimed abruptly. "I don't give a damn whether you take it or not."

"That's a relief," Brewer said. "Because I'm not going to take it."

"I wish you'd reconsider," Court said.

"There are a dozen people who can help you with this," Brewer said. Bitter cold air rushed into the car as Brewer opened the door. "I don't do off the books. And I don't take assignments in the backseat of a car." He stepped out into the night and shut the door.

Court held both hands up in despair. "For Christ's sake, Sauer. Are you out of your mind?"

"It killed me to hear you begging that bastard," Sauer said.

"He was going to say yes!"

"Bullshit."

"Sauer, you're so pissed off, you can't even think straight anymore. That guy outranks us by a mile. He's up for Bobby McCall's job. And he's got a reputation for being a dangerous guy. I warned you not to tangle with him. So what do you do? You try to order him around like a clerk. Even an idiot could tell that you were trying to make him refuse. And now he did!"

They watched Brewer's car pull away. The two red taillights disappeared in the darkness.

"You've ruined us, Sauer."

"Maybe if everyone else refuses the job, they'll let us go back and find the bastards in Vienna."

More snowflakes fell out of the darkness into the light of a streetlamp.

Chapter 6

Brewer drove in heavy traffic over the Potomac and entered the Pentagon parking lot. In the southwest corner of the southwest sector of the South Parking Area, away from all other vehicles, as instructed, at precisely 4:00 P.M. he parked and waited. A whistling frigid wind pushed against his car.

A few minutes later a Pentagon parking-lot shuttle bus approached and stopped at the designated bus stop. The driver looked at Brewer then looked at the far distant Pentagon entrance. He pointed a questioning finger.

Brewer shook his head and the bus drove off.

He studied the faint smudge of sunset in the black clouds and felt the wind rock his car. A snow sky at dusk. In the arctic breeze a cardboard coffee container bounded along like an escapee. He told himself that he should follow the container and flee the place. The instructions ordering him here were the most absurd he had ever received. If they hadn't been relayed by his own case office, he would never have obeyed them.

"Okay, Brewer. I'm going to read these instructions to you just as I got them. Ready? You're to be in the Pentagon parking lot, southwest corner of the southwest sector of the South Parking Area at precisely four P.M.—that's 1600 hours. Park and wait for a charcoal-gray stretch limousine. The chauffeur of the limousine will step out with a newspaper under his left arm. He'll walk over to a navy-blue escort car and get into the backseat. You will then get into the front seat of the stretch limousine. Do not attempt to look into the backseat. Repeat: do not attempt to look into the backseat. Got it?"

"What is this—amateur night at the legion hall?"

"Sounds like a kid's game, Brewer, but that's what it says on this paper."

"Is this one of your cases?"

"Nope. I'm just a messenger boy on this one."

"This have anything to do with that slide show I was shown the other day?"

"Beats me."

"Who is it? Who am I going to talk to?"

"How would I know, Brewer? Whoever he is, he obviously doesn't want you to see him."

Slowly, from behind him, approached a charcoal-gray stretch limousine with dark one-way windows, followed closely by a navy-blue Chevrolet sedan right out of the federal motor pool. The two cars crossed in front of Brewer's car then drove in a circle around him, slowly, studying him.

The chauffeur parked the limousine six spaces away from Brewer's car. When he stepped out, a great puff of tobacco smoke came with him and blew away in the wind. The chauffeur walked over to the navy-blue Chevrolet, holding the bill of his cap against the biting wind. The edges of a folded newspaper fluttered under his left arm.

Brewer walked over to the limousine and got into the driver's seat. The interior was filled with cigar smoke.

"Don't you have an office?" he asked.

"Don't get shirty," said a voice in the backseat. "There's a good reason for this."

Brewer didn't recognize the voice.

"Now listen, Brewer. They tell me you're very good at what you do, and you'd better be because I'm about to bet the farm on you. It's that simple."

The accent was monied New England, Boston, with a private-school overlay. Choate, Harvard. Not a civil servant. A presidential appointee probably. A ranker. Now listen, Brewah.

Brewer said, "Nothing is that simple."

In the failing light the chauffeur, in the backseat of the escort car, chatted with the driver. Two silhouettes in silent pantomime.

"All right, Brewer. Now listen carefully. I have a very very

very important assignment. It involves the Soviets. It's going to be a tough, dirty fight. The action is going to be very fast and there's going to be a lot of hard hitting. It's going to be dangerous. It's going to mean working outside regular channels, and that means working without a net. I want to emphasize that, Brewer. No net. Clear so far?"

"Yes," Brewer said. It was clear. There was to be no crapping around. A heavyweight from the front office in a big car had come to preach the gospel bluntly to his sin-blackened soul: Do this job, do it now, do it right, and don't talk back.

The man's voice said, "If you get into any kind of a sticky situation, you know there are people in high position who can protect you. You have my word on it—even though you don't know me."

Brewer smiled. In Washington there was only one thing worth less than a man's word. A stranger's word. "I know all about the protection of people in high position," he said.

The voice ignored that. It went on—accustomed to commanding, to persuading, to applying pressure, accustomed to speaking bluntly to subordinates. "We have to have a man who really knows the ropes. Someone resourceful, who can work with minimum direction—out of sight of the mother church. Someone who has a lot of contacts in all the intelligence organizations, here and abroad—and who can call in old favors. Do you understand me?"

"Yes," Brewer said.

"I went over your record very carefully. The job I have in mind fits you to a tee. You have a strong background in Soviet military high-tech, you have an excellent record in counterespionage. You've done this kind of job before—countering Soviet thefts of U.S. technology. And you've got a brilliant record as a smuggler yourself, so you know how smugglers think. You have a reputation for keeping your mouth shut. You come with the highest recommendations from a number of sources. So you're a known quantity I can trust and rely on. In short, on paper you're perfect for the job. Okay so far?"

"Yes."

"Before I tell you another word about it, you have to make a decision. You can walk away now and no hard feelings. Or you can stay and take the assignment. If you stay, you're in for keeps. There's no way to back out. You stay until the end. Clear?"

"Yes," Brewer said.

"Now listen, Brewer. I won't say that if you refuse this we won't be able to find someone else to do it. But on such short notice, that's pretty close to the truth. The normal channels are paralyzed. The bureaucratic infighting is the worst I've ever seen. The two department heads who should be cooperating to stop this problem in its tracks won't talk to each other and are refusing each other's phone calls. The Congress has bottled up a bill in committee that might help, but I hear it could take two years and probably never come out at all. Meantime we're hemorrhaging technology to the Russians. The Soviets are on the biggest looting spree in history. Okay so far?"

"Yes. Were you the one who ordered me to see that slide show?"

"Yes. I wish I could give you more time to think it over, but I can't. I have to know right now."

"Nothing happens until my record is cleaned. I want my name cleared of the prison record."

"Yes, yes. And you want the McCall appointment."

"No. I don't want the McCall appointment. I want my name cleared, as promised."

"Now wait. Listen Brewer. I can take care of your name and record immediately. That's not a condition. About the McCall job—"

"Forget McCall's job. I'm no longer interested in it."

"May I ask why?"

"I don't let people coerce me."

"That's not our intent."

"I'm supposed to start Monday at McCall's desk. Instead you're here to bend my arm into taking an off-the-books assignment. That means you're holding up the McCall job. That's blackmail."

Several clouds of cigar smoke came sailing into the front seat.

"Okay, we'll discuss that later," the voice said. "What do you say? Can you make a decision this fast?"

"Yes."

"Okay. What is it?"

Another cardboard coffee container went bounding across the parking area. A second warning. Brewer looked over at his car; he considered walking back to it and driving away.

"Clear my record first," Brewer said. "Then call me." He opened the latch on the door.

"I'm calling you," the voice said. "Here." A thick brown envelope was extended over Brewer's shoulder. "Shut the door."

Brewer pulled the door shut and took the envelope.

"It's all there, Brewer. The petition to the court. A transcript of the hearing. Official documents. Testimony of witnesses. Unequivocal evidence of the framing. The judge's response. The official court order. A full pardon. Correspondence to all the official bodies and records-keeping authorities and their letters of compliance. A written apology from the United States government. A salary check covering the entire period you were imprisoned, including every penny in back pay plus interest. Restoration of time on your pension. A copy of your current personnel record, with no record of your false imprisonment. And a press kit containing a complete coverage of the events. Everything your attorney, Madeline Hale, asked for. Your name is immaculate."

Brewer studied the papers carefully, doubtfully.

"Miss Hale sends you her fondest regards, by the way."

Brewer fanned the papers. At last. Delivered in the backseat of a car. He fitted them back into the envelope.

"The announcement of the pardon will be on the six o'clock news tonight, per Miss Hale's instructions. Now—" Another bank of smoke filled the car. "The question is, are you in on this deal or not?"

"Yes."

"You're in?"

"I'm in," Brewer said.

"You are a perplexing, nettlesome man, Brewer."

"Are you calling me a pain in the ass?"

"Yes."

Brewer heard the rear window roll down. A cigar struck the

paving with a brief shower of sparks and rolled away in the waning daylight.

"Okay," the voice said. "I want now to apologize for Sauer's behavior last night. I wanted him to handle this so that he could win back some of his self-esteem. I failed to realize how angry he was. My apologies. Now I'd better tell you what the assignment is. The moment I do, you're at the point of no return. Clear?"

"Yes."

"Christmas Eve in Vienna, the Russians stole nearly a million dollars worth of incredibly sensitive military computer equipment that was illegally shipped there by smugglers in the United States. They not only got matériel we badly wanted them not to have, they made a laughingstock of us in Europe. If you listen, you can hear the German guffaw, the British titter, and the French sigh."

"I've heard them laugh before," Brewer said.

"Yes. The Russians have been making fools of us for years. I've read your reports, Brewer. All of them. You obviously feel there's one person smuggling the most sensitive technology."

"Yes."

"So do I. What I want you to do is find that man."

"That's it?" Brewer asked. "Find one man?"

"That's it. Find him. Above all else, find Mr. X."

"Why?"

"I can't tell you."

"Why?"

The man sighed mightily. "Brewer, you are as maddening as a gored bull."

Brewer waited.

"All right," the man said. "We have something coming down."

"What?"

"Something new and sensitive." Smoke from a fresh cigar came in waves now. "You're going to say, Why don't we turn this problem over to our counterintelligence people? The answer is, if I put this assignment in that loosey-goosey bureaucracy, it'll leak all over the place. And the Soviets will have the damned thing in Zeleenograd by breakfast tomorrow. So I can't go through regular channels."

"How many people know about this new and sensitive something?"

"Two."

"The White House?"

"The White House!" the man said. "Listen. There are so many cuckooboo chatterboxes in the White House, I can't even tell the President about this at this juncture. Not yet anyway. The only reason the Russians haven't been able to find the damned thing is I haven't told the White House."

"I'll need to talk to Sauer again," Brewer said.

"Sauer? Yes. Of course."

"When can I see him?"

"How about tomorrow morning? I'll arrange it. And I'll tell him to polish up his manners."

"I can handle him. From here on I report to you?" Brewer asked.

"You report to me."

"And who are you?" Brewer turned around and looked into the backseat.

He needed only a glimpse. He didn't recognize the man, but he recognized the type. The rumpled suit, the bow tie, the watch chain across the vest that covered his rotund belly. But most of all he recognized the expression on the scowling face: haughty, patrician, arrogant. Faces like that washed into Washington in great waves with every new administration and washed out again a few years later, defeated by the enduring capital bureaucracy.

From a face of about sixty under sparse gray hair, two quick-tempered eyes looked back at Brewer.

"They warned me about your insolence," he said. "You were told not to turn around."

"Do you have a name?"

"Limoges."

"When do I start?"

"Right now."

Carrying the thick brown envelope, Brewer walked over to his car and drove off.

••• Chapter 7

At dusk all of Washington hurried home. The rising wind was hurtling a bitter cold front into the city, blowing trash cans, tattering flags, whistling in the shroud lines, rocking loose windows, reaching through the thickest coats—effectively shutting the city down tight and promising a heavy snowfall by morning.

Police vans cruised up and down, trying to coax street people into the warmth of shelters. Weathermen speculated that the Potomac might freeze over for the first time in many decades.

When Brewer opened the door to Margie's apartment, she observed him from the kitchen. He shoved the manila envelope up onto the shelf of the closet then hung up his coat.

"Hello," she said softly.

"Hi."

"Is that what I think it is?"

"Yes."

She turned back into the kitchen. "Okay, Brewer," she called. "Stand by. The time has come." She came back with a small bottle of champagne and two glasses. "I've been saving this bottle for the occasion." Deftly, she unwound the wire, squeezed her eyes shut and pressed her thumbs on the cork. It flew across the room with a loud pop.

"Here's to you, Charlie," she said. She handed him a glass. "Congratulations. A very dirty piece of business is laid to rest." She toasted him.

"Thanks," Brewer said.

"You're all put back together, Charlie. Humpty Dumpty finally beats the rap." She poured more champagne into his glass. "Monday morning you start a new job, a new career. The past is past. You can walk away from it all."

Walk away. He looked solemnly at her. Walk away from the Limogeses, away from the McCalls, away from the blackmailing and false imprisonment and the mounting madness. Walk away from everything but memory.

And how was he to walk away from his own personality, which had gotten him into the whole mess? The character traits that had him fenced about like a cage—the fool, the gull, the ass.

After dinner he said, "I decided I don't want the McCall job."

"Oh."

"It's time for me to get out," he said.

"Out? Out like in leave the government?"

"Yes."

She nodded slowly. "You should have gotten out long ago, Charlie. Before McCall shoved you into prison." She took his hand. "Where will you go?"

Where would he go? He'd never had to ask himself such questions before. He was a mole emerging from its burrow for the first time to stare at the stars, unable to comprehend such vast spaces.

"I have to talk to some people," he said.

She searched his face again. "Can you really break away, Charlie?"

"Why not?" he answered. "Meantime, I've got one last assignment."

"One last assignment."

"Yes."

"You wouldn't kid a public servant, would you, Charlie?"

"It's the last job."

"Get out now," she said.

"One more job," he said.

Margie had fallen asleep in her gown on the couch, her Boston grandfather's clock prating the seconds behind her. He had picked his way slowly through the papers in the brown envelope, finding Madeline Hale's touch on every page, every paragraph. And on every page, every paragraph, was memory; his arrest in Central Park, the trial and prison—mostly prison—the bars, corridors, faces of prison, the suicide of Jason Poole.

Still half asleep, Margie stood and pressed her face against his cheek and yawned. He watched her weave her way to the bedroom.

Nearly eight hours after their meeting, he could still smell Limoges's cigar smoke on his clothes. One sniff of his sleeve brought back the whole surrealistic conversation in the limousine. Brewer shook his head at the image of Limoges. Riding around in his limousine to evade eavesdroppers while trying to sneak a new invention into the national arsenal, Limoges was the prime symbol of the twentieth century: another bringer of unwanted gifts to the world, the bearer of another new weapon to be thrust into man's bewildered arms. Here was yet another stroke of the brush that was painting the entire world more and more into the same tight, explosive corner.

"Without a net," Limoges had told him. "I want to make that perfectly cleah, Brewah." A high-wire act without a net. The secret was never to look down.

He removed his clothes and got into her bed with her. She stirred, full of sleep, and pulled off her nightgown. "I love you," she said. "Love you. Love you." She kissed him. Lovingly. Longingly. Lingeringly.

She slept in his arms, holding his hand on her breast.

I love you: He had never said that to anyone. Never felt it. Passion, yes. Fondness yes. But a thundering, rocketing, downtown, brass-band love? No.

Yet she did: love unabashed, unreserved, uncomplicated. Flat out, with nothing held back. How her face would light up whenever they met. She glowed with her affection for him. It was carved on her heart with a clasp knife: M.L. loves C.B. Complete with cupids and a fretted lace doily.

In his heart was warfare—maces and shields: he'd picked his battle ground; he'd picked his weapons; he'd picked his adversary. But was there no room left for love?

He awoke in her arms. His head and chest were soaked.

"You were having a nightmare," she said. She got a towel

and dried his face and hair. Then she put the light out and held her arms around him. "It's going to be okay," she said.

"No," he said. "It's never going to be okay again. I can't get back to that place where I was before prison. I can't get out of my head the sound of those heels kicking on the wall when that kid hung himself. I can't see with the same eyes as before."

"Then see with my eyes," she said.

"Love," he murmured.

"Yes. Love."

"You have to be very crazy or very brave to love someone," he said. "You know you're going to take a terrible beating. I had it once and walked away from it. I thought it was a trap."

"The alternative is worse," she said. She stroked his hair. "I love feeling love. It's like a purr here." She pulled his hand between her breasts. "Right here. It's the only thing that can help you live with those nightmares in your head." She kissed his brow. "It's the only thing that can make life worth living."

Before dawn he heard snow grains tapping on the windowpane. Snow at the window, seeking the way in. Malice patiently waiting.

The President lay asleep in the White House. His cabinet dozed in their beds. The Congress snored. The members of the Supreme Court slept the sleep of the just. And all about town the foreign ambassadors in their multitudes slumbered toward another day. In the morning all would rise, rub the sleep from their eyes and begin to push the great creaking, lumbering cart of history another mile on its reluctant squealing wheels. Each would try to push it in a different direction.

He asked himself yet again what he was to do with this lump of life called Brewer. What was he do with the rest of his days?

When Margie woke, she stepped to the window and peeped under the shade.

"Good God," she exclaimed and slipped back in bed. "Not fit for man nor beast. No school today, sports fans."

"The CIA will never make it without you," Brewer said. "Langley will never be the same."

"A pox on the CIA," she said. "Listen, Brewer, you've got a

naked broad in your arms, and she definitely does not want to discuss her cockamamy research job in Langley."

Listen Brewah. Her Boston accent echoed Limoges's.

"You should call her," she said.

"Who?"

"The lawyer who cleared your name. Madeline Hale."

When you have a naked broad in your arms talking of love, should you be thinking of Madeline Hale getting married in Vermont?

Chapter 8

"**Y**ou been a bureaucrat too long, Brewer."

"Have I?"

"'Have I?' You want the truth, Brewer, or you want bullshit?"

"Are you giving me a choice? Which do you do best?"

"Hey, Brewer, let's cut the comedy. You want jokes, call Las Vegas. You interested in a deal, a nice deal, you call me. Okay?"

"Wonderful."

"Okay. Here's the deal. I got this client. He's looking to sell. He's getting on in years, and he has this nice security agency on the waterfront in a city along the East Coast. His customers buy his security services against pilferage. Larceny. Highjacking. He probably saved his clients upward of eight million last year alone. You know what that does to insurance rates, Brewer? It brings them down. Way down."

"What city?"

"I'll tell you later. This is a good deal, Brewer. You could make some real bucks. Better than the fishcake you get from the Fed. You interested? I could get you a financial statement."

"I'll let you know."

••• Chapter 9

Within hours city traffic was paralyzed. Schools were closed. Businesses that had managed to open, shut down a few hours later. The federal government dismissed its army of civil servants officially before noon, although few had actually come in.

By one o'clock seven inches had fallen and it was still coming down thickly. The streets belonged to the wind-driven snow. Brewer walked the six blocks to the delicatessen, clambering several snowdrifts on the way to his meeting with Sauer. The front of his overcoat was soon snow-caked, and he entered the delicatessen slapping it off with his cap. There were only a few people in the place.

In the last booth Sauer sat alone. Head on chest, arms folded, one leg cocked over the other, the man scowled at the floor, the picture of desolation: the battle lost, the stock market crashed, the dice crapped. Beside him on the seat was a thick brown envelope.

Brewer rapped a knuckle on the booth table.

Sauer grunted.

"Is that the file?" Brewer asked. He sat down and looked directly at Sauer.

Sauer raised his head and looked irritably back at Brewer, like a man roughly awakened from a deep sleep.

"Let's skip the crap," Sauer said. "My orders are to show you this file on the Vienna job."

Brewer pictured himself going down a dark alley, backed up by this slouching desolate figure opposite him. The thought made the hair on the nape of his neck prickle. Sauer the brooding backup.

"Goddamn snow," Sauer said. "If Russia was in a warm climate, I'd defect."

The waiter brought a sandwich—a mound of corned beef topped by a high hump of leaking cole slaw and Russian dressing between two thick slices of rye bread. Sauer studied it solemnly then roused himself.

As he shook out his napkin, Sauer looked appraisingly at Brewer. "So you're the kind of hairpin that likes long odds, hey?"

"What brought that on?" Brewer asked.

"This is the Game of the Cornered Rat," Sauer said. "And you look like the type that's hooked on it. No sane man would take the assignment you've got."

He spread the paper napkin on his lap. "We're all set," he said, patting the thick envelope by his side. "I'm going to eat and you're going to have fun."

"Fun," Brewer said.

Something in his tone made Sauer look attentively at Brewer's face. Sauer cleared his throat carefully. "Okay. Joke's over. Where would you like to begin?" he asked.

Brewer watched Sauer bite into his sandwich. He had met many Sauers—sometimes German with pale hair, sometimes British with a time-ruined face or American with a purple whiskey saddle over the cheeks. Whatever the type, there were always deep lines of sourness between the brows and around the mouth: an intelligence man who had spent too many days looking into the void, surrounded by talk of Armageddon and gotterdammerung. Then one day he looks into the void once too often and loses his nerve. After that he clings like a limpet on a seawall, holding on until retirement day. Sauer was a limpet.

"Start at the beginning," Brewer said.

"Okay." Sauer put down his sandwich, chewing. "You wanted information? Okay." He opened the brown envelope. "Here's information." From the envelope he pulled out a file folder. "I was the one who got the original complaint. That's why I was put on the case. We got it from the Department of Commerce in November. From a computer-parts wholesaler in Texas. He thought there was something fishy about this outfit in

Kansas City that's buying parts from the no-no list for cash. So Court and I flew down to Kansas City. 'Kay?

"After we looked the situation over, I called it in. I said that we might have found a smuggling operation. This outfit—Three Tee it called itself—consists of three guys with a rented house and garage, a white Toyota van and a brand-new checking account. They've been there less than two months. They're not listed in any industrial directory. They don't have a track record of any kind, and the telephone is listed under the name John Paul Jones. On their purchase orders they list themselves as a V.A.R. A value added repackager. They're a customizer of high-tech equipment for medical schools and hospitals. 'Kay? But what they're ordering doesn't have medical applications. It has military applications. You see what I'm saying?

"So upstairs told us to camp on this for a while and see where it goes. We figured we could nail them anywhere along the way. Here." Sauer slipped the topmost sheet from the folder and handed it to Brewer.

"Three Tee always attached to their orders this Department of Commerce form," Sauer said. "It covers the export of high-tech equipment." He pointed at the printed text. "The form declares that the equipment is intended for medical purposes, domestic use only. No export. You've seen these before, right?"

"Many times," Brewer said.

Sauer handed Brewer another copy—this time of a check.

"And they always sent a check with the order," he said. "Like this. Drawn on a small bank in Kansas. Nice clean deal for a wholesaler. All the paperwork done and cash in hand. 'Kay?"

Sauer pulled another sheet from the folder. "Each one of these wholesalers did the same thing," he said. "They processed the check and filed the government form away with the invoice. The minute the check cleared, they sent the merchandise by air freight with a waybill. Like this. Always air freight."

Brewer looked at a copy of Waybill number 458–88643–2124, conveying an itemized order to Three Tee in Kansas City from a supply house in Texas.

"Is this the whistle blower?" Brewer asked.

"That's him," Sauer said. "See? Nothing big. A small part

here, a little unit there. Nibbles. But it adds up big: they've placed a lot of small orders with a lot of high-tech wholesalers—all over Texas and all up and down the West Coast. 'Kay? But this Texas dealer was different. He took the money, shipped the goodies—then blew the whistle. One phone call did it.

"So Court and I hung around the Kansas City airport. And every day packages were arriving for Three Tee. And every day a guy in a white Toyota van would claim them. He drove the stuff to a garage behind a private residence. Three guys in a garage. The list of stuff they were buying was impressive—hardware no hospital ever needed. Every few days they packed all the stuff up, put labels on it and drove it to the airport. Then they would assemble another load. So we decided to follow one of their shipments. This time they list the stuff as air-conditioning equipment. Seventeen cartons and crates. They shipped it all by air right out of the country, contrary to their sworn statements."

"Where did they ship it?" Brewer asked.

"To Toronto, Canada, addressed to an air-conditioning and heating firm that turned out to be ficticious." Sauer slipped out another sheet—a waybill—and handed it to Brewer.

"I even rememer the number," Sauer said. "Waybill number 339–14256–9538. Right?"

Brewer looked at the waybill number. "What happened in Toronto?"

"Guess who claimed the merchandise in Toronto?" Sauer asked. "You got it. The same three jokers—Three Tee. They drive up to the common carrier's airport loading platform and drive off with all seventeen pieces. They take the whole load to a loft a few miles from the airport, and—sure enough—they repacked and relabeled everything all over again, this time as repair parts for home heaters. They shipped the stuff to Europe in four different cargoes." He handed Brewer another sheet.

"This is one of them," Sauer said. "Waybill number 4356–95995–5138—from Toronto to Stuttgart on Lufthansa airlines. Including all the correct customs forms."

"These three men were Americans?" Brewer asked.

"One was Canadian."

"Go on."

"So Court and I flew to Stuttgart," Sauer said. "And there different people claimed the shipment. Two German nationals and an Englishman. One of their regular contacts was a Russian, from the Moscow ExImport Company—so you don't need to guess where the stuff was going."

"Mashproborintorg," Brewer said.

"Yeah. Mashproborintorg in Cologne. This Russian's name was Revin. One of the Germans met him for a drink one afternoon. Then right after that, wham—these three smugglers repacked and redocumented the stuff yet again with new labels and—" He cued Brewer with a pointing forefinger.

"A new waybill," Brewer said.

"Head of the class." Sauer slipped out another sheet of paper with a flourish. "Number 7767–85674–2321. The stuff now went to Austria—all seventeen items. They moved it three times inside Austria—and eventually shipped it to a freight office in Vienna. That's when I got nervous. Vienna isn't all that far from the border to Czechoslovakia and Hungary.

"So we get the Austrian authorities involved at this point. And when the stuff arrives in the Vienna freight office, we secretly go over it. Everything's in order. We're all set. We're ready to follow the shipment to the border and grab whoever claimed the merchandise. Then we can roll up the operation all the way back to the three jokers in Kansas City. See what I'm saying?

"It's cold in Vienna. So goddamn cold. Sitting in cars, standing in doorways and freezing around the clock. And the stuff sits there. Just sits there. Day after day and night after night. Everyone's bitching. We all want to go home. Then one snowy afternoon we enter the warehouse and check the merchandise. And that's when we find out the cartons are all empty.

"Beautiful, ha?" Sauer asked. "The bastards let the stuff sit there until everyone got bored and careless. Then they would sneak away one item at a time. And replace it with a duplicate carton that was empty. One by one they got all seventeen, and we ended up watching seventeen empties. This was with someone inside the warehouse at all times watching the whole shipment."

"Sleeping," Brewer said.

"Who knows? My Christmas stocking ends up with a hole in it." Sauer snorted angrily at Brewer. "Know what that operation cost the American taxpayer? Just the surveillance. More than one million U.S. dollars. And it cost me everything."

Sauer looked up at the ceiling, remembering. "I wanted to take the whole crew in and sweat them," Sauer said. "But I was voted down. There were Americans and Austrians involved. They said it could cause an international incident."

Sauer felt Brewer's eyes studying him and looked up. "So?"

"So what did they get?" Brewer asked.

"Who?"

"The Moscow smugglers. In Vienna."

"Oh." Sauer pulled out a folded sheet of paper. "Confidential, of course."

Brewer studied the list then glanced at Sauer. "You know how bad this is?"

"You're the computer expert, Brewer. You tell me."

"This is state-of-the-art, top-of-the-line computer technology. The latest computer-operated soldering station. A prototype unit for disk drives. Vital parts for two central processing units."

"So?"

"So this helps the Russians make state-of-the-art electronic components for space weapons—Star Wars stuff. It's just the kind of capability we don't want them to have."

"It's that bad?"

"If they've managed to swipe the software to go with this, they're in production right now, making military hardware to use against us."

"We were set up," Sauer said.

"How were these units wired—like this clean-room contamination indicator?"

"For East European voltages and plug configurations . . . just as you would expect."

"What's been done about the Americans and the Canadian and the two Germans and the Englishman?"

"Who knows? Interrogations didn't help a bit. They all said they were hired by telephone and paid cash up front."

"In Swiss francs?"

"Yeah," Sauer said. "How did you know that?"

Two policemen came into the delicatessen, stamping their feet and shaking snow off their greatcoats.

"Doesn't make sense," Sauer said. "You see what I'm saying?"

"No," Brewer said.

"All our brilliant minds turning out all these brilliant inventions and discoveries, and all we can think of doing with it is making fearsome weapons or building a network of television stations so that a roofer's apprentice's wife can watch a moronic quiz show between other roofer's apprentice's wives. Yet we can't devise a system to stop our enemy from stealing it."

Sauer studied Brewer's eyes for a moment, then put down his sandwich and pushed the plate away. He dipped a paper napkin into his water glass to swab his fingers and palms.

"This thing looked like a dream operation to me," he said. "See what I'm saying? I was in the doghouse anyway. A few years ago my marriage was in bad shape. Too many trips away from home. So I began to turn down assignments to spend more time with my family—wife, mainly. My bosses noticed, and I was put on the shelf—desk jobs with no travel. Didn't help—my marriage went bust anyway. So there I was—a failure in private life, a failure in my job. Then the divorce rocked me pretty good. I had a tough time with the solitude. Anyway, I tried to get back into the game. But it was tough. I drew down a couple of things, but nothing noticeable. I was down in Panama for a while. Then we picked up on this Kansas City thing. I figured I can make myself look good. Instead, what a goddamn mess it made of my life."

"This is no worse than a number of other smuggling jobs the Russians have pulled off," Brewer said. "What's all the fuss about?"

"Something's coming down," Sauer said. "And they don't want those Rooskie pickpockets swiping it."

"What's coming down?"

"I don't know. Something. All I have is a word I overheard." He looked at Brewer. "'Cassandra,' whatever the hell that is."

"Cassandra," Brewer echoed.

Sauer folded his arms and sighed. "How am I ever going to live down those empty cartons?" he murmured.

"You did your job," Brewer said.

"I was the one in charge," Sauer replied. "It's my ass that was on the line." Sauer looked out at the sheets of snow that blew past the delicatessen window. "It was a goddamn disaster. Those Russian smugglers made me look like an asshole. And now you come swooping in to find him. You'll get all the glory. And I end up the back end of a horse act."

"Have you told me everything, Sauer?"

"Yep. Everything."

Brewer watched Sauer reach into his pants pocket to pull out a mound of coins. With them came a small pink baby rattle with a small pink bow. Almost absentmindedly he pushed the baby rattle back into his pocket and stood up.

He hadn't told Brewer everything. Brewer sensed it. Something had been omitted.

"Got to phone the pickle factory," Sauer said. "Be right back. 'Kay?" He stood, then hesitated.

"What's the matter?" Brewer asked.

"Nothing," Sauer said. "I wish things between us were starting out different. They say you're pretty good. They used to say that about me."

He walked over to the phone.

•••Part Three

●●● Chapter 10

A s planned, the dinner was given on the night of the full moon. The occasion for the dinner, a superb Bernier oil just acquired by the host, Eric Marten, stood on an easel on the terrace under a soft studio light. It was a celebrated Bernier—a view of a full moon shining down on the snow-covered Swiss Alps—and it stood on its easel on the terrace under a real moon shining down on the real snow-covered Swiss Alps. Black clouds bringing snow squalls sped across the European sky.

In evening dress, discussing the oil painting on the easel and chatting amiably, were the guests: the editor of a major German art magazine and his wife; a book publisher from Paris and his wife; a Swiss banker and his wife; the curator of an American museum; and filling the role of hostess, a young woman wearing a gown of the thinnest silk, filmy, floating, nearly transparent, and held up by the thinnest of spaghetti straps.

Under the glass canopy that covered the ancient stone terrace, amidst the murmuring voices and tinkling glasses, waiters circulated with cocktails and canapes. The butler was supervising a young pantry boy who was placing several more logs on the fire. Outside, held at bay by the glass canopy, a wintry night wind prowled.

Gogol stepped over to the fireplace and spoke to his butler in a low voice. "I am expecting a very important telephone call from America," he said. "No matter what I'm doing, be sure to interrupt me the moment it comes."

"I will, Mr. Marten," the butler replied.

Gogol now walked over to his new oil painting and stood beside it. He held up his glass. "To Didier Bernier's moonscape," he said.

"And to the money that bought it," his banker said. "Here's to many more, Eric."

Gogol smiled. "To paraphrase an old joke, there are nine hundred Berniers, of which three thousand are in the United States." He watched them smile.

The banker's wife turned her husband away from the others with a hand on his elbow and walked him along the terrace. She spoke to him in a low voice, confidentially. "I thought we had been invited to a small skiing chalet," she said. "I had no idea we were coming into the midst"—she swept her hand—"of all this."

The banker nodded. "I thought you'd like the surprise."

"He's quite handsome," she said. "How old? Thirty, thirty-five?"

Her husband shrugged. "Perhaps."

"But who is he?" she asked. "And where did he get his money so young?"

The banker shrugged. "His credentials are real enough. In the few years I've known him he seems to have become richer by the hour."

She gazed about the stone terrace they stood on, then up at the recently added glass canopy supported by gleaming copper ribbing. "A four-hundred-year-old stone monastery on top of a mountain in the Swiss Alps. He must have paid a fortune for this."

"Fixing it up cost another fortune," said her husband. "This glass dome alone cost a king's ransom."

"But where's he from?" his wife insisted. "Is he German? Austrian? What?"

The Swiss banker shrugged. "Marten? The name could be German, Austrian, even Swiss—if that's his real name. All I know is, his money is real enough. He keeps much of it in my bank. I know he owns several computer software firms, a computer components plant, and an interest in a shipping company. And they're all very profitable. And he has an equally sound investment portfolio."

She stared at Eric Marten. "I can't believe you haven't delved into his background. It's not like you."

"No one seems to know much about him," the banker said.

"They say he has a brilliant mathematical mind. Some say he was educated in German universities, some say he attended Harvard. I've heard it said that many influential men consult with him. Grauff says there is no doubt that Bonn confers with him on sensitive high-tech matters. Schmidt in Cologne says he is the son of a German count but conceals his background to make it on his own. Hornblower says he is an American whose mother was a German war bride."

"But don't they ask him?"

The banker shook his head. "The money's real. The talent's real. The businesses he owns are real. If you try to find out more than that, he smiles and changes the subject."

She looked at the publisher's wife. "Giselle says he speaks German with a faint Hungarian accent." She turned her eyes to Marten. "He's quite handsome. He's one of the few men I've met who wears a beard well. And very pretty blue eyes."

"They're not so pretty when you're across the conference table from him."

"Imagine," she said. "A million and a half dollars for a painting." She looked appraisingly at Gogol then at the young woman standing next to him. "And the girl—who is she?"

"From Cologne. Her father is a university professor. Oh, he's real enough. Professor Schmidlap is his name. She went to university. She worked on Fritz's art magazine for a while. Now . . . I suppose she just lives here with Marten."

"You know she's stark naked inside that silk gown."

"She's hardly inside that silk gown," the banker replied.

"Leah, are you serious?" the publisher asked the young woman. "Numerology?"

"Yes," Leah said. "In Cologne. When I finished college, I took the job as a lark. Her name is Madame Strega. She does castings for many people. Famous people."

"You can't be serious," the editor declared. "Are you telling us that major political figures and leading businessmen in Germany consult a—a—witch?"

"And leaders from other countries too," Leah said.

"But that's preposterous," the editor protested.

"They believe her numbers," Leah said.

The publisher stepped closer. "What are her numbers telling them?" he asked.

"War," she said. "They predict a terrible world war within two years."

"Now wait," the editor said. "Are you saying that many European political leaders are expecting a nuclear war? Based on numerology?"

"Yes," she said. "I am."

"Dear God," the banker's wife sighed.

"Explain that," the publisher demanded. "How does numerology work?"

Leah said, "You have to calculate all the cyphers in a given year—like 1990—with a certain formula she uses, to see if it produces a thirteen or thirty-nine. Thirteen or thirty-nine always foretells doom."

She had their complete attention. "Go on," the editor prompted.

"So far, the formula has predicted all the war years of this century. World War One—1914. World War Two—1939. Korea—1950. Vietnam—1961. The formula for this year shows both a thirteen and a thirty-nine, and that means a great war. Armageddon, in fact." She looked at their solemn faces. "The other numerologists are all saying the same thing—that catastrophe is coming."

"Preposterous," the banker said. "I deal in numbers all day too. And my numbers point to a very strong Swiss franc with peace and prosperity."

The others barely smiled.

"It is absolutely preposterous," the editor said. "Predicting the future with numbers. Absurd." His eyes looked for support from the others.

Leah said, "It isn't just the numbers. It's the mushrooms too. Many people are talking about the size of the wild mushroom crop in Russia this year."

"How's that for irrationality?" the banker asked. "Are you serious? Wild mushrooms in Russia?"

"When it comes to predicting war years," she said, "there's a perfect correlation between numerology and mushroom harvests."

"Explain about the mushrooms, please," the editor's wife said. She stood next to her husband and took his hand. "I have children."

Leah said, "Russian peasants believe that when the wild mushroom crop is large, war follows. They say there was a bumper crop in 1914. Another in 1939. Another in 1950. Another in 1961. And this year Russia and much of Eastern Europe had the largest mushroom harvest in history."

The banker frowned skeptically at her. "Peasants and numerologists. Two unimpeachable sources."

"If it isn't convincing," his wife protested, "it's frightening."

In their minds armies marched. The earth shook. War drums thundered. The splendid Bernier in moonlight was forgotten.

Gogol seemed amused by their dismay. He clapped his hands for attention. "Dinner is served," he said. "And the numbers predict a wonderful meal. Follow me to the feast."

With Leah, he led the way to the dining room. As they entered, the guests exclaimed with delight at the sumptuous table setting, the tableware, the silver service, the huge bowls of fruit, the banks of candles and the staff of servants that awaited them.

The wife of the editor stood beside Marten. "Don't you believe in numerology and mushrooms?" she asked.

He made a face at her. "No scientist would touch such evidence with a stick," he said. "Come, enjoy your meal."

"That's a relief," she said.

"I'm sorry," Leah said to the table, "if I said anything to upset you."

"In that dress," Gogol replied, "you say anything you want."

They all laughed.

Gogol put his arm around Leah and patted her hip. He smiled at his guests. "Can you imagine this in a convent school, being taught all about the seven deadly sins by the sisters?"

The men laughed.

"Please," the editor's wife said. "What exactly are the seven deadly sins?"

"The seven deadly sins," Leah replied, holding up her hands to list them on her fingers, "are Pride, Covetousness, Lust, Anger, Gluttony, Envy, and Sloth. Isn't that ironic?"

"Why ironic?"

"Well," Leah said, "Nietzsche says when man ceases to believe in God, all things are lawful. And that's exactly what's happened. The seven deadly sins have become the leisure time pleasures of the twentieth century."

"Tell me again what they are," the banker's wife said.

"Pride, Covetousness, Lust, Anger, Gluttony, Envy, and Sloth."

"My God," the banker's wife said. "She's right."

"I'm all for that," Gogol said. "Let's start with some gluttony." He looked at the butler. "Remember what I said about the telephone call from America."

The butler nodded.

"No, no, Eric," the Swiss banker said to Gogol across the table. "Your exquisite Bernier may turn out to be an excellent investment. But if I want to make money, I invest in high tech, particularly medical high tech. Major breakthroughs are coming in the U.S. and Japan. A new artificial heart, flushing machines for washing chemicals and cholesterol from the blood and dissolving fatty deposits in the cardiovascular system. New knees and joints. And pharmaceuticals. Lots of new pharmaceuticals. Arresting the aging process. New antibiotics—the bugs are becoming immune to the old ones. I have a simple rule of thumb. I put the most investment dollars where the most research dollars are going. And that's medical high tech." He looked at Gogol. "What do you invest in?" he asked.

"Oh, myself, mainly." Gogol looked about for his butler. Where was the phone call from America?

"But that doesn't produce a predictable income," the banker said.

"My predictable income comes from finding a need and filling it," Gogol said. "And I have customers with limitless needs." He smiled. "Limitless."

"But don't you consider medical tech a good investment?"

Gogol looked with a sly grin at the banker. "I wouldn't seriously consider investing in medical high tech until they perfect the brain transplant."

"Why?"

"Because that will create a limitless need that someone will have to fill."

"Why that kind of a transplant in particular?" the banker's wife asked.

"Take the case of an old man," Gogol said. "A sick old man. He lies on his death bed. His heart is hanging by a thread. His lungs are on half power, his liver is all but dead from cirrhosis. His stomach will hold only a little oatmeal. His brain is dying from lack of blood carrying dopaminergics because his rotting old body can't supply them anymore. Up he gets and out he goes. It's time to do a little shopping."

"Shopping?" the banker asked with a wary grin. "What are you leading to?"

Gogol smiled back. "The old man visits a local gymnasium and gazes at all the young men with their superb physiques, lifting weights, running in treadmills, and he sees exactly the young body he wants and points his palsied finger." Gogol pointed with a quaking hand and said with a hoarse voice, "'That one. I'll take that one.'"

"Dear God," the banker's wife said.

"So," Gogol continued, "kidnappers seize the protesting young man and drag him to the hospital, and a doctor takes the young man's brain out. And he replaces it with the old man's brain. In a few days the old man's brain is walking around in a twenty-year-old body."

"God," the banker's wife said. "You can't be serious."

Gogol laughed at her. "If you believe in numerology, you'll believe in anything."

They all smiled uncertainly.

Gogol looked at the butler, who stood in the doorway then returned to the pantry. "Consider the case of the homely woman of wealth," Gogol went on. "She can go to a nightclub and point at any one of the gorgeous girls dancing in a chorus line and say, 'Put my brain in her body.'" He smiled at their doubtful expressions. "Do you suppose a homosexual and a lesbian could make a swap?"

After a pause, the table laughed.

"The possibilities are enormous," Gogol said. "Imagine yourself meeting a ravishing blond girl at a cocktail party and make an overture and she says, 'Don't be ridiculous, Frederich, I'm your mother.'"

The table laughed louder.

"And you say to her, 'I'm not Frederich.'" The table laughed again.

Leah watched their laughing faces. "One thing we will never be able to transplant," she said.

"What?"

"Our personalities. What you get at birth you are stuck with for life."

"Oh, people can develop," the banker said. "Don't you think so?"

Leah said, "The Greeks say character is fate. Your character determines the life you will lead. Modern psychologists mean the same thing when they say personality is destiny. That means you are what you're born. You can't change your personality."

"Predestination?" the banker's wife asked doubtfully.

"But surely," the editor said, "environment plays a role."

Leah shook her head. "If you are born with a conservative nature, you will be conservative for life. An introvert cannot become an extrovert. You become what you were born—a brilliant mathematician or successful banker, or even a failure. Or a suicide. And that's your existential cage—a life sentence. You're trapped inside the personality you're born with. You can't get out of it, and so it decides your life for you."

"Predestination?" the banker asked. "Is that what you say?"

"Well." Leah hesitated. "Determinism, anyway."

"My little Cassandra." Gogol toasted her with his wineglass. "She brings us such happy thoughts." His laughter made them laugh, and they returned happily to their food.

"Oh look," the editor's wife said. "It's snowing again." They all looked at the snow whirling around the glassed-in terrace. "What happened to that beautiful full moon?"

The butler leaned over to Gogol and whispered a message in his ear.

Gogol smiled. "Please excuse me," he said, throwing down his napkin. "I'll be right back." He went to his study.

"I got it," said a voice. "The whole conversation."

"On tape?" Gogol asked.

"Yes. On tape. I'm sending it by the courier. He's leaving Washington within a few hours."

"Then I'll see him"—Gogol looked at his watch—"in the morning sometime."

"Yes. This tape is going to blow out all the doors and windows of a certain building I could mention."

"Marvelous," Gogol said. "Simply marvelous. How is my friend Limoges?"

"For once he talked too much."

"We'll see," Gogol said. "In the morning."

He walked back to his guests with a light step. Snow was whirling at every window.

Later, alone, at bedtime, Gogol watched her step out of the filmy silk gown, leaving it on the tiles of the bedroom floor, abandoned. "Which deadly sin is this?" he asked her.

She paused beside the bed. "You are guilty of all seven."

He walked over and put his arms around her. "There's only one sin I'm interested in right now—how many times I can make love to you in my lifetime."

She looked at the stone wall beside the bed. "You're doing very well so far." Scraped on the wall were a row of tallies, each with four vertical marks and a fifth drawn diagonally through them.

"I want to fill the whole wall," he said.

"And how about the other deadly sins?"

He laughed. "You really softened up the stuffed shirts with that one. But your list of sins is outmoded. I have a list of deadly sins for modern times. I've made my own list."

"You are evil."

"No, not evil. Just sensible. In this world you have a very short time, and as your friend Nietzsche says, 'All things are lawful.'"

"Let me hear your list," she said. She smirked expectantly.

"Well, the first of the seven deadly sins is Poverty. . . ." He watched her smile broaden.

"Two. Boredom . . ." He paused.

"Go on," she urged.

"Hunger."

"That's three."

He smiled at her nude figure. "Chastity."

"You wicked man. That's four."

"Growing old."

"Ah-ha! You did believe what you were saying about brain transplants, didn't you?"

"Slow cars . . ."

"That's six," she said.

"And the seventh is living in Russia."

He watched her laugh, a superb smile with a deep, knowing chuckle. She touched his beard and looked into his eyes.

"Lovely pale blue," she said. "Much too pretty for a man." She patted his beard. "Be careful, Eric. You like danger too much. You are riding a tiger."

"I get off when I wish."

She shook her head. "You can't. You were born to ride the tiger."

"So? What's so bad about that?"

"The tiger always comes back alone."

••• Chapter 11

The courier arrived in Zurich on the morning flight from Washington. He pressed past the sauntering passengers, worked his way through passport control, skirted the baggage-claim area, and the NOTHING TO DECLARE customs desk, and hurried to a waiting automobile. The driver carried him quickly to Zurich on the auto route along the Limmat River then to an apartment just off Universitat Strasse. It had begun to snow again.

The driver let the courier out in front of a small apartment building, and waited with the motor running while the courier admitted himself with a key. He walked through the lobby and mounted a short flight of stairs. At the top he unlocked an apartment door and entered.

Gogol sat on a couch, arms folded, his heavy winter coat neatly folded over the back of the sofa, a briefcase by his side— like a traveler waiting patiently for a train.

The courier crossed the room and handed him an audio tape cassette.

"Will that be all, Mr. Marten?" he asked in Russian.

Gogol nodded.

"It's begun to snow again, sir," the courier said. He turned and left.

Gogol carried the cassette to a dining room table, put it into a tape deck and pushed the play button.

When the taped conversation began, there was a muffling of some sort over the microphone, but the two voices were clear enough. After a few sentences he was able to differentiate between Brewer's voice and Sauer's. Then he remained standing by the table impatiently.

"So what did they get?" Brewer's voice asked.

"Who?"

"The Moscow smugglers. In Vienna."

"Oh." A rustling of paper. "Confidential, of course."

There was a long pause.

"You know how bad this is?"

"You're the computer expert, Brewer. You tell me."

"This is state-of-the-art, top-of-the-line computer technology. The latest computer-operated soldering station. A prototype unit for disk drives. Vital parts for two central processing units."

"So?"

"So this helps the Russians make state-of-the-art electronic components for space weapons—Star Wars stuff. It's just the kind of capability we don't want them to have."

"It's that bad?"

"If they've managed to swipe the software to go with this, they're in production right now, making military hardware to use against us."

Gogol's impatience drove him to pacing. As the conversation wound on, he strode up and down the small room.

"Something's coming down," Sauer said. "And they don't want those Rooskie pickpockets swiping it."

"What's coming down?"

"I don't know. Something. All I have is a word I overheard . . . 'Cassandra,' whatever the hell that is."

Gogol clapped his hands together and settled into a chair. "Bravo!" he cried to the tape deck, applauding. "At last. Cassandra." When the tape ended, he rewound it and started it again. Then he called Revin in Cologne.

"I have momentous news. A major breakthrough. Yes yes. I'm very serious. Where shall we meet? How about my favorite city? No, not Paris. Zurich, Viktor. Zurich! We'll visit my money." He laughed easily. "Tomorrow? Of course. I'll pick you up at the airport. The evening flight. Auf Wiedersehen, my friend. When you hear what I have, your hands will tremble."

Chapter 12

Brewer called Dore Hesse at the National Security Council.

Hesse said, "My kid's in a high school play tonight. I can't see you."

"A drink at Khyber Pass."

"Is this important, Brewer?"

"In twenty minutes."

"Damn."

The faces strung along the bar at the Khyber Pass were like a living photo album of Brewer's past: men he'd worked with during his fifteen-year career. Some saluted him silently with the wave of a glass. Others spoke to him. Some thumped his back.

Dore Hesse entered and strolled along the bar, pumping hands like a politician working a crowd.

"The last time I saw you here, Charlie," Hesse said, "you were sitting at that table having lunch with Bobby McCall. It couldn't have been more than a few weeks later that he slapped the knife into your back. It's very good to see you all put back together."

"Thanks for the recommendation," Brewer said.

Hesse made a sour face. "What the hell does that mean?"

"Come on, Dore. Your fingerprints are all over the gun."

"Charlie, I can't talk to you about this."

"You put my name in the hat."

"Charlie, I want to say two things to you. Don't ask questions now. And go do what you have to do."

"Limoges has seen too many spy movies."

"No comment."

"Why did you give him my name?" Brewer asked.

"I wasn't the only one, Charlie. He asked everyone in Washington, and your name headed every list."

"You know what the job is, Dore?"

"No."

"A high-wire act with no net."

"Look, Charlie. I'm sorry. I didn't know what he had in mind when he asked for recommendations."

"You should have asked. Tell me who Limoges is."

"He's an academic—Ivy League colleges mainly. Contemporary history, political science, something like that. He writes thick books on Russian intelligence that no one reads. So everyone uses him as a consultant. He's been involved in the usual alphabet stuff. He's chairman of the Technology Export Control Committee at NSC."

"A yo-yo. You gave my name to an authentic, certifiable industrial-strength yo-yo."

Hesse rubbed his face thoughtfully and was silent. Then he said, "Charlie, you have the fatal flaw of having the unique characteristics he was looking for."

"What characteristics?"

"Cheers," Hesse said, holding up his glass.

Brewer touched Hesse's arm. "What was he looking for?"

"Someone who likes playing long odds—"

"What makes you think I like long odds?" Brewer asked.

"Come on, Charlie. I've played poker with you. I've been to the races with you. You're a genuine Silky Sullivan, running dead last, then in the home stretch pulling the trigger and beating the pack. That's what Limoges wanted. Come from behind, never say die, and a tremendous homestretch kick. You not only like long odds, you're addicted to them." Hesse sighed. "What did you want to see me about?"

"I need everything you have on Russian high-tech smugglers and their styles. Cases they've been involved in."

"If you're trying to stop high-tech theft, you're taking on the whole Directorate T." Hesse snorted. "Charlie Brewer versus twenty thousand Russian spies."

"How do you like the odds?" Brewer replied. "Is that Silky Sullivan enough for you?"

"Listen, Charlie. A French team of specialists was sent up

against Directorate T. You know about this? One of them was found in a trunk in a railroad station in Milan. Another was found dead in his car on the corniche near Monaco. And two others disappeared. The French are smarter than we are, Charlie. When they realized that Directorate T was behind the murders, they shut the Reds down, booted them out of France, and that was the end of that problem. And here we are, standing on our border, waving them in. Directorate T is nothing to mess with if you don't have solid backing from the front office. And you don't. Okay?"

"Case histories, Dore."

"Charlie, I didn't know what the job was. I apologize. Don't take this assignment. Hear? You'll be all alone."

"Case histories," Brewer said again.

"Okay, okay," Hesse said at last. "I'll get what I can. If you get caught with it, it's my ass."

"Are you playing the violin for me, Dore?"

"Get a Woodcrest attaché case. Model 1212-B. Buffalo brown." Hesse wrote the number on a paper bar napkin. "And bring it to the British Embassy tomorrow at four. And one last time—I promise you I'll never put your name in the hat again if you'll do one thing for me. Call Limoges and tell him you quit. Don't take this assignment."

•••Chapter 13

Gogol couldn't get to the Zurich airport fast enough. He smiled every time he thought of the expression he was going to put on Revin's face. Yet road conditions frustrated him. The autobahn was clear and dry all the way to Zurich, but in the winter twilight, great clouds of wind-blown snow were spinning off the white fields and pouncing on the roadway, momentarily blinding the drivers.

Gogol had a sudden yearning for hot sun—for a few days in Greece or perhaps St. Kitts. He thought of Leah bathing topless at St. Kitts.

But first—Zurich.

During those young years in his clerk's cubby in Moscow, quietly raging against the system that moved dull, plodding incompetents ahead of him—the son of an admiral, the grandson of an old Bolshevik, the daughter of a committee chairman—he dreamed of this moment. It was time at last to make his move against his enemies.

He touched the tape in his pocket again.

Like Ulysses, he was now barring the door, and inside the banquet hall, he was turning to confront his band of enemies with his bow and basketful of arrows. None would escape.

His price for this coup would be a basketful of Moscow heads. He would have them mounted on pikes and erected on the walls of the Kremlin. Particularly Arnoski, Tolenko, Bronowski.

He had learned that living well isn't the best revenge. Revenge is.

                              *   *   *

Revin was standing at the pickup station when Gogol arrived
at the airport. Gogol stepped eagerly out of his Porsche and
came striding around to Revin with that remorseless gusto, en
costume, fully dressed for the part in custom-made knee-high
snow boots, a custom-made loden coat, the end of his merrily
striped scarf sailing over his left shoulder, and his left hand holding his alpine hat on his head, dauntless as the figurehead on a
stormbound ship.

Like Pan he was, invincible, inevitable, piping the spring no
matter the weather. The spirit of fun. Was there ever a more
improbable relationship than this one between Gogol the Merry
and the grim-faced committee of Directorate T? As he watched
Gogol approach, Revin was put in mind of catastrophe.

"Viktor," Gogol said, clapping Revin on both shoulders.
"We are going to have an historic visit."

As usual the impeccable Swiss had cleared most of the new
fallen snow from the city walkways and roads of Zurich. Gogol
strolled with the impatient Revin along the Bahnhofstrasse. The
evening was star-filled, still, and sharply cold—made for walking—and he led Revin from one decadent shop window to another.

Revin didn't look well. He had dark patches below his eyes
and his pale face had deep fatigue lines that Gogol hadn't seen
before. He looked older than his forty-five years. Officially, Viktor Revin was attached to the Moscow technical acquisitions
company, Electronorg-Technika, but his primary job was working, through Mashproborintorg, with Gogol.

"We are walking over my gold, Viktor," Gogol said. "Right
under our feet in the bank vaults of Zurich."

"Your money is Russian money," Revin said. "Wrung from
the peasants a penny at a time."

"So? Isn't that the same place our esteemed leaders in the
Kremlin get theirs?"

"Emil," Revin said. "Do you realize that it was in this city
that Lenin conceived the Russian Revolution? He walked along
these same sidewalks that we are, over the same obscene piles of

gold, brooding over the slaughter of young men that was going on in the trenches all over Europe. Lenin sat in the Zurich library, studying the techniques of revolution in the history books, while all about him the First World War raged."

"Hurrah for literacy."

Revin assumed his paternal tone. "Would he be very proud of you, Emil, using your great gifts for self-aggrandizement?" Revin answered his own question with a shaking head.

"Well, I'm very proud of him," Gogol said. "After all, if it hadn't been for him, I wouldn't be where I am right now."

Revin looked away. "You are trying to irritate me." His eyes observed the parade of brilliantly lighted shop windows—the cascading diamonds, the lavishly dressed mannikins, the expensive cameras, the gilt-framed paintings, the magnificent Persian carpets—an endless array of enticements, all freshly tumbled from a giant cornucopia.

"Greed has made its masterpiece in Zurich," he said.

Gogol stopped Revin, put his hands on both shoulders and turned him face to face.

"Do you remember my first trip to the West, Viktor? It was Vienna. It was a summer's night on that marvelous promenade of Karntner Strasse. You've been there."

"Yes, yes," Revin said.

"All the outdoor cafés were open. And the shops. An abundance of things—a feast for the eyes. It was like nothing I had ever seen before. Vienna. Lights everywhere. And out on the promenade was a group of American university students in red-striped blazers and straw hats playing New Orleans jazz. It had this driving beat and a pulse. Overjoyed music. Free! Right there on the promenade, playing for no reason except the fun of it. And all those happy faces, strolling up and down in the summer night, stuffed with food, wrapped in expensive clothing. And on either side of Karntner Strasse, expensive shops like these as far as the eye could see. And I stood there and knew I could never go back to Russia and my clerk's job again. I didn't see greed. I saw the good life." He shook Revin. "Viktor. You can't get the genie back into the bottle."

Revin shook his head at Gogol. "How can we see things so differently? You see the bright and shiny toys, and I see the corruption and greed and selfishness. I see the sadness under all this trash."

Gogol laughed. "Trash," he said, "A good meal will cheer you up, Viktor. How about a rack of lamb at the Jockey Club? No? Not the place for a good communist. And certainly not the filet of veal flambéed in kirsch at the Kronenhalle. Some of your bosses eat there, Viktor, whenever they visit."

"Don't be absurd."

"Not the Ermitage? And not the Eden au Lac? What would Lenin say? Then we shall go to the Alpiner Stube—it's just a quiet small place, Viktor, with a cheery fire, justly celebrated for its wonderful fondue." Gogol took Revin's arm again to lead the way.

"Loosen up, Viktor," he said. "Even communists are allowed to enjoy themselves."

"What is this news you want me to be so excited about?" Revin demanded.

"Let's eat and talk," Gogol said. He felt for the tape cassette in his pocket. In his other pocket he touched the necklace. The nineteen-thousand-dollar necklace. Revenge.

Revin liked cheese. Sitting at the table with the fondue pot between them, he forked the squares of bread into the bubbling pot of melted cheese and ate them with pleasure. As he chewed, his eyes moved from the wavering flame under the fondue pot to the dancing flames in the fireplace. The Alpiner Stube was filled with the odor of burning applewood. There was frost in the corners of the windows, a murmur of contented voices in the air. The cheese was delicious.

As they drank the last of the wine, Gogol asked, "Viktor, how did you like that wine?"

"Fine. It seemed fine. Although I have no taste for wine."

"You have no taste for anything. You're a worker ant. You never lift your eyes up. A bowl of peasant soup or a rack of lamb—it's all the same to you. Do you know this wine costs one hundred dollars a bottle? And to you it could be cold tea."

Gogol looked at him and shook his head slowly. "Nothing is worth a hundred dollars a bottle."

"Can you name the two leading importing countries for that wine, Viktor?"

"I can't say that I care."

"The United States and Japan. But the third country, Viktor, that should interest you. It's Russia. I can hear the corks popping all over the homeland right now, at the tables of the party faithful. Hundred-dollar bottles of wine, wrung from the peasants a penny at a time."

"Why are you telling me this now? What is your motive?"

"The human heart is not what Marx said it was," Gogol replied. "The worker is not the noble creature he pictured, corrupted by capitalism. The human heart is very very flawed, my friend, even in Russia. Man can't measure up to Marx. Our own party leaders don't believe in the earthly communist paradise. Man can never be that good. Controlled environments and psychological conditioning cannot create a new man."

"Somehow, Emil, you've missed the point."

"Have I?" Gogol laughed. "You walked the Bahnhofstrasse with me. You saw all the bright and shiny things people have their hearts set on. Monkey hearts. Look where you are in the communist hierarchy, Viktor. Where is your career? While you are working for the common man, your friends in Moscow are drinking expensive wines behind closed doors."

Revin's face flushed.

"Your career is stalled," Gogol said. "Just like mine was. And all you do is brood about it. Viktor, you know what your problem is? You care. And that makes you odd man out. Look at Moscow. It's every man for himself."

"Enough."

"Viktor. Let's talk about you. Let's talk about making you rich along with me. Quietly rich. I can make you as rich as an emperor. Right here in Zurich." He pointed at the floor. "Serve your country Viktor, but serve yourself too. The two things are not incompatible. You agree?"

"I don't want to hear such talk."

"Grandson of one of the founders of the Revolution and son-in-law to a general, and what have you got to show for it?"

"Enough," Revin said.

"How is your sweet wife, Viktor? Lovely girl. Much too

good for you. And you treat her terribly. Here, Viktor. For her. Your wife. With my deep affection." Gogol put the purple velvet jeweler's case on the tablecloth and pushed it slowly over the table with a forefinger to Revin.

Revin opened the jeweler's case and gazed at the contents. He looked at the price tag. Stunned, he looked at Gogol. "Are you insane? You spent nineteen thousand dollars for this? My wife can't wear it."

"Oh yes, she can. You know how such things are managed. You put that in your pocket, Viktor. And take it to her. Take it to her. You tell your superiors that I personally bought it for her and expect to see her wearing it next time we meet. They will not permit me to be offended, Viktor. I am their little goose that lays the golden eggs. And you are the official goose tender. You are entitled to rewards and perks. Don't ask, Viktor. Don't petition. Demand. They will understand that."

"Demand what?"

"Demand your place in the sun."

"Why? For what reason?"

"For saving the Soviet Union from destruction. After tonight you will have plenty of reasons. After tonight they will all fall all over themselves to give you what you want."

"I fail to see—"

"Viktor. Viktor. Viktor. Listen to me. Every little bureaucrat in Moscow tucks himself into his bed at night secure and warm because of the air defense technology I smuggled into Russia. Do any of them write me a note and express gratitude? Where are my medals? I'm worth twenty divisions in the field. Who says so? Zeitzov says I am worth twenty divisions in the field. Me. Me, Viktor. Me."

Revin nodded reluctantly. "That's true," he said.

"Of course it is. Everytime the MiG Foxbat flies with its American look-down/shoot-down system, you have to think of me. Everytime your computers skip happily through ABACUS, you have to think of me. Every really crucial piece of high-tech equipment in Zeleenograd came through me."

"Emil, I concede all this."

Gogol pushed on. "After Arnoski botched it three times, and lost millions and millions of rubles in the process, didn't I deliver to you an entire microchip factory? One hundred percent built from spare parts which I painstakingly assembled from all over the world and shipped into Russia personally. Is that not right? Brilliant, wasn't it?"

Revin waved a dismissing hand. "Yes yes. Brilliant. We all agree."

"And after those idiots in Directorate T fumbled and fumbled and failed to get that ABACUS software, getting three of our best agents kicked out of the U.S. in the bargain, who was it that got it in one weekend?"

"Yes yes, Emil. I have already conceded all this. What has it got to do with this necklace?"

But Gogol wouldn't be placated. Using his fingers, he continued to toll off other smuggling coups. The list was long, and Revin knew Gogol could extend it endlessly. "And just recently, Viktor, who conceived and operated that Vienna job, leaving the American agents watching a bunch of empty cartons?"

Revin sighed. "So—come to the point."

"When your wife goes to another function, I want her to wear this little bauble. I want those people in Directorate T to know where it came from, and I want them biting the rug with frustration and envy. This little bauble will be like a beam in the eye to them."

"I still fail to see," Revin said. "We have made you rich beyond your dreams. You have villas all over the world. For all I know you gargle every morning with hundred-dollar wine. If you wish, you could encrust your potty with diamonds. We paid you four million American dollars for that Foxbat radar system alone."

"A bargain! An incredible bargain. You know it cost the Americans fifty-two million to develop it."

"You charged the Poles a million dollars for that computer system you sold them."

"They were eager to pay it. How much do you think it was really worth? You Moscow bureaucrats have a stupid streak, Viktor. You're so used to stealing what you want, you resent paying even a dollar for a device that could change the course of world history. Huge egos. You decorate yourself with others' feathers."

Revin's face flushed. "Don't denigrate your own country, Emil. Russian technology has created wonders. In just forty years we took our nation from the ashes of war to one of the leading powers in the world. I could list all night what we're doing. And we now have our own computer. The Ryad Two—"

"Oh come, Viktor. It's a bad copy of the IBM."

"There are thousands of them in use."

"Are there, Viktor? Where? The Ryad Two is good enough to sell to the Bulgarians and the Poles. But do we use the Ryad Two to operate our military defense systems? What computer guards Moscow? And Leningrad? And all the other vital centers of Russia? Is it our Ryad Two? No, Viktor. IBMs, many of which I smuggled. Big Blue protects Russia."

Revin raised his head. "We could defeat the West now if we went to war."

"Only if it's a short war, Viktor. We can't even maintain our equipment. I have to smuggle the IBMs back into the West so that Western technicians can get them operating again. We don't have the spare parts for a long war. What would we do if our Moscow air defense computer went down? Call IBM in New York for a repairman? A two-month war would wipe us out. No. What's going to wipe us out is your Russian capacity for self-delusion. If you want to prevail, you'd best start telling yourselves the truth. Self-criticism from your internal critics. You'd best learn to listen to those voices. The nation that silences criticism commits suicide."

"You are mistaken, Emil. Russia will prevail. Remember what Lenin said: the West will sell us the rope we need to hang them with. We are not only acquiring Western technology. The West is lending us the money to buy it with. And now our technology is catching up. And soon will surpass the West. I tell you one thing: we put Sputnik up first, and we did it with lesser technology than the Americans had then. We make do with what we have. And that's our secret. That's how we'll win. You'll see." Revin touched Gogol's arm. "You may be Eric Marten, the great European computer expert and wheeler-dealer. But back in Moscow you are still Emil Gogol, a member of the Directorate T team."

"Am I, Viktor? Am I just another Arnoski? A Tolenko? A Bronowski?"

"Directorate T has a long memory, Emil. And a long arm."

"Then let them remember all I've done for Russia—more than that entire pack of incompetents could do in ten lifetimes."

"This is not the time or place to—" Revin looked down at Gogol's extended hand. "What's this?"

"The necklace, Viktor. For your wife. I want her to wear it." Gogol leaned over and gripped Revin's cuff with his fist. "And Viktor, that's nothing compared to what else I want."

"And what else do you want?"

In reply Gogol held up the tape cassette. "It's time to talk, Viktor."

"No no," Revin said. "I want first to hear what you want. If it isn't great wealth, what is it?"

"Power."

Chapter 14

Gogol opened the door to the apartment with a great flourish.

"Now," Revin said, "we'll see what this momentous event is."

"Patience, Viktor," Gogol said.

Revin stepped into the apartment, sallow-faced, his exhausted eyes looking out from under bristling brows at the furnishings. All this odd miscellany of furniture, much of it here from the old days. It had been the setting for countless crises over the years, as Directorate T had fumbled for ways to get its hands on desperately needed American technology—until they found Gogol, a born thief and confidence man, an inspired dissembler and intriguer, right there in his little cubby in Moscow. If the furniture could talk—the thought made him sigh. Was there no end to these crises?

"Tea," he said to Gogol. "I want a cup of tea." And he went familiarly to the kitchen. "This week," he called from the kitchen, "I flew to Moscow to report to the committee."

"And . . ." Gogol searched the shelf of the hall closet for the tape deck. He found it where he'd put it—under a pillow, enwrapped with wires.

"I was grilled for two hours," Revin said.

"So . . ."

"They think that you're playing." Revin stuck his head out of the kitchen and looked pointedly at Gogol. "They think that you should have found Cassandra by now."

"Ha!" Gogol looked to the ceiling for mercy. "Half of Russia is looking for Cassandra. And they think I should have found it by now."

Gogol plugged the tape-deck wire into an outlet. Then he slipped the cassette into the tray.

"It was only a few days ago," he said loud enough for Revin to hear, "that I stole that desperately needed microchip-manufacturing equipment. It gives them a capability they never had before. They haven't even gotten it all out of the crates and cartons yet. Do I get phone calls of congratulation, medals, a posh dacha in the woods? No. I get a complaint that I haven't found Cassandra yet."

"That's always been the way," Revin said. "Since we all climbed down from the trees. A bureaucratic system is never grateful."

"When I get Cassandra, they're going to be grateful," Gogol replied. "The whole committee will file past me and each will plant a resounding kiss on my bare ass."

"I will bring a camera," Revin said.

"Here," Gogol said. "I want you to listen to something."

"What?" Revin walked up to the tape deck and watched Gogol push the play button.

"So what did they get?" Charlie Brewer's voice asked.

"Who?"

"The Moscow smugglers. In Vienna."

"Who am I listening to?" Revin asked.

"Two American agents," Gogol said, "one named Sauer and the other named Brewer."

"Brewer? Charlie Brewer?" Revin sat down in a chair. He listened with the fingers of both hands on his lips. Periodically he grunted.

"You know how bad this is?" Brewer's voice asked.

"You're the computer expert, Brewer. You tell me."

"This is state-of-the-art, top-of-the-line computer technology," Brewer's voice said. "The latest computer-operated soldering station. A prototype unit for disk drives. Vital parts for two central processing units."

"So?"

"So this helps the Russians make state-of-the-art electronic components for space weapons—Star Wars stuff. It's just the kind of capability we don't want them to have."

"It's that bad?"

"If they've managed to swipe the software to go with this, they're in production right now, making military hardware to use against us."

Revin cleared his throat. "Brewer is a very dangerous agent," he said. "The committee will be very unhappy about this." His face seemed even grayer.

They listened for several minutes in silence, then Gogol held up a finger to call Revin's attention to what was to come.

"Something's coming down," Sauer said. "And they don't want those Rooskie pickpockets swiping it."

"What's coming down?" Brewer's voice asked.

"I don't know. Something. All I have is a word I overheard . . . 'Cassandra,' whatever the hell that is."

"Cassandra," Brewer echoed.

Gogol stopped the tape. He pointed at Revin. "Cassandra," he said. "I want you to remember two things, Viktor. With every intelligence service in Russia looking for this brain and not finding it, I want you to remember that I was the person who found the first clue that Cassandra exists. I found it. And also, the price tag this time is my price tag. Money's not going to do it."

"Oh? What is?"

"First of all I want you to have the status of a general who commands twenty divisions in the field."

"Do you really think they'll do that?"

"Do they want Cassandra?"

"They don't want trouble," Revin said. "Brewer is the last man we want to face. He knows as much about stealing and smuggling as you do. We've had great trouble with this man before. Arnoski considers him one of the most dangerous men in American intelligence."

"Arnoski either overrates or underrates everybody, Viktor."

"Tolenko agrees with Arnoski. He tried to have Brewer assassinated a few years ago."

"Tolenko wants to assassinate everyone," Gogol said.

"Emil, you mustn't minimize this man. He's a bone in our throats."

"Perhaps I'll be a bone in his throat."

Revin looked away with smoldering irritation. "Your ego has become enormous."

Revin often found Gogol's preening self-confidence annoying. But time and again in the past when the committee's projects had collapsed, when desperately needed American technology had been stopped at some border or other, huge sums of money lost, discouragement and weariness at hand, Gogol—with that driving self-confidence and his brilliant stratagems—had galloped in, snatched up the banner, and carried the field.

Time and again, at the committee table, faces of chagrin and fury had been pasted over with paper smiles. Hands that wanted to kill were forced to applaud. How they envied Gogol and his successes, how they needed him, how they feared his failure and yet how fervently wished for it. Their little goose that lays the golden eggs had gotten completely out of control.

The proof of his enormous success was in the Gogol Express—that network of European roadways over which capitalist trucks and trains and vans carried vital Western war matériel to the very gates of Russia—a flow of smuggled goods that flooded unabated even as they sat talking. Emil Gogol—as Eric Marten, the quintessential capitalist—had created the greatest shell game in espionage history. And it was powered by the boundless self-assurance of his brilliant and irritating ego. But Gogol had never faced a Charlie Brewer before.

"I think you should understand the threat that this Brewer poses," Revin said. "I will give you one illustration. A few years ago Brewer was free-lancing around the world. You may remember the arms dealer, Mann."

"Oh yes," Gogol said. "He was a Swiss. Right here in Zurich."

"Yes. Mann was sick and old, and the people in the arms business had taken advantage of that. Several dozen independent arms sellers owed him great sums of money. Mann hired Charlie Brewer to collect the money for him." Revin looked closely at Gogol. "Are you listening, Emil?"

"To every word."

"When the word got out that Brewer was collecting, many of those men paid up on the spot. Others ran for their lives. They went into hiding. But Brewer found every one of them, Emil. In Cape Town, Buenos Aires. Hong Kong. New Delhi. And he collected every penny. One of those men was never heard of again."

"Good for Brewer," Gogol said.

"But not good for you, Emil. Have you ever seen a ferret go after a rat, Emil? Have you?"

Gogol smiled. "No. I don't think I have."

"Well, go see for yourself. Then you'll know how Brewer works, and you'll know why so many men are terrified of him. It will remove that smirk from your face."

"And maybe Brewer will end up terrified of me."

"I wish you good luck, Emil."

Gogol laughed. "Viktor, shall I ever return to Russia?" he asked.

Gogol's self-image was accurate: Revin felt he *was* watching a mischievous genie escaped from his bottle, on the loose in the land—and about to cause a catastrophe. How do you get a genie back into the bottle? How do you get the toothpaste back into the tube?

"The question is," Revin said, "will you find Cassandra before Brewer finds you?"

"Doubt, Viktor? Do I hear doubt in your voice?"

"This Cassandra affair could bring catastrophe," Revin said. He went and stood by the window. If catastrophe came, it would come not with earth-shaking drums and rippling black pennants, full of rushing action and terrible noises, like a war or a volcano or a burst dam. No. That's not the way things happened in the intelligence world. Cassandra would lug disaster onto the stage with no fanfare: the bubonic flea hopping onto the clothing of passersby, a drop of water between two hull plates, a lone rider cresting the horizon.

"What catastrophe, Viktor?"

"The murder of Charlie Brewer."

Gogol frowned. "Who wants that?"

"The committee will," Revin said. He looked down at the

parking area. Snow was falling again. Swirling out of the blackness and into the streetlights. The cars in the parking area were rapidly being covered. It would snow all night.

Revin longed for sun and fields of flowers, far away from crises. He looked at Gogol. "You know what they'll say. They'll order Brewer's death. And to tell the truth, that's what's needed."

Gogol shook his head. "But it may be unnecessary. Do you understand how difficult it will be for this Brewer to find me? First he has to find Eric Marten. And that's very unlikely. Then he has to discover that Eric Marten is Emil Gogol of Directorate T. And that's even more unlikely. Even if he manages to do it, it will take him a very long time. We should have found Cassandra by then. Killing Brewer can cause worse problems than not killing him. It would be a war of spies." Gogol unwrapped and dropped into his tea a lump of sugar as Revin watched. Then he unwrapped another and dropped it into the cup.

"You don't want him killed?" Revin asked.

"As you said, killing Brewer would be a catastrophe," Gogol answered.

"Ah," Revin said. "But not killing him may be a grave mistake."

Gogol chuckled. "The classic no-win situation." He dropped a third lump into his tea and unwrapped a fourth. He smiled at Revin's disapproving eyes. "When I get diabetes," he said, "I will have nothing but twenty-four-carat-gold needles. Viktor, if the committee wants Brewer killed, I can't stop them. But I have one request. See to it that the job is done properly. Don't use the usual cut-rate killers. This has to be a first-class job. I can get you just the man, if you want. Shall I?"

"No no." Revin was thoughtful.

Gogol took the tape out of the deck and pressed it into Revin's palm, then carefully wrapped Revin's fingers around it. "Play this for that absurd committee."

"It's almost like a joke," Revin said. "It contains good news and bad news. Cassandra and Brewer." Revin looked down at the tape in his hand. His face was very pale.

"What is it, Viktor?"

"For one of the few times in my life, I'm filled with foreboding."

"You need a vacation."

"We all need a vacation. The whole world needs a vacation from this cold war. It has gone on too long. It should have ended long ago. One way or the other."

"I warn you again about Brewer," Gogol said. "Don't miss."

Chapter 15

Brewer bought an attaché case at Shapiro's the next afternoon. Woodcrest Model 1212-B. Buffalo brown. Then he took a cab to the British Embassy on Massachusetts Avenue. In the embassy cloakroom he fitted the empty case on the lower hat shelf between two other attaché cases.

The reception room was crowded with a hodgepodge of Washington diplomatic people, mostly young, mostly lower rung—third secretaries from some twenty embassies smouching stale gossip from each other. The British were fishing for something. And there were a lot of East Bloc nosybodies in the crowd, come to see what it was the British were looking for.

The scotch was better than the standard level of bad booze usually served at these lesserling's sessions. Already the murmuring voices were growing strident.

In his book, Krowbin, the Russian defector, stated that he picked up some of his most valuable leads from embassy gargles. The Russians rarely held them, and when they did, they loaded them with KGB.

The British military attaché strolled up to Brewer. "Your presence is noted, Brewer," he said. "How are you?"

"Checking out the wastebaskets," Brewer said.

"All you'll find in mine are the rejects from other wastebaskets."

"Lots of Bloc people here."

"Yes. I've noticed. Poles and Russians, mainly. I think the Poles are here to watch the Russians, and the Russians are here to watch the Poles. They're all very goosey lately."

"What about?" Brewer asked.

"Who knows? I hear there's been a lot of pushing and shoving behind closed doors. It all involves the Czechs somehow."

At four-thirty Hesse arrived with a very pretty woman. A few moments later Brewer went to the cloakroom and looked about. His empty Woodcrest attaché case was where he had left it on the lower shelf. Directly above it was a duplicate Woodcrest. He pulled it down and walked out with it.

Hesse had been thorough. The packet of papers was over an inch thick, and most were classified documents. Some were secret. On top of the file was a handwritten note: "Khyber Pass, 7 P.M. Without fail." Hesse had given him less than three hours.

He sat on a stool in his kitchen, put the papers on the counter and slowly went through them. There were pages of reports on specific acts of smuggling, mainly in Europe—all brief and lacking in details. If there was a Mr. X behind any of the dozens of cases, there was no hint of in these papers.

Most of the reports were useless—repackaging information cribbed from other reports that had been cribbed from previous reports. Most of the information was old. All the studies expressed great concern with the problem but were very short on specific information.

Several white papers recited old background material. One recounted the history of Directorate T and its formation by Andropov in 1974 specifically to acquire American technology, after Russia realized that it had fallen alarmingly far behind the United States.

Another paper described the beleaguered state of the Department of Commerce, which was assigned the task of stopping the outflow. Another reported on the administration's determined efforts to stop the smuggling, efforts that ended in frustration. That paper predicted that the volume of Russian smuggling would not only continue, but increase.

There was nothing that would show Brewer a pattern or point toward an individual. After several hours Brewer put the papers back in their folders and put the entire file in the attaché case. At seven he drove to Khyber Pass.

There was something arrogant about Hesse. Making a pass

involving two identical attaché cases in a pub frequented by professional spooks from many different branches of government—many of whom had made many similar passes on numerous occasions—was the height of smugness. The move was bound to be spotted by a number of knowing eyes.

Hesse sat at a bar stool talking to four or five others. Brewer sat next to him and joined in the conversation. A few minutes later Hesse bowed out, took his attaché case up and left, leaving Brewer's new attaché case between the stools.

Later that evening, when he got home, Brewer opened the attaché case before pushing it up on a closet shelf. Inside he found a rabbit's foot.

•••Part Four

●●● **Chapter 16**

Margie watched Brewer's preoccupation. There was something he wasn't telling her. Something troubling and personal. One evening when he kissed her, she touched his lips with her fingertips. "Your kisses have sadness in them lately, Charlie," she said.

Everytime she hung her coat up, she noticed the brown envelope up on the shelf where Brewer had put it. It looked abandoned. Forgotten.

Perhaps the answer lay there. She lifted the envelope down, carried it over to her couch, and pulled all the documents out onto her lap. Writs. Interrogatories. Stipulations. Transcripts. Extracts. A fugitive arrest warrant for Bobby McCall. Proclamations. Copies countersigned. Official seals. A parade of papers generated by a parade of people. Clerks of the Court. Judges. Attorneys. Chief of Detectives. Warden. Register of Documents. It all should have made him happy. But it hadn't. Humpty Dumpty was pushed, he said.

To her surprise, the check was still there, near the bottom of the pile, accompanied by a statement of account—columns of figures headed by code numbers, glossary on the back. It was a check for his lost time, his other perquisites and emoluments, restored pension time—a large sum of money which could have remained in the envelope for years. How casually Brewer had pushed it into the envelope and out of his mind. He had a total lack of interest in money.

When she restacked the papers to put them back, a white envelope fell out. It was addressed to Mr. Charles Brewer. "Personal & Confidential." In the upper left-hand corner was the office address of Madeline Hale. The note itself had been only half pushed back into the envelope. Slipping it into the other papers, she put the pile back on the shelf.

Margie went into her bedroom, changed her clothes, changed her shoes, carried a load of wash to the washer in the bathroom, then crossed the living room back to the closet and lifted down the pile. Finding the white envelope, she sat down on the couch with it.

Without hesitation she unfolded Madeline Hale's note and read it.

> Charlie.
>
> These are all the papers concerning your pardon. Every jot and tittle has been taken care of. I hope you can get all this behind you now and get on with your life. I'm sorry about us. We could have made it work. I wanted to. I put no conditions on our relationship. Take care of yourself, Charlie. I'll always remember you.

Margie put the envelope back in the pile, shoved all the papers into the manila envelope and restored it to the hall closet. Then she went into the bathroom and loaded the laundry in the washer. A few moments later she returned to the closet, took down the letter once more, and reread it. And read it again. By the time she returned the note again, she had memorized it.

It was her practice, periodically, usually after a shower, to stand before her full-length bathroom mirror to take inventory of herself and analyze the way she fit into the world. She felt it was time to do it again, and now, while reloading the washing machine, she took off all her clothes and tossed them in too. Then she looked at her figure.

"A little cellulite there, doll," she said, poking a finger at her thighs. She pinched the flesh around her waist. "Remove two inches." She looked at her breasts. "Add two inches." She twitched her mouth. "But then—he likes them." She saw her face in the mirror: plain girl-next-door style. Not cover-girl material. Things never got better: lately, very faint lines around the mouth and eyes. Gather ye rosebuds while ye may. She looked at herself from head to foot. "From nose to toes, doll, you're no competition for Madeline Hale. So what makes him stick around?"

She looked at the woman in the mirror who looked back at her.

"Poacher," she said.

She awoke one night and found him beside her wide awake, arms behind his head, staring at the ceiling.

"What time is it?" she asked.

"Three o'clock."

"You okay?"

"I always wake up at three o'clock."

"Why?"

"In my head it's always three o'clock in the morning and I'm still locked in that prison cell. And I still hear that kid's heels kicking the wall next to me when he hung himself."

"You have to get past what Bobby McCall did to you," she said. "He framed you. He let you go to prison. And now you're out with a full pardon. That's that. It can't always be three o'clock, Charlie."

"Once upon a time," he said, "I thought I was Archimedes."

"Who's Archimedes?"

"A Greek mathematician. He said, 'Give me a place to stand, and I can move the earth.' That was me. It was all cops and robbers. The good guys versus the bad guys. And all for fun. A meaningless game. I could move the earth."

"And. . . ?"

"And then I went to prison."

Chapter 17

T he next morning Revin sat in a coffeehouse in Cologne, reading a paper and periodically looking at his watch, waiting for ten o'clock. At last he paid his bill and carefully buttoned up against the cold. Then he walked toward the cathedral.

His head was pushed deeply into an astrakhan fur hat. Seldom, even in the coldest parts of Russia, had he felt a wind as fierce as this. Just as the snow seemed to be stopping, the wind pounced with another snow shower that for minutes on end could white out the whole city. He stood on the steps of the cathedral, grateful to be out of the wind and watching for the two of them to come across the cathedral square.

It would not be hard to see them. That numbing wind, whistling up the river, had swept the streets clear of all but the most stubborn pedestrians.

They came at last, the most improbable pair Revin had ever seen, their figures a grotesque contrast.

One was tall, nearly seven feet, limbs as thin as sticks, wearing a long black overcoat only partly buttoned, coat skirts billowing in the wind. A flapping wide-brimmed black hat sat on his head like a black halo. The ends of a long crimson scarf sailed like pennants behind him. A grimace exposed huge white teeth in an olive face. He was so tall and emaciated, he appeared even taller, a man striding on stilts. He seemed unaware of the cold.

The other, walking on massive legs in blue jeans that rubbed together with each step, wore an expensive sheepskin shortcoat buttoned up to his throat and tightly belted around his broad waist. His hands were like great paws in their sheepskin mittens. On his head, a sheepskin hat with earflaps tied under his chin.

Yellowed teeth showed under a huge black Turkish moustache and a scimitar of a nose, very red. He shivered.

Revin had misgivings as soon as he saw them. He clicked his tongue in dismay. Where had Tolenko gotten them? Cut-rate cutthroats from a human bargain basement somewhere in the Middle East. Just what Gogol had warned him about. It must be a first-class job, Gogol had said.

Revin let them step up out of the wind. This was going to be a very quick meeting. He held the red bound book prominently on his chest as they crossed to meet him.

"We bring greetings from the sunny clime of the Bosphorus," the heavy one recited in demotic French. His towering companion stared at Revin remorselessly with dilated pupils. Revin decided he was on something—a hard drug of some kind.

Revin held out an envelope, and it was taken by the tall one's bare hand, grotesquely long and thin.

"In there," Revin said, "you'll find two passports. Yours is Syrian"—he glanced at the tall man, then at the other—"and yours is Algerian. You'll also find two airline tickets—round trip, Cologne to London. You will wait in London at the hotel noted in that envelope until you get further orders. Other people are setting things up. Understand?"

The heavy one nodded, then shivered even more violently.

Revin tapped the envelope held by that impossibly long, phthisic brown hand. "You will receive airline tickets in London and further instructions. You have already discussed the job and all its details, is that not so?"

"That is so," the heavy man said. "Including the man's name, Charlie Brewer, and the city, Washington, and the agent who will meet us in Washington. We've been briefed a number of times."

"Are you sure you understand it all?" Revin asked.

The heavy man nodded his enormous black moustache up and down. "I can walk and chew gum," he said, and hooted a deep laugh.

Revin worried some more. "Change all your money into American," he reminded them, and watched the stout man's nodding face. "And carry nothing but the money, the two passports, and the two airline tickets. You are to cut all the labels from your clothing. Do you understand?"

The heavy man grinned broadly with chattering teeth. "I speak five languages," he said. "And understand them all." He looked at the desperately thin face of his companion, who stared down at Revin without expression. "And he understands what I tell him."

Revin went on. "When you get to London, memorize the information in the envelope. When you leave for Washington, destroy everything but the airline tickets and passports," he said. "Understood?"

The heavy man nodded. The tall one stared.

"When you meet our agent in Washington, he will give you the rest of the details." He looked at their two faces. They seemed to be expecting him to say more.

"That's all, then," he said. The meeting was over. He watched them walk back the way they had come; the tall one swaying his stick limbs inside his fluttering trousers and coat, the ends of his crimson scarf fluttering before him; the other, a rolling tun bundled inside sheepskin. From his coat pocket protruded the cover of *Playboy* magazine. They disappeared in a sudden whiteout.

Revin hurried off to a warm fire and hot tea, filled with foreboding.

••• Chapter 18

The lastest episode in Eastern Bloc quarreling in Washington finally leaked into the newspapers. It was reported in Penny Pine's column on embassy news.

The Russians are denying it, but last night a young diplomat attached to the Czechoslovakian Embassy blackened the eye of a Russian diplomat during a reception in the Polish Embassy. The Czechoslovakian was hurried onto the next flight home. 'Tis said that behind closed doors Mr. Karlov, the Russian ambassador, is still raising cain about the incident. Here in Washington lately there has been a considerable amount of quarreling going on among the East European nationals behind those firmly closed doors. No one will say what the quarreling is about. To be continued . . .

Brewer recalled what the British military attaché had told him. Goosey Russians following sullen Poles watching hostile Czechs. Brewer sent a message to a contact in the Czechoslovakian Embassy. Then he went to the National Gallery to wait.

At three-thirty his Czech contact came strolling down the stairs from an upper floor of the Gallery, carrying a visitor's guide. He went traipsing along the corridor through the bookshop, where he studied the array of framed reproductions then bought four children's coloring books. He strolled past the cafeteria, stared at the waterfall, then stepped onto the moving walkway to the new wing. Brewer waited by the waterfall as the Czech rode the walk to the end. There he turned right to the rest rooms.

Brewer walked back to another rest-room area by the book-shop and entered a phone booth with a sign that said OUT OF ORDER. He waited. A moment later the phone rang. Brewer lifted it off the hook.

"What can I do for you?" the Czech asked.

"What happened Tuesday night?" Brewer asked.

"Punches. My friend Alexandr just had a stomachful of this arrogant Russian bastard and put one right—what's the expression?—right on the chops. Broke his nose. Really shut his mouth. All the Czechs there applauded. Then the stupid Russian bastard gets up, still mouthing out. And Alexandr landed another and broke some teeth. Finally he picked up this heavy metal lamp, and was going to break the bastard's head open, when we stopped the fight. He might have killed that crazy Rooskie."

"What's the problem?" Brewer asked. "What's going on?"

"They're crazy. The Russians are crazy. They're screaming at everyone. They're using everyone. . . . They're searching our wastebaskets. They're accusing our intelligence people of hold-ing back information. They're calling us traitors. They're look-ing for something, and they think we know about it, laughing behind their backs. Paranoid bastards."

"What do they want?"

"I don't know. They're obsessed with getting more intelli-gence on American military stuff. They can't get enough. I tell you, they're looking frantically for something."

"What?"

"I don't know. Something."

"What are they looking for?" he asked again.

"I don't know. Something. Star Wars stuff. They think the Americans have some Star Wars stuff. They want to steal it. Something called Cassandra. I tell you, Charlie, you people are as crazy as the Russians. Do you think they would let you come into their country and steal their technology? Go to Zeleenograd and see what they would do. They have a mine field around the entire city and the tightest security on earth. Try to steal a secret from them and you'll get both legs blown off. And that's what you should do to them. Shoot them. Cut them off at the knees. Everyone wonders why you let them get away with it. You let their airliners routinely fly over your military sites, but you see what happens when an airliner flies over one of theirs. They shoot it down. Like that Korean airliner. They not only shoot it down, but then in full view of the whole world they pin a medal on the jet fighter pilot who did the job. A medal for killing women and babies."

Brewer waited patiently for the excited flow of words to stop. Then he said, "I need more information about what they're looking for."

"I can't help much longer, Charlie," the Czech said. "My tour of duty is up soon. I want to defect, but my wife won't hear of it. She doesn't want to be cut off from our families. The children's grandparents would go crazy. So it's back to a Russian police state again for us. So. Okay. I'll see what I can find out."

Brewer put the phone on the hook thoughtfully. That was twice he had heard that word—Cassandra. He called Hesse. "What do you make of this fistfight in the Polish Embassy?"

"The Czech got in some good shots. Broke the Russian's nose and some of his teeth, and broke two bones in his own hand doing it. Tempers are hot. Things are getting out of control. So something's up."

"What?"

"I don't know, Charlie," Hesse said. "The Russians are driving everyone crazy. They're looking for something."

"Find out."

"I don't even know what I'm looking for."

"Try Cassandra," Brewer said.

Chapter 19

I t was an old Victorian house, top heavy with extra bedrooms originally intended for children and servants. Wearily it stood watching the ceaseless traffic, not far from Heathrow Airport. All about it, the rooftops of London were covered with snow, and the streets were under several inches of frozen slush.

Over the door was a sign, badly weathered, that said:

Mehtma's London House
Bed and Breakfast
Full Pension Available
Special Weekly Rates
Indian Cuisine a Specialty

The two of them stepped from the cab and looked at the building and at the sign. The stout one paid the driver then lugged his canvas bag up the steps and rang the bell.

The tall one, with his black overcoat slung over his shoulder and his black hat cocked on the back of his head, mounted slowly behind him, bearing his bag. Around his neck was draped his crimson scarf.

They would wait at Mehtma's until they received a telegram.

Mehtma himself, thin as a thread, with a Buddha's belly, stood in the doorway, chafing his hands against the cold. Air as warm as a hothouse and heavy with cooking odors flowed through the open door. Mehtma spoke to the stout one with a clipped, quick, Indian accent, nodding and beckoning and taking his bag. Then he looked up at the tall one, glanced at those staring eyes and the toothy grimace, and didn't look again. He drew them both inside, leaned out through the doorway to glance furtively up and down the street, then shut the door.

Chapter 20

Brewer decided it was time to call Chernie in New York.

Another major snowstorm had hit the East Coast, and there were more than six inches down when he walked to the public pay phone on M Street in Georgetown. He pulled up the hood of his parka and turned his back to the blowing snow as he dialed. He rang Chernie's number in Manhattan once, redialed, rang three times and hung up. Then he waited.

The snow had driven most traffic off the streets, and the few cars that were out went by at a crawl. From long habit, Brewer scanned the doorways and parked cars. The streets were empty.

Shortly later, Chernie called him from a phone booth over on East Forty-third, near the United Nations building.

"This is the shirtmaker," Brewer said. "We have a new selection of shirting materials to show you."

"When can I see them?"

"Any time, sir."

"Today."

Brewer hesitated. "Yes," he said. "Today is fine."

There was something urgent in Chernie's voice. So Brewer tried to get a seat on the air shuttle to New York. But the shuttle flights were canceled because of the mounting snowstorm. Brewer hurried to Union Station to get a train.

The station was packed. Thwarted air travelers from the Dulles and the Baltimore-Washington International airports had hurried there. They were joined by rail passengers arriving from the south who were shuffling into the main waiting room, trying to make connections with other trains west or north. Lining the walls and reclining on benches were Washington's street people, with their bags and rags, bedrolls and knapsacks, driven inside by the snow and the relentless wind.

The travelers stood spraddle-legged over their bags in the middle of the waiting room, studying the huge black train-schedule panel like bettors before a racetrack tote board calculating their odds. And the odds were against them—the long list of trains told the story: Late. Delayed departure. Canceled. The East Coast railway system had been snowed in. Brewer noted that trains to New York were hours behind schedule.

One woman said to another, "My husband's called every hotel in Washington, trying to get a room. Nothing. Absolutely nothing." She looked around. "My God. We can't sleep here with these people."

Brewer stood in the aisle all the way to New York.

It was nearly four when he got to Penn Station. After he called Chernie, he took the subway up to Forty-second and then the shuttle crosstown to Grand Central. He walked back to Madison. From the rear door he entered the shirt shop, hung up his coat, walked through the stockroom to the front and nodded silently to the owner. He busied himself with trays of regimentals in the glass case.

The owner stood by the window, watching the crowds hasten by. "I never saw so much snow in a single winter in my whole life. And it's not even January yet. You know what this has done to my business?"

Chernie arrived five minutes later in a rush, his eyes darting everywhere. His tie was crooked. The left lens of his eyeglasses had a large fingerprint on it. He carried a rolled magazine like a club. Almost breathless, he leaned on the counter and pointed down at a tray of ties.

"I was followed," he said.

"Easy does it, Igor," Brewer said. "You've been followed before." Pulling out a tray of ties, Brewer glanced at the proprietor, who stood watching the street. "How are we doing, Artie?"

"Seems clear. No surveillance."

Brewer looked back at Chernie. "How do you know you were followed?"

"I recognized him. But I think I lost him."

Brewer picked up a tie and held it up to Chernie's chest. "How's your list coming?"

"Very slowly. I wish your people would accept some of the other things I offered them."

"I keep bringing your proposals to the jolly green giants, Igor, but they say you aren't offering much . . . not enough to justify a new life, a new business, and a new identity somewhere in the U.S."

"They're so hard to please."

"No, that's not it, Igor. By the time you get your hands on something important, they've already got it from another source. It's just bad luck."

"Well, what can I do? They're on to me. I'm being followed everywhere. My mail was opened. I found a tap on my phone at home—"

"Calm down, Igor. This has all happened before. As long as you're the Russian Secretary for Scientific Affairs at the U.N., your people are going to do routine checks on you."

Chernie shook his head. "This is different. This is more re-lentless. They suspect something, I'm sure." His eyes couldn't rest. They darted around the room, seeing everything, noting nothing, just this side of panic.

"Charlie," he said, "does anyone know about me besides you?"

"No. Some people know that I'm working with someone who wants to bring over a big score to set himself up. But they don't know who."

"I wonder if there's a leak back to my people," Chernie said. "Your entire intelligence system has been penetrated."

Brewer said, "Your people don't know anything. You are absolutely safe and clean. They won't find anything, and then they'll stop. Calm down."

"Your system is full of leaks, Charlie. I keep telling you, and you don't believe me. There are leaks at high places."

Brewer watched Chernie and read the familiar signs. Fear. Drenched with it. Too long on the high wire. Loss of nerve.

The man took a breath. "I can't stand it."

"Yes, you can." Brewer reached up, straightened Chernie's tie and fixed his collar. "You can do anything."

"That's easy for you to say. Taking risks is your business. You thrive on it. I see the way your eyes dance when there's danger. I'm a diplomat. I can't handle this. I want to defect now. Take me in. Tell my wife to meet us somewhere, and take us both in."

"Okay. I can get you sanctuary. But that's all." He watched the agony on the man's face. "You know, Igor, you don't have to go through with this."

"Don't be ridiculous, Charlie. I can't back out now. Someone in your group could talk. Even years from now. If I went back to Russia, I would spend my life expecting that sudden tap on the shoulder. Do you know how much priming I had to do with my wife? The weeping at night . . . abandoning her family in Russia. You must not torture people like this."

"This is a world I never made, Igor."

Chernie put a clenched fist to his mouth. "Do you know what it's like? Do you?"

"Yes. I know. I've been there. I walked the same path you're walking many times. You just do it. And one day it's finished."

"I hope my new life in your country is worth this."

"Why did you call me up here today?" Brewer asked. He held another tie up to Chernie's chin.

"Anna is going to have a baby."

Brewer made a sour face. "Your timing is great, Igor."

"Well, we finally found a doctor here in New York who knows about such things. Turns out it was only a minor problem. And so she's pregnant. But now she wants to go home to Russia."

"How much time do you have, Igor?"

"A few months. I have to make a big score fast. Help me, Charlie."

"Well, it just so happens that maybe I can."

"What?" Chernie looked hopeful. "What is it you want?"

"We're interested in a guy . . . a Soviet spy. He's a master smuggler and thief. We think he's responsible for getting such things as the look-down/shoot-down radar system. He got all kinds of microchip capabilities into Russia—masks and VAXs and IBMs. He's certainly working out of Directorate T."

Igor shook his head and shrugged eloquently. "Ah! Directorate T? It might as well be a foreign country, Charlie. They live in their own private world, and no one else is admitted. I can't get you anything on Directorate T."

"This guy's special," Brewer said. "He's their goal maker. We think he brought off that Vienna coup."

"Oh, Vienna. Bloodied your nose, they did, Charlie. Pushed your face in the pie." Chernie shook his head grimly. "Your people are fools to put up with that. A pox on both your houses." The light showed the fingerprint on his left lens again. "What can you tell me about this goal maker?" he asked.

"Nothing," Brewer said. "We don't have anything on him. We just sense he's there."

Chernie braced both arms on the glass counter. "How can I—what—I mean give me something to go on."

"I can't. But I can tell you one thing. There's very little chance my people will learn about this guy from another source. If you get his identity, it will be fresh news. And we're ready to pay off big, Igor. Write your own ticket. There must be a lot of secret traffic in the coding room on this guy. Everybody must be clamoring to use him."

"But you know that our intelligence officers do their own decoding. Alone. In the decoding room. No one else is allowed in there when one of them is decoding. And that includes other Directorate T people. You know this. I have told you. You must understand I have no way of getting into the decoding room."

"Find a way." Brewer watched him writhe.

"I can't!" Chernie exclaimed.

"Igor, this is a very dangerous game for people like you. I can't help you play it. If you can't stand the tension, you shouldn't mess with it. Understand?"

"I know. I know. If you can't stand the heat, get out of the kitchen. But I want to start a new life."

"Then do it. Go to the nearest U.S. office and ask for asylum."

"Then what? Starve here? Oh no. I know what I need. I need a business, a guaranteed job of my own. I have to have that . . . especially with the baby."

"Then you have to do what you have to do. Take a deep breath and go do it."

The shop owner cleared his throat.

Brewer bent over the case. "How many?" he asked.

"One," the owner said.

Brewer led Chernie by the elbow to another counter. He picked up a large swatch of blue broadcloth shirting and held it up to Chernie.

Chernie was panting, a man who had discovered there was a trapdoor under his feet.

"Don't look at the windows," Brewer said. He took a tape measure and measured Chernie's neck.

"Would you believe," Chernie asked, "I wanted to perfect the Ryad One computer? I wanted to take all the bugs out of it."

"It's not worth fixing," Brewer said.

"Yes! Yes! I could do wonders for that Ryad. There are some good things in. We did not follow correct procedure in designing it."

"Come on, Igor. The Ryad One is a damned bad, completely unreliable copy of the IBM 360. Russian scientists didn't have the technology to make a decent copy of it. And the RYAD Two is an equally poor copy of the IBM 370." He glanced at the owner. "Still there?"

"At the corner."

"Russia is constantly playing catch-up," Chernie said. He seemed to be talking to himself. Perspiration made his brow glisten. "Why reinvent what has already been invented? It's more expedient to use what exists. You mark my words, Charlie. Someday the Russians are going to be important manufacturers of high-tech equipment."

"Not this year, Igor."

Chernie belonged in a coffeehouse down in the Village, with a beard and turtleneck sweater, playing chess and arguing about Russia with other emigrés. An ardent man, a passionate man, an excited man, a born intellectual.

Brewer put the tape around Chernie's torso to measure his chest. "Keep your eyes away from the windows," he said. Then he measured Chernie's waist.

"You've lost weight, Igor," he said.

"I feel as though you're measuring me for my coffin."

                            *   *   *

Later, on the way back to Penn Station, Brewer decided it was the red umbrella that had alerted him. Or maybe it was her face. He had seen her first when he'd arrived in New York.

Coming back up the stairs from the subway shuttle, he saw her again behind him. Instead of going into the station, he took the escalator to street level, walked out on Thirty-third Street and turned toward Eighth Avenue.

In the dark it was still snowing. The city was sheeted up and the streets were empty. A strong wind was creating drifts as quickly as the snowplows cleared the roadways. He struggled through the banked snow to cross Eighth Avenue and walked in half-filled tire tracks along the side of the post office. Ahead were the lights of the diner on the corner of Ninth Avenue. He paused several times to look back. She wasn't following him.

In the diner three uniformed security guards were sitting in a booth drinking coffee. A fourth was making a telephone call. Brewer sat at the counter with a cup of coffee and watched the door. He waited for ten minutes. No one came. He stepped out once again onto Ninth Avenue then retraced his steps along Thirty-third. He found a second set of footprints, smaller, with a narrow heel—a woman's shoe.

He slipped and slid in the narrow tire tracks, following the two sets of footprints back to Penn Station, and took the escalator down to the crowded waiting room.

A few moments later the woman arrived, caked with snow, her head wrapped in a plastic shawl tied under her chin. She was wearing a short leather jacket, a pair of black slacks, and low heeled shoes which were soaked. Under her arm she carried the same furled red umbrella.

She made a phone call, nodding and waving a hand. An argument. Brewer guessed at it. She was telling someone that Brewer had spotted her. And the other person was saying they didn't have a replacement for her. Then she joined the group and stood, smoking a cigarette and shivering.

He looked at the umbrella again. Imagine fighting a snowstorm with a small round disk of red plastic. And wet feet. She'd had a tough day.

Brewer looked at her bleakly. If she'd uncovered Chernie,

she had done some real damage. When the station man opened the gate, Brewer descended the stair to the Washington train. She followed him and sat five rows behind him. But when the train pulled out, he looked back. She was gone.

Later, between Newark and Trenton, he took a stroll the entire length of the train. He never found her.

At midnight he was standing in Margie's kitchen, drinking a can of beer, when he noticed three cup-sized depressions in the carpeting in front of the three front legs of her couch. Someone had moved Margie's furniture.

He checked her telephone for bugs, then took the elevator down to the phone junction box in the basement.

Brewer once estimated that he had installed over a hundred wiretaps in his career, most of them in Washington. Yet when he opened the door to the telephone junction box in the basement of the apartment building, he was surprised to find not one, but two taps on Margie's line. He had the eager attention of several people.

He left both of them in place and went to bed.

●●●
Chapter 21

In Mehtma's, meals were served in a basement dining room; and, throughout the house, the odor of curry was so pervasive, it was said the bricks could be cooked and eaten. Most of the patrons, Orientals newly arrived from the airport, preferred to dine with chopsticks.

The two of them waited for the telegram to come.

The stout one slept much of the day on his bed under the eaves, wrapped in two white blankets. Often he just stared at the streaked white wall and thoughtfully tongued the gaps in his upper row of teeth.

Before his trip to Cologne he had rarely seen snow, and whenever the white flakes flurried out of the dead white sky, he would go to the window to watch. Sometimes he would open the window and stick his tongue out to catch them.

The tall one, wearing his round black hat, sat all day down in the entry hall in a creaking wooden chair under a ticking clock, waiting; he rarely moved and never spoke, never wore any kind of an expression on his famine face. In the afternoon he took a long solitary walk through the streets of London with that slow, stiltlike stalking gait, his black hat cocked back, his black coattails swaying behind him, the crimson scarf around his neck.

Each day they waited expectantly for the telegram to come.

Chapter 22

Brewer waited in the dark parking lot of the Pentagon. The pyramidal mounds of snow piled by the plows had gotten higher with each successive snowstorm. Under the streetlamps they hulked like icebergs.

The approach of Limoges's limousine and the escort car reminded Brewer of an Al Capone movie. He shook his head as they reenacted the ritual: the two cars circling Brewer's car, the chauffeur getting into the backseat of the escort car, Brewer getting into the front seat of the limousine.

"Well?" Limoges asked.

"Nothing," Brewer said. "Lots of warnings."

Limoges pumped cigar smoke and waited, watching Brewer with calculating eyes.

"This Mr. X is buried too deep," Brewer said. "I can't dig him out with the usual tools."

"So? I told you go to any lengths you have to. Maybe I haven't made myself clear, Brewer. We're going all the way on this one. If we go down, we take the Reds with us. We all burn together."

"Have you consulted the rest of mankind about that scenario?"

"We mustn't stop now, Brewer."

"You can't stop. What you do was decided in your mother's womb."

Limoges sighed. "What do you want to do?"

"I'm going to try to follow one of his smuggling operations like a piece of string—from the U.S., across Europe, and even into Russia if need be. At the end of the string I should find Mr. X."

"Which one?" Limoges asked. "Which smuggling operation?"

"The most recent," Brewer answered. "Vienna."

In the morning Brewer went over to see McMasters in Export Control, a section of the Commerce Department's Bureau of East-West Trade which was charged with issuing export licenses.

McMasters was sitting exactly the way he was the last time Brewer had seen him—feet on his desk, arms folded, phone cradled between ear and shoulder, talking. He reached out his right hand to Brewer, still talking on the phone.

"Okay, okay," he said into the phone. "Call me back." He put the phone down and stood up. "Look, Brewer. I understand what you're after. But how the hell am I going to help you? These Russians are everywhere. We're beset with bees. And nobody cares. Congress says we're exaggerating. And the rest of Washington has its own problems. As for the Europeans, forget it. They don't care that Russia is stealing U.S. technology."

Brewer asked him, "What can you tell me about the way the Russians operate? Tell me about the Vienna thing."

McMasters sat down and put his feet back on his desk. He pointed at his phone. "You know what that phone call was all about? They just picked up a Russian touring a microchip plant in California. Imagine a Russian in California. In a microchip plant. God knows how he got inside, but there he was, taking pictures of everything with a miniature camera. As they were escorting him by the elbows to the door, he was still trying to take pictures. And when they took the film from his camera, he tried to get physical. Here he is, breaking ten or twelve federal laws, he can be sentenced to five years in the pen, or at least kicked out of the country, and he stands there and yells his head off as though we were depriving him of his rights to spy on us. What do you do with people like that?"

"What can you tell me about Vienna?"

"Got a week?" McMasters answered. "That Vienna thing is so goddamned tangled—with wheels within wheels—we don't even know where to begin. Maybe you ought to talk to Kane over in Customs. He's supposed to be doing the workup on it."

"What have you got?"

"Me? Couple of forged documents. Some stray pieces. We're pretty sure there was a group of men—three of them in Kansas City, but the primary one was in L.A."

"Are you going to do any follow-up?"

McMasters shrugged. "Come on, Brewer. We don't have the manpower to check into every potential supplier who might have sold stuff to this group. And if we did, we'd find borderline infractions. Nothing to get your teeth into. Go see Kane in Customs."

Brewer made a lunch date with Ted Kane, who worked for the Strategic Investigation Division of the U.S. Customs Service, Treasury Department.

Kane liked Chinese food, and he met Brewer at a Chinese restaurant in Georgetown.

He told Brewer, "I don't think there's any way to stop the Russians. Once they set their sights on a piece of equipment or a design, they use every trick in the book. They do credit checks and financial studies on the target companies to find out if they're underfinanced and in need of cash. They dig into the private lives of executives. They find out who's in debt over his head, who's a closet gay, who's black and facing an invisible wall of discrimination. They pry out your deepest secrets. And they use them to force you to give them what they want. Nothing is sacred to them. No crime is too low for them to stoop to. And they always get what they want sooner or later. They never miss. Never."

"You ever hear of a master smuggler in Directorate T?"

Kane shrugged. "Who needs a mastermind? With the way we work, children could do the smuggling. It's as easy as stealing pencils from the blind."

"Then how come the Russians miss the target so often?"

Kane shrugged. "I just read where six times out of ten the cheetah misses his target."

"But what if there's one cheetah who never misses?" Brewer asked.

"Brewer, I don't think there's a Russian mastermind. But if you're going to look for him, I have two words for you. Good

luck. Why don't you try chopsticks? It's very easy. See? Hold
one stick like so, and the other—"

"Tell me about Vienna."

"We haven't completed our report yet," Kane said. "Maybe
we never will. The trail is cold. We're short of manpower, and
current cases take precedence. You know how it is, Brewer. So
far we're pretty sure that Vienna thing started in Los Angeles.
In fact we're pretty sure it was a guy named Bobby English, who
has since skipped with a suitcase full of money. And I'm personally pretty sure he had at least one contact here in Customs. I
mean, I think someone right in my office warned him to get out
of town. How do you like this moo goo gaipan?"

"Were there others?"

"In Kansas City. Three others. Aren't you going to eat your
fried rice? Give it to me."

"But you haven't checked?"

"Right. I haven't checked. And I'm probably not going to."

"What do you have on Bobby English?"

"He scamped long ago. He's a very small fry, anyway. We're
convinced he was directed by someone else, probably from Europe, maybe from Moscow. He's not worth all the paperwork
and trouble to extradite him. Besides, he's dropped out of sight.
After he left L.A. he was in Vegas, kited a bunch of bad checks
there. Then he was in Germany, then we heard he was in
Athens, heading east. Now we've lost track of him."

"You and McMasters have been a big help."

"Come on, Brewer. We're buried. The fort is besieged. Is
there anything else I can do for you?"

"Find Bobby English."

Kane shrugged. "I can put it in my weekly bulletin. Okay?
It's an in-house memo that gets pretty wide circulation."

"Will it do any good?"

"I doubt it."

After lunch Kane brought Brewer back to his office for conversations with the Customs people in Kane's division.

Customs specialists, eagerly rooting through their files,
showed him case after case of stolen technology. Everywhere,

tales tumbled from their lips about the swarming, insatiable Russians.

After an hour of recitation one of the Customs men said, "If the shoe had been on the other foot, the Russians would never have let us do this to them. We wouldn't have gotten one screw head. We just never took what they were doing seriously enough. They're much better at this game than we'll ever be."

"It's that bad?"

"Brewer, if we'd stopped the Russians from stealing all our technology, they would have fallen so far behind us, I'm convinced they would have had to come to the bargaining table ten years ago. The cold war would be over. And we wouldn't have spent—what is it?—trillions of dollars in defense. They've helped push the American economy to the brink of collapse."

Late in the afternoon Brewer took the Blue Bird out to the CIA at Langley and poked through their library. Crawley found him there in the biography stacks. Stooped, with cigarette stains on the fingers of his left hand, Crawley looked at Brewer with his exhausted hound's eyes while his deep, gravelly voice murmured tales of Russian depredations.

"When the history of this century is written, it's going to say that Russia conquered the world in back alleys, in the dark, by stealth, by breaking and entering, by mugging, by murder, torture, beatings, blackmail, and psychological violence, without a major battle, without ever firing a shot, while we spent ourselves into poverty preparing to fight a war that never came."

"Don't bet on the wrong horse, Andy," Brewer said. "Maybe neither of us will come out ahead on this one."

Three nights later, while he was sound asleep, the phone on the night table rang. He pulled the whole phone in bed with him and put the headpiece to his ear.

"Hello," he said.

"Is this Brewer?"

"Who's this?"

"My name is Bobby English."

Brewer took the red-eye late the next night to L.A., where he went to meet Bobby English's flight from Hong Kong.

He waited by the exit doors from customs. In the shuffling crowd, he recognized English immediately: tall, thin, pale blond, about thirty-five and anxious, his brown eyes quickly skimming the faces around him.

His eyes had just found Brewer's when four men stepped from the crowd. One of them stopped English with a pointing finger. Holding out a badge, he spoke briefly to English. Then the four of them formed up and quickly walked English away.

Brewer followed them along the main concourse to a side corridor. They walked English down the corridor to the men's room and pulled him inside. One of them remained outside and waved people away.

"There's a men's room in the next corridor," Brewer heard him say.

Brewer walked briskly toward him.

"Use another men's room," the man was saying. Brewer strode past him to a fire extinguisher, unsnapped the straps and pulled it down. Making a quick half turn, he slammed the end of the extinguisher tank into the man's belly. When the man doubled over, Brewer brought the end of the tank down on the back of his head. Then he used his shoulder to push open the door.

They had English in one of the toilet stalls. All the doors and partitions were shaking as they pounded at him. One of them raised a club and swung it inside the stall. Another was using brass knuckles.

Brewer upended the fire extinguisher and aimed the long blank nozzle. A cloud of vapor rushed out. He held it up to their faces and watched them rolling and ducking to get away, shouting and covering their faces with their hands.

Brewer used the extinguisher as a battering ram, aiming for their heads and their kneecaps. Two of them broke and ran. The third retrieved the club and swung it. It just missed Brewer's head and dented the door to the stall. Brewer swung the extinguisher and caught him full in the face. The man turned stumbling and ran with a bloody hand covering his nose.

Brewer ran out into the corridor and threw the extinguisher after them. Then he went back inside.

English was jammed down between the toilet seat and the wall, panting. His face was weeping blood from a number of contusions, more blood flowed thickly from his scalp, and his raincoat was covered with large circular red stains. One lapel was torn almost off.

"Oh my God," English murmured. "Oh my God." Brewer gripped the front of his raincoat and pulled him up and away from the wedge. He let him settle to the floor.

Two airport security men pushed open the door and entered. "What's going on?"

"I came in here to pee and there's four guys working this one over. With that bat."

The two of them looked down at English writhing on the floor, then at the wooden billy. One of them put a two-way radio to his mouth. "Got a four-two-two here," he said. "Men's room, corridor four. Call an ambulance."

In the waiting room of the emergency ward, the doctor read aloud to Brewer from a form on a clipboard. "Most of the pain he's feeling is from massive contusions to the major muscle groups. They'll heal. The three cracked ribs will take care of themselves, but he won't be able to take a deep breath for a while. There's trauma to his right kidney, causing some impairment to renal function, but we think that will heal. We hope so. There are a total of five broken fingers on both hands . . . the splints will take care of them. He's got bone fragments in his left wrist. It's too soon to talk about the ligaments. Some were nearly torn from their moorings. Permanent damage there, we think. As for the kneecap, he's going to be on crutches until he has an operation to make it function again. Even then it's in the doubtful column. He's got a jaw fracture, but amazingly enough, no broken teeth. He's got a hairline fracture over his left eye. The whole eye is shut and we're not sure how much damage there is to it. He's very lucky to be alive. One more shot with that fungo bat would have scrambled his eggs for him. And that would have been the end of that. He's probably going to walk away from this one. Not tomorrow morning. But he's going to walk away." The doctor laid aside the clipboard. "A man was brought in here three o'clock yesterday morning. His car had gone over a guardrail and fallen two stories down. The list of things wrong with him filled two pages—and he was in

better shape than Mister"—he referred to his clipboard—
"English."

Brewer nodded and waited.

The doctor said, "This laundry list of damages isn't the real
problem. People who are beaten like this go into severe depression—sometimes for life. And this man is severely depressed. I
suspect he was depressed even before this attack, which makes
the problem infinitely worse. Anyway, the resident shrink will
have to figure that out. Now—Mr. English says it's urgent that
he talk to you. He's nearly frantic. You can have ten minutes
with him. I don't want him talking for more than that. And if he
gets more upset than he is, you have to leave immediately. He's
very close to the end of his rope."

English's one good eye focused on Brewer as he walked up
to the hospital bed. He was panting shallowly. "You Brewer?"

"Yes."

"I have to talk and I have to talk fast. Okay?"

"Yes," Brewer said.

"Christ. Look what they did to me." His right eye filled with
tears. "Maybe I would have been better off if I had taken that
last shot from the fungo bat. Things aren't looking so good for
me. I haven't cried since I was a little kid. And now I can't
stop."

"Take it easy," Brewer said. "And take your time."

"They nearly tagged me in Hong Kong," English said.
"They just missed me. So I knew I had to get back here and spill
my guts. I want to talk. I want everyone to know what I know.
Then I won't have any secrets, and they'll leave me alone.
Where do you want to start?"

"Who were you working for?"

"I never met him. It was all done by phone."

"Come on," Brewer said. "You'd have to be an idiot to
touch a deal like that."

"I had no choice." English heaved a great sigh. His eye filled
again.

Brewer watched and waited.

"I screwed up," English said. "In Chicago. Last year. I was a
purchasing agent in a company making robots. I took a few
goodies from some suppliers."

"Kickbacks?"

"Nothing big. No cash. Presents. A TV set. Weekend in Las Vegas. Then a microchip company I was dealing with went into Chapter Eleven and the records came out. I was on their good little boys' list. I got a suspended sentence, probation for five years, but I lost my job, my reputation, everything."

English swallowed several times. "Oh Christ, everything hurts so much . . . I came out here to the West Coast to get a fresh start. And one day I get a letter, and in it there's a photocopy of one of the checks I wrote in Chicago. People in Chicago didn't know about the bad checks or I would never have gotten off with just the suspension. If they ever saw it, they'd throw me right in the sneezer. So when I pull this bad check out of an envelope, I go into a real sweat. There's a note in the envelope. 'I will call you Thursday evening.' So you bet your bippy I'm home on Thursday, waiting for the call. I know I'm in deep shit. Guy says I want you to do a job. And I will pay you very well. When you're through with the job, you walk away clean with money in your pocket, and you got the original check to tear up."

"So you did it?"

"Does a monkey eat bananas? It was the carrot and the stick. I was hurting for money. I wasn't doing so great on the West Coast. My past kept after me. And here was payday."

"What was the deal?"

"Purchasing. Military supplies. High-tech equipment. That was my specialty as a purchasing agent. This guy on the phone set up a checking account, and I went out and rented an office. Had a bunch of fake letterheads printed. Purchase-order forms, business cards, the lot. Eureka High-Tech Enterprises was one I made up. And Condor Medical Software Company. There were others."

Brewer wrote the names on a pad.

"I was caught in a trap," English said. "I was supposed to buy stuff on the forbidden list. If I don't, the Voice calls Chicago. If I do, I'm a big-time criminal. If I get caught, I'm looking at five to ten plus another two to five on the suspended from Chicago. It was one long nightmare. I mean long. It's—"

English sighed then inhaled sharply. "Oh Christ." He suppressed a sob.

Brewer put a box of tissues on the bed.

"I'm okay," English said. "Okay. One day a list arrives in the mail from the Voice. It's a list of parts, every damned one of them illegal. Buy these, says the note. Don't be obvious. There's also another list—of companies—military component manufacturers and defense contractors. Those are the companies I'm to buy from. And every damned one of them was having financial difficulties. Cash-flow problems. Slow pay. Bad credit. Several were in Chapter Eleven, fending off the wolves. These outfits are all desperate. They'll sell for upfront cash plus some fake papers without asking too many questions. To make it even easier to buy from them and cover their asses, I set up a third party as a V.A.R."

"Value Added Repackager?"

"Yes. These are guys with customized manufacturing capabilities. They buy components from various sources and repackage them for specialty markets. See? So I would order stuff, claiming to be buying it for a V.A.R. who in turn was repackaging for the ultimate buyer—a major corporation with a defense contract. . . . So I would send in a purchase order with a check and an affidavit that the merchandise was destined for a bona fide defense contractor and would not be exported. Understand?"

"Go on," Brewer said.

"So I start. Buying small. A piece here, a piece there. When I got the parts I ordered, I would use a series of fake companies that took title, so no one would ever be able to figure out where the stuff went. Finally I would ship the stuff using false labels—dishwashers or plumbing supplies."

"Where?"

"To an outfit in Kansas City. So far as I know, the operation in Kansas City would ship the stuff out of the country under other fake labels."

"Customs never checked?" Brewer asked.

"These were small orders. That was the secret. The Voice told me to never buy anything big or noticeable. A few parts here, a few components there, but when you looked at the total list, you could see instantly that he could assemble all the stuff and end up with significant capability."

"Did the Voice have any kind of an accent?"

"Yes, but it seemed American. You know what I mean?"

"You ever meet the people in Kansas City?"

"No. The Voice never let you near anyone else. But five will get you ten that they were in the same boat I was in. Blackmailed."

"So what happened?"

"Things got worse—that's what happened. What I was doing was bad enough. If just one person began to ask questions, I'm in the sneezer. But there was some stuff I couldn't order over the transom. And I told that to the Voice. So he told me to steal it. Steal it. God Almighty." English seemed bemused, and stared away without speaking.

"Go on," Brewer said.

"I balked. I told him I didn't know how to do that. So I got another letter from the Voice with a copy of another one of my checks. He must have bought them up—the whole lot. That's when I crashed. This guy owned me. All he had to do was send copies of those checks to Chicago and my chain is yanked. So I couldn't stop. Yet I knew one day I would get caught." He stopped talking again. His mind seemed to be wandering.

"Go on," Brewer said.

"One thing I couldn't do was burglary. I mean it's a skill, you understand? So I hired some second-story men to steal for me. You ever go out on the street and try to hire some burglars? I mean, you don't just run a classified in the local paper. And these weren't a few juveniles in sneakers. These were hardcase hoods. Fifty percent earnest money up front, balance on delivery. I didn't crap around with this stuff. When I got it, I slapped fake labels on it for the waybills and shipped it fast to Kansas City."

"Now you've got a big operation going," Brewer said.

"A mountain of small stuff," English said. "A nibble here, a nibble there. I got in deeper and deeper. I'm dealing with real criminals now. I didn't trust a one of them. I knew if those hoods got caught, they'd finger me to cop a plea."

"Suppose you had to get in touch with the Voice?" Brewer asked.

"There was a phone number with an answering machine where I could leave a message. Some place in Europe. Germany."

"Go on," Brewer said.

"One day a miracle happened. Would you believe it? The Voice called me. Shut it down, he said. Burn all the papers. Everything. Pay off everyone. A check is in the mail. He tells me I did a good job. I'm free! Glory be to God. I'm off the hook. Life began to look good again." English paused and swallowed, and more tears welled.

Brewer waited. English tried to dab his eye with tissues but the splints on his fingers and wrists stopped him. He dropped the tissues, defeated.

"So," he said. "The check comes. It's another cashier's check from a New York bank. Nice fat check, more than I expected. But none of my bad checks from Chicago. So he's still got me. I call the number in Germany and leave a message. But there's no reply. I decided to take the money and run before he changes his mind and gives me another job."

"You went to Las Vegas?"

"Yep," English said. "I went to Vegas. I'm in bad shape, man. I mean I have some money, but I know I'll never work on a legitimate job again or lead a normal life. I have to spend the rest of my life on the run, hiding from that nightmare voice on the phone."

"So you've been running ever since?"

"Oh no. It wasn't that simple. Vegas was a big mistake. Big mistake. You know there are people who make a living gambling? That's their occupation. So I figure if I can't go legit with a regular nine-to-five somewhere, I'll make my daily bread at the gaming tables. Like I said others do. You know what my father does?"

"No," Brewer said.

"He's a minister, man. A minister. He believes in the goodness of every single person. And now he's got a criminal son who's a professional gambler in Las Vegas. My father doesn't really believe that Las Vegas actually exists." English stopped again, struggling to stop the tears. "How am I doing?"

"Just great," Brewer said.

"Twenty-one got me. Blackjack. Got my bankroll. Now I'm desperate. I'm hiding. No dough. And no way to get any. So, I bought stolen credit cards. They're not expensive, and you can live like a king if you have nerves of steel and an instinct to know when to lay off a card."

Brewer nodded.

"It gets worse," English said. "I figure I can't keep this up forever. I just don't have the skills to be a criminal. So what do you think I decide? Let me show you how smart I am. I decide to contact the Voice again. Bright? The brass ring? Sure. I figure if I can get those checks back, I can try to go legit again. I flew to Germany and I called the number and I left a message and I waited. Just by pure luck, I'm coming back from dinner when I see these goons enter my hotel room. You know the kind? No neck. A nose like a banana. Knuckles dragging on the ground. And the pants are stuffed full of these colossal legs. You see them in your nightmares. In Vegas they call them the Sunshine Boys. Like those animals in the airport. So, I just turned around and got the next flight out of Germany."

"Athens?"

"How'd you know?"

"Go on."

"They followed me to Athens. How? I don't know. So I skipped again."

"Hong Kong?"

"Yeah. That's when I decided to come back and face the music. Even jail's better than that. Got the picture?"

"I got the picture," Brewer said.

"They nearly tagged me in Hong Kong. So when I took off, I knew they had me pegged. There would be a welcoming committee in L.A. when I landed. I figured I was a dead man. And damned near was." English paused to control his voice. "Listen," he said. "I want to tell you something. I mean—" He wept softly. "I want to say—" He paused and gathered himself again. "Everytime I see a fire extinguisher, I'm going to kiss the blessed thing." He laughed. A giggle. "So help me Christ." He laughed again. "Maybe I'll even carry one strapped to my waist. How's that for a picture? Me coming down the street lugging a fire extinguisher." He giggled then sobbed.

He tried again to get tissues from the box by his side with the finger splints. Brewer pulled some out for him. "Here," he said.

Bobby English attempted to speak again. "I want to say— Listen, I want to say—" He sobbed. "Honest to God, man. I owe you big. When you hit them with that fog, I knew I was delivered like Moses and his people in the wilderness. I owe you big, man. Big."

English tried to reach Brewer with a hand. "No man should do to another man what they tried to do to me. These guys don't mess around, man. They're mean. I mean sick mean. They meant to kill me.

"Right now, you can bet the Voice has dozens of other fake companies operating here—all shipping a steady stream of small packages out of the country. The smuggling goes on and on. It'll never stop. A bunch of poor bastards like me. You get him. For me. Get him. Monster. A Russian monster."

"How do you know he was Russian?" Brewer asked.

"Reach into that drawer," English said. "Right there. The top one." Brewer found a bank note, a Russian ruble. "They found this in my coat pocket down in the emergency ward. A calling card. It's Russian, isn't it?"

Brewer nodded. "Russian," he said. He looked at it thoughtfully, then at the purple face on the bed.

Brewer got the evening flight back to Washington. As his plane took off, a man with a bandage over his nose made a call from an airport pay phone. "He's airborne," he said. "Bound for D.C."

●●●
Chapter 23

On Wednesday evening the stout one and the tall one were in Mehtma's dining room eating tandoori chicken with curried rice and chapaties. A new group of Orientals had arrived at mid-afternoon. Tiny people, they sat around the round tables, still bundled and shivering from the unwonted cold, drinking quantities of hot tea, scraping the rice from small white bowls into their mouths with chopsticks.

Mehtma's third son, with his furrowed brow, entered the dining room. He crossed to their table and with his quick, small hand put the telegram down beside the stout one's plate.

The stout one picked up the telegram and opened it with a table knife. He read the message then nodded at his partner.

The next morning, after breakfast, they cut the labels out of their clothes with a razor and took a taxi to Heathrow for the ten A.M. flight to Washington. They carried no baggage.

●●●
Chapter 24

They were asleep when the telephone rang once—a long, sustained ring.

"I never heard a phone ring like that before," Margie said.

"Neither did I." Brewer picked it up and got a dial tone.

He was almost back to sleep when the telephone rang again. Three very long rings.

"Sounds more like a burglar alarm," Margie said.

Brewer picked up the phone; there was a three-second pause before he got a dial tone. He stood up and pulled on his pants then walked down the apartment stairs to the basement. In his bare feet he strode down the rows of the apartment storage units, following the overhead lines along a steel I beam to the telephone junction box. The cement floor was cold.

The door to the phone junction box stood open. There were now three taps on Margie's telephone line.

He felt a draft of cold air, and turned and walked to the back of the basement to the rear door. It was standing open. He climbed up the dozen outside steps to the alley. The snow froze his feet, and the cold wind on his bare torso made him gasp as he glanced up and down the alley under the clear, cold sky filled with stars. There was no one to be seen.

He locked the basement door, shut the door to the phone junction box, and returned to bed.

"Your feet are like ice," she said.

He lay beside her, holding her in his arms and shivering.

The blanketing snows and the hard freeze in the wetlands were driving flocks of starving birds to the salt marshes along the coast. Newspapers advised people to fill their bird feeders more

often and to put out extra food for the larger birds. All through
the winter Margie fed the crows.

On some mornings Brewer would walk with her to the park,
carrying the bird feed in a large paper sack. Under the grim and
gray cloudy sky, he would stand in the middle of the park and
watch her trudge in her red boots over the deep snow, her red
plastic scoop strewing pellets of bird feed. Flocks of silent crows
on swift, silent wings seemed to materialize out of the gray sky
to come flying down through the winter-bare trees like Greek
furies bringing retribution. As they landed on the snow around
her, they raised a din of squawks and caws.

"What is this?" he asked her, hefting the bag.

"Dog Kibble," she said. "Tuna-flavored. They love it."

He held the bag so she could refill her red scoop.

She studied his face for a moment.

"What?" he asked her.

"When you walk, you don't look up or down," she said.
"You stare straight ahead as though you were seeing something
awful. You're like a man with tunnel vision."

"That's what you need when you're in a tunnel," he said.
And he felt he was in a tunnel, a man racing through a tunnel
from birth to death toward a destination unknown, on rails laid
by some other. He felt he was unable to change, unable to alter
his course. Programmed like a robot from the day he was born.
He looked at the throngs passing through the park. Was everyone created on a set of tracks?

"Life is passing you by," Margie said. "Lift up your head
and see what's going on around you."

"Do I want to see what's going on around me?" He looked
again at the straggling lines of office workers shuffling on the
salted slush through the park to their jobs. The ant people. Is
that the life that was passing him by?

A car pulled up at the curb and a man got out from the
passenger side, wearing a long black overcoat and a wide-brimmed
black hat. Around his neck was a scarlet scarf. Above the car
the street sign read: FIRE LANE *No Stopping or Standing.*

The tall man stood by a partially open car door, speaking to
the driver as he watched Margie sow the pellets over the snow.
Pointing at crows, he shook his head at the driver.

Then he slammed the car door, and all the crows leaped into the air with great flaps, cawing with alarm. Watching the birds doubtfully, the man turned and strolled through the shuffling crowd, talking to himself.

Brewer set the bag of bird feed on the ground and stepped in front of Margie, watching the man attentively. Striding into the park, the man stepped off the path, out of the way of the pedestrians, and with his hands at his sides, cocked his head at Brewer. With slow deliberateness he pulled the scarlet scarf open then unbuttoned his long black coat. Hanging from his neck on a leather strap inside his overcoat was a nine-millimeter Uzi.

He unsnapped the strap and slipped it from around his neck. Solemnly, he raised the weapon. Without haste, he pulled back the lever and cocked it. Then, with bent arms, he aimed it waist high at Brewer. The crowds shouted and ran in all directions.

Brewer shoved Margie to the ground then leaped and rolled in the snow, waiting for the shots. Nothing happened. The man checked the weapon. Then he tugged at the top-mounted cocking mechanism. Brewer clambered to his feet and ran.

The man struggled again with the mechanism, then saw Brewer crossing the snow, sprinting right at him. Still tugging at the weapon, he turned and trotted back toward the car, shouldering past people as he went. At the edge of the park he squared off to aim again as Brewer leaped at him. Again the weapon failed to fire. Brewer drove his head and shoulders into the man's torso and flung him out on the roadway, face down. The Uzi went sliding across the ice, trailing its strap.

Brewer jumped up and leaped after the man. They both were trying to run on the rutted ice after the Uzi. They went slipping and sliding across the road, pushing each other, falling and entangling themselves in the legs of the pedestrians and knocking many down.

They struggled to their feet, wrestling each other, then fell again. Brewer seized the Uzi. The man fell on top of him, trying to punch him. Brewer brought the Uzi around and clouted him on the temple. Then again. As the man fell back, Brewer slammed him across the mouth with the weapon. He got to his feet. The man was on his knees, holding his hands to his bloody mouth. Brewer hit him once more on the side of the head then turned to the car.

The driver, holding a pistol in his upraised hand, was furiously cranking his car window down. As the window lowered, he extended his arm and took aim at Brewer. Brewer aimed the Uzi and they both fired. The Uzi blew holes in the door, and the driver fell away inside the car. Brewer ran across the road at the car and shoved the Uzi through the window. The man lay still on the front seat.

Back behind Brewer the other gunman lay sprawled in the street. He'd been shot through the head by the driver. The crowd, immobile, stared at Brewer in terrified silence while the crows, circling in a silent panic above, slowly settled again in the snow. In the middle of the park he saw Margie standing in her red boots, covered with snow, holding the empty red scoop at her side, staring back at him. At his feet lay a scarlet scarf.

Afterward he remembered all those eyes staring at him, and the profound silence.

•••Part Five

Chapter 25

Margie's reaction was very simple and uncluttered. She did what her family in Boston always did when a relative died, a father lost his job, a daughter divorced. She made a pot of tea and sat in her kitchen holding the teacup in both hands and, staring at the wall, confronted the fact.

Brewer, sitting across from her, could see her mind working, explaining and accepting. A car veers off the road, a great dam bursts—a sparrow loses a feather. A trigger fails to fire. God's will. When she put the cup down, the affair was over. She was ready to go to her office. God hadn't called her this time.

But Brewer, in his chair, his tea untouched, was absorbed by a different vision—one that would haunt him: Margie lying under a red police blanket in the snow in the park while above her a congregation of crows crouched in the trees, observing. Only the jammed firing mechanism had saved her. Fortune. Luck. Chance.

If that trigger mechanism hadn't jammed, the gunman would have killed them both. And if it hadn't fired at the car when he'd pulled the trigger, the driver wouldn't have died. Instead the driver would have killed him. He had missed death not once, not twice, but three or four times in a row. How contingent it all is. Incredible luck: a lifetime supply of luck used up in forty-five seconds. Would he be overdrawn tomorrow at the luck bank? In a business where luck was more important than skill, had his luck run out? Margie's luck?

He'd violated his own rule, and she almost paid for it: he had let his private life get mixed in with his job.

It was time: he had to leave Margie or leave the job. But the only way to leave the job was finish the assignment. Find X before X finished him.

Brewer spent the day in a microfiche in the Library of Congress, going through microfilm reels of newspapers, including the *New York Times* and the *Washington Post,* then *Aviation Age, Electronics,* and *Purchasing World.* By four he'd filled the pages of a pad with notes on Russian industrial espionage and smuggling, but he hadn't gotten one inch closer to X. The next step was a tour of European intelligence files.

That evening he watched Margie sewing. She and three other women were making cloth drapes for the church. She was needlepointing a multicolored crosier on a royal-blue field of silk. Behind her, draped over the couch, was another needlepoint— this one of a small lamb she had done in white on the same blue silk field. He watched the serene expression on her face as she watched her hands sewing.

She was stability, home, love. But where were the children, the husband, the fireplace? She sat, a childless widow, making a church pennant while her live-in scurried in the walls of the great rat wars.

How was he going to tell her that they had to separate—at least until his assignment was over?

"A penny for your thoughts," she said.

He was thinking of Kipling's couplet:

Down to Ghehenna, or up to the Throne,
   He travels the fastest who travels alone.

If he'd told her, she would have asked: "What's Ghehenna?"

"Hell," he would have said.

What he did say was, "I have to go to Europe for a few days."

In the morning, lying by his side, she confronted him. "Charlie?"

"I'm here."

"I'm sorry about the park."

"Yes."

"I hope it doesn't change anything between us," she said. "Do you hear me?"

He nodded.

"I feel bad enough about your unfinished business with Madeline Hale," she went on. "I don't want this thing in the park to come between us too. Did you call her?"

"No. Not yet."

"It's my choice, you know," she said. "To stay or leave. Not yours." She grabbed a fistful of his hair. "Right?" She rocked his head in assent. In a deep voice she answered her own question: "Right, Margie."

She sat up and looked at him. "If you decide to leave me, can I go with you?"

At noon he left for London.

London was buried in snow. Siberian winds rocketed through the streets and drove people inside. Everyone was talking about the tremendous snowfalls in the English midlands. "In the memory of the living," an editorial noted, "there has never been a winter like this before. And, we fervently hope, never one like it again."

But in the intelligence community in London the talk wasn't about the weather. It was about the missile standdown. Brewer found things greatly changed: suddenly, Russian armies and not Russian rockets were the threat. Europe, expecting soon to have no nuclear missiles to protect it, now found it had no conventional defenses to replace the missiles.

After forty years the parameters of the cold war were changing. And the bureaucratic machinery was creaking. After forty years the most crucial problems have a way of becoming domesticated. They become a sort of solution in themselves. Necessary. After forty years habits of mind were reluctant to relinquish the comfortable old troubles. And reluctant to take on hard-edged new ones. Unknown ones. Unsettling ones. It takes so long to readjust. Bureaucracy hates change more than it hates democracy.

He found an air of foreboding everywhere. Even the amiable Mrs. Walmsley was in a mood to scold someone. As Brewer explained his mission, she kept twitching the loose green sweater across her shoulders. Up on a shelf behind her, her favorite cat watched her. Its marmalade tail twitched.

"There are three of our men you can talk to in particular," she said. "But it won't serve any purpose. You'll find that the only Russian pattern for smuggling is just smash and grab. Street tactics. What you ought to be worrying about is the new policies Washington has forced on us."

Brewer shrugged. "Too bad for Europe. The old policy was a bargain for you all these years."

"What did you expect Europe to do?" she demanded. "You and Russia wanted to play the mad game of outspending each other. Coming over here year after year insisting we spend more on a larger European defense budget. Absurd. Spend and spend and spend. Purse-proud Americans showing the poor old folks how. If we had done that, the European economy would be in the same pickle yours is in. The wisest thing we could have done was what we did—stand aside and let the two of you go at it. Do you know what Europe spent on defense last year? Eighty-three billion dollars. Do you know what your country spent on European defense last year? One hundred sixty-seven billion dollars. That's a huge military welfare program to give to Europe's middle class. You thought your money would never run out."

"Then you've lost a very good deal," Brewer said. "Now it's you who are going to have to spend and spend and spend."

"You people are gadget obsessed," she told Brewer, pulling her sweater back over her shoulders. "It's going to take more than a few stolen radar units for the Russians to beat us." She pointed down the hall. "You can do your interviewing in the office next door. The first man I'm going to have you talk to has handled more than one hundred cases of Russian technological espionage during his career. He ought to be able to tell you something."

"A hundred cases? Is this what you call a few stolen radar units?" he asked.

"What would you have us do?" Mrs. Walmsley demanded.

"For the last twenty years," he said, "you've needed a public gadfly like Winston Churchill again. Someone crying up the streets, tolling his bell."

He sat in the office late into the afternoon, listening to the three British intelligence men one at a time discuss Russian espionage. It was tailored, of course. They weren't going to tell Brewer anything sensitive. Mrs. Walmsley brought him a cup of tea, twitched her green sweater back across her shoulders, and left with a sniff. Things were in a state, and someone had to be blamed.

Brewer did get some information. The matériel that Bobby English had purchased in Los Angeles had gone to Kansas City and then to Montreal. Some of it then transited through Britain as plumbing supplies, heaters, aircraft navigational equipment. From Britain it had gone to the Continent. And there he would follow it.

He looked eastward through the window, across London. Down in the streets, bundled Londoners clumped from their offices homeward at dusk, fleeing the iron bite of the evening air. Was there really a Mr. X at the end of the line? The three British intelligence men thought not.

Lord Spatfield administered corporate punishment to the body politic of America. "Russia and the U.S. have exhausted each other," he told Brewer. "The wounds you've inflicted may be fatal. My intelligence group has just completed a study of Russia's medical establishment. Medical services are in ruins in that country, cash starved because of military spending. People dying from bad medical practice and no drugs. Plenty of rubles for arms yet no money to install running water in their rural hospitals. Infant mortality rate climbing—one of the highest in the world, in fact. At the same time, America's stunning trade deficits, according to many economists, are signaling the end of your economy. By the year 2000 Japan will have a larger gross national product than the U.S."

That day a London journalist, Winston Matters, in his column, "Matters Military," ran a cryptic note about espionage.

The Smuggling Commandos. It's now quite clear that the West never achieved a significant edge over Moscow in the missile race. One of the reasons, it may not be so obvious, is the relentless technological espionage program Moscow always mounts. And a key reason within that reason may be Moscow's secret intelligence commando team that specializes in difficult acquisitions. So effective is it that a recent defector from Russia values this commando team as worth five divisions in the field. Perhaps more. Perhaps much more. If there's a war, it seems clear that the nation that wins on the battlefield must first win in the intelligence field. And the Russians are in a clear lead here.

Brewer tried to reach Matters by phone. "Mr. Matters is away on assignment," he was told. "He is expected back the day after tomorrow."

In the evening he took a cab to Chelsea and went to her pub. When she saw him, she never took her eyes off him as he walked up to the bar.

"Hello, Charlie," she said.

She still had that splendid rosy color to her face and those marvelous eyes—delft blue with a sly mirthful expression. Plump pink arms. A feast of a woman nearing forty.

She served him a pint of lager. "Haven't had one of those in a while, I'll wager."

"You're looking fine," he said.

She nodded. "I'm rid of him," she said. "The army took him." She scowled at his scowl. "Well, that's what an army's for, isn't it, taking other people's mistakes? But they sent him to Belfast, and him only nineteen. And now I'm feeling that guilty."

"I wish him well," Brewer said.

"I doubt it. He certainly doesn't deserve your good wishes." Her eyes watched her hands fill a pint glass with lager. "I'm sorry about it all. It was my fault. Letting Arthur break up a marriage like that. You were the best thing that ever happened to me, Charlie. Here, Stanley, for the two in the booth."

"It wasn't Arthur," he said.

"He didn't help. But I suppose you're right. That night that Thomas came in here looking for you with those cold February eyes of his, I knew I'd lost you." She smiled. "Truth be known, the pubkeeper's life wasn't the life for you. But any time you want to come back, Charlie, it'll be no questions asked. Here, Stanley, clear that table and let them sit there." She studied Brewer's face. Nothing ever seemed to escape her gaze. "I cried for you more than once, Charlie, my love," she said.

"Save your tears for Arthur in Belfast," he said.

"You're back into the same old game, is it?"

"I'm doing fine."

"That's not what your face says, Charlie."

That night it snowed again in London. His flight for Frankfort the next morning took off an hour late.

Brewer moved carefully in Europe. Another attack on him could occur anywhere, anytime. In airports a man with a coat over one arm and a newspaper can conceal a pistol and a silencer. Step up, raise the pistol under a folded newspaper, fire. Target falls down with a hole in his back, assailant, in the confusion, passes the weapon in the folded newspaper to another, who quickly passes it to a third person while the assassin disappears in the crowd. A skilled man with a knife can kill in an elevator, on a seat on an airplane. A hotel bedroom is a Whitman's Sampler of opportunities for a killer. Cabs, staircases, parks—the opportunities are abundant.

On the Continent he found the same foreboding: Russia without missiles seemed stronger and more threatening than Russia with missiles, conventional warfare more likely. Everyone was aware that there was a new game to be learned—and an old game to be laid aside, the worn playing board and counters so much impedimenta to be left in history's storage bin. The Europeans now counted divisions, not warheads, and talked of troops and logistics, terrains and tactics. They weren't interested in smugglers.

"What are you looking for?" agents in Frankfort asked him.

"Patterns," he said. "Habitual strategies. The Russian way of doing things. I'm looking for the man behind it all."

In Bonn Schneider made a skeptical mouth. There was no man behind it all. He blamed Russia's great smuggling coup on European indifference—particularly CoCom.

"The Committee for East-West Trade failed to impose embargoes on vital strategic matériel," he prated. "They just let it all flow across Europe into the Russian war machine. They still are. CoCom sat there in Paris and did nothing. How could it? What were there? A mere dozen political appointees, from as many different countries, against thousands of Russians. They met in Paris and agreed that nothing could be done." He spanked the air with a beating forefinger. "The CoCom was a political do-nothing slapped up by diplomats. Its sole purpose, now it can be told, was to shut up the American caterwauling. We didn't want embargoes. We wanted all that fat trade with Eastern Europe. Bonn has become very dependent on East-West trade." He looked at Brewer. "Truth is, Mr. Brewer— American businessmen wanted that trade too. They sold as much to the Russians as we did."

Schneider's people were reassessing Russian conventional army strength, and everywhere they turned they found that strength immeasurably increased by stolen American technology.

Schneider told him not to bother checking CoCom records. "Every one of its moves are at least three years too late. Have you ever seen their embargo list? Absurd. Absolutely absurd." He shook his head and clicked his tongue. "Now there's a great cry to have CoCom put firm embargoes in place. Now. Isn't that ironic? With the imminent missile standdown, Europe is suddenly regretting every last disk drive and radar unit that had been smuggled into Moscow. All of it is now ranged against us."

"Meantime," Brewer said, "the smuggling goes on—more than ever. Someone must be orchestrating it."

Schneider shrugged. "I have no reason to believe in a Russian mastermind. Truth is, we really have no idea how much matériel has flowed into Russia. If we did, we would probably believe there are a hundred Russian masterminds. It was done on such a vast scale—as we now see."

Brenier in Paris blamed it on American policy. "How many times did we adopt an American policy," he demanded, "with great reluctance I might add, only to see Washington abruptly abandon it, most times without even advising us? Ha? How many times? If there was a mastermind, we gave him more help than he needed."

Brewer didn't find a single official on the Continent who knew anything about a supersmuggler. A war-matériel concertmeister? A pied piper of technology? Farfetched. None of them believed there was such a thing.

He tried others—people outside the intelligence services. In Holland, in Germany, Switzerland, Austria, he talked to freight-office managers, drivers, warehousemen. In spite of their silence and their furtive glances, he felt he glimpsed the truth: people had been bribed to push the American matériel down the road to Moscow. All done by telephone. A man would call. An envelope would arrive. And things were accomplished.

Brewer went to question the three smugglers in Germany who had received the shipment from Kansas City and pushed it on to Vienna.

His name was Ruskin and he was part English and part German, the issue of a British soldier and a German war bride. The German authorities were holding him on charges stemming from a serious and growing problem in Germany—drugs. Ruskin had been arrested trying to smuggle nearly a half-million dollars in cocaine through German customs.

No one was interested in Ruskin's record of smuggling high-tech matériel to Russia.

In prison Ruskin looked like a man accustomed to losing. He had a large beak of a nose and a bitter sunken mouth, gaps between crooked teeth, acne scars, and strands of long oily hair. A lifelong outsider.

"They're going to throw the key away," he told Brewer. "No deals. I've got all kinds of information on high-tech smuggling, but they're interested in drugs only."

"What about your two partners?"

"Who? Wolf and Muller? They walked. We all walked. We were hardly questioned about that high-tech stuff."

"Where are they now?"

"Dunno. Not drug dealing, if they're smart."

He seemed glad of the company, reluctant to see Brewer go. He had been smuggling for years, driving across borders in trucks with false papers. Nothing sensitive. Stolen goods mainly—Japanese radios and tellies. Did a lot of it for a group of German businessmen. He got started on war matériel with one phone call.

"Never met him," Ruskin said. "Just a voice. Tried to black-mail me. Said he had a lot of information on my smuggling. I didn't care. Told him so. But the money he offered made me listen right enough. And I did know the ropes. So we did busi-ness. And money arrived in small envelopes."

"Swiss francs?"

"Right. How'd you know?"

"So what did you do?"

"The shell game. You know—we shuffled the goods from place to place until no one could untangle it. We'd pack the shipments in different cartons and different papers. It was easy." He smiled. "We even used the shipping containers of ma-jor German corporations and shipped it across borders in their own trucks with the customs seals wagging behind—without anyone knowing it. Safe as a baby in its mother's arms. A few pounds here, some marks there—it accomplishes marvels. Easy money for people in shipping departments. Easiest way in the world to make lots of stuff just disappear."

"How long were you doing this?"

Ruskin shrugged. "Couple of years. We moved a hell of a lot of matériel, to Switzerland and Holland, but most of it into Aus-tria."

"Vienna?"

"Mostly, I'd say." He grinned. "These Germans are half mad about the drugs in their country. But if I were them, I'd be more worried about the military stuff we sent to Russia. Just the three of us alone must have armed several Russian divisions—and they can raise more hell in Germany than all the drug push-ers in the world. Think of how many other groups the man on the phone was operating. Half of Europe must be smuggling for him."

From memory, in a very bad handwriting full of misspellings, Ruskin wrote down pages of information on the history of those seventeen chameleon cartons from Kansas City. He laughed just once during the whole interview.

"He really pushed your face into the pie, didn't he?" he said. "I heard about the empty cartons." He twisted a hank of hair around a finger and laughed happily, like a small child. "Wish I had thought of that."

"What was his nationality?"

"Hard to say. He spoke mostly German. Good educated German. But he often spoke English to me—although he knew I was raised in Germany. I'd say he had an American accent."

When Brewer was ready to leave, he took a long look at Ruskin. "Why don't you give them what they want?" he asked.

"What?"

"Information about the drug ring."

"Oh. I can't. It's the same man, isn't it?"

"Who?"

"The man on the telephone. The same one who had us smuggling the high-tech equipment."

"You mean the Russian smuggler is also a cocaine dealer?"

"That's about the size of it. And there's nothing I can tell them about who he is. I haven't got the foggiest, do I?"

As Brewer was walking away, Ruskin called after him. "He's much too smart for them, you know. They'll never find him. Nor will you."

In Munich Brewer tried to reach Winston Matters again at his London newspaper.

"Yes, he is back in London." The speaker said she was Matters's secretary. The day before, Brewer had been told Matters had no secretary. "But he's out for most of the day," she said. "He rarely stays in the office. Perhaps you'd like to leave your name and phone number. And what did you say it's about?"

With Sauer's documents and Ruskin's notes, Brewer rented a car in Munich and continued his Easter-egg hunt. He followed the trail across Austria. The first stop was Salzburg.

It was the same story there. Labels on top of labels. Warehousemen conveniently looking the other way, indifferent or bribed. The voice on the phone was well known. Very friendly. Sometimes he sent envelopes with money for no reason. Mr. X had built and maintained his own well-greased underground transport system across Europe, and through it contraband poured into Russia. Brewer drove to Linz. He drove to Graz. And finally he drove to Vienna.

He stood in the warehouse with the owner, gazing at the spot where the seventeen cartons had stood. The owner was very distinguished-looking, with an aristocratic face. He could have been a stand-in for the old emperor, Franz Joseph. In his hands he held one of the empty cartons. He hefted it.

"The others are gone," he said. "Thrown out, I suppose. They're of no significance now, in any case. This one I've kept in my office."

"How did he steal seventeen cartons?" Brewer asked him.

"Ah," the owner said. "But he didn't, don't you see? He replaced them."

"How did he replace them."

The owner smiled at him. "One at a time."

"Right in the middle of the floor?"

The owner pointed upward, at the double rows of skylights. "As you can see, the light is not the best. Especially on these snowy winter days. With a number of people and hand trucks and such going on—well, you can see. It would be easy."

"How do you think it was accomplished?" Brewer asked. "Especially with a man up there in the offices doing nothing but watching."

The owner shrugged. "Police. A boring job. And a cold one. Day after day. Time out for a trip to the toilet. A pause for coffee. You must remember they were waiting for someone to drive up with a truck and claim all seventeen cartons. Would a man notice that a full carton had been replaced with an empty one while he was in the toilet?"

Brewer walked the length of the great warehouse then stood by the main doorway. For the seventeen cartons the trip had started in Los Angeles, gone across the continent and up to Canada, then to Germany, then through Austria to here, then out this door to—where? He looked northeastward. Zeleenograd.

He took out Bobby English's ruble note. The end of the string, and no Mr. X. The face no one had ever seen. The only tangible thing he had was this piece of worn currency pushed into Bobby English's coat pocket in Los Angeles.

Back in his hotel room Brewer dialed the German telephone number English had given him. A recording replied, "At the tone, please leave your message." Brewer hung up.

He tried Winston Matters's London newspaper again.

"Mr. Matters received your message. He has left a Paris number for you to call."

Chapter 26

It was finally too much for Gogol's patience: the botched assassination attempt meant that the next try against Brewer would be infinitely more difficult. And meantime, Brewer was moving closer to him while he was getting no closer to Cassandra.

The way home lay through Limoges's automobile. That was obvious. The man conducted all his secret meetings about Cassandra in that limousine. Gogol had to find a way to listen in.

Over the objections of Nevans, the chauffeur, Gogol disobeyed expressed orders from the committee and flew to Washington. He arrived late on a bitter cold Sunday morning and went to their customary rendezvous—a quiet motel down by the Potomac. He had never before seen so much snow in Washington.

The motel overlooked a winterscape, the river banks deep in snow under pallid sunlight, ice along the edges, while above, flocks of small birds fluttered along the scribbled black lines of bare branches. This was not the Washington he liked to remember. He preferred the springtime Washington of his sixteenth year, when he first came to the city with his father from Teheran, en route to Moscow. Three months that now in memory seemed like a year. Three months that changed his life.

He made three raps on the door.

Nevans thrust his head out and glanced up and down the hallway. "Were you followed?" he demanded.

"Yes, by the President himself and his entire cabinet. You are getting far too nervous for this business."

Two pillows were propped against the headboard of the bed, and sections of the Sunday paper were scattered over the counterpane. On the night table was a pot of coffee and a cup. How domestic. Sunday morning in Washington D.C., reading the newspaper.

Even in sweater and slacks Nevans looked like the perfect chauffeur. Quiet, reserved, with an obedient expression on an ordinary, forgettable face under thinning hair. It was a face that rarely smiled, never told a joke, never got into quarrels at traffic lights. But the eyes had changed since Gogol's last visit. Bland calmness had been replaced by the furtive sidelong glances of a man under siege. Too long in the trenches. This was a face that said in the mirror each morning while shaving, "Today may be the day my luck runs out." Each day a little more confidence slowly sifts away like the salt through a hole in the bag, until one day all the salt is spent, all the confidence gone. Nevans was living the old saying among agents: when the nerve fails, the luck runs out. He badly needed a good starching.

"That Brewer is unkillable," Nevans said.

"I'll take care of Brewer," Gogol said. "All I want you to do is concentrate on Cassandra."

"That's all I ever think about," Nevans said.

"Do you have the pictures I asked for?" Gogol asked.

Nevans walked over to his jacket and, from the inner pocket, slipped out an envelope. "There's a close-up of every piece of equipment that's in Limoges's automobile trunk."

The envelope contained a set of Polaroid photographs, and Gogol looked at them slowly one at a time, placing each in turn in a row on the bed. "I don't believe I've ever seen anything like this before," he said. "Limoges has one of the biggest collections of anti-listening devices I've ever seen. It's a miracle they were able to fit all this junk in that trunk."

"It takes them an hour every morning to check it out," Nevans replied. "You'll never ever record one word in that limousine."

Gogol resumed his study of the photographs. "Some of this stuff I've never seen before," he said. "I could find a ready market for it." He started through the photographs again, casting a smile at Nevans. "You're right. This is going to be difficult."

"Impossible," Nevans said. "I told you that. The engineer who put that stuff in the trunk told Limoges that he didn't know of any listening device that could penetrate that system."

Something in Nevans's voice made Gogol look at him. A man on the edge.

"Relax, Nevans," he said. "You're doing a fine job. Just keep it up, don't take any risks, and let me do the worrying. Your position is perfectly safe."

"I want a reassignment."

"Soon, Nevans. Soon."

Gogol spent the next hour trying to reassure Nevans. A little while longer, he told him. Things were coming to a head. Nevans was safe. There was no chance of exposure. This was his last assignment. Medals and kudos were waiting for him.

But Nevans was hard to prop up. Gogol finally identified the problem: Nevans was afraid of Brewer.

"He's already tracked that job from Los Angeles to Vienna," Nevans said. "He talked to Bobby English. He talked to that British smuggler in prison—I told you to take care of him. This Brewer is like some kind of a fiend. He's already learned more in a few days than they had learned in two years. He could find you at any moment. And when he does, he'll find the rest of us. He should be taken care of now. Today."

"Brewer's probably very good," Gogol said. "But he's just another human being. Not a fiend. He has no special powers. And I'll take care of him. Trust me."

"I won't trust anyone until Brewer's in his grave."

"He will be. Soon."

When they were finished, Gogol said he wanted to see the park where the failed assassination took place. Nevans was reluctant.

"A brief look," Gogol said.

Nevans carried the Sunday paper in an untidy pile down the corridor of the motel with him to the parking lot and threw it in the backseat of his car.

"How are the Orioles doing?" Gogol asked.

"What Orioles?"

"The baseball team. I heard they were dealing for a new left-handed relief pitcher."

"I don't know," Nevans said. "I don't follow baseball." He frowned at Gogol. "What do you know about baseball?"

"You haven't seen anything until you've watched a really

great relief pitcher at work in the ninth inning with the bases loaded and a .300 hitter at the plate. Where is this park?"

"Just follow me."

Gogol's eyes took in the park terrain. A frigid wind was soughing in the trees, rocking the branches and ruffling the feathers of the perching crows. A weak sun was dodging in and out of thin clouds. The streets that framed the little square were covered with old snow, bracketed by icy crosswalks.

"He stood here and Brewer there?" he asked. "That's twenty meters, wouldn't you say? No more than thirty. Point-blank range with an automatic weapon. And the firing mechanism jammed?"

"Jammed," the chauffeur agreed. "It was an early model nine-millimeter Uzi. Very old and in very bad condition. He would have gotten better results if he'd beaten Brewer to death with it."

Cut-rate Russian assassination all over again, Gogol thought. Everything on price. It cost a fortune to set this up: the surveillance teams that followed Brewer; Nevans's selection of the site and the timing; the transporting of two killers from halfway around the world, then getting them within twenty meters of the target; and Directorate T caps it off with a worn-out weapon that misfires.

"Your choice was excellent," he said to Nevans.

"The firing mechanism may have been stiff from the cold," Nevans said. "If they'd let me provide the weapon, Brewer would be dead."

Only a worn-out, bargain-basement weapon misfires, Gogol thought. And the consequences were fearsome. Brewer, instead of being killed in this park, flies out to Los Angeles, where he gets valuable information from a man who is also supposed to be in his grave, not once but four times—in Munich, then in Athens, then in Hong Kong, then in Los Angeles. And who saves his life there? Brewer—the man who is supposed to be dead in this park. Gogol felt haunted by the living dead.

Nevans looked unhappily at the frozen footprints in the snow of the park. "Brewer is the one who can track you down," he said quietly.

"I hear you."

"He's very dangerous," the chauffeur said.

Gogol flapped a hand at the park. "He's very lucky," he answered.

To the chauffeur's intense relief, Gogol parted from him at the park.

"Brewer is the one who can track you down," he said again to the departing Gogol.

Periodically on the flight back, Gogol studied the Polaroid photographs Nevans had given him. Then he studied a brochure, *Surveillance Equipment: A Catalog of New Industrial Technology*. Somewhere in those pages there had to be a device that would penetrate Limoges's defenses. A device that would enable him to listen in on Limoges's conversations about Cassandra.

From his case Gogol withdrew tear sheets of Matters's London newspaper columns. Another problem. The meeting between Matters and Brewer had to be stopped. They simply could not be allowed to match notes.

Gogol had never had the feeling of being stalked before. For the first time he had a momentary sense of vulnerability. He heard the chauffeur's words ringing in his ears. "Brewer is the one who can track you down."

Brewer called Matters in Paris. He was in Berlin. Then Matters called Brewer from Rotterdam.

"Yes, yes," Matters agreed. "Russian smuggling is just not that efficient. Someone very gifted is orchestrating a smuggling program of the most sensitive matériel from America, across Europe to Zeleenograd. Don't you see?"

"Do you know who it is?"

"Someone brilliant, Mr. Brewer. Directorate T couldn't do it. They're too bureaucratic and musclebound. This program is being conducted by a virtuoso."

"Do you have a name?"

"I'd rather not say any more on the telephone."

"Where can we meet?"

"Paris. Got a pencil? I'll give you the address."

*   *   *

There was less snow in Paris, but the city suffered from freezing rain that had coated the streets and walks with ice. The chestnut trees along the Champs Elysées were wrapped in an icy glaze which slowly dripped in the weak sunlight. Walking was dangerous.

Brewer called Matters as soon as he got out of the taxi from DeGaulle.

"I'm more convinced than ever that there's a fixer in the Russian system somewhere," Matters said. "A brilliant fixer. And I may be on his trail right now. Listen, Mr. Brewer. Why don't you check into your hotel, then come around to my place, say about eightish tonight?"

"Have you had your phone checked for taps?" Brewer asked.

"Taps? I have no idea. I suppose it could be tapped very easily. I'm in the phone book."

"Have you been followed?"

"I don't bother with things like that, Mr. Brewer. If anything happens to me, there are other journalists who will step right in and continue the search."

"That won't impress the Russians," Brewer said. "If they decide to silence you, they'll kill you and a hundred other reporters to boot."

"I understand," Matters said. "I've been threatened before."

"These people don't threaten," Brewer answered. "They don't warn. They just do. If you're going to keep digging, you'd better get yourself a bulletproof vest. Or even better, a bulletproof body. See you at eight."

As an encore to the ice storm that evening snow began to fall in Paris. More than an hour before he was expected at Matters's flat, Brewer emerged from his hotel and stood in a soft, feathery snowfall. Matters's insouciance was dangerous: Brewer had decided to check the columnist's apartment for surveillance before keeping the rendezvous. He decided against taking a cab. Instead he took the metro.

When he reached street level, he waited at the stair top to

see if he had been followed. He went back down the steps to see if anyone on the street came down after him. Then he took the metro one more stop and mounted to street level. So far so good.

He looked at his watch; forty-five minutes early. The snow was getting deeper.

"I don't bother with things like that," Matters had said. As Brewer walked, his thoughts were on another journalist he had known—Bernie Parker—who did bother with things like that, but in spite of all his precautions, was murdered on the metro steps down by the Champs Elysées.

When he got within several blocks of Matters's building, Brewer paused. He stepped into a doorway and looked carefully at the dark street ahead of him. He stared at every doorway. He looked into every parked car. He waited a few minutes and re-examined the doorways and cars. Then he stepped out and continued his walk toward Matters's apartment.

When he reached the building, he paused again, checking cars and doorways. Then he looked at the names on the bells. Matters lived on the third floor. Brewer stepped back into the middle of the narrow street and looked up at the lighted windows on the third floor. The apartment was not a good place to meet. In fact, it was a trap.

Walking and looking into every car and doorway, Brewer shuffled through the snow to the next intersection, circled the block and came around again to the building. There was no surveillance on Matters that he could find. Brewer beat the snow off his coat then tried the front door, found it unlocked, and opened it. Inside was a vestibule, then the stairway up, and beyond that, a corridor that led to a basement door. Brewer went down to the basement.

It was an old foundation, made of brick, with brick support piers for the old chimney stacks. Water pipes, sewer pipes, and electrical wires crisscrossed the ceiling, while the telephone wires and junction box were mounted on the back wall. And there, like a leech, a wiretap was attached to Matters's phone line.

As Brewer mounted the basement steps, he heard a car pull up in front of the house. Footsteps. Front door opening. Steps mounting the stairs quickly. Brewer stepped into the hallway and looked up. From behind he saw a man carrying a small valise, hastening up the stairs on light feet, two steps at a time. Brewer could hear the motor of the car still running. A few moments later the man came bounding down the stairs. Brewer withdrew to the basement doorway and watched him hurry out of the building. The car sped off.

Brewer ran up the stairs to the third floor. He pounded on Matters's door.

"Matters!" he yelled. "Pitch it out of the window. Matters! Throw it!"

He raised his fist to pound on the door again. But it was too late. The bomb went off.

It was one A.M. when Gogol got word from Revin.

"It did only half the job," Revin's voice said from Cologne.

"Which half?"

"The wrong half."

"What happened to the other half?"

"Not a mark," Revin said.

"Then we still have the same problem."

"Yes," Revin said.

"That means it's a bigger problem than ever."

"Yes," Revin said. "Bigger than ever."

Chapter 27

The snow piles in the Pentagon parking lot seemed deeper than ever to Brewer when he drove to the rendezvous point. And the wind seemed stronger. Behind him came the limousine and the navy-blue escort car.

He watched the chauffeur, with the fluttering newspaper under his arm, walk over to the backseat of the escort car and get in.

"What made you go down to Matters's cellar?" Limoges asked.

"I was checking for phone taps."

"Did you find any?"

"Yes."

"That's good," Limoges said. "Because that's what saved your life. They waited for you to enter the building, then they delivered the bomb. If you had gone up to his apartment as you were supposed to, instead of down to the cellar, the bomb would have got you both. That's twice you got lucky. You'd better watch your little po-po, Brewer. You can't be that lucky a third time."

"That was about the thirtieth time," Brewer said.

Limoges lit a cigar. "What did you get?"

"A good case for Mr. X," Brewer said. "Let me show you a few examples." Brewer took a sheaf of papers from a file folder. "The Russians were hot to get two PDP-11's from Digital Equipment Corporation for computer-designing microchips. They used a fictitious front company to buy them and tried to ship them out of New York. But U.S. customs intercepted them. So they bought two more and got them as far as Amsterdam before they were stopped. They made a third try out of Milan.

And they failed again. Three misses. Then out of the blue from London, they get the two units. And Western authorities didn't even know this until months later.

"Here's another example. They urgently needed a micro-chip-soldering production line—a series of soldering stations. Same story. Customs nailed them. Twice. Then voilà. They get it." Brewer handed another piece of paper to Limoges. "Same story with six high-pressure ovens. They got them as far as Berlin, then lost them to Western customs agents. Next time they didn't miss—they got them through Vienna. And I've got two pads full of other case histories. Two or three misses, then success. And those are just the cases we know about. No one knows how many VAXs have been smuggled into Russia. Or IBM 360's and 370's."

"What are you getting at?" Limoges asked.

Brewer said, "I believe there's a single person behind all this—a Mr. X. He's their super goal maker. When the regular troops botch a job, the Reds send in their fixer. And he never fails them." Brewer pointed to his list. "He's done a lot of damage to the West. For example, last May he smuggled a complete set of photolithographic masks of computer circuits into Zeleenograd from California via Vienna. At the same time, through another source in California, he got the copiers and the etching equipment that transfer the circuits from the masks onto silicon chips . . . Amsterdam to Strasbourg to Vienna to Mother Russia. He's a master of the shell game. He just keeps moving the pea until it disappears. Listen to these moves: he shoved a supply of microprocessing spare parts from Chicago to New York to Montreal through Genoa to Austria then back to Switzerland and finally to Vienna to Hungary and into Zeleenograd. It took a group of CoCom investigators weeks to follow the trail of these spare parts. And by that time they were already inside Russian equipment. You may have noticed that Vienna is his favorite city.

"Here's another piece of smuggling. Five tons of equipment essential for chip making—including crystal-cutting saws and scribers to separate the wafer circuits. That material was wandered in small batches back and forth across the U.S., then went to Europe by way of Amsterdam. Then it was relabeled and reshipped to Coblenz. Relabeled once again and reshipped to Salzburg then to Vienna, where it disappears.

"And here are four more tons of equipment—through Frankfort to Zurich to Vienna. Computer-controlled design systems that plan integrated circuits. Here's an interesting shipment—ion implantation gear, lead-bonding tools, solderless connectors, solder mounting tools. All shipped to Vienna, where they disappear. Here's another shipment through Munich to Zurich, then by air to Vienna, where he slipped it across the border into Czechoslovakia and on to Zeleenograd. Here are high-pressure oxidation ovens for microchips . . . and on and on and on, a steady flow of high-tech equipment pouring out of U.S. plants into Europe to Vienna and then into Russia. And he always plays the same game: button, button, who's got the button? Nothing stops him."

"How do you know one man is doing all this?"

"The style. The finesse. The techniques. The pattern is always the same. He sets up a bunch of fictitious little companies here in the U.S., blackmails Americans into operating them, then orders what he wants through them. Each of his fake little companies make small, unobtrusive purchases here in the U.S. Nothing that will draw attention. A machine here, a tool there. Then he always covers these purchases with falsified Department of Commerce documents. Forged disclaimers. And he always sends cash with the order. Checks from little banks in rural areas."

Brewer passed Limoges sheet after sheet of documents. "First-rate forgeries of waybills and certification. Quick relabeling and reshipping, with turn-around times of a few hours to a few minutes. Slick, smooth, and without a hitch. But when you put the circuit masks from here with the crystal-cutting saws from there and the soldering stations from someplace else, it all dovetails perfectly into a complete factory."

Limoges's lap was filled with papers.

"Look at this little masterpiece," Brewer said. "He wanted a clean-room air filter for making microchips. But he couldn't buy one without military documentation. And those are papers he couldn't forge. So what did he do? He went to the spare parts department of the same company, and over a period of six weeks sent in seventy orders from eleven different little companies, got all the parts piecemeal that he needed to make a complete air filter, and shipped it to Zeleenograd.

"But he's not perfect. He leaves little clues. For example, he always orders the equipment wired for East European voltages. And he never buys service contracts. They would be useless to him in Russia. And because he doesn't buy complete systems from one source, he usually doesn't get complete service manuals. But back in Zeleenograd they need those service manuals when they do their reverse engineering of American equipment. So he leaves another trail—stolen service manuals.

"He breaks into the offices of legitimate companies all over Europe and the U.S. Very selective break-ins. He never touches anything else in those offices. He ignores valuable equipment, often hefty sums of cash, and even negotiable securities. He steals just one thing. Service manuals. How do I know? When these companies find their manuals missing, they call the original equipment manufacturer for new ones. But the OEMs are very reluctant to provide new ones—because they're on the embargo list along with the equipment. So right after a load of equipment is smuggled into Russia, OEMs get requests from legitimate companies for replacement of manuals.

"There's also an unavoidable trail of straw men, fake companies, doctored contracts—he even has used the shipping channels of legitimate companies by bribing shipping clerks, truck drivers, or even executives of common carriers.

"Sometimes, the people he uses get caught. They all say the same thing. They were hired by telephone, paid in cash in advance, usually Swiss francs, and they never saw the man who hired them.

"So he leaves a pattern. First he illegally purchases a piece of equipment. Then he uses forged papers and fake identities to ship it back and forth in Europe until no one is able to follow his trail. Then he smuggles it across the border. Then shortly later, he steals service manuals."

"One man can do all that?" Limoges asked.

"One man can orchestrate all that," Brewer replied. "Look here. In a six-month period last year he was smouching up everything in Europe from microchips to mainframes. All kinds of

CRT capability. Even command technology for missiles. A variety of computer-manufacturing methods. Machinery plans—blueprints by the pound. Tooling, all kinds of tooling that they can reverse engineer. Disk drives. Communications hardware and software—all of it centering on one thing: microprocessor manufacture and design. In a little over a year Mr. X got enough equipment into Russia to give it a formidable military microchip capability. All of it taken from the heartland of the U.S. It's been like the sacking of Rome.

"Lately he's been focusing on Star Wars hardware, and especially trench capacitance on megabit chips. You know what's number one on his shopping list? Four-bit machinery. It's brand-new technology. We've just made the first machines for this—IBM and a few others. Maybe the Japanese. And Mr. X is on hand, trying to swipe it already."

Limoges stared at the pile of scattered documents in his lap.

Brewer said, "Let me tell you how good this guy is. On at least three occasions he smuggled VAX 10's back into the West. And two IBM 370's. Complete mainframe computers."

Limoges smiled skeptically. "Reverse smuggling?"

"Yes. The Russians can't do maintenance on the American computers they've stolen. So when they need servicing, Super Red smuggles them over the border into a Western European country, sets them up in a phony factory setting, then has American-trained European technical staffs unwittingly service and repair them. Then he smuggles them back into Russia.

"On one occasion he assembled an entire anti-microcontamination plant in a factory building in Austria and set it working. Next he smuggled in a complete team of factory managers from Zeleenograd and demonstrated it. Then to modify it according to their directions, he went out and swiped other machines they asked for, crated the whole lot—tons and tons of matériel—and slipped it across the border to Hungary and then into Moscow. He's Moscow's ace in the hole—Mr. Nevermiss—the invisible man. Yet there's no record of him anywhere. You never see him or hear of him. He just leaves a shadow. A trademark. A style. All these smuggling jobs I've shown you have the imprint of the same mind. He's a brilliant operator."

Limoges looked at the pages of documentation that littered

his backseat. "Looks like you got everything except the key piece, Brewer," he said.

"What?"

"His name."

Brewer smiled grimly at him. "That's going to be the hard part," he said. "Your prayers are earnestly solicited."

In the rear of the computer-repair shop, Gogol stood looking at an array of anti-eavesdropping devices ranged on a workbench. He looked again at the Polaroid photographs Nevans had given him.

"Everything's on there," the engineer said, pointing at the workbench. "A duplicate of everything from the trunk of that car is on that workbench." He held out a list.

"I understand that," Gogol said. "My question is, how do we penetrate it?"

The engineer made a sour face at the workbench. "We don't," he said. "There's no way in the world."

••• Chapter 28

Brewer didn't move in with Margie again. He went to his own apartment. He even delayed calling her to let her know he was back. Live together. Die separately.

His living room now looked like a war room. All around the walls he'd pinned up maps of the U.S. and Europe. On each map, with felt markers, he'd traced a different one of Mr. X's smuggling operations. The felt markers in blue and green and red zigzagged across the motor routes of the U.S. and Europe. X's patience and cunning were evident in every move, every switch of cargo, every relabeling, every forged manifest, every document.

Limoges was right. Brewer could tell a great deal about Mr. X—his favorite trucking companies in each country, his product interests, his method of operation, his method of finding people to blackmail, and his technique of blackmailing them. He could tell something of how Mr. X's mind worked and how he timed his operations. Gazing around his living room, it was obvious: he knew a great deal about Mr. X's methods. But he didn't know a thing about Mr. X.

The only tangible fact he had—the only hint of a personality, the only individual touch—was the ruble note that had been pushed into Bobby English's suitcoat pocket. Brewer put it on his kitchen counter and stared at it. He smoothed it with his fingers, read the legend.

Somewhere in all this welter of facts—shipping dates and product lists, airline schedules and names of people who had handled the cargo—somewhere in there was a clue to X's identity.

Brewer crumpled the ruble in his fist. I'll get you.

Was Mr. X tall or short? Thirty or forty or fifty? Dour? Humorless? Flamboyant or reserved? Did he drink with the boys or drink alone? Married? Children? And why did he have the thugs in L.A. push a Russian bank note into English's pocket? Was it a personal message to English, or something more revealing—a romantic flourish?

Sauer had gotten close to Mr. X—in Vienna. Was there some clue that Sauer had omitted—even unwittingly? There was one way to find out.

Brewer went to Sauer's apartment. He tapped on the door.

"Who is it?" Sauer asked through the panel.

"Brewer. It's eight o'clock."

"Just a minute." There was a long pause. Then Sauer called through the door, "I'll be right with you, Brewer." After another wait, the door swung open. Sauer stood there, feet bare, his shirttails out.

"Sorry," he said. "I thought you said nine o'clock. Come on in." He shut the door behind Brewer.

The shoulder strap of a woman's slip dangled from under a seat cushion. A woman's high-heel shoe lay on its side under a chair. On a kitchen chair on a pile of newspapers lay a red umbrella. The door to the bedroom was closed.

"I want to ask you some questions about the Vienna affair," Brewer said. "I won't stay long."

"That's okay," Sauer replied. "There's something I want to go over with you too." He had been drinking, and spoke in a loud voice.

"What is it?" Brewer asked.

"Something personal. 'Kay?"

"Go ahead," Brewer said.

"Have a drink."

"No."

"One. Just one."

Brewer nodded. He watched Sauer walk into the kitchen. A quick bob of Sauer's head: a quick pop of booze for the bartender. Then he made the drinks. Was it the eye or the hand that announced it?—a man in free fall, out of control. Blaming others, blaming the world, blaming anyone but himself—a man about to crack. Who did this?

On a table, framed photos of children. Young people holding babies. A youthful, smiling Sauer with a youthful, smiling wife—a studio portrait. When our hearts were young and gay.

Sauer handed him a drink—scotch on the rocks.

"Cheers," Sauer said.

"God bless all in this house," Brewer said, glancing at the bedroom door.

"I want to talk about a deal with you," Sauer said.

"Okay," Brewer said. "Shoot."

"I want in. You see what I'm saying? I want to be part of the operation."

"What part do you want?"

"Any part I can get. A good part. I want to be in for some of the credit if it comes off." He watched Brewer's face. "Suppose I said please?"

Brewer considered that. Finally he said, "Sauer, you don't want any part of what I'm working on. Bet the rent money on it."

"I don't care what it is—whatever it is, it's the road back for me. See what I'm saying?"

"I'm not sure I can talk about this now, Sauer."

"Why not?"

Brewer stood up and walked over to the bedroom door.

"What are you doing?" Sauer demanded, jumping to his feet.

Brewer opened the door and looked into the bedroom. A woman was sitting on the edge of the bed in the dark, nude except for the pillow she was clutching.

"Hello," Brewer said. "Nice to see you again." He pulled the door shut.

Sauer shrugged at him. "A friend of mine."

"I see." Brewer picked up the red umbrella.

"Okay. She's the one who followed you to New York. It was Limoges's doing. You weren't coming around fast enough, so he put a tail on you. He didn't give her any notice at all. She didn't even have time to get some warm clothes. In the middle of a snowstorm he yanked her out of the office as is and stuck her on the train."

Brewer silently studied Sauer's face.

"She's the best we've got, Brewer. They say she's the best tracker in the business. She sure stayed glued to your ass." He took a long pull on his drink. "'Kay? She's a tracker, she's a friend of mine, and that's the whole story."

Brewer nodded. "Okay."

"What about me joining you?"

Brewer shook his head. "You won't want any part of it. What I'm working on is all off the books. You know what that means—really means?"

"Being off the books?" Sauer asked.

"Yes."

"Yeah. I guess I do. No cover. No protection. No net."

"Have you ever been off the books?"

"No." Sauer shifted in his seat.

"Then you don't know what it means. What it means is you're a renegade. You're outside the legal system."

"I know that."

"You're on the run and you're absolutely all alone—fair game for anyone who wants to take a pot shot at you."

"I know that too," Sauer said.

"If you get caught, all those people who promised to help will look the other way, and you can go to prison for a big number."

"But—"

"Your name gets in the paper. Congressional committees will demand an investigation. The entire intelligence system gets a bad name. So every intelligence officer—all your friends and associates—everybody you ever knew marks you down as a criminal and a traitor. Even your old kindergarten teacher puts you on her shit list. You're a rogue agent, free-lancing with America's safety. A sellout. And do you know what's the worst part?"

"What?" Sauer asked with great patience.

"All the smilers and promisers who put you up to it—the ones who make vows to help you—walk away clean. None of

them ever heard of you. They have complete deniability and
total amnesia. You're the goat for their mess. You do the time
for their crime. Got it? It's called the Washington Walk Away."

"Then why are you doing this?"

"You want the best advice you ever got in your whole life,
Sauer? Withdraw your request. Go back to your desk and the
bureaucracy and make your mark on the world in some other
way."

"I can't," Sauer said. "This is the last chance for me."

Brewer shrugged.

"You're a deep one, Brewer," Sauer said. "No one gets inside, do they?"

"Drop it."

"I can't. It's the last train out of town for me. I told you—I
screwed up my marriage, I screwed up my career, I screwed up
my own emotional life, and if I don't get things straightened out,
no one will want to work with me. Who wants to work with a
loser dogged by bad luck?"

"Are you sure it's your mess you're cleaning up, Sauer?"

"If I want to get back in," Sauer said, "I have to climb back
out of the pit. And I can't do that sitting at my desk waiting for
the phone to ring. I have to be part of this. See what I'm saying?
I understand the chance I'm taking if I join you. But I'm taking
a bigger chance doing nothing. You have a reputation. You're a
golden boy. You live a charmed life. That's what I need. Break
the jinx. Beat the bad luck. You're going to be my lucky penny.
See what I'm saying? A career has momentum. And I've lost
mine. I'll do anything I have to, to get back on the track. 'Kay?"

"It can't be that bad, Sauer."

Sauer nodded. "Back to the wall. Cornered rat. Last chance
with the team." He looked levelly at Brewer. "And last chance
with myself."

"What do you mean—yourself?"

"With myself," Sauer said. "Maybe it's too late already." He
raised his chin and looked defiantly at Brewer with his frightening eyes. "'Kay?"

"'Kay," Brewer said.

"Am I in?"

"I'll think about it."

"How long do you need?"

"Not long."

Sauer nodded angrily at him. "It's a turndown, then."

"No, it isn't," Brewer said.

"Uh-huh." Sauer averted an angry face. "'Kay. What did you want to see me about?"

"Vienna."

"What about it?"

"What made you check the cartons?"

"I knew you were going to ask me that sometime." Sauer stood up and opened a drawer in the small table. The framed photographs rocked on their stands. He pulled out an envelope. Then he hesitated. "When can I know if I'm in or not?"

Brewer looked at him appraisingly. Who did this? A pariah, a penitent seeking redemption, filled with guilt, quaking with anger against himself and the world. Who put that desperate expression there, who put those terrible eyes in that flogged face?

"Soon," Brewer said.

Sauer took another long pull on his drink. He drained it. "Here. This was put in my mailbox at the Kaiserin Elisabeth Hotel in Vienna."

Brewer opened the envelope and slipped out a white sheet of folded paper. One word was written on it. In Russian. *Cpaceeba.* In the folds was a Russian ruble note.

"You know what *cpaceeba* means in Russian?" Sauer asked. "It means thanks."

So there it was: the winning ticket to the Irish Sweepstakes, an unexpected legacy from an unknown aunt, a fat gold nugget in the pan. A ruble note to go with the one that had been tucked into Bobby English's pocket in Los Angeles. A ruble note at the beginning of the line and another at the end. Moscow's high-wire star performer couldn't resist: he had taken several little bows. Moscow's star was an exhibitionist. A grandstander. A hot dog.

Gotcha.

Brewer called Chernie in New York.

"You don't have to get into the code room," he said. "I have an easier way for you."

"Tell me. I'll do anything to get out of this nightmare."

"The guy we're looking for is an exhibitionist. His bosses in Directorate T have a tough time keeping this guy in line. They're putting up with a lot they wouldn't put up with in ordinary team members. So this guy is someone special. Chances are no one knows exactly what his assignment is or what he's doing. He's something of a man of mystery with secret assignments. He operates outside Russia, mainly in Europe. I would say a lot of his superiors can't stand his guts, but none of them makes a move against him. What you need to do, Igor, is listen in on the gossip in Directorate T. If you get his name, I can get you the whole package you're after. One more clue: the word 'Cassandra.'"

••• Chapter 29

Tolenko sat in the chair in Revin's office in Cologne, one fat leg cocked over the other, the roll of fat at the back of his neck making him thrust his pugnacious head forward as he talked. He was so angry, he said everything in an indiscreetly loud voice.

"The committee says you must not miss," Tolenko boomed.

Revin waved a hand at Tolenko to signal him to lower his voice—his words could carry down the corridor and into who knows whose ears. But Tolenko took no notice.

"This must be a flawless piece of work," Tolenko went on.

"I understand," Revin said in a low voice. Almost a whisper.

But the fool still did not get the message. He boomed out another ukase. "The committee doesn't want this traceable back to the Directorate or to the Soviet Union. They don't want to start a game of reprisals with the Americans. So they want this to look like a death unrelated to the intelligence world or to Russia." He shook his head scornfully at his own words. "Reprisals, bah!"

Sitting in that chair far inside Germany, Tolenko the hammer, who had no fear of the Americans and their reprisals, in a voice loud enough to be heard back in Moscow was telling the committee what he thought. He was being forced to deliver this absurd message to Revin. No reprisals. Absurd. Absurd. Absurd.

"Brewer," Tolenko said. "I would like to untwist his head." His two huge hands untwisted air.

But after two failures Tolenko was obviously being superseded by Bronowski, who was much more prudent. Cautious. Timid, even. And Bronowski did what he always did with a hot potato. He threw it—this time to Cologne and Revin.

No reprisals. Revin wondered why the committee didn't think of that before they let this human battering ram send those two animals from the Bosphorus to Washington and then order that inept bomb attempt in Paris that killed Matters, the British journalist.

After a few more shouted orders, the angry Tolenko strode down the hall to the elevator, his bulk threatening to split the seams in his badly cut and wrinkled suit.

Revin watched with dismay as the man left. He had never handled an assassination before.

Yes, he had been involved in several—as a hand-off man, or occasionally a deliverer of messages. As he had been with the two from the Bosphorus. But he had never been assigned the job of finding a killer and aiming him at a target. Brewer would be his first direct murder.

Revin considered his assignment. The committee had said, Here, clean up this Tolenko mess. Kill Brewer. Kill him now. Don't miss. And make it look like someone else did it.

But this Brewer was not only a particularly dangerous target; with Tolenko's two botched attempts, Brewer was also now fully on the alert—and that was going to make him infinitely more difficult to kill.

Revin drew the palms of his hands down the sides of his face in agitation. Obviously the first thing he had to do was find a killer.

Revin went about this new assignment as he did every other one. Systematically. Step one was to gather information about assassins. He allowed himself three days for this.

He conferred with six fellow espionage officers. Klusak was the most helpful. Always discreet, he adopted a academic tone, as if their conversation were between two professors having an intellectual discussion. He never once asked a direct question.

He came to Revin's office and drank tea and for three hours, hands folded calmly in his lap, stared absently at the ceiling and delivered a learned dissertation on the art and craft of killing a fellow human being, copiously illustrated with anecdote and specific details.

"First," he said, "the capo will state the purpose of the action. Is it to punish? To make an example of? To eliminate an obstacle? Second is the methodology. How is it to be done? Third is the agent. Who is to do it? Then the planning. Before the hit. The hit itself. And most important, after the hit."

New words entered Revin's vocabulary. Wet jobs. Bounce backs. Executive action. Deniability. Soft landing. Hard landing. Open-ended contracts. Closed-loop contracts. Bird dogs. Setups. Pay outs: money, drugs, new identities, manumission of sins. And most important: deniability. Brick-ups. Daisy chains.

The key part of Klusak's discourse was the list he uttered of known killers and their techniques. There was an amazing quantity and diversity of killers looking for work. Revin sedulously made notes.

So-and-so uses a twenty-two-caliber handgun—a modified Brestin with suppressor. A single shot in the base of the skull—the signature of the paid professional. So-and-so uses a garrote. There's a husband and wife team; she's called the black widow because the assassination takes place during seduction in the boudoir. Another choice: an acrobat—a former circus performer—is singularly adroit in entering secure buildings, usually from the top. Another uses karate. Another specializes in untraceable murders.

The list of available terrorists who would car-bomb, strafe, and torch was too long to write down: casual slaughterers they were, strolling players who free-lanced for anyone. Another had a diplomatic status with a Mideast country, and guaranteed that he could kill anywhere, anytime, because with diplomatic immunity, he could not be arrested or tried.

"In Rome," Klusak said, "there is a man—Adolphus is one of his names—who is a talent agent for the crème de la crème of world-class killers. As part of his sales presentation, he shows a videotape of a training camp somewhere that turns out proficient killers in all types of mayhem. On this same tape he also shows several actual killings as they took place—graduation exercise, I suppose. His killers are totally anonymous. No previous history. No criminal record. Not one of them has ever been caught, he claims. Not one has ever been seen by a witness. He even reeled off a long list of successful hits. I must admit I was slightly sickened by him and his videotape. But he can get the job done." For the first time Klusak looked pointedly at Revin.

Klusak's list seemed endless. He mentioned the names of several men who specialized in killing with overdoses of heroin, so it looked like a drug addict's death. "Many many people in high places are addicts," Klusak assured Revin. "These specialists provide pure heroin to unwary addicts who are used to street heroin that has been cut down to twenty to thirty percent of pure. The hundred-percent dosage almost always proves lethal. Of course, the target has to be known to be a user."

Klusak knew of four men who specialized in untraceable poisons—particularly valuable in insurance cases. Another man killed with an ice pick in the ear, untraceable to all but the most diligent medical examiners.

As a finale, Klusak handed him a catalog of assassination devices. It was incredible the many ways man had devised to kill his fellow man. Explosive devices containing actuators, switches, sensors, or fuses. Devices that could be detonated by telephone, by light, by voice or noise, by doorknob, by laser beam, even by mail. One device, called Dawn Patrol, was designed to explode at sunrise. "Guaranteed to work even on stormy days," the brochure promised. Included were the standard props of the trade: sniper's rifles with scopes, assassin's pistols with suppressors, knives, and pages of other weapons.

Revin felt like a man who had wandered into a slaughterhouse.

What's a suitable place for a meeting between a spy and an assassin? Revin didn't know; no place seemed appropriate, because it was essential that the two of them not be seen together. So in the end Revin set the date for Thursday in London, and under a false name reserved a room for the meeting in the old Gascoigne-Sandford Hotel.

He had the hotel set up a small table with two chairs in the middle of the room. When he arrived, he set up a metal frame that screwed to the edges of the table. Into the frame he slipped a nylon screen. The whole conversation was to be conducted without Revin showing his face. Revin regretted the arrangement. He would like to have looked into the eyes of a man who makes a lucrative career from killing people.

A few minutes before two-thirty that Thursday afternoon, he sat waiting for his visitor. He took a folded piece of paper from his inner coat pocket and studied the schedule of events he had set up for arranging Brewer's murder. He was a day ahead of his schedule. So far so good. The next move depended upon Chessmann's time availability.

At two-thirty—you could have set your watch by it—there was a soft, firm knock on the door.

"Who is there?" Revin called.

"Deeter Chessmann."

"Enter, please."

The door opened.

"Mr. Chessmann, I do hope you will understand these precautions."

"I do." Chessmann, an indistinct form through the screen, walked across the room and sat down opposite Revin. He slid a calling card under the screen. "I presume I am addressing Mr. Moltke?"

Revin read the card: *Deeter Chessmann. Confidential Business Matters.* "Yes, Mr. Chessmann, you are." Revin pushed a business card back under the screen: *Franz Moltke. Imported Technical Items.*

"Mr. Chessmann, would you describe your method of operation to me, please? I understand your reluctance to discuss such sensitive matters by telephone, so I know of it only imperfectly through a third party."

"Yes. I would be pleased to." Chessmann had a soft voice, almost unctuous, and he spoke good French—the agreed-upon language—with a definite but unidentifiable accent, perhaps Greek. "I call it stagecraft. A scenario. Things are not what they seem. Perhaps to get specific, I should describe the program you asked me to work out . . ."

"That would be excellent, Mr. Chessmann."

"Well, to begin. The subject—Mr. Charlie Brewer—will be

fitted out with certain props in his home and on his person that will establish him conclusively as a secret drug trafficker."

"You mean you will frame him?"

"Precisely. At the same time, I will set up another place—an apartment in a marginal neighborhood in Washington. This will be staged with props that make it clearly a place where drugs are sold at retail to the local addicts. There is a known drug pusher in that city with the name of Waley. I will arrange to put a liberal supply of Waley's fingerprints in the apartment. And also a liberal scattering of Mr. Charlie Brewer's fingerprints there. A key to Waley's shooting-gallery apartment will be left on the body of Mr. Brewer. The weapon—an ordinary police thirty-eight—will be left at the scene of the crime with Mr. Waley's fingerprints all over it. Mr. Charlie Brewer's death will be blamed on a quarrel between him—a drug importer—and Mr. Waley, a long-time street pusher. If I do my job effectively enough, you will be rid of your problem and Mr. Waley will go to prison for murder."

"I see. How will you obtain the fingerprints of these men without them knowing about it?"

"Stagecraft, Mr. Moltke. One of the secrets of my trade."

Revin sat in thought.

Chessmann cleared his throat. "Mr. Moltke. Perhaps I can reassure you on several points. As I explained to you, it is very difficult for me to present references from satisfied customers, but I know that you did receive endorsements from two gentlemen who are in my general line of business. I can also assure you that I have never had a failure. I am very careful. I do a great deal of planning and preparation. The results of my stagecraft are so convincing, even Mr. Charlie Brewer's own people will believe that he was secretly a drug trafficker. I have done these scenarios so many times, I am an absolute master of the art. I set the highest possible standards for myself. I will not fail you."

Revin raised another question and another. He was concerned because there were too many elements out of his control. Chessmann could chose to abscond with the money, and there would be no way of recovering it. Worse, he could fail. Failure could prove disastrous for Revin. The committee would be vengeful, to say the least. Then, afterward, he worried about confidentiality. Suppose Chessmann were caught. What was to prevent him from plea bargaining?

"With what?" Chessmann asked. "I know nothing about you. I don't even know what you look like. I wouldn't be believed."

The conversation lasted for several hours. Revin, with some reluctance—but impelled by necessity—opened an attaché case and took out several piles of currency. Half in Swiss francs and half in Japanese yen.

"Mr. Chessmann, a word about the money."

"Yes. I know what you are going to say, Mr. Moltke."

"Since you don't really know who I am, you cannot in confidence expect to find me after the fact in order to be paid."

"Exactly."

"Therefore, Mr. Chessmann, I am going to pay you the entire amount before the event. Half now and the second half when you have set things up in Washington and are ready to proceed."

"Excellent. You understand, of course, that I will not proceed with the final event until full payment is made."

"Yes. I do understand." Revin pushed the packets of currency under the screen to Chessmann. "Mr. Chessmann, I ask that you count it to the last sou in my presence."

Chessmann used two fingers to riffle with great speed through the pockets of francs and yen. "Quite right," he said at last. Revin could see his hands putting the packets in a soft leather carrying case.

"Just one last point, Mr. Chessmann," Revin said. "It is often said that a fool and his money are soon parted. And you could believe I am a fool for paying in advance. But it comes down to one of us having to trust the other. Either you have to trust me to pay you after the event. Or I have to trust you to do the deed after full payment. Obviously you are in the stronger bargaining position here, so I must do the trusting. Threats are an empty gesture at best. But perhaps a warning is not out of place here. If for any reason you fail to produce the results I seek, you will be expected to return the money— all of it, to the last sou. My warning is, do not fail to return the money promptly. If there is any doubt in your mind about this matter, let me assure you that my organization is international and notorious for finding people who believed they could not be found."

"Mr. Moltke," Chessmann said, "let me in turn assure you. While this fee is quite substantial, it is not enough to retire on, not enough to hide with. I cannot afford to operate my business while being pursued by a dissatisfied client. So, Mr. Moltke, satisfaction guaranteed. Satisfaction guaranteed or your money back."

Chessmann exited, leaving only the sound of the door shutting behind him. Revin remained awhile longer, thinking of the two men from the Bosphorus who now lay in unmarked graves in Washington.

Revin's reputation was rooted soundly on his ability to think through all aspects of a problem. Others sometimes called him Mr. Options and Alternatives. And Mr. What If?

As he sat in the hotel room in London, whiling away the time before going back to the airport, he briefly entertained a different sort of What if?

What if there were an after-life? A Judgment Day of Christian mythology. He had never seriously considered such a possibility. "Besides," he had once said, long ago in college. "Am I not dedicating my life to the service of mankind? I would have nothing to fear from such a day."

After this meeting with Chessmann, he would not be so sure.

Chessmann left that night for Washington, and the next day, a few hours after landing, he set about creating his scenario.

He sat down with several newspapers, a map of the city, and a set of crayons. Then he began making phone calls.

"I see you have a furnished apartment for rent," he said. "I need one for about a month. Too short? A lease? Tell you what. I can make it worth your while. I will give you double your monthly rent plus expenses."

After the third phone call he struck a deal with a landlord. Triple the monthly rent plus double the expenses. In cash. Upfront. And no questions asked.

He put the money in a plain white envelope, addressed it to the landlord, and summoned a local messenger service.

"Hand him this envelope," he said to the messenger. "And he'll give you a set of keys. Bring the keys back to me."

An hour later Chessmann had the keys to a furnished apartment he had never seen.

••• Chapter 30

C hessmann went to the neighborhood where his furnished apartment was located. The snow, a dirty gray, was mounded everywhere and formed long, frozen walls between the sidewalks and the roadways. A cold wind rolled a rogue trash can down the street.

Chessmann quickly found what he was looking for: the B&B bar. It was housed in a battered old brick building on a corner, with a row of four outside telephone booths along the side wall. Men stood bundled and shivering in small groups by the phones, answering them when they rang, then entering the bar with white slips of paper. Other men sat in parked cars with the motors running. As quickly as one car drove away, another would take its place.

Chessmann looked at the scene with satisfaction. The advice he had gotten was excellent. This was exactly what he wanted— a thriving drug business with a phone-order delivery service. Now he wanted to see the proprietor. He checked a piece of paper in his pocket: Skits Waley was his name. He went into the bar.

Inside he ordered a drink. The men with the white slips of paper came into the bar from the phone booths and went into a back room. Seconds later they would emerge, pocketing small packets of drugs, to be driven away in one of the cars at the curb.

It didn't take Chessmann long to identify Skits Waley. He fit his description exactly. Sitting at the bar across from Chessmann, the man could easily have been mistaken for a successful politician. Big, with a ready smile and a hearty laugh, he greeted everyone with open arms, knew everyone's name, slapped backs and asked after the health of family members in either Spanish or English. He was dressed in a custom-made gray pinstripe suit, and wore, in the breast pocket, a huge purple handkerchief in a floral print that matched his necktie. On both hands he wore diamond rings.

Waley operated a string of runners who covered much of official Washington. Deliveries were made mainly in the lavatories of office buildings and in shops. In a city like Washington, Waley paid particular attention to the politicians and their staffs, who considered drugs as important to a successful party as liquor.

To operate a thriving drug business like this out in the open, Waley was known to be liberal with bribes, discreet, and adept at good relations with everyone—never using force where negotiations would serve. It was said he himself did not use drugs, and watching him, Chessmann suspected that Waley had a different problem: alcohol.

In a booth behind the affable Waley sat two very large men who watched everyone with wary eyes. They often took long looks at Chessmann.

Chessmann felt no need to stay longer. He'd found his target.

For verification, he went next to a neighborhood lawyer whose name he got from the phone book. He called, said his business was urgent, and was admitted to a consultation.

"It's my daughter," he said to the lawyer. "She's infatuated with a man. And I'm very suspicious of him. We have been here in the United States only a short time, and we don't know how things are done. What I would like to know is, can you find out if this man has a criminal record?"

The lawyer nodded. "Yes. I would need complete identification. And any vital statistics."

"But I have none. Only his name. Waley."

The lawyer raised his eyes from his pad. "Waley? Skits Waley?"

"You know him?"

"Everyone in Washington knows him."

"Then what can you tell me about him?"

"He has a rap sheet that goes back at least twenty years.

He's been accused repeatedly of being a drug pusher, pimp, and gambler. His list of arrests fills pages for everything from general mayhem and suspected murder to bribing public officials. But so far as I know, he's never had a conviction."

"Oh dear."

"'Oh dear' is hardly the word, sir," the lawyer said.

Eureka would be a better word, Chessmann thought. In Skits Waley, he'd found just the man he needed.

Chessmann returned that evening to the bar. He told the bartender he had just moved into the neighborhood, and a few minutes later Skits Waley stood by his side, holding out a large hand.

"Welcome to our neighborhood," he said. "My name is Waley. You can call me Skits. And I'm pleased to meet you."

Chessmann took his hand. "How do you do. My name is Moltke and I'm pleased to meet you."

"When did you move in?"

"Just today. I'm a writer from Germany and I'm doing a book on American civil rights."

Mr. Waley was very interested in civil rights, and he talked volubly about them. In the process, he very adroitly pulled quantities of information from Chessmann. Waley bought Chessmann another drink. His disappointment was clear when he had to excuse himself abruptly: he was summoned to the back room. "We'll talk some more, Mr. Moltke," he said with a huge smile and another handshake.

Chessmann congratulated himself on his great good luck: Waley had left his glass on the bar, right beside Chessmann's. Unobtrusively he put a handkerchief around it and slipped it into a side pocket of his suit jacket. A few moments later he left.

The apartment Chessmann had rented was unprepossessing. The furnishings were of mediocre quality and rather shabby. There were two bedrooms, a living room, and a combination dining area with Pullman kitchen. There were roaches.

Chessmann placed a small food scale on the counter of the kitchen, put a pound package of marijuana in a cabinet with a supply of cigarette papers. He spilled some white heroin powder on the counter then blew on it to spread it out. Next he took a roll of clear plastic tape, unrolled a length of it, and held it up to the light. Barely discernible on the tape were faint fingerprints—Skits Waley's fingerprints, dozens of them in a row, reproduced on the adhesive side of the clear plastic tape, all taken from a few master prints from Waley's drinking glass.

Chessmann occupied himself for the next fifteen minutes placing the tape on various surfaces then rubbing the back of it with plastic stick to transfer the fingerprints to various surfaces. He quickly put Waley's fingerprints everywhere—on the table, on the counter, on the doors, on the bathroom sink, on the toilet. On the counter he dusted several with heroin powder.

Getting at Charlie Brewer was an entirely different matter. He scouted Brewer's neighborhood early that morning then sat in his car waiting. When Brewer came out of his apartment building and drove off, Chessmann went up to the front door and with a lock pick quickly admitted himself to the building. He hurried up the steps and unlocked Brewer's door.

Brewer wasn't much on furnishings. His was the apartment of a man who is rarely in it. There wasn't even a television set anywhere. But pinned on the walls were dozens of papers—long sections of road maps, American and European, with routes marked off in colored felt pen—as well as receipts, checks, manifests, cargo-claim certificates, export and import forms—most in either English or German. There was one bed, unmade, articles of men's clothing scattered about the bedroom and more hanging in a closet. In the bathroom cabinet were male toilet articles for one person. No cosmetics or other female paraphernalia. Chessmann learned what he wanted to know: Brewer lived alone.

He spent an hour dusting the place for clean fingerprints. There were layers of prints, one overlaying the other, but it was difficult to find a clean set. He tried the kitchen, the bath, the glasses and dishes in the sink, cans and jars of food. He found a number of borderline prints. Finally, in the trash, he found a clean set on an empty coffee jar.

Before leaving, he checked the windows of the apartment.

He went up to the next floor and then to the staircase to the
roof. Picking his way around the television antennas, he examined the fire escapes and the chimney stacks, then looked down
the side of the building where Brewer's windows were. He
would soon be ready.

Brewer returned late in the afternoon, entered the building
vestibule, unlocked his mailbox, then walked back to his car,
sorting the envelopes as he went. He drove to Bonnie's Billiards
and Bowling in Crystal City. Chessmann followed him.

At Bonnie's, Brewer had several glasses of beer at the bar as
he ripped open his mail. He soon had a pile of crumpled papers
before him.

"I can get vitamins at half price," he said to the bartender.
"And I can get a credit card from a Kansas City bank with ten
thousand worth of credit. And I can get a weekend for two in
Atlanta including Sunday brunch, a real old-fashioned southern
dinner in the Confederacy Room, and tickets to a tour of the
city."

"And I can get you another beer," the bartender said.

Later Brewer went into the billiards room. At six-thirty he
met with another man, had dinner with him in the hotel across
the road, then went home.

Chessmann was satisfied. He'd had a good long look at
Brewer. He was ready for the last phase of his assignment.

All this talk of death and violence stirred old memories for
Viktor Revin. So did the appalling winter that was tormenting
all of Europe—the winter in particular haunted him. Even when
it wasn't snowing, the wind blew the loose ground snow so fero-
ciously that Cologne seemed to be living in an unending blizzard.

He woke at night often now, remembering his childhood
when the Russian war was on . . . the snow, the blowing snow
and the freezing weather, and the frozen bodies of the soldiers,
and the frozen bodies of the horses, the people cutting the meat
off the horse bones with cleavers and axes. Day after day the
war and the winter slaughtered more people.

When he woke, he thought of Chessmann. What manner of

man was that? Making a career of taking other people's lives. Probably in the morning he would hear from him, and he would have to give him final authorization and final payment. Revin wondered how he would live with himself after that.

He tried to picture himself in his old age back in Russia, a little place out in the country, perhaps, growing bent and gray and slow and recalling old sins and crimes. Would he then be conscience stricken?

He had watched the old revolutionaries age into their graves, almost all with that bemused look of 'What have I done?' For some of them, a look finally of fear.

If murder is necessary for the survival of Russia, then that's tragic. Unlike others, he couldn't order murder casually. He felt himself a misfit.

Revin's guess was right: before noon Deeter Chessmann called him.

"I'm fully prepared to proceed," Chessmann said.

"When will it be?"

"Tomorrow night. During the night."

"Where shall I send the package?"

"To my hotel. I will give you the address. Once I receive it, I will complete the operation. I am sure the Washington newspapers will be full of it. Another drug crime."

Revin traveled to Zurich for his monthly meeting with Gogol.

Revin admired Gogol as one admires a tiger, a splendid predator, ideally suited to his times and environment. But although Gogol could kill with no qualms, he was not a Chessmann; he wouldn't kill for a living. Revin wondered if Brewer could kill without qualms.

The purpose of his meeting with Gogol in Zurich was to go over the Blue List of Acquisitions issued by the committee each month.

Gogol became irritated with the length of the list. "That committee will ride a willing horse to death. What do those people think I am, a human railroad? Look at all this nonsense. Have all the other supply lines broken down?"

Gogol sighed. He was tired, and not eager for this quarrel. "As you know, there's a customs crackdown all over Europe. They've finally awakened—the Germans, the French, the Austrians, the Italians—all of them. They talk of nothing else but the conventional military posture of Russia. After years of selling us billions of dollars in weaponry, now no one wants us to have so much as a nut or a bolt. It's taxing the resources of the whole Directorate to get matériel through the new customs barriers."

Gogol looked sourly at Revin. "You know, Viktor," he said, "if that committee were a herd of horses, there would be more horses' asses than horses." He cast the Blue List aside. "As a condition of existence, every committee on earth should be flogged once a week. How much more difficult they make things."

"We will give you some relief soon, I hope," Revin said.

"How?"

"Brewer. We will soon finish him off."

"Skip it, Viktor. The time to have killed Brewer is past."

"I don't understand."

"Brewer's more valuable alive than dead."

"That's absolute nonsense! There's too much at stake. And Brewer is too dangerous. I don't approve of contract killing. You know that. But in this instance, it must be done."

"How will they do it this time? Maybe the committee is going to stone Brewer to death with marshmallows."

"No. I handled the details personally this time. I'm using a highly experienced professional named Chessmann who is going to make it seem a drug-related death."

"I see. And when will Chessmann make this drug-related death take place?" Gogol asked.

"Tonight. Late tonight."

"In Washington?" Gogol asked.

"In Brewer's car."

Gogol folded the Blue List and pushed it into a pocket. "This is the last time I handle a list this long. You tell the committee I simply cannot maintain my effectiveness and at the same time deliver the absurd quantities they are asking for. Tell them that for me, Viktor. Revoir."

In a mink-lined trench coat, in a mink fedora with a quail's plume, in a long white scarf, always like Pan piping the spring, Gogol exited.

From his car Gogol telephoned for plane reservations: a flight from Zurich to Paris and then a Concorde flight from Paris to Washington.

He drove directly to the airport and there awaited his flight. Shortly later, he received an overnight bag from the estate chauffeur.

"Did you break my speed record?" he asked the chauffeur.

"Never," the chauffeur said. "The road is snow-covered in the passes again. Have a good trip."

Less than an hour later Gogol was airborne to Paris. With great good luck he would arrive in Washington just in time to stop Brewer's assassination.

Chapter 31

C hessmann took a last, careful walk through the furnished apartment he'd leased, murmuring to himself as he went.

"Brewer has been smuggling heroin into the U.S. for some time. And selling it to Waley. After his last trip, he met with Waley here. Their fingerprints are all over the place, with traces of heroin and some marijuana paraphernalia." He pointed at the kitchen cabinet with a gloved finger. "They have a strong disagreement over money. Brewer gets nasty and makes threats, and Waley decides to kill him personally."

Chessmann went to a briefcase and took out a pistol with a suppressor. He had made a change of plans; Brewer's apartment posed too many problems; therefore he would kill him in his car. At least, he would stage it so that Skits Waley killed Brewer in his car. From the backseat. One shot through the back of the head.

"After he kills Brewer in his car, he needs to get off the street quickly. So he brings the weapon back here, planning to get rid of it later." He walked into the kitchen. "He wipes the prints off it and wraps it in this cloth and puts it in the cabinet under the sink, behind the garbage disposal unit. But, due to haste, he leaves a clear thumbprint on the barrel of the suppressor. A fatal error for him."

Chessmann walked back to his briefcase and lifted up the roll of clear tape with Chessmann's fingerprints on it. "I'll put the fingerprint on it after I bring the weapon back here." He turned around and looked at everything. "The keys from the landlord." He struggled to get his gloved hand into his overcoat pocket and lifted out the two keys the landlord had sent to him by messenger. They were tied together with a piece of green grosgrain ribbon along with a plastic tag that gave the address and apartment number. "These are left at the scene of the crime, in the backseat of Brewer's car. And this extra set of keys I will use to get back in here to put the weapon under the sink. I throw these keys away and board my flight back to Germany. Now—rehearsal for the murder." He pushed the weapon into the briefcase, took one final look around the apartment, and went out.

The parking lot behind the bowling alley in Crystal City was already filling when Chessmann got there. It was just after dark, and he carefully checked the lighting. It was poor, a number of the lamps on the poles were out, yet there was still too much light. Chessmann got a pellet gun from his glove compartment and stepped out of the car. He scanned the parking lot, saw no one, and aimed at one of the lamps. It went out like the wink of an eye. He gazed about and shot out another. And another. Six, all told.

Then he got into the backseat of his car and examined his costume. Black overcoat, black socks and shoes, black gloves and black ski mask. In his hand he held a swivel-headed mirror on a long wand. He lay on his back and side on the floor of the backseat and pulled the black ski mask over his head. He raised the mirror by the wand and studied the appearance of his body by the poor light of the parking lot. His entire figure was a dark blob, an unreflective black mass that blended with the darkness of the backseat. Perfect. "Camera and action," he said. He pushed the button on a stopwatch.

"Brewer shoots pool and comes back to his car and gets in. When the door slams, Waley sits up, aims the gun"— Chessmann slipped the weapon and suppressor from his coat sleeve—"at the back of Brewer's head, gangland style, and pulls the trigger. Pfft! No sound." Chessmann raised himself higher. "Brewer slumps forward over the steering wheel. And Waley puts another bullet into the back of his head for insurance. Waley then gets up and out of Brewer's car, goes over to his own car, and drives off to the apartment where he will conceal the weapon." Chessmann stepped out of his car. "Twelve seconds." Chessmann looked about the parking lot. "But Waley has forgotten one thing. Brewer's keys to the apartment."

Chessmann dropped the keys with the plastic tag on the driver's seat of his car then sat down on them. "When the police pull Brewer's body from the car, what do they find but this set of keys—which leads them to the apartment and the gun and Waley's fingerprints and the other incriminating evidence." He opened the door to the backseat and got inside. "Once more with feeling." He laid down, clicked the stopwatch, and went through the motions again. "Eleven seconds."

Chessmann got into the driver's seat and started the motor. "And now for the finale," he said, and drove to Brewer's apartment.

At the airport Gogol stood by the cab stand. Almost immediately a car drove up and Gogol stepped inside.

"The pistol is in the glove compartment," Nevans said as he drove off. "Brewer's address and a map are in there also. The map has an X where Brewer lives. When you're finished, park the car back here in parking section A and leave it. I'll take care of it."

"Where's Brewer?"

The driver looked at his watch. "In about forty-five minutes he should arrive home. He gets his mail then drives over to a bowling alley in Crystal City where he spends his evenings shooting pool. I think what you are doing borders on madness. Brewer should die. You don't appreciate how dangerous he is. The last thing you should do is save his life."

"Enough," Gogol said.

Nevans stopped the car at the edge of the airport parking lot and, without a word, stepped out and walked over to a parked car.

Gogol walked around to the driver's side and got in. He drove fast to Washington—to Brewer's house. If you want to find a mouse, go to a mousetrap. From there he was going to have to improvise. He had one primary advantage. Surprise. The killer was not expecting him to interfere.

Gogol parked beside a fire hydrant where he had a clear view of Brewer's building and turned his lights out. The headlights of passing cars illuminated the parked cars ahead of him, and he soon realized that a man was sitting in a car across the street, with his lights out and his motor running. Gogol decided it was Chessmann. A few minutes went by. The bitter cold penetrated the car, and Gogol started his motor to operate the heater. A car went by and stopped in front of Brewer's building.

The man who got out was unmistakably Brewer. He stepped into his vestibule, opened his mailbox, then returned to his car. When he drove off, the other driver followed him.

"Ah-ha," Gogol said. "The cat and the mouse." Now he was sure it was Chessmann. He followed them both.

Brewer drove quickly through the streets and over the bridge to Crystal City and entered a parking lot behind a billiards parlor and bowling alley. It was very dark. Chessmann went slowly by then circled the block and came back. He parked too. Gogol circled the block once more and drove back slowly with his lights out.

Brewer's car was empty. Chessmann was standing beside it, scanning the area. Brewer was nowhere to be seen.

Gogol weighed his chances. It was quite dark. There were no pedestrians. Brewer had walked off somewhere. Gogol opened the glove compartment and pulled out the pistol. There would be no finesse to this. He would drive as close as he could to Chessmann, take aim and shoot. Even if he failed to kill, a serious wound would stop him.

He checked the chamber of the pistol, screwed on the suppressor barrel, and was about to drive when Chessmann turned and went back to his own car. And there he paused. He scanned the area again, opened his car door, abruptly ducked his head and got inside.

Gogol began to drive slowly, his car lights out. He rolled down the window as he approached Chessmann's car. Chessmann had become almost invisible: he wore a black ski mask over his face. Suddenly Chessmann flung his arms violently. In the bad light Gogol saw a pistol and suppressor in Chessmann's hand. He was trying to aim it behind him, toward the backseat. The gun went off and the back window shattered. Chessmann cried out and pumped another shot backward. His legs were up now and his heels were kicking at the passenger's front window. Another shot collapsed a back window.

Chessmann's whole body was thrashing and struggling. At last Gogol understood. Brewer was in the backseat of Chessmann's car with his arm in a stranglehold around Chessmann's neck. And Chessmann was trying to shoot behind him with his free hand.

Chessmann struggled furiously and finally kicked out the passenger window. His raised hand kept pulling the trigger, but there were no more bullets. The kicking slowed. Then stopped. Gogol quietly backed his car away and waited. Brewer stepped out of the backseat, entered his own car, and drove away.

Now Gogol pulled up to Chessmann's car and looked in. The body lay against the door with one foot stuck out of the broken window. He still wore the black ski mask.

Gogol looked after the red taillights of Brewer's car as they moved away. For the first time he felt a chill in his gut. He remembered Revin's question: "Have you ever seen a ferret go after a rat?"

"Ego!" Revin cried. "What have you done? Do you have any idea?"

"I did nothing," Gogol said. "Brewer took care of it himself."

"But you went there to save him," Revin said. He pulled Gogol by the arm along the walkway outside the Zurich airport. Everytime he spoke, vapor exploded from his mouth.

"I told you," Gogol said. "Brewer is valuable now."

Revin shook both fists in air. "I will tell you what you have done. Just when your country needs your help most desperately, you have put your own ego first. You know we have to win this issue. We must! We need every advantage. You know how dangerous this Brewer is. We simply cannot let him be a threat any longer." Revin stopped and turned Gogol to face him.

"You wanted to save him for your own ego," he said. "You want to beat the best they have in front of the whole world, rub the committee's nose in the shit again. What you are doing is grandstanding—gratifying your own ego. A selfish little boy showing off." He held a finger under Gogol's nose. "If you fail, you won't have one voice to speak up for you on the committee. Not even mine!" Revin turned and walked away.

Gogol shrugged. "I can beat him," he said.

•••Part Six

Chapter 32

B rewer was taken by surprise when the call from Chernie came. He was in the middle of his living room, surrounded by the maps he'd hung up, sitting in the midst of countless copies of waybills, freight vouchers, and other documents, carefully piecing together all of the Russian smuggler's many operations, identifying his habitual procedures, listing his predictable behavior patterns, when his beeper went off.

"Your cleaner called," the message center told him. The message couldn't have come at a worse time. A second snowstorm, stronger than the first, was heading directly for the East Coast. It was just a few minutes after noon. He put on his coat and went down to his car. The new storm had already started, and the stark whiteness of the new snow was already covering the dirty gray mounds of the old.

He drove past three pay phones before he felt safe. Brewer's Law Number Three: all phones in Washington are bugged, especially pay phones. He rang Chernie's Manhattan phone twice then waited five minutes to allow Chernie to get down the street to the pay phone by the all-night pharmacy on Forty-third Street. He dialed that number.

"I have what you want," Chernie said. "What you asked for."

"Fine."

"Special delivery. Personally. Right away."

"Of course. Give me a little time to set it up."

"I haven't got a little time," Chernie said. "It must be right away."

"Yes," Brewer said. "Right away."

"Today. It must be today. And it must be you. No substitutes. Your system is riddled. Soviet informants. Don't trust anyone, Charlie. You come alone."

"Stay where you are. I'll get right back to you."

Brewer stood in the freezing phone booth in the middle of Washington in the midst of a growing snowstorm and felt a great elation. "I have what you want." Chernie knew who X was. But Chernie also sounded desperate. Panicked. Brewer wondered if he could get to the man in time. He dialed another number.

"This is Brewer," he said. "You wanted in? You're in. And I hope you don't live to regret it."

"I'm ready," Sauer said. "What's next?"

"We need at least two more."

"How about Court and Maida Conyers."

"How well do you know Court?"

"I've known him about four years," Sauer said. "He was with me in Vienna."

"Conyers is the lady with the red umbrella?"

"She's better than ninety-nine percent of the men in this business."

"Get them. I'll call you back."

Brewer needed a helicopter. He dialed another number.

"Now?" the voice asked. "Today? Brewer, tell me you don't want it now."

"What's wrong with right now?" Brewer asked.

"Wrong? Look out of the window, Brewer."

"So? You can't get me a bird?"

"The bird I can get. The pilot crazy enough to fly it in a snowstorm with high winds—that's what I can't get."

"Come on. It's just snow."

"Snow? The Midwest is paralyzed. All the airports as far east as Pittsburgh are closed. Dulles expects to be socked in within a few hours. So does JFK in New York. This storm is a lot bigger than the last one. Where do you want to go?"

"Manhattan. The top of the Pan Am Building."

"Brewer, are you crazy? That Pan Am pad's been closed for years. The FAA closed it because it's too dangerous. And you want to land on it in a snowstorm. Those winds will slam the bird against the walls of the building."

"If that happens, I'll be very unhappy."

"Pick another pad."

"East Side in the Forties near the U.N. building."

"I don't think I can put this together today, Brewer. Can it wait twenty-four hours?"

"We have to move now. My man is halfway out of his skin. He could be in a real jam."

"Ho-boy. I'll have to get back to you."

"Make it fast. And don't fail me."

"Brewer, you're the only guy on earth who could get me to try this. Listen. You have any idea what they'll do to me and a lot of other people if anything happens to that bird?"

"You have any idea what will happen if I don't rescue my man?"

"I'll get back to you, Brewer. And remind me not to owe you any favors ever again."

Brewer called Chernie. "This is the cleaner, sir. We can pick up your cleaning in a few hours. It depends on the weather. I'll call you shortly with a definite pickup time."

There was a pause. Finally, Chernie spoke in almost a whisper. "Come now."

"As fast as I can, sir."

"Come now," Chernie whispered. Brewer put the phone on its cradle. It was now one-twenty.

The new storm settled in. Remembering the tangled traffic horrors of the first, working Washington had already fled. Even so, before the first light coating, the major arteries—including the Beltway—were jammed and crawling.

Brewer called Sauer then met him in a bar in Georgetown.

"Things could get pretty wild," Brewer said. "If that backs you down, now is the time to tell me."

Sauer stared at Brewer, trying to read more information from his face. "I told you I'm on a one-way street. I can't back down from anything."

"Your friend," Brewer said. "What's her name?"

"Maida Conyers."

"How tall is she?"

"About five-four," Sauer said. "Weighs about one twenty."

"This may turn out to be a street brawl," Brewer said. "How old is she? Does she work under fire?"

"She's about forty and she carries her end of the piano," Sauer said. "She and Court are both on their way." He chafed his hands and looked out on the street. "Goddamn snow."

Brewer called again. "Do I have a bird?"

"Coming up, Brewer: one helicopter, two pilots as crazy as you are, one pad near the U.N., and up to two feet of snow."

"Grazie."

"The bird will pick you up at National Airport in half an hour. Good luck."

"Thanks."

"You know, Brewer, sometimes I think you really like the long odds."

At three they got out of a cab at the Washington National Airport on the edge of the Potomac River.

Brewer went to a pay phone and dialed Chernie's number, let it ring twice and hung up. He waited five minutes for Chernie to run down the stairs of his apartment to the pay phone on the street corner. Then he rang that number.

"Hello," Chernie's voice cried breathlessly.

"I'm on my way," Brewer said. "I'll be there in a few hours. Here's what I want you to do. Take your wife and leave the apartment."

"Yes yes."

"Don't take anything. No bags, no packages. Just walk out as though you're going to do some shopping. Got that?"

"Yes yes."

"Go to Bloomingdale's and buy a couple of things. All right?"

"Yes."

"Stop for something to eat. Is that Russian language film still at the PanCinema Theater in Times Square?"

"Yes."

"Good. Do you both have parkas?"

"What?"

"Parkas? Do you and Anna both have parkas?"

"Oh. Yes."

"What color are they?"

"Red. They're both red."

"Good. Wear your parkas and boots. You have boots?"

"Yes yes."

"Sit in the rear row of the theater and stay there until I get there. No matter how long it takes. Stay right there. Got that?"

"Hurry," Chernie said. "Hurry."

Brewer led the way through the airport and out to the helicopter pad.

At three-fifteen the helicopter left National. It had no military markings, and both pilots wore civilian clothes. Flying through the snowstorm was like flying through a white blur.

Brewer thought of Chernie in New York—sitting in the theater with his wife, eyes not seeing the film before him, ears not hearing the sound track. Slowly dying.

Sauer leaned close to Brewer's ear. "When are you going to detail the job to us?"

"When we get there," Brewer said.

The co-pilot spoke to Brewer. "We're going to be flying along the coast all the way to New York. We've passed over Chesapeake Bay and we're over the Eastern Shore now. We'll be over the water somewhere around Bombay Hook."

There was nothing to do but wait. And think of the terrified Chernie, glancing over his shoulder each time someone entered the theater, fearing the awful tap on the arm by a KGB man, hoping at any moment to see Brewer's face wearing the smile of deliverance, and periodically giving his wife's hand a reassuring squeeze. All this for a few words inside Chernie's head: "His name is—" Brewer felt powerless.

"A world I never made, Igor."

••• Chapter 33

When the helicopter arrived over Manhattan, the city was already under five inches of snow. As it approached the landing pad on the east side of Manhattan, the helicopter swung like a kite in the buffeting winds.

The co-pilot shook his head at Brewer. "It's going to be tricky," he said. "Wind shear."

The helicopter made a tentative pass at the landing pad and swung off as the wind rocked it. Then, turning and approaching from the other direction, the two pilots tried to land again. At the last moment the helicopter was borne away.

"Try once more," Brewer said. The two pilots conferred, studied the landing pad, then conferred some more. Brewer looked down through the storm to the street. He thought of Chernie and his wife sitting in the theater, terrified and ready to bolt, waiting to be rescued.

Skepticism was written all over the co-pilot's face as he glanced back at Brewer. He and the pilot talked at some length while hovering over the landing pad. The wind was pushing the helicopter like a frail toy. The pilot turned to Brewer then held up crossed fingers.

"I'm terrified," Maida Conyers said.

"So am I," Brewer said. He nodded at the pilot. "Do it."

The helicopter circled the pad again, rocking in the seething wind. As the pilot tried to settle the craft on the pad, the gusting wind pushed it aside. At the last possible moment the pilot dropped it on the pad. A hard landing.

"I'll never do that again," the pilot said. "Pure luck."

Brewer had to restrain himself from running. They were not far from the United Nations building, but there were no cabs at the cab stands. He considered calling the theater and paging Chernie, then rejected the idea.

The wind was blowing great clouds of snow through the streets and piling curved drifts at the intersections. Snow grains cut their faces. It was snowing harder than ever.

"Are we going to have to walk?" Sauer asked.

"No," Brewer said. "We're going to do what everyone else in New York is doing. We'll take the subway—the crosstown shuttle." He led the group up Forty-third Street and into Grand Central Station. They followed him down the subway stairs past the Lexington Avenue line to the shuttle line. And there, as they stood on the platform, he detailed the job to them.

"We're going to pick up a man in the PanCinema movie house in Times Square." He looked at Sauer. "You know it?"

Sauer nodded. "Foreign language movies."

"That's the place," Brewer said. "The man is waiting in there with his wife. He's a Russian who wants to defect. If he's in the clear, then we simply escort the two of them back to a safe house on the east side. Okay so far?"

They all nodded.

"Trouble is," Brewer said, "there's a chance a couple of Russian security people may have followed him."

"Then what?" Sauer asked.

"They'll probably try to kill the man. He knows too much."

"What's his name?" Court asked.

"Chernie. Igor Chernie."

"The Science Officer?" Sauer asked. "On the Russian U.N. delegation?"

"Yes," Brewer said.

"You're right," Sauer said. "He knows too much."

"Why don't we get a busload of agents and rush the place?" Conyers asked.

"Because they'll kill Chernie on the spot before we can get to him," Brewer said. "We're going to have to finesse the two of them out of that theater." He looked at Maida Conyers. "Conyers, what I want you to do is change clothes with Anna Chernie in the ladies' room. And you, Sauer, you'll change clothes with Chernie in the men's room. That means you two will be wearing their red parkas and they'll be wearing your coats. Okay?"

Nods again. "Decoys," Conyers said, and they all nodded again.

"When I signal you," Brewer said, "zip up the hoods so your faces are partly covered. Wrap scarves around your mouths so that only your eyes show, and walk out of the rest rooms to the front door of the movie and north toward Forty-fifth Street. That's in the opposite direction from the subway-shuttle entrance. If there are any Russian security people around, they should follow you."

Brewer looked at Court. "The moment these two red parkas go out the front door, you take Anna Chernie out by the side door and walk her south back to the shuttle entrance and down the steps. As fast as you can."

Court nodded. "She speak English?"

"Fluently," Brewer said. "Take the shuttle back to Grand Central, then transfer to the Lexington Avenue local, downtown. So far so good?"

Court nodded. "Where are we taking them?"

"To the safe house off Third Avenue," Brewer said.

"I know where that is," Sauer said. "Down in the twenties between Second and Third."

Conyers and Court both nodded. "Brownstone," Court said. "Been there."

Brewer looked at Court again. "While you're taking care of the wife, I'll be taking care of Chernie himself. I'm going to lead him out the other side door of the movie, around the corner, and follow you back to the subway shuttle. We should be right behind you and Anna Chernie. Clear?"

"Clear," Court said.

Brewer looked again at Conyers and Sauer. "Once you two leave the movie, if you're being followed, just keep walking north. If you're not being followed, turn back and follow us back to the shuttle. You know the route now?"

Both of them nodded.

Brewer looked at their faces. "Just one thing," he said. "Now that you know what's going on, nobody makes any phone calls from now until we have the Chernies safely housed. Got that? Don't even look at a telephone." He watched their nodding heads.

"Sounds like you don't trust someone," Sauer said.

"I don't trust anyone," Brewer said.

He handed out a supply of the subway tokens he'd just purchased to the three of them. "When you come back, you're going to need these to avoid the lines at the change booths. If you have any problems, just step over the turnstiles and keep moving."

When they entered the subway car, Brewer looked speculatively at Sauer and Court.

Court stood with his head bowed, hands in pockets, avoiding everyone's eyes. His actions formed a familiar pattern that Brewer had seen before, and he tried to remember where. He wondered if Court was about to come apart.

Sauer idly read the car cards above his head.

Brewer felt as though he were going into action accompanied by the town drunk and the village idiot. And himself, the biggest fool in the asylum, leading them.

"I never rescued anyone by subway before," Maida Conyers said. She looked levelly at Brewer. "And I'm inclined to hope I never do again."

When the shuttle stopped at the Times Square station, Brewer said, "Okay. Break up and enter the theater one at a time."

He walked by himself up the subway steps to the street. The blowing snow was blurring the bright lights of Times Square. There was the sound of spinning tires as cars skidded and slid in the deepening snow, fighting for traction. Several people were pushing a car. Most of the businesses were closed, and few pedestrians were about. He hurried toward the theater, head down, feeling the snow crystals blown into his face. As he walked he noted a man standing in a doorway of a record shop. There were two others under the marquee of the Charter House Hotel next to the PanCinema Theater. Two more stood in a doorway on the other side of the theater entrance. Chernie's fears were justified.

Brewer bought a ticket and entered the lobby, opened the inner door and walked up to the low back wall. He looked over into the last row. Chernie and his wife looked back at him. Mrs.

Chernie sighed audibly, almost a sob. Brewer slipped into the seat next to Chernie and whispered in his ear.

"Igor, I want you and Anna to walk out into the lobby, where you can be seen in your red parkas from the street. Hoods down so they can see your faces. Look out at the storm then turn around and come back in. Go into the rest rooms and change clothes with a man and a woman who will be waiting for you. Understood? Then follow my signals. Understood?"

Chernie spoke to his wife and the two of them got up, put on their red parkas, and went to the lobby. They looked out at the driving snow then turned back into the theater and went to the rest rooms. Maida Conyers entered the theater and went to the ladies' room. Then Sauer entered and went to the men's room. Court was a long time entering. When he passed Brewer, he leaned over and said, "I counted at least five." He sat down a few rows ahead of Brewer.

A few minutes later Brewer nodded toward the rest room doors. Sauer and Conyers, wearing the Chernie's red parkas, hoods zipped up, walked out of the rest rooms. They crossed the foyer quickly, walked through the front lobby and out on the street and turned right.

Court led Mrs. Chernie, in Maida Conyers's beige storm coat, to the side exit. The door opened briefly and the two figures stepped through and were gone.

Brewer beckoned Chernie and led him to the left side door. They stepped through onto Forty-fifth Street.

"Head for the subway," he said to Chernie. They turned the corner and looked. None of the five men were there. Ahead of them, Court and Anna Chernie were stepping through the deep snow.

"Pay dirt," Brewer said. "They followed your red parkas. Keep your head down, Igor, and keep walking." Anna Chernie turned to look for her husband. Court held her arm and urged her forward. They went down the stairs and disappeared into the shuffling crowd.

Brewer looked back. "So far so good," he said. They descended the steps and hurried toward the shuttle entrance. A long line stood at the change booth. Shorter lines were pushing slowly through the turnstiles. Brewer looked repeatedly to the rear. "So far so good," he said again.

At the turnstiles he turned again. "Hurry up, Igor. Here comes trouble."

Two men holding walkie-talkies were pushing violently through the crowds, kicking over pails of fresh-cut flowers, running into people at the hot-dog stand. One pointed at Chernie and the other yelled into the walkie-talkie.

Brewer shoved Chernie ahead of him, pushing people out of line, and steered Chernie up to the turnstile and through it. Sauer came running down the stairs in his red parka and hurried up to the two men.

"Run," Brewer said to Chernie. Brewer looked back once and saw Sauer struggling to hold the two men. One of them raised his walkie-talkie and backhanded it over Sauer's head.

"Get out of the way!" Brewer yelled at the crowd as he pushed Chernie ahead of him. "Clear the way!" The two Russians were climbing over the turnstiles. Sauer, from behind, grabbed one of them around the neck and pulled him down.

At the stairs to the shuttle, Brewer paused. The cars of the shuttle stood at the platform below him, doors open. Crowds were filling the cars. Chernie pushed and shoved and ran down the stairs with Brewer running after him. Chernie ran right into his wife's arms on the crowded subway car.

Court looked at Brewer doubtfully. "They'd better shut these doors soon. I'd hate to have to start shooting in this crowd." More and more people were filling the cars.

There was a melee at the top of the stairs. A number of people were pushed from behind and fell. The two men with walkie-talkies were struggling to get down the steps, with Sauer trying to wrestle them to the ground. They fell in a writhing lump and rolled partway down the stairs. Right behind them came another agent. Conyers had her arms around him from behind and was trying to pull him backward. Amid the shrieks and cries, they rolled and tumbled on the stairs. Conyers ended up on the bottom next to Sauer, struggling with two men. They fought their way to their feet.

The other man turned and lunged toward the doors of the car. They shut.

He forced an arm through the rubber buffers of the double doors, gripped the lapel of Chernie's coat and pulled him against the door. He was shouting in Russian at him. The train started, and the man ran beside it with his arm still grasping Chernie's coat. Then the arm withdrew.

Anna Chernie looked at her husband. "There," she said. "It's done. I've made my commitment. Good-bye to Russia forever." She stood holding her head against his chest, weeping.

Brewer looked at Court and finally recognized the expression on his face. Guilt. Court's eyes avoided his. Had he tipped the Russian security people outside the theater? If he had, they'd already had plenty of time to make their way to Grand Central Station to intercept Chernie and his wife.

"You okay, Court?" Brewer asked.

"Yeah. Fine. Fine."

Fine.

Chernie was trying to console his terrified wife. He managed a tight grin. "We're okay? Yes?" he asked Brewer.

"A little while longer, Igor."

Chernie whispered to his wife in Russian. She nodded and wiped tears off her cheeks. She held his hand tightly.

The train rushed through the tunnel, picking up speed, then it slowed, and crept into Grand Central Station. A crowd on the platform pushed their way in the moment the doors opened. The passengers struggled in clots to get off.

"There they are," Court said. Several men with walkie-talkies were standing at the top of a stairs, searching the faces in the crowd.

"Stoop, Igor," Brewer said. Chernie crouched in front of Court. Brewer turned Anna Chernie away from the door, put his arms around her trembling shoulders and pulled her face against his chest. She was as small and fine-boned as a young girl.

"Igor, keep your head down," Brewer said. "And go with the crowd, away from those stairs."

"We sure could use Sauer and Conyers," Court said.

Brewer hurried Court and the Chernies into the midst of a

mass of moving bodies to another flight of stairs. At the top of the stairs he turned and looked back. The two men had seen them. With arms raised, they pushed through the crowds down the steps and along the platform, like two men wading in a deep surf.

Brewer led his group back down to the platform by another staircase then to another flight of steps. At the top he turned and looked. The two men were nowhere in view. He led the way along a gallery then up a long ramp to the Lexington Avenue subway platform. Their timing was perfect. As they reached the platform, a train was pulling in.

The four of them stepped on board. Brewer and Court looked out on the crowded platform.

"So far so good," Brewer murmured.

As the doors began to close, Court abruptly stepped off the train and turned. He raised his pistol and shot Chernie in the chest. He shot twice more, then turned and fled. All Brewer remembered ever after was the horrified, staring eyes of Anna Chernie crouching over her husband as the train doors opened again. A crowd gathered as the doorman came running down the platform. Anna Chernie raised her head to Brewer, staring at him with both hands over her mouth.

He was holding her, turned away from Igor Chernie's body, feeling her slight arms around him, feeling the great sobs of her body against his, hearing her muted cries.

Sauer came in a rush. Behind him came Conyers. They stood looking at Chernie's body.

Sauer had dried blood on his forehead. Conyers had a badly bruised eye and cheek. The red parka she wore was torn and stained with mud and wet.

"Court?" Sauer asked.

Brewer nodded. "Court."

"They shot him," Sauer said.

"Who?"

"The Russians," Sauer said. "They shot Court. Right there at the foot of the stairs."

••• Chapter 34

Limoges flew up from Washington in a helicopter. He reached the beach house at ten-
fifteen that night, after the snowfall had
stopped, and in a blinding rush of whirling snow landed on the
pad next to the other helicopter. Brewer climbed on board.

Limoges, in a tuxedo, sat behind the map table, watching
him. "They yanked me out of my favorite opera for this," he
said.

"Maybe they'll give you your money back," Brewer replied.

Limoges peered through the window at the other helicopter.
"That pilot had to be nuts to fly that thing in the height of a
storm to New York. And you have to be as nuts as he is to fly
with him. It's a wonder you weren't all killed. Where is she?"

"Inside. Hysterical."

Limoges studied the house. It was a large old seashore
house, covered in weathered cedar shakes. Lights blazed at
every window and all around the grounds. There was over a foot
and a half of snow on the sand dunes.

"Who's with her?"

"Sauer, Conyers, and a small army of others."

"Well," Limoges said, drumming his fingers, "it's making the
front page of every newspaper in the world. Pictures of dead
spies on subway steps and subway cars. The U.S. and Soviets
are already calling each other every name in the book right out
in public. Because of Court our counterespionage system has
been compromised. Damage Control tells me it's going to be
months and even years before they can assess the harm that's
been done. God knows how long its going to be before they
clean out all the turncoats in our ranks. They have no idea how
many more Courts there are. I thought he was too stupid to turn

his coat. And I've already heard from that claque in Congress that wants to kick the United Nations out of the country. That was quite a night's work, Brewer."

"Court was one of your boys."

"I told you not to trust the system," Limoges said.

"So did Chernie," Brewer said.

"The critical question is, where are we?"

"Nowhere yet," Brewer said. "We lost a priceless property in Chernie. It took me two years to develop him. A year ago he was trying to give us Court and everyone else in our system who's been turned. But no one would listen. For one god-damned year I tried to tell those idiots they were missing the espionage coup of the decade with Chernie. If they'd listened, Court would be in chains and Chernie would be singing his head off. Instead, Chernie's dead and we didn't get that name we were after."

"Give me some good news."

"Good news?" Brewer shrugged. "The Soviet system has been compromised too. They must be going crazy right now in Moscow trying to figure out how many more Chernies there are. Also, now we know that there really is a Mr. X. But he pushed our faces in the pie. Again. So round two goes to him."

"What about Chernie's wife? What are we going to do with her? We can't give her back unless she requests it. We can't keep her unless she asks for asylum."

"This isn't the best time to ask her," Brewer said. "She's in pretty bad shape."

"I don't know how much longer State can hold the Soviets off," Limoges said. "They're saying an American agent mur-dered Igor Chernie in front of dozens of witnesses and that we kidnapped his wife."

"What are we saying?"

"We're contending that they sent Court to kill Chernie to keep him from blabbing about the Soviet's penetration of our intelligence system. And we're saying they then killed Court be-fore he could be arrested and spill the beans. Their story is a pack of lies and ours is the truth."

"Their story sounds more believable."

Limoges untied his black bow tie. "Okay, Brewer. We just

laid a big egg, we still have our problem, and time is almost up. What's your next move?"

"We don't have many pieces left on the board."

"Don't tell me your troubles, Brewer. Earn your pay. I want a miracle and I want it now."

"She's pregnant."

"That's no miracle."

"She didn't want to defect," Brewer said. "He did. Now he's dead and she's locked out of her own country. Where else will she go?"

"Why are you so worried about Chernie's widow?"

"If she decides to return to Russia, she'll be no help to us at all. But if I can convince her to stay, she's holding the biggest bargaining chip in the world."

"Don't play games, Brewer. What are you talking about?"

"Anna Chernie knows who Mr. X is."

When Brewer reentered the beach house, Charles from the State Department was still there, sitting in the living room, shaking his head. His attempts to talk to Anna Chernie had come to nothing. She refused to tell him where she wanted to go—Russia, the U.S., or anyplace in between. She flatly refused to speak. She refused food. She wept.

She stayed in a bedroom on the second floor of the old beach house, sitting in a chair, staring at the ocean.

"Maybe you haven't given her enough time," Brewer said.

"Lord love a duck," Charles said. "There isn't any time! The Russians are raising hell. We can't just give her back unless she tells us. And we can't just keep her here unless she requests it. The pressure is unbearable."

"She hasn't said anything?"

"Not a boo. Candidly, Brewer, she has to do something. With each hour, the Russians are getting more propaganda value out of this. If you can get her to talk, I'll personally create a special medal with your name engraved on it."

Brewer stood in the bedroom doorway and looked at her. She sat immobile, her back to the door, looking even smaller than he remembered. Love is a purr, here, between the breasts,

Margie had said. Brewer watched Anna Chernie's sad face. Love is an agony—a knife between the breasts. What we do to each other in the name of love.

He stepped into the room. "Anna."

She turned to look at him.

He walked over to stand beside her chair.

"You'll have to make a decision soon, Anna."

She didn't answer him.

"You either have to go back or start a new life."

She squeezed her mouth into a button of anger. "What new life? He was my life. He was all the life I ever wanted." She angrily wiped away the tears. "This was all his idea. He talked about nothing else. Freedom. Freedom. Freedom. And what happened? He's dead. Dead. And now I'm alone in a foreign country. What has he done to us?"

"He was giving you a new life, Anna."

"Without him, there is no life. Every morning when I woke up, the first thing I would do was look at Igor and think how lucky I was to have him." She wept.

"Anna. What about the baby?"

Her mouth opened to protest. "How did you know about that? Did he tell you? It was our secret!"

"He couldn't help himself, Anna. He was so happy."

"Is he happy dead? He'll never see his baby."

"He didn't want to raise the baby in Russia, Anna. He hated the repression, the gulags, the surveillance . . . you know all that. He wanted a fresh start."

"Igor was a dreamer," she said. "I have no reason to leave my country. That's not my country—the Kremlin that he hated. The gulags. The repression. My country is my parents and my family and relatives. It's the place where I grew up. It's where I went to school. And all my friends and their families and their children. That's my country. I want to see my mother's face when I put my baby in her arms. I want my father to kiss me and tell me what a wonderful thing a new baby is. I never wanted to defect. I just want to go home."

Brewer put his arms around her, feeling again those racking sobs he'd felt when he'd held her in the subway.

"I want my Igor and I want to go home," she said.

"Maybe you can't have either of those things, Anna."

"Either?"

"Maybe you should stay here and take what we promised Igor."

"Why?"

"You know what we promised him. It will be a good life."

"But I want to go home."

"You can't go home, Anna. You know too much. And they'll find out."

"What do you mean I know too much?"

"Igor said he had pages of material, but when he came out of that movie, he had nothing with him. I know he didn't carry it in his head. He had a terrible memory for things. He couldn't remember simple telephone numbers."

"The information died with Igor."

"No, no, Anna," Brewer said. "The information didn't die with him. If Soviet security had known the truth, they would have sent Court after you."

"What do I know?"

"You know everything."

"No."

"He said he put the information where Soviet security would never find it." He held her chin. "He had you memorize everything."

She tried to shake her head.

Brewer said, "You have a photographic memory, don't you?"

She turned her face away.

"Anna. He got that information to start a new life with—for the three of you. You can use it too. You can't go back to Russia. You'll never be trusted again. Igor has burned your bridges behind you. They'll realize you have a photographic memory, just as I did. You can't go back. You can go only forward."

She wept. "I don't know what to do. Who can I trust? You. Can I trust you?"

"Trust yourself," he said. "We have a lot to talk about. Why don't you try to sleep for a little while?"

But when he returned an hour later, she was still awake.

"You didn't sleep?"

She studied Brewer's face. Then she nodded. "Everything you said is true. I can't go back. If they find out what I did, they'll put me in prison. Or worse. I have to make a new life for myself here in America." She stood up. "And you're also right about me. I have a photographic memory. Igor called me a walking computer."

"What did he give you to memorize?"

"For the last few weeks, each night he brought home papers and he had me memorize them. I memorized all the embassy codes. I memorized lists of Russian personnel all over the world. I memorized lists of names of Americans the Russians use for spies, dozens of them." She tapped her temple. "Pages and pages of material."

"Did he tell you the name I asked him for?"

"Yes. He told me."

"What is it?"

"The name is Gogol."

"Who is Gogol?"

"I don't know."

"That's it? Gogol? No title? No other information. Wasn't there a whole dossier?"

"One name," she said. "Gogol. Emil Gogol. That's all he had."

Chapter 35

Brewer walked into the meeting room carrying a pile of reference books. In the gray winter daylight slanting through the window, Sauer and Conyers sat silently waiting. They watched as he crossed the room and put his burden on the tabletop.

"So," Sauer said.

Brewer nodded. "So."

"Who are we looking for?" Conyers asked.

"Gogol," Brewer said. "His name is Emil Gogol. And that's absolutely all we know."

"That's why Court shot Chernie?" Sauer asked. "For a name?"

"What I want you two to do," Brewer said, "is a name search. In our official file system. Check the Diplomatic List. The Consular List. The U.N. List. Check visas. Since we don't know anything about Gogol, we can't even assume what his nationality is. So we're going to have to check visas from all East European countries, including East Germany.

"Most visa applications stay in the American consular office of the originating country," Conyers said. "I know. I've been through a few of them."

"Check the key American consulates in the Bloc countries—especially the office in Moscow," Brewer said. "Also check the Visa Violations File here in Washington. Check Passport Control. If this Gogol has ever been in the U.S. as part of the Soviet diplomatic corps, there should be a record. If he's been working through one of the Bloc trading companies—Elorg, Mashproborintorg, Metronex, Unitra, Tungsgram, Isotimpex, or any of the rest—his name would be on their lists. If he's been in this country during one of his smuggling operations, there may be a record. If he's been getting export clearances with falsified documents, the Department of Commerce could have his name on a list on one of the Stipulator Forms—that's Form 823B. We're even going to check the Chief of Protocol records in the White House."

Brewer held up his list. "So—by the numbers," he said. "Start with the State Department. Examine all their files, including the Deputy Secretary for Political Affairs, Office of Munitions Control. Go through their application forms for munitions registration—that's Form DSP-3. And do the SPLEX file, all of it. And the Foreign Correspondents list in the Bureau of Public Affairs, the U.N. Correspondents list in the Office of International Affairs—he may be passing for a *Pravda* correspondent. And don't forget the Visa Lookout Book and the Master Index of the Immigration and Naturalization Service—"

"There's forty million names on that list," Conyers said.

"Do just the A file," Brewer said. "Nonimmigrants who departed from the U.S." He continued reading from the list. "After that, go over to the Registration Section of the Internal Security Division of the Department of Justice. I want you to check out the Foreign Agents Registration. If all else fails, there's the CIA at Langley. And there're still the newspapers— *New York Times, Washington Post,* Paris *Herald Tribune.* And the newspapers of the foreign capitals. And there's the Johnson file."

"What's the Johnson file?" Conyers asked.

"It's a list of known political illegals," Sauer said. "East Europeans, mainly. People who went underground when their visas ran out. Foreign students who never went back home. Suspects. Wetbacks. Probable sightings. Aliases. Thousands of names."

"How about the files of NATO countries?" Conyers asked.

"I'll take care of them," Brewer said. "I'm going to call in a few favors."

"It's like looking for a needle in a haystack," Conyers said. "And Gogol may not be on any of these lists. Directorate S of the KGB puts Russian underground agents into the U.S. all the time. There must be thousands of them here, living like ordinary citizens. And none of them would be on any of these lists."

"While you two are checking the files out," Brewer said,

"I'm going to try something else. A long shot. I'm going to hunt Gogol with a camera."

"A camera?" Sauer frowned at him. "How?"

"If you were Gogol," he said to Sauer, "and you didn't want me to find you, what would you do?"

"You mean murder?" Sauer asked.

"Someone tried to kill me twice," Brewer answered. "I must have at least one surveillance team following me. If it's Gogol, I can find him. Just by myself."

"How?"

"I'm going to take his picture."

Brewer called Hesse at National Security.

"I need a favor."

"I thought you'd never ask."

"I want a name search. All European files."

"A full search?"

"Particularly Paris—the Direction de la Surveillance du Territoire," Brewer added. "They've had their innings with Russian piracy."

"Shit," Hesse said.

"Maybe next time," Brewer said, "when people like Limoges ask you for names, you'll be smart enough just once in your life to keep your mouth shut. Is that possible, Hesse?"

In the State Department, Sauer and Conyers went to the Records and Services Branch of the Office of Security in the Office of the Deputy Undersecretary for Administration.

"We'll divide this up," Sauer said, looking at the list. "You check the Visa Office. 'Kay? Check the nonimmigrant visa applications. 'Kay? Then check the Visa Lookout Book and then the SPLEX file. See what I'm saying?"

Conyers nodded.

"I'll go over to Political Affairs," Sauer said, "and go through the File on Violators of the Munitions Control Act."

"You want me to do the Visa Frauds file too?" Conyers asked him. "And the Passports Fraud file?"

"'Kay," Sauer said, checking the list. "We're supposed to go through the main security file repository too."

"All of it?" Conyers looked doubtful.

"Why not?"

"There are over a half-million files there," Conyers said. "And about a million-and-a-half index cards."

"Read fast," Sauer said.

The rendezvous was set for four-thirty in the morning. Light grains of snow were slowly covering the old, frozen dirty-gray snow as Brewer drove in the darkness out to CIA facility in Langley. The meeting place was the Langley parking lot, Sector J, Rank 12, File G.

A photographic van, lightly dusted with snow, was parked in that slot. He opened the door to the van and looked in at a complete photographic laboratory on wheels, plus a small galley for cooking, and a lavatory. Turned away from him and bending over in tight slacks was a young woman. She straightened up.

"Good morning," he said doubtfully.

She looked at her watch. "Yes, it is, isn't it?" she said. "I keep thinking it's nighttime."

"Where's Tommy Allen?" Brewer asked.

She held out her hand. "I'm Tommy Allen."

"Tommy?"

"Tomasina."

Tommy Allen was not yet thirty. She had a very pretty face, a good figure, a highly intelligent expression, and a wedding ring.

"You're my photographer?"

"Yes." She watched his doubtfilled expression. "You asked for the best photographer in the section," she reminded him.

"And I got him, ha?"

"And you got him, ha," she said.

"Listen, Tommy Allen. Are you clear about this assignment? We're liable to be spending a lot of time cheek by jowl in this tiny box, eating in here, and even sleeping here."

"I hope you can cook," she answered.

Brewer climbed into the van. "Did they tell you anything about this assignment?" he asked.

"Nothing except it's clandestine photography and it's a break from the usual CIA routine."

"This is a very different assignment," Brewer said.

"Okay."

"What we're going to do is very simple," Brewer said. "You're going to ride around in that van with all your photographic equipment, following one man. Me. Whenever I get into a crowd scene, you're going to shoot pictures of all the faces in the crowd. Airports. Restaurants. Street scenes. Shoot pictures of people sitting in cars, standing in doorways. People in shops looking out at the street. Even cars in traffic. License plates. Then we're going to pin up the pictures and compare different scenes to see if any faces appear in more than one scene. If we find any, there's a good chance we've found a tail." Brewer looked at her. "Simple?"

"No," Tommy Allen said. "It's anything but simple." She smiled. "But it's interesting."

"I'm taking the morning air shuttle to New York today," Brewer said. "I'll be back late this afternoon. So that's where we'll begin—at the airport—when I go and when I come back. Let me see your photographic equipment."

"Okay," she said. "This is the key piece. And I invented it myself." She took out a canvas airline bag and showed Brewer a lens cover that had been sewn into the wall of the bag. She held it up to the light and squinted through it. Next she placed a thirty-five-millimeter camera inside the bag and snapped the lens cover over the lens. Then she extended a long shutter cable from the camera in the canvas bag up the right sleeve of her coat, across her back, and down the left sleeve to her left hand. Now she could operate the camera that was concealed inside the canvas bag by operating the shutter-cable end concealed in her pocket.

"This is for inside work," she said. "All I have to do is hold the bag on a counter or in my lap or under my arm. I can take all the pictures you want and no one will know it. On the street I can shoot from inside this van from any of these windows, a full three-hundred-sixty degrees." She opened a cabinet. "I have all kinds of telephoto lenses and a mess of other equipment, including a computer and a scanner." She opened a door to a small compartment. "That's a darkroom. I can make prints and transparencies and anything else right here. This is a complete photographic laboratory—compliments of our own very dear Uncle Sam."

When Brewer arrived at the airport for the shuttle flight to New York, he saw Tommy Allen standing by a check-in desk with the canvas bag on the counter. She was already at work.

The passengers arrived for their flight, dripping with melting snow. As they checked their bags and handed over their tickets, Tommy Allen was photographing them all—passengers, well wishers, passersby, and airport employees.

In the Office of the Undersecretary for Political Affairs, Sauer had a long talk with the custodian of the File on Violators of the Munitions Control Act.

"Most of that kind of smuggling would be under Military Electronics Violations," the custodian said. "That's one of the largest files of all. It'll take a while."

Sauer looked out at the snow in the street. "I wasn't going anywhere anyway," he said.

On the early evening shuttle flight, Brewer returned from New York. For one brief moment when he came off the transit bus into the terminal building, his eyes gazed candidly at Tommy Allen, who was standing at the same counter with her canvas bag, busily shooting.

An hour later Brewer arrived at the Langley parking lot. He found her in the van, with contact prints hanging from lines strung from wall to wall. They sat hunched over a light table and studied the contact prints from both shooting sessions.

"This is a hell of a lot of faces to remember," she said.

"You'd be surprised how many you can remember," Brewer said.

They spent over an hour squinting through the magnifying glasses. Finally Allen put down her lens. "Goose egg," she said. "There's no face in this crowd that was in the other crowd."

Brewer went over each face again as though trying to memorize them.

"You've got the patience of a saint," she said.

Brewer looked at her thoughtfully. "No," he said at last. "I've got the dedication of a fanatic."

They met at Slim Jim's tavern in Georgetown at four the next day. Brewer read their faces as they arrived.

Conyers sat down in the booth with a great sigh and stretched her legs in the aisle. "I want a cold beer."

"We found one Gogol," she told Brewer. "Anton. On the Soviet staff at the United Nations, 1985 and 'eighty-six. He's dead."

"We also found a Valentin Gogol from 1972. He was here for a brief time after a tour of duty in Iran."

"Iran?" Brewer asked.

"Yep. Iran as in the Shah of Iran." Sauer shrugged. "We're running out of places to look," he said.

●●● Chapter 36

V alentin Gogol 1972, and Iran: it was a slim lead, probably so slim it was valueless, but Brewer couldn't afford to ignore it. He called Bobby Burns, military attaché to the British Embassy.

"Bobby, when were you in Iran?" Brewer asked.

"Oh, let me see . . . 1969 to 1972."

"Did you ever hear of a Valentin Gogol?"

"I do believe I did. What can I tell you?"

"That's what I want to know, Bobby. What can you tell me?"

"Ah, well. Let me see. I need to chew on this. Talk to Amalia. She remembers all kinds of things I've long forgotten. Let me call you back in a while."

In the CIA library Conyers was going through diplomatic and consular lists, past and present. She raised her eyes occasionally and looked out at the blowing snow. A scouring wind was picking up clouds of white flakes and chasing them in great dervishes across the Langley parking lot.

Sauer was also in the CIA library, going through the CIA Biographic Register, a huge file on foreign personalities, culled from CIA reports, foreign and domestic newspapers and periodicals, and many other sources.

"Will you accept variant spellings?" the librarian asked him. "G-O-G-G-O-L. G-U-G-O-I-L. And so forth."

"'Kay," Sauer answered. "We don't know for certain how the name is spelled."

"There's another file you should know about," the librarian said. She led them to a room full of cabinets with card drawers.

"It's all on card files?" Sauer asked.

"I'm afraid so," the librarian said. "It's slow going. A lot of Washington hasn't been computerized yet." She smiled softly at him. "If you think this is bad, you should see the National Archives."

Sauer looked around the large room. A wooden wall of cabinets surrounded him. A vast cardboard army of names, annotated, cross-referenced, and keyed to a multitude of other files all over Washington.

Sauer stepped up to the first file with a sigh. Emil Gogol, where are you?

Amalia Burns mounted the stairs to her attic in Leesburg.

She studied the ceiling first. No telltale water stains under the shingles. No squirrel nests; no birds' nests; no leftover hornets' nests. Everything seemed in order. She gazed out through the dormer window at the snow falling over the countryside. It was almost twilight, and the crows were circling before they settled for the night, circling in the snow-filled sky, black coronals over the bare trees. It all reminded her of her native Surrey when the rooks would return to their roosts at the end of the day. She watched the snow thoughtfully. It was the strangest winter she could ever remember.

She turned her attention to the trunks and cartons, old framed prints, paper-wrapped parcels—impedimenta from a lifetime of living around the world in government service. She looked at one carton labeled IRAN, 1969–1972.

Thoughtfully, she opened the flaps and reached inside to lift out a photo album. She turned the pages. "Ah," she said. Carrying the album over to the half light of the window, she examined one photograph closely. Then she went downstairs to call Bobby on the telephone.

The next morning Brewer received a message to call Bobby Burns at the British Embassy.

"This is worth at least one lunch, Charlie, my boy," Burns said. "Perhaps I can even finesse it to two."

Brewer met Bobby Burns for lunch at the old Basford Club in downtown Washington. Built originally by railroad magnates to lobby the Congress, everything was oversize and overwhelming. Brewer and Burns sat by one of the huge bowed windows that faced on the street, and dined on oversize dishes with oversize silver tableware, with oversize heavy linen napkins.

Brewer's seat gave him a clear view of the unmarked photographer's van parked down the street between two high mounds of snow.

Everything about Bobby Burns said military: the trim moustache, the Sandhurst poker-straight back, the commanding upraised chin, and the scowling falcon's eyes. He had more than twenty years experience as a military intelligence officer with the British diplomatic corps.

He sat across from Brewer, a relaxed, anecdotal man, a born raconteur who loved the confidential murmuring tone. Whenever he made a significant point, he would touch Brewer on the arm with his index finger. Then his raking eyes would glance around the dining room fiercely to catch eavesdroppers. He talked of Iran, of the early seventies, when he and Amalia were stationed there, and of Valentin Gogol.

Burns reached into his pocket. "Maybe this might help," he said. He handed Brewer a photograph. "Amalia found this in one of her photo albums. This was taken in 1972, at a British Embassy party in Teheran. That's the Soviet Third Secretary of Cultural Affairs from the Russian Embassy. His name was Valentin Gogol."

Brewer studied the photograph. A man about forty. High cheekbones and deep-set intimidating eyes.

"See who's next to him?" Burns asked.

"The boy?"

"Yes. That's his son. I should say about ten or twelve . . ."

Brewer nodded. "And his name was Emil?"

"Right you are," Burns said with delight. "Charlie Brewer, meet Emil Gogol."

Brewer went to the CIA library and got out the Soviet diplomatic lists, going back year by year. Burns had guessed that Valentin Gogol had served briefly in Washington in 1973. And there, on a Washington list for that year, Brewer found the name Valentin Gogol, Third Secretary Cultural Affairs.

Brewer contacted a friend in the State Department.

"I have his record here," his friend told him. "This Gogol was evidently a bit of a mystery man. He was suspected of being in the KGB—aren't they all? Anyway, according to the records, he came here from a tour of duty in Teheran. He had his wife with him and a son, Emil, age thirteen. Most unusual. Soviet kids go home to Russia at the age of five or six. Mandatory. Anyway, the father was returned to Russia after less than a year here in the U.S. Reason given was ill-health."

Brewer caught up with Leslie Drinker at his home in Silver Spring. He was wearing his overcoat and hat when he greeted Brewer at the door.

"Watch the bags," he said. "We're catching the afternoon flight to St. Thomas. Can't take the cold weather anymore." He shut the door. "You'd better make it quick. Our cab to the airport is on the way."

Brewer nodded. "Gogol. Valentin Gogol."

Drinker removed his hat and sat down on the steps to the second floor. "Gogol. Third Secretary Cultural Affairs. That must be twenty years ago. Or more. He was a man far over-qualified for his post here, and he was suspected of being a high ranker in the KGB. As I recall, there was something else. He was not well. Heart, was it?"

"What do you remember about his family?"

"Oh yes. His wife. Very quiet. Kind of a washed-out blonde. And a boy. Oh . . . ah. Most unusual. The kid was far beyond the age limit for Russian children abroad. Seems to me he was about twelve or fourteen. Certainly no more. You know, it's usually very hard to get at Soviet families. They keep to themselves. But this boy was very open and eager to come forward. Blessed if I can remember his name, but he had these hot dancing eyes full of enthusiasm. And he went American with a vengeance. Loved baseball. There was a rumor that he fought like hell about going back to Russia."

"Was that the last you heard of him?" Brewer asked.

"Let me see." Drinker stroked his chin thoughtfully. "Just before I retired—that's ten years ago—I remember talking to Dawes about a trade mission to Moscow. We had a kind of détente going then with the Soviets. And I believe that Dawes saw the Gogol boy in Moscow. Why don't you ask him about that? My memory plays tricks on me."

Dawes had a habit of drawing his lips back and exposing his teeth in a grimace of pain when concentrating. And it took a prolonged grimace before he remembered Emil Gogol. He looked at the Teheran photograph and grimaced again. "It could be him. Yes. That's probably the same person. A new clerk he was when I met him in Moscow—in his early twenties, I'd say. Skinny as a sapling. Had to have been right out of school. Just a little nobody at that time. He was kept in the background and not allowed to talk. You know the Russian style. But he had a kind of irrepressible air about him. Eating the world with his eyes."

"What was the meeting about?"

"Trade. It was a trade talk with Elorg. You know that company—Elorg? Electronorg-Technica. It's one of the major Soviet companies in the electronics industry. And I believe Mashproborintorg was involved. The Soviets had just signed the Helsinki accords on human rights. It was the usual Russian cynicism. They had no intention of abiding by the human rights agreements. They only signed those accords to thaw things out so they could get easier access to American technology in return. They were desperate for our technology. George Anders spoke with Gogol. They had quite a chat, as I recall. Go see him."

George Anders had left government and was now teaching political science at Georgetown. He greeted Brewer from a small cubby that he shared with another faculty member. There were so many books in so many piles, there was no place for Brewer to sit.

Anders removed two piles of books from a chair and stacked them out in the hall against a wall. Then he studied the photograph of the twelve-year-old boy with his father.

"Oh, yes," he said, "that could definitely be the same person. The eyes are the same. I remember Emil Gogol quite well. The most untypical Russian bureaucrat you've ever met. He had to restrain himself from talking too much. And he was very curious about the West. He was at pains to use American idioms when he spoke English. He was like a magpie. He cocked his head when we talked, listening to our slang expressions, then tried to use them himself. If he had had enough exposure, he would have gotten a creditable American accent down pat in very short order. His eyes never missed a detail: our wristwatches, jewelry on the women, our shoes. He felt the fabrics of our clothes and studied the details and fittings on our attaché cases. He noted the slightest details."

"Anything else?"

Anders nodded. "He surprised me when he asked how the Baltimore Orioles were doing. Asked about a particular player, a relief pitcher, I've forgotten the name."

"The Orioles?"

"Oh yes. He was passionate about baseball. He made a very strange comment to me about it. He said, 'In my next incarnation, I want to come back as a relief pitcher for the Baltimore Orioles.'"

"Relief pitcher," Brewer said. "Did you get any news about him after that?"

"No. Not a word. I would guess he's about thirty or so today. Disappeared into the Soviet woodwork, I suppose. Without connections, you don't go far in the Soviet hierarchy. Especially people like Gogol. He just didn't fit the mold. Too exuberant. The Soviets don't know what to do with people like that. Neither do we, I suppose."

Anders smiled at Brewer. "Imagine a little clerk somewhere in the vast bowels of the Soviet bureaucracy, dreaming of being a relief pitcher on an American baseball team."

Brewer sat in his car in the Georgetown U. parking lot and looked thoughtfully at the photograph of Emil Gogol, aged twelve. A seventeen-year-old photograph of a Russian boy who liked American baseball and now was a Soviet clerk somewhere without the connections to get ahead. Maybe this was the wrong Emil Gogol. Brewer put the picture back in his pocket.

Tommy Allen called Brewer that night to ask him if he could meet with her in the photographic van to go over a collection of contact prints—prints from a number of sessions: Brewer at lunch with Bobby Burns in the Basford Club, Brewer in the corridors of the Pentagon, Brewer in the lobby of a hotel in Crystal City, Brewer driving on the Beltway around Washington, Brewer at Langley.

He met her in the parking lot at Langley late that night. They worked together in the photographic van until after two A.M. before they had all the prints assembled and roughly sorted. The two of them sat hunched over the tables, going from batch to batch, looking from photo to photo. Brewer kept shuffling them, eliminating the duplicates, winnowing the piles down, then poring over them with the magnifying glass.

After several hours Tommy Allen sat back and gazed patiently at him. "What do you think?" she asked. Brewer sat back and shook his head at the pictures. Nothing, he said to himself. They had found nothing.

"What a wild-goose chase," she said. "We must have looked at thousands of faces. I don't want to see another face for a year." She stood up and stretched. "It's nearly four o'clock," she said.

Brewer pushed his chair back and stood up. Every avenue had led to a dead end. Sauer and Conyers had come up empty. The European name search had come up empty. The U.S. Embassy visa file in Moscow had come empty. The lead from Burns had led nowhere. And these pictures surrounding him revealed nothing. All they had for their troubles was a pile of contact prints and a picture of a twelve-year-old boy taken more than seventeen years ago.

He hated to call Limoges. "A flop," he'd have to say. "A wild-goose chase. We're right back at the bottom of the hill."

He passed his eyes over the photographs on the walls. He could shut his eyes and call forth many dozen faces from memory. Gogol wasn't in any of those photographs on the walls, not in any of the crowded scenes in airports and luncheons. Emil Gogol, where are you?

Tommy Allen went to the lavatory and stayed in there a long time. When she came out, she said, "Oh, shit."

"What's the matter?" Brewer asked.

"I just tossed my cookies." She scowled at Brewer. "I think I'm pregnant. Oh, Bobby, I could kill you."

She picked up the phone. "Wake up, Bobby," she said. "Do I have your attention? I have good news and I have bad news. The good news? Okay. The good news is you're not sterile. Damn it." She listened for a moment and whispered something. Then she said, "Are you really pleased, Bobby. I mean are you really really pleased? You don't sound pleased. Really? Are you sure? Say you're pleased."

Brewer pulled on his parka and strolled up and down the parking area. Bureaucrats, equal rights, and pregnancies in the spy craft. As he walked, he remembered something about two of the photographs.

When he got back into the van, she said, "We decided it must have been that weekend in Chincoteague. It sleeted and we were stuck in this motel room. Turned out to be a great weekend after all." She patted her hair. "I put Bobby right up the wall. I'm a real handful when I get going." She smirked at him. "Am I embarrassing you?"

"Terribly."

"You know, you're quaint . . . not fooling with married women. Right? Victorian morals. Very proper. Don't discuss sex with the opposite sex. Is that it?"

"Talk's cheap."

"Oh-ho! I see. Talk's cheap, and no action while on duty— so that's that, hey?" She leaned over and kissed him on the lips slowly. "And that's that, buster." She touched his cheek. "If I'd met you before Bobby—well, that's for you to wonder about."

Brewer quickly shuffled a pile of prints. He scanned the pictures on the wall, his eyes stopping at one of them. He pulled it down and studied it, scratching his throat. He pointed at a pile of brown envelopes. "Hand me that pile of prints, Tommy," he said.

She handed him the large brown, flapless envelope from the stand-up rack. "See something?"

"I don't know. It's a scarf someone's wearing." Brewer reached for other sets of prints and spread them on the light table. He adjusted a lamp over the prints and sat looking at them. He selected several sheets of prints and pushed them back into the envelope. Then he studied another batch.

She leaned on her elbows next to Brewer and stared at the two pictures, "You're right—same scarf," she said. "But a different face. Do you know, it's getting close to five in the morning?"

Brewer assembled all the photographs of the two men wearing the plaid scarf.

"See?" she said. "He's wearing glasses. And he's wearing a moustache. Different guys."

Brewer asked her, "Can you operate that computer and the scanner?"

"Of course."

"Then put these two photographs in the scanner," Brewer told her.

She turned on the computer and put the two photos in the scanner. A short time later both photos appeared on the screen of the computer.

"Take the moustache off that guy. And the glasses off that guy."

She magnified the moustache in one photo until it was a series of dots. She then wiped away the dots. When she reduced the photo again, the moustache was gone. Then she magnified the other photo and dot by dot removed the glasses. She placed the two photos side by side again. "Not the same," she said. "Completely different hairline."

"One may be a wig," Brewer said. "Put one of those pictures on top of the other."

Slowly, on the computer screen, she drew one photo over on top of the other. Then she adjusted them to make them the same size. With the exception of the hairline, it was the same face.

Tommy Allen was delighted. "It's the same man."

"Yes," Brewer said. "And I just realized I know him."

Brewer ordered enlargements of a dozen photos just to make sure. But there was little doubt. The man was about thirty, with a broad, flat face and bland eyes. An all-purpose anyface.

In one photograph he was standing about ten feet away from Brewer in Dulles Airport, unwittingly looking right at the camera. In the Crystal City hotel photo he was standing to the left of Brewer, staring right at him. In both photographs he was wearing the same scarf.

There was no doubt about it. The man in the two photos was Limoges's chauffeur. Nevans.

Chapter 37

Brewer discussed the situation with Sauer and Conyers. He wanted to form a daisy chain—Sauer and Conyers to follow Nevans, who was following Brewer.

"We want to know everything about Nevans," Brewer said to Sauer and Conyers. "He's tailing me, and we need to find out why. So get on him but don't let him know it. And don't let Limoges know it."

Nevans's job entailed long hours, but also long periods of free time. Limoges used his limousine as an office because it was his only place in Washington that was virtually impregnable to electronic eavesdropping. Nevans was on duty from early morning, frequently to late at night. But Limoges was often out of town or embedded in meetings in the Pentagon or several other places, during which time Nevans was dismissed for the day or even the week.

For Sauer and Conyers, following Nevans was cold, boring work. First there was the time he spent chauffeuring Limoges around. Nevans had an infinite capacity for waiting—at curbside, in public garages, in open parking lots. He carried a pocket chess set and a book of master games that he simulated while bathed in the warmth of the automobile heater as the winter wind chased rooster tails of loose snow skyward. He also studied the racing form by the hour and placed bets by phone. He placed at least one bet every day.

"I wonder," Sauer said to Conyers, "if he wins."

Then there was the girlfriend. Whole evenings of that. She worked as a typist/word processor for the Department of Agriculture, and she was married to a State Department limousine chauffeur who worked usually in the evenings.

Nevans was quite at home in his fellow chauffeur's apartment with his fellow chauffeur's wife. Sauer and Conyers took turns sitting in a car or standing in doorways while Nevans and the girlfriend spent their evenings in bed with bowls of pretzels under a winking television set. The nights he visited her seemed to be determined by the television schedule.

"I suspect that Nevans isn't much in the love department," Conyers said. "She has a husband and a lover, and she still looks bored."

Sauer suffered from the cold. He wore thermal underwear, wool socks, rubber overshoes, a heavy, pile-lined blizzard coat, two scarves, a ski patrol cap, and skiing mittens. Even so, when he and Conyers met with Brewer, his teeth chattered on the rim of his hot coffee cup and he talked endlessly about Panama. He carried a hip flask with brandy to lace his coffee.

"I just hope that bloody bastard is as cold as I am," he would say.

Nevans was a solitary. Except for the girlfriend, he rarely spent any time with anyone. When he could, he went in the late afternoon to a cafeteria to settle with his bookie. He often ate an early dinner there or ate with the girlfriend.

He spent little time in his own apartment, and then mostly to watch television.

Nevans followed Brewer on a random available-time basis. He sometimes waited during the morning rush hour for Brewer to come out of his apartment, then followed him for a while. In the evening he would cruise by Brewer's apartment to see if he was home. In his own apartment Nevans had a wiretap tape deck that recorded Brewer's phone conversations. Sauer put a wiretap on Nevans's phone which would play back the phone messages on Brewer's answering machine.

"Maybe he's trying to set you up for another park episode," Sauer said to Brewer. "Or else he's hoping you'll lead him to the prize, whatever it is."

"I think," Conyers said to Brewer, "he's sending routine reports to someone on your activities."

"That's what we need to uncover," Brewer said. "Who he's reporting to. And how."

Whenever they met, Brewer studied Sauer with attention.

The man's behavior was often spiritless. He was frequently pen-
sive—even cast down. And his breath was heavy with brandy.
Brewer wondered if he were also on something else.

In Zurich Gogol received a phone call from his electronics
specialist.

"Can you come now?" he asked Gogol. Gogol went immediately to the man's workshop.

"I think I may have found something," the specialist said.
He opened a case and took out a small carton. He pulled the
flap and slipped out a thin U-shaped metal component. He went
over to the worktable holding the collection of anti-listening devices favored by Limoges and slipped it into the tape deck.

"This little frame clips inside the cavity of the tape deck of
the limousine. Like so. See? You can't see it once it's in place.
And it doesn't affect normal play of ordinary tapes. But what it
does is turn the tape deck into a voice-activated tape recorder.
So when you're out of the limousine, the tape deck will record
conversations that take place inside. It has astonishing sound
resolution."

He pushed the rewind button on the tape deck then pushed
play. "This little frame," said his voice from the tape deck,
"clips inside the cavity of the tape deck of the limousine. Like
so. See?" He erased and rewound the tape.

Gogol tried it. He asked the specialist a number of questions. He walked up and down past the anti-listening devices.
Then he asked more questions. And he tried the little unit in the
tape deck again.

Even after the specialist answered all his questions, he was
still skeptical. "What about all that detecting equipment in the
limousine trunk?"

"It can't detect this," the specialist answered patiently, "because once you clip it in place, it becomes part of the same system as the equipment in the trunk."

"How do I know it's going to work?" Gogol demanded.

"Because it has been extensively tested and proven under
the most challenging circumstances by its inventor, who also
happens to be the world's leading expert on sound equipment."

He held it out to Gogol. "Compliments of its inventor—the United States Navy."

One night Sauer followed Nevans to a motel down by the Potomac. He summoned Conyers, and while she covered the front of the motel, Sauer walked along the boat promenade to look in Nevans's window. The drapes were only partially drawn, and Sauer could see Nevans in his room talking to another man. Conyers summoned Tommy Allen.

Sauer approached the window of Nevans's room and fitted the suction cup of a bug on the glass of a window. From their car Conyers was able to tape the conversation in the motel room.

When Tommy Allen arrived in her photo van, she and Sauer tried to position the van so that she could shoot pictures of Nevans's visitor through the partially open drapes.

"I doubt it," she kept saying.

"What's the problem?" Sauer asked.

"His back is turned and all I'm getting is his shoulder and the back of his head."

Several hours later the man left. And Nevans left. Sauer followed Nevans. Conyers in her car and Allen in her van followed the visitor, who drove to Dulles Airport. After he turned in his car and entered the terminal, Conyers went to the auto rental to get his name and address.

"Marten," the desk clerk told her. "Eric Marten. He's Swiss."

"Did you get his passport number?" Conyers asked.

"And his driver's license number, and home address, and credit card number, and a lot more." The clerk showed Conyers the application.

When Brewer arrived, he found Tommy Allen in the photography van.

"Get anything?" Brewer asked.

"Yes. Gorgeous stuff," she said. "Very handsome man. I love the beard. And those blue eyes. Yum."

Brewer and Conyers waited while she developed the film. The prints were excellent. Then they shuffled through all the previous contact prints. There was no match up.

"That face is too distinctive," she said. "I would have re-membered it if I had seen it in any of these other pictures. Handsome man like that."

Brewer held out several of the close-ups. "Can you put these in the scanner? And this?"

She studied the third print. "Old picture. Grainy. What is it you want? The man or the boy or both?"

"Just the boy. A close-up of his face. Sorry about the graininess. It was taken sixteen, seventeen years ago in Iran."

"They're not the same," Allen said. She put the photos in the scanner then watched them appear on the computer screen. "See. He has a full, fleshy face with a thick beard. And the boy's face is skinny. It's all cheekbones and teeth."

"Take away the beard," Brewer said. He and Conyers watched as Tommy Allen selected then eliminated the beard on Marten's face.

"I want you to select the boy's eyes and the ears. That band from the middle of his face." They watched her select a broad oblong from the boy's face.

"Now," Brewer said, "make them the same size as the eyes and ears on the man's face." Allen increased the size of the oblong.

"Okay," Allen said. "Now you want me to put the boy's eyes over the man's face?"

"Yes."

She moved the strip and placed it over Marten's face. It was too small. She increased the size in the computer.

"Perfect fit," Conyers said. "The eyes and ears are identi-cal."

Brewer nodded. "Eric Marten is Emil Gogol."

●●● Chapter 38

Conyers played the tape recording she made of Nevans's meeting with Gogol in the motel.

Nevans's voice fit his face: it was soft and bland, with faint inflections. Gogol had a rich speaking voice which he used with dramatic effect.

"Wait until you see this," Gogol's voice said.

"What is it?" Nevans asked.

"A way to get around Limoges's toys," Gogol said. "This is a listening device that will bypass all that junk in Limoges's trunk. See how thin it is? Just stick it inside the tape deck with a cassette and it makes the tape deck a voice-activated tape recorder. Every time Limoges sends you out of the limousine, you push this into the tape-deck cavity. When you come back, you have a tape recording of the conversation."

Nevans wasn't delighted. He was afraid it would be discovered. "They check that equipment in the trunk every morning," he said. "Two experts go through every unit."

"So? They won't find this. It'll be in your pocket."

"How do I know it won't set off one of the sensors in the trunk?"

"Because we tested it over and over. Trust me, Nevans. Do you know how important this is? All the major business dealings concerning Cassandra take place in that limousine. We'll be listening in on every major conversation, thanks to you. We'll learn the inmost secrets about Cassandra, thanks to you."

"Brewer is still alive," Nevans lamented.

Brewer called Limoges. "I have some information."

"Will it keep until morning?" Limoges asked.

"Meet me by the Jefferson Memorial," Brewer said.

"I prefer to meet in my car."

"Behind the Jefferson Memorial," Brewer said. "In half an hour."

"It's freezing cold out there."

"Wear a very warm coat," Brewer said.

Around the Jefferson Memorial the pedestrian walks were scraped to the paving, wide paths through the deep snow. In the sharply cold air the walkways were empty. A red winter twilight was fading to rose.

Limoges clambered out of his car, out of his element, walking awkwardly, coat collar up, homburg hat pulled tightly down against the chilly night air, puffing a cigar. He didn't belong there.

"Why are we meeting here, of all places?" he complained. "No one in his right mind is out here in this weather."

His shoes crunched angrily on the footpath through the snow. He stepped crabwise, leading his body with his right shoulder as though he were being pulled along by the cigar in his mouth.

He walked in silence for a few moments in feigned patience, with Brewer at his side. At last he threw down his cigar and asked again, "What are we doing walking around in this freezing cold park?"

"We're here to talk," Brewer replied.

"Well, then, talk. You called this meeting." Limoges pulled up his coat collar.

"Your limousine is bugged."

Limoges stopped. He placed his hands over his kidneys, showing his frog's belly, and stared with disbelief at Brewer's face. Then he turned and looked back at his limousine. "Are you saying that there's a tape recorder in my car?"

"Yes."

"Recording all my conversations?"

"And all your phone calls."

Limoges slowly rubbed his nose. Through the frozen snowbank beside him the leafless branch of a shrub stuck up like the skeletal hand of a drowned man in a farewell salute.

"Then you are saying that Moscow has a pipeline into my car. That I'm a security risk." He pointed a finger at Brewer's face. "You'd better be able to make that stick or I'm going to come after you full bore." He took Brewer's elbow. "Show me. Right now." He tried to walk Brewer back to the limousine.

Brewer withdrew his elbow. "After you," he said. Crows flew overhead, journeying to their roosts in the twilight.

Limoges stomped angrily toward his car, between the snow-banks, under the bare branches, under the gray winter sky, past the summer benches. In the still air he paused to look back at Brewer and to beckon him with a flapping hand. "Come on. Come on." Then he walked on again. "God help you if you're wrong."

As Limoges approached his limousine, Nevans got out and got into the escort car. Limoges followed him to the escort car and spoke into the driver's window. Then he watched the escort car drive away with Nevans in the backseat.

"Come here," he said to Brewer, hauling out a ring of keys on a long key chain. He unlocked the trunk of the limousine and pointed at the boxes of electronic gear. "This stuff could pick up a mouse fart a half mile away. Every anti-eavesdropping device known to man. There is no way in the world that my chauffeur or anyone else could slip a tape recorder into this car. But help yourself, Brewer. You've got fifteen minutes before they come back."

He watched Brewer walk to the driver's door and slip into the seat behind the steering wheel. Limoges clambered into the rear compartment of the limousine and fell back in the seat, his overcoat flung open, his chest panting, happy to be in the warmth. As he pulled another cigar from his leather pouch, his thick lenses magnified the anger in his eyes.

"God help us all if this security system has been penetrated," he said.

Brewer pushed the play button of the tape deck.

A moment later Limoges's recorded voice said, "God help us all if this security system has been penetrated."

"Oh Christ!" Limoges said.

Brewer pushed the eject button. When the tape cassette came out, he reached his fingers into the lip of the deck. With two fingers like tweezers he plucked the flat metal piece from the deck.

Limoges watched with a face becoming empurpled with choking rage. He leaned forward to study Brewer's upheld hand. His agonized eyes studied the thin metal piece. Brewer held his finger to his lips for silence. He returned the metal strip to the tape deck then pushed the cassette back in. He signaled Limoges to step outside again.

Limoges stared at Brewer. "How did you know that was in there?" he demanded. He buttoned his overcoat and pulled up the collar, pacing the length of the limousine, making a mental inventory of the many conversations that had taken place inside. "Oh, my God." He walked completely around the vehicle, bent, his head down, hands plunged into his coat pockets. "Oh, my God."

He stopped at Brewer's side. "Okay, Brewer. Maybe you'd better start at the beginning."

Overhead, so silently, crows flew and settled on the sycamore branches. History's witnesses come to witness.

Brewer held out the earphones to Limoges. "Listen," he said. Then he pushed the play button on the portable tape deck in his hand. He hung the shoulder strap over Limoges's head and let the unit dangle on Limoges's ample belly.

"Who is this?" Limoges asked.

"Just listen," Brewer said.

Limoges listened. "My God," he said at one point. "It's Nevans!" He strode up and down, puffing great clouds of cigar smoke that hung unmoving in the still air. "Like hell!" he said at another point. At last he yanked the phones off his ears. "Who is that other voice?" he demanded.

"Mr. X," Brewer replied.

Limoges stared at him. "And what is his name?"

"Gogol," Brewer said. "Emil Gogol."

"And where will I find Emil Gogol?" Limoges said with icy anger.

"In Switzerland, under the name of Eric Marten."

Limoges pressed the portable tape deck into Brewer's hands and walked back toward his limousine, puffing cigar smoke.

"Would you like his picture?" Brewer called.

Limoges circled back and held out his hand.

"Hurry up," he said, turning his back to the wind. "My hands and feet are freezing."

Brewer handed him an envelope with the photographs of Eric Marten. Limoges turned and walked away once more. As he watched Limoges's retreating figure, hunched against the cold, Brewer knew exactly what the man was going to do.

"Judge, jury, executioner," he said. "God."

•••Part Seven

Chapter 39

The man parked his car and, with a pair of binoculars, walked out on a small promontory to gaze up at the Swiss mountain range that confronted him. As he studied the mantle of deep snow, he felt the immensity of terrain and the relentless cold that pressed against him. He zipped up his parka.

Only one road was kept open in the winter through the mountains. The others—the higher ones—were all closed until spring. And the open road—a steep switchback—was the one Gogol used on his frequent trips between his estate and Zurich.

From the promontory the man looked through his binoculars to his left at the series of eight hairpin turns where the road switched back and forth steeply down the mountainside. Firing distance less than a hundred yards.

On either the third or fifth turn—the two steepest—a rifle shot could catch Gogol's left front tire at the moment of maximum stress and deformation. A single shot then would cause the tire to explode, the left side of the car to drop, the car to roll over and tumble down the steep-sided mountain: an accidental death caused by a blowout at high speed on a curve. But the shot would be successful only if he made the correct allowance for the constant mountain wind; only if sun glare on the snow didn't affect his visibility; and only if he hit the tire at the right moment in the curve. It was not a simple assignment. In fact, it would be the most difficult shot he had ever made. But with the right weapon he could do it.

He got his camera from his car and took a number of photographs with a telephoto lens. Then he returned to his car and drove toward Germany.

"It's a fine piece," the colonel said, pointing at the rifle on the gun bench between them. "A modified Russian Dragunov. It's equipped with the Kalashnikov action and a new Ultra-Simplex telescopic sight. It has a barrel length of sixty-one centimeters. Out in the open, with a likely strong wind, I particularly like that, and I like the weight of the bullet. It has an effective range of nine hundred meters, and that gives it good throw and good carry in unpredictable air. The old Enfield sniper's rifle, for cxample—the L42A1—has a range of only five hundred meters. If you need it, this Dragunov can be fitted with the Starlight scope." He patted the barrel with his fingertips. "Very reliable," he said. "You can trust it."

The colonel stood over the piece in his custom-made uniform, trim-waisted, with shooter's sunglasses, smiling with perfect white teeth as his large, well-made hands picked up the piece. "The Dragunov was born for sniping," he said. He held it out.

On the firing range the man pushed the ten-round magazine into the chamber and adjusted the strap on his upper right arm. He assumed the prone position, pulled the stock against his shoulder, and aimed through the telescopic sight at the target down range.

"Squeeze," the colonel said. The man fired, and they both looked at the target.

"Good," the colonel said. "A little down and to the left."

The man adjusted the sight to correct it.

"Squeeze," the colonel said. The weapon barely kicked.

"Yes," the colonel said, looking at the target. "I can see you've done this before. Quite nice."

The man fired round after round for more than a half hour.

When the colonel was leaving, he crouched down and touched the man's shoulder. "This meeting never took place," he said softly. "Luck."

Back in Switzerland the man stayed in a small inn in a skiing village near the switchback road. From his window he could see the black to-and-fro line of the road descending the white mountainside. Seated in his chair in his room, he studied the terrain with his binoculars then studied the enlarged close-up photographs of the road curves that he had arranged in a row along the counterpane of his bed. Most of the photos were of the third and fifth curves.

Just before dawn a fresh snowfall began, and by afternoon another eight inches of snow were down. The innkeeper warned his skiing guests to stay on the marked ski trails to avoid avalanches.

At lunch the man observed a woman with two teenage girls. Mother and daughters, he decided. Definite facial resemblances: the two girls had the woman's eyes and sensual mouth. The younger had her profile. Both had inherited her excellent figure. Before hearing them speak, he tried to guess their nationality. They didn't hold their forks in the American style like a spoon, but inverted, European style. Definitely European. Not English, though. And not Mediterranean. German. Perhaps Austrian. He observed their skiing outfits and jewelry—the earrings, bracelets, and watches. Wealthy.

He listened attentively. They spoke German—Austrian, was it?—with a heavy sprinkling of Italian words. Then he had it: they were Austrian Italians. From the Dolomite Alps in Italy perhaps. From Bolzano possibly.

The woman took one long look at him and didn't look again.

The man went skiing cross-country in the snowfall, alone. In the profound silence of the mountains he heard only the sound of the snow grains and his own heavy breathing. One wrong turn, a slip and a slide into a chasm, and he would be quickly covered with snow and frozen. He might not be found until spring, if ever. The sense of danger made his skin prickle—it added to the sense of excitement.

He paused periodically to gaze at the mountain, always the mountain, the implacable challenger looming before him, a gray shadow in the snowfall. The switchback road that marked its face was not quite visible.

Late in the day, with twilight pressing around him and darkness not far, he turned back toward the village. He saw the mother and two daughters skiing. The two girls were good skiers; the mother was excellent. She attacked her curves with grace and surprising strength, leaving long, sweeping ski trails behind her. She had great style. She skied—he searched for the words—with an animal joy.

Just before sunset the skies cleared and the sun came out, a brilliant sunset, and he watched the long shadows that stretched across the valleys and declivities. He timed the sunset and the darkness that climbed up the mountainside to slowly smother the switchback road, calculating with his watch the last possible moment he could get his single shot off. There would be no chance for a second.

In the evening, after his meal, he sat in the game room with brandy, aloof from the skiers who clustered, talking and laughing, around the snapping fire. The woman sat with her two daughters and discussed the ski trails with a group of two German families.

News of the new powdery snowfall had spread, and all evening more and more guests arrived with skis on the racks of their cars. By ten o'clock the innkeeper's wife was turning people away. The inn was full.

At nine the moon rose—sailed—in the frosty sky. From his seat, over his brandy, he gazed periodically at the mountain and the faint line of the road lit by the clear moonlight. His confidence was at full flood. All he needed to do now was wait for the phone call.

The woman adroitly changed seats with one of her daughters so that the two girls were sitting next to two teenage boys in the German party. The woman had one last brandy then bade everyone good night. She gave the man another searching look as she left.

He went to bed without speaking to anyone, and slept well.

Brewer stood with Gustav on the old pier and looked out at the rafts of broken ice that floated down the Hudson River.

"Mostly," Gustav said to Brewer, "I stay here on the Jersey side of the river and the bay." He pointed along the waterfront at the busy piers. Across the Hudson River was the skyline of Manhattan. "Counting Newark Bay and Staten Island, that's about twenty-five miles. For a waterfront security business like mine, that's enough. There's enough excitement for a lifetime. Ten lifetimes. This is one of the most active stretches of waterfront in the world. The amount of crime—theft, smuggling, bribery, blackmailing—is astronomical." He looked at Brewer. "The local talent has developed some smuggling tricks here that maybe even you haven't seen. And when it comes to knock offs, some of this stuff you have to see to believe. The other day they found a shipload of counterfeit encyclopedias that are so close to the original that even the publisher of the real encyclopedias had trouble telling them apart. I've seen knock offs of televisions and computers that cannot be detected by the ordinary waterfront type of customs man or security officer." Gustav looked up and down the piers. "I built my business from scratch five years ago. It was scary as hell at times, but it was a lot of fun too. And I think the next five years are going to be even better. It's a shame. I wish I could stay. I hate to give it up." He pointed at his car. "Come on. I'll take you down to Port Newark."

On the Jersey Turnpike south, Gustav asked Brewer to drive. "I'm not supposed to drive anymore. The excitement. I can't handle it. Traffic on this pike gets more like the German autobahn every year. Average speed is over seventy. I got the car for it but not the ticker."

At Port Newark Brewer stood on the piers and watched the huge overhead cranes offload containers the size of freight cars from the decks of freighters. Behind him jet planes roared into the sky from Newark Airport.

Gustav's uniformed security guards were everywhere evident as he led Brewer from station to station.

"I could sell out for big bucks," Gustav said. "But it would mean selling to frontmen for some of the hoods I've helped chase off these docks. They'd love to get their hands on my company, if for no other reason than to put it out of business. Fortunately for me, there's one deal I'm very interested in. It's a consortium of reputable businessmen—men I know personally—who are interested in keeping the company going, and they're willing to buy me out for a good price—if I can find a successor who can handle everything. And that's where you come in."

After Port Newark they went to Port Elizabeth. Gustav introduced Brewer to several of his people, standing beside a partially burned pier shed.

"My Director of Investigations," he said to Brewer. "And the other one is my Marketing Manager. We're making a proposal here for a new client. He had a fire of suspicious origins—read arson—and some other major problems that we can clear up for him."

Brewer looked at them and at the fire scars. The client had enemies—serious enemies. "He'd better be ready to do more than just add security guards."

Gustav smiled at him. "You have a nose for this business, I see. We're going to do a lot more for him than just security guards. My God, it's cold on these piers." He led Brewer back to the warmth of his car.

"They're all good people," Gustav told him in the car. "I hired them myself. But none of them can take over. And even if I was dumb enough to recommend them, the consortium would never accept any of them in the top slot."

He took Brewer back up the Turnpike to a restaurant on the waterfront not far from the Lincoln Tunnel. They sat at a table beside large windows facing the Manhattan skyline.

"I've showed you most of the operation," Gustav said. "Industrial security. Armed payroll. Even executive protection and dockside crowd control. We have our own communications network—guards and patrol vehicles, our own alarm systems, closed-circuit TV, guard dogs, metal detectors, and even our own industrial intelligence force. Four hundred people work for me.

"Let me tell you, Brewer, I've been on both sides of the fence. I've been in the FBI and I've been in private industry. There's nothing I've found that gives me the satisfaction I get from owning my own company. You come on board and take over, and you'll see what I mean. You'll never go back working for the Uncle again. You got a twenty-five-mile playground here, and you'll never once look back."

He watched Brewer drink his beer. "What have you got? I know. I've been there. It's always three A.M. You've got airline tickets by the night table. You're in bed wide awake, listening to the clock ticking and the wind at the window. And down the street there's someone waiting in a doorway. Stuff it, Brewer."

Brewer looked out at the ships and barges and tugboats that were slamming through the choppy, ice-ladened gray water, and beyond, at the misty outlines of the Manhattan skyline. To the south he could see lower Manhattan and New York Harbor. Playground.

Gustav drove him back to Newark Airport to catch the shuttle flight to Washington. "I used to love to drive." He looked at Brewer then tapped his chest. "You think I got this building my own business? No no. I got this from too many years in the FBI. I should have gotten out ten, fifteen years earlier. I'd be a healthy man today."

Inside the airport, as Gustav shook his hand, he told Brewer, "Think about it. I can tell you you're exactly what the consortium is looking for. You say yes and you're in. You'll be rich before long." He shook Brewer's hand once more. "Give me a call in a day or so. If you have questions in the meantime, call me. Anytime. But you have to make up your mind soon." He tapped his chest. "I can't put off this operation much longer."

Brewer stood leaning against a wall, waiting to board his plane. He slung his overcoat over one shoulder, folded his arms and tried to think about Gustav and his twenty-five-mile playground and all the toys in it—the tidal flats, the Jersey meadowlands, the piers and docks and the freighters and trucks and freight trains and fences and security cameras and the unremitting warfare—the thefts, the smuggling, the bribery, the subornation, the savage beatings behind packing crates, the power plays and the swollen savage egos, the muscle and the cunning.

"Beat the system," Gustav had told him. "Get out while your ticker works, your pecker works, and you still have your sanity. Come play in the world's biggest sandbox."

He tried to think about the playground, but his mind was elsewhere. It was on Gogol.

He suspected he knew how Limoges would do it. Using expert help, Limoges would try to make Gogol's death look like an accident. Limoges was hoping that if the death were convincing enough, it could preclude reprisals from Directorate T. Or maybe he hoped that Directorate T would think Gogol's death was a reprisal for the two attempts to kill Brewer. Even-Steven. But Gogol was their paladin. They would not accept his loss casually. He would not be easy to replace.

Then as he stood there leaning against a wall in Newark Airport waiting to board his flight, Brewer saw that killing Gogol was all wrong. Inviting reprisals from Directorate T was all wrong. He now knew what the answer was. There was a better idea. A better way. Gogol was worth infinitely more alive than dead.

He walked over to a telephone and made a call, then came back in time to join the crowd climbing on board the Washington shuttle. Gustav's waterfront security business was far from his thoughts.

The man waited all morning, sitting at a table in the glassed-in café, reading Swiss newspapers and drinking demis of strong coffee. The skiers came and went, and the sun climbed in the cloudless sky. It was just after noon when the phone call came. Gogol had left Zurich and was driving his Porsche on the mountain roads, homeward bound.

The man had lunch in the café, a cheese omelette with a glass of white Burgundy. He was having another demi of coffee when she entered with her daughters and the two boys and another woman. She cast another look at the man. During lunch, while she was watching, he put the key to his room on the edge of the table.

The two daughters, chattering gaily, went off skiing with the two boys. The other woman went away with several magazines. The woman finished her coffee, stood and walked by him, plucking his room key from the table as she passed.

When he got to his room, she was standing by the window, nude, looking out at the mountain. Her figure was superb, and she watched with delight as he drank it in. She kissed him ardently, hungrily. They never spoke.

When the late afternoon sunlight was on the wall of his

room, and she was half asleep in his arms, the second phone call came. Gogol had driven through the little ski town on the other side of the mountain. In about a half hour his red Porsche would crest the mountain pass and start down the switchback road.

He turned and looked at her inviting smile. Half an hour. He kissed her.

He awoke abruptly to look at the sunlight on his wall. He leaped from the bed. Less than ten minutes. He quickly shrugged into his clothes, yanked on an extra sweater, and hurried from the room. The woman waved a hand at him as she sat up.

He cursed himself for a fool. He'd let himself be distracted. He could fumble this gig and lose his reputation.

The man hurried down to his small sports car and sped out of the little village and along the road to the promontory. He parked well off the road, to conceal the car, then hurried out to the ledge with his binoculars. Gogol's red Porsche was not in sight. Had he gone by so soon? Gogol would have had to have driven like a demon to do that.

The man quickly checked the terrain. Shrubs half buried in snow completely hid him from the road. He lay down on the snow and looked across at the switchback road. The site was satisfactory. But now there were complications: a strong wind was out of the northwest. He returned to his car, took out a small anemometer and set it up. The small hemispheres whirled in the breeze, measuring a steady twenty knots and rising, a cold wind pressing against his left side as he lay on the shooting ground cloth. The sun was behind him and dropping quickly. It would be a bitter cold night.

He looked up at the top of the switchback road where Gogol's Porsche would first appear. He looked at his watch. It should be right now. But no Porsche appeared. It was already a little past prime light. Darkness would come with that mountain abruptness, and if Gogol was delayed, the man would have to scrub the shoot. The possibility that Gogol had already passed by nagged at him. Fool. For a woman. He might have jeopardized everything.

The four right-hand curves stuck out at him stacked like the four knuckles of a fist. No traffic. A bird circled high up.

He returned to the car, took the Dragunov from the trunk and carried it back to the ledge. He checked it out by the numbers, then checked out the sniperscope before fitting it to the rifle.

He was reluctant to do any firing, but he needed to do some check shots for correcting the gun sight and for wind drift. In waning sunlight he picked out a small white spot on an exposed rock more than one hundred seventy yards away. He checked the gun sight, aimed prone, and fired. It made a pinhole in the snow. Off by a half foot. He adjusted the sight and aimed again. Squeeze. The white spot disappeared. He chose next the dried seed pod on a windblown stalk. He corrected for wind and fired. The seedpod disappeared. He wished for a moving target.

The bird in the sky he judged to be a predator of some type, looking for ground animals in the failing light. It drifted lower along a lengthy slope of mountain, then began to drop faster and faster. The man sighted, adjusted, sighted again, leading the bird, anticipating its rate of speed, then squeezed. A moment later the bird tumbled and fell, kicked up a little puff of snow when it crashed.

He felt no elation. The shot at the tire was infinitely more difficult. He was going to try to hit a band of rubber little more than four inches wide, spinning at very high speed and moving through three planes—coming directly at him, turning broadside on the curve, then swinging sharply away from him. He had at best a second. More likely a fraction of one second. With a capricious, rising crosswind, in bad light.

If his shot was just a few inches off, he would hit the roadway—a complete miss—or hit the metal wheel rim itself, or even the hubcap, to no effect.

It was growing colder. The sun was dropping fast. The man zipped up his sleeves and ankles and pulled up the padded hood of his parka. His fingers were cold, and he pulled on his shooting mittens, flexing the trigger finger on his right hand. There were only about five more minutes of usable light.

He decided that Gogol had already passed. He'd blown it.

Back at his inn the skiers would be coming in, glowing, feeling loose, gathering around the crackling fire in soft chairs with drinks, talking about the runs as dusk filled the streets.

The man checked his watch. It was almost too late. Gogol should be cresting the ridge. Minutes went by. The man gazed anxiously behind him at the setting sun. Already part of the sun was below the mountain peak.

The switchback road was still lit from top to bottom in a soft golden light. But the shadow in the valley was rapidly climbing the side of the mountain. Two or three minutes left. That was all. Lights gleamed in the windows of the widely scattered ski lodges.

He looked once more at the setting sun. When he looked back, a car crested the mountain and began its descent. It was not Gogol's car. The man watched it with attention as it swung through the curves, descending. The third curve was the steepest and sharpest, the perfect place. With binoculars he watched the left front wheel turn into the third curve. "Fttttt!" he said as he mentally pulled the trigger. The car turned at the far end of the road and came around toward the fifth curve, swung around and made a long run to the next curve, into the twilight, out of range.

At last the light was past its prime. The man sat up. He'd blown it. Gogol had already gotten by him. And even if he came now, it was too late. The northern slopes were already in dark shadow. Gogol had unwittingly saved his own life. The man stood up.

The red Porsche appeared. It crested with its headlights on. One glance through the binoculars told the man it was Gogol. He looked appraisingly at the road, at the last glow of sunset above the crest. Might there be enough light? He decided against it, watching Gogol descend. He was approaching the first curve. The sound of his engine and the shifting gears carried clearly. The fifth curve was too dark, but the third . . . There might be enough light.

The man seized the Dragunov, put his arm through the sling, dropped to the prone position and put his eye to the telescopic sight. He could just make it. Gogol's car turned through the first curve. He took it cautiously. He approached the second curve. The gunman aimed, then paused to watch Gogol wheel through the second curve. He watched the red car drive back across the face of the mountain toward the third curve. It was a perfect position; the wind had died back but the light was inadequate. With a great deal of luck and one squeeze on the trigger, he would tumble Gogol down the side of the mountain.

The gunman raised his rifle and aimed. Gogol reached the curve accelerating. Distantly, the gunman could hear the gears shifting as the Porsche shot into the curve. The gunman had the car in his gunsight. He put his finger on the trigger. No. Not enough light.

He squeezed. The rifle jerked. He watched. The Porsche spun through the curve and kept going. He'd missed. Missed. He looked at the fifth curve. There was even less light down there. He would never make it. It was over.

He felt a tap on his shoulder and looked up behind him.

A man in a skier's outfit stood over him.

"The shoot's been scrubbed," he said.

Without a word the man stood up and carried the rifle and the anemometer and the shooting cloth back to his car. He glanced once at the red Porsche as it reached the eighth curve and drove off into the darkness of the valley. There was just a touch of sun on the tip of the mountain.

Now, no one would ever know that he had missed. He promised himself a warming brandy at the inn.

"Buy you a drink," he said.

••• Chapter 40

At Brewer's insistence Limoges met him in the Air and Space Center of the Smithsonian. Crowds of schoolchildren brought by the busload were darting from one exhibit to the next. The din of shrill voices would make voice recording impossible.

Limoges bared his teeth at the noise. He stood in the middle of the main room, his watch chain across his bulging vest, the familiar cigar in his right hand unlit, his hat in his left hand, his heavy overcoat draped over his left arm. He looked tired and old, and his face sagged over his blue polka-dot bow tie. His chest was heaving from the short walk from the entrance.

"Okay," he said to Brewer. "So far all you've done is save Gogol's life. He was less than one second away from Good-bye Mommy on that switchback road. This idea of yours better work."

"Your prayers are solicited," Brewer said.

"It's not up to me, Brewer. You're going to have to sell this idea to someone else a lot more knowledgeable than I am. If he doesn't buy it, I send my man right back to that switchback road in Switzerland and blow your Mr. X away."

"Blow him away." Brewer looked sourly at Limoges.

"I didn't invent this game, Brewer," Limoges said. "I inherited it."

"I hope you don't have any heirs."

"Truth be known, Brewer," Limoges said, "we're both addictive games players. The play is more important than the principle."

Brewer nodded. "And you have to play the game according to the personality you've been dealt. Shooting Gogol or slipping him a fake, they're both the same size to you."

"Don't play the holy innocent with me, Brewer. Some things have to be done to win. It's the weight of office."

"Win," Brewer echoed. "Win what? What do you think it is—a giant soccer game? The Moscow Monsters versus the Washington Frankensteins? History isn't going to care much who wins."

"I care who wins," Limoges said.

"There's something more fundamental I care about," Brewer replied. "If you can kill a Gogol, you can kill a Brewer."

Limoges stood looking at him. Then he nodded. "Okay, Brewer. I'm going to arrange for you to meet someone. And you can try to sell your plan to him. To do that you'll have to be the world's best salesman, because this guy is the world's toughest skeptic. You know whom I'm talking about?"

"I'd guess it's the man who invented Cassandra."

It was Sauer who arranged the meeting.

"Be at the deli on M Street at three this afternoon," he told Brewer, "and I'll take you to the guy personally. 'Kay?"

Sauer arrived complaining. "Can you believe this?" he demanded when he saw Brewer. "More snow." He shook his overcoat. "I hate it. I hate the snow. I hate the cold. I hate the winter."

Two waiters stood at the window, looking out at the storm. Behind them the delicatessen was nearly empty. One of them walked back to take Sauer's order while the other yawned and stretched.

"Coffee," Sauer said. He hung his coat on a wall hook and sat down across from Brewer. "Why can't we hibernate like bears?"

Behind the counter, with scissoring hands, a bored sandwich man skimmed a knife blade along a sharpening wand.

"'Kay," Sauer said. "This guy you're meeting—he's a computer scientist, maybe the top computer scientist in the world right now. 'Kay?"

"Go on."

"'Kay. The bad news is, he's flat-out crazy. Owns his own two-wing airplane and loves to barnstorm at air shows. Stunt flies it all over the place. Everytime he gets into that old kite, the government wets its pants. 'Kay? What else can I tell you?"

"His name."

"Coles," Sauer said. "His name is Coles. Ever heard of him?"

"Of course."

"I never did." Sauer watched two policemen enter the delicatessen, slapping the snow off their greatcoats. They sat in a booth near the door. "That's all I know," Sauer said. "No one told me why you're meeting him or what you're supposed to do or what. From here on in you're on your own. See what I'm saying?"

Brewer nodded at him.

"Now," Sauer said, "if you want to meet him, just walk down to that booth with the two cops in it and sit down. He's the one with the gray hair. The other one is a bodyguard."

"Costumes," Brewer murmured.

"Be thankful for the snow," Sauer said. "Limoges wanted you to be decked out like a firefighter, but the uniform rental closed on account of the snow. Lucky you."

Brewer walked to the booth. As he approached, one of the policemen got up and walked past him to go sit with Sauer. Brewer stood looking down at Emmett Coles, head of the world-famous computer-sciences research center, Mobius Laboratories.

The man was very big. He had a large shaggy head set on a full barrel chest, and heavy arms and thick fingers. It was hard to picture him fitting himself into the cockpit of a biplane. Even more improbable was picturing him in front of a computer, designing new software configurations. He didn't look as though he could comfortably add two numbers together. What he looked like was a tough, no-nonsense career policeman.

"I'm disappointed," Coles said. "I expected at least a pirate or a goblin."

"Saved by the snow," Brewer said as he sat down.

"I wasn't that lucky." Coles patted his uniform. "But this isn't so bad. My grandfather was a New York policeman. He's probably getting a big laugh out of this."

"I'm glad someone is," Brewer replied.

Coles studied Brewer frankly. "So you're the latest solution to the big problem."

"Am I?"

"How about telling me about your background?"

"There's not much to tell," Brewer said.

Coles pointed a thick finger at him. "No games, Brewer. I came a long distance in a snowstorm and put on this silly uniform to talk to you. I have to know what kind of a background you have."

"Am I auditioning for a job?"

"That's about the size of it."

"What's the job? Maybe I don't want to apply."

Coles looked curiously at Brewer. Then he gave his head a short shake. "Maybe I don't want to apply." He shook his head again. "Give me a hint, Brewer. Just a little thumbnail of yourself."

"Come on," Brewer said. "You've been thoroughly briefed on me. My background is primarily arms control. Lately, sophisticated weaponry and high-tech capability. Do you want to talk about this plan or play twenty questions?"

"Okay," Coles said. "Before we get off on the wrong foot, Brewer, let me say I'm very interested in a plan to stop the Russians from swiping Cassandra. What I'm not interested in is another idiot from U.S. intelligence with another unworkable plot."

"And you think I'm the scrapings from the bottom of the barrel?" Brewer said.

"Well, let's say you're the latest in a long list." Coles looked thoughtfully at Brewer. "I've got a personal case against the Soviets," he said. "They've stolen a number of inventions of mine. Some of my colleagues have had their life's work stolen and used by Moscow. So we're taking this looting as a personal affront. You understand?"

Brewer nodded.

"I wonder if you do," Coles said. "How would you feel if a missile guidance system you invented to defend your country is on a Russian missile outside Moscow aimed right back at your granddaughter's crib?" Coles waited for a reply. "You don't say much, do you?"

"The answer to your question is obvious," Brewer said.

"No matter," Coles said. "My biggest complaint is against my own government. American scientists have dumped into Washington's lap the greatest cornucopia of technology in history. Hundreds and hundreds of technological treasures. Any one of them would have given the U.S. a commanding military lead for decades to come. And these idiot politicians have let Moscow come in here and steal it all."

Coles frowned at the snow that filled the windows. "These people in Moscow shouldn't be the power they are in the world. They should still be trying to figure out how to make garden rakes. It's absurd. Are you aware that a number of our best scientific minds now won't work on weaponry or any military equipment?"

"Tell me about this new item," Brewer said.

"You don't like sermons, hey? Fair enough. Cassandra may be our last chance to get so far in front of the Soviets they won't be able to catch up. Does that get your attention?"

"Yes."

"I have finally drawn the line," Coles said. "I told Limoges that I'm not releasing this item until he comes up with an iron-clad defense. I want assurances that I won't see Cassandra in the next May Day parade in Moscow."

"Nobody can give you that," Brewer said.

"Then the impasse continues. This has been going on for months. They've come to me with one absurd plan after another. They've suggested everything from underground manufacturing capabilities in the middle of the desert to a floating factory in orbit. None of them are feasible. Have you heard any of them?"

"No," Brewer said.

"Okay. I've told Limoges I'm out of patience and he's out of time. If I don't hear a plan from you that makes sense, I'm going to destroy Cassandra. Neither side will get it. So, weigh every word before you speak."

Brewer studied Coles. "How do I know you can recognize a good idea when you hear it?"

"That's a fresh wrinkle," Coles said. "You're the first one to ask about my credentials. Am I detecting a glimmer of intelligence in you?"

"Maybe you've already heard a good idea and didn't recognize it," Brewer said. "Maybe you're not qualified to judge. What kind of a background do you have in intelligence?"

"That's not the issue here."

"Before I tell you about my idea," Brewer said, "I want to be sure you know a good idea when you hear one and that you're ready to accept it."

"Okay, Brewer. I've got good native intelligence and a good dose of common sense. I can assure you I have the equipment to evaluate your idea. I may even be as smart as you are."

"I'm not smart," Brewer said. "I'm experienced. And you're not."

"Okay."

"You shouldn't be deciding on the plan to protect Cassandra."

"Neither should the U.S. government."

"How much do you know about Russian high-tech espionage, Coles?"

"Too much," Coles said. "I'm a victim of it."

"That hardly makes you an expert."

"Brewer, if you want to put your idea into practice, you have to deal with me. Tell me what it is."

Brewer nodded at last. "Okay. What you need to know is, the Russians have a time-lag problem. After they steal innovations from us, it takes a while for them to digest them."

"Go on."

"If they get Cassandra, it will take them a year or so to make it operational."

"So."

"So—if they get a defective item, it will take them a year to discover it."

"So?"

"So there's our chance to give them indigestion."

"You'd better explain that, Brewer."

"Right now there's only one plan on the table. Limoges wants to assassinate their top thief. In fact he almost did."

"Yes yes."

"My idea is not to kill him but to use him."

"Go on."

"I'm not sure I want to go on at this point," Brewer said. "This is not an ironclad, foolproof plan. It can backfire."

"You have to sell it to me, Brewer. Or there's no game."

Brewer studied Coles's face then nodded. "Maybe you're right. Maybe you should destroy Cassandra."

"That's one way to make the Russians happy," Coles said.

"It's certainly one way to make mankind happy."

"Okay. I must admit you've got me really intrigued. How about telling me your idea?"

"The idea is very simple," Brewer said. "This smuggler wants Cassandra. So let him steal it. Let him carry it back to Moscow. Let Moscow install it."

"Go on."

"It takes Moscow a year to discover they've stolen a fake Cassandra."

"A fake?" Coles looked at him with astonishment. "A fake? Are you . . ." He paused. "I think you'd better spell this out for me."

"A fake," Brewer said. "With a very serious flaw or two in it. While they're preoccupied with the fake Cassandra, we'll have the year you need to get everything in place. When the Russians wake up, we'll be confronting them with a completely operational system, and they'll be confronting us with a system that's so full of flaws they won't dare use it."

Coles chewed on a knuckle. "Huh. A fake."

Brewer asked him, "Can you make a fake Cassandra that the Soviets will have to chew on for a year or so?"

Coles looked at the floor then twisted his coffee cup. He turned his eyes to Brewer. "Sure I can. Can you make the thief swipe it?"

Brewer nodded. "That's likely."

Coles snorted. "Likely. Yes or no. Can you manage to slip the mickey to him?"

"Yes."

"How?"

"By telling him I'm going to slip him a mickey."

Coles smiled. "Are you crazy or are you kidding me?"

"I'm crazy."

"Brewer, you'd better explain this to me."

"Okay. The problem is, if we make it easy for Gogol to swipe Cassandra, he'll be suspicious. We have to make it tough on him. Challenging. So he'll be convinced that he eluded our trap with the fake in it and swiped the real McCoy."

"Go on."

"To set things up, we'll let him discover that we've set a fake out for him and that we're waiting for him to come and take it. He'll ignore it, go around the back door and steal what he thinks is the real Cassandra."

"But what if he doesn't come in the back door, but the side door or a window?"

"That's the risk," Brewer said.

"He could wind up stealing the real Cassandra?"

"Yes."

"But that's the very catastrophe we're trying to avoid."

"Yes."

"I don't like it." Coles turned away and chewed again on his knuckle. "You're asking me to take an incredible risk here, Brewer."

"Any plan involves a risk."

The two waiters in their aprons and vests, and the counterman in his whites, stood cross-armed at the restaurant window, looking out at the blizzard, murmuring to each other, then looking at the empty booths. Windblown snow rushed furiously at the window, and the day seemed to have grown darker.

Coles signaled for more coffee. He looked very unhappy. He asked more questions. He listened. He nodded. Then he asked still more questions.

"This Russian," Coles said. "He's supposed to be one of the smartest men in the business. Brilliant, is the word Limoges used. And we're supposed to outsmart him?"

"Yes."

"That means you think you're smarter than he is."

"I told you. I'm not smart. I'm experienced."

Coles brooded over his coffee.

"I understand you like to fly," Brewer said.

"Yes."

"You do stunt flying."

"Yes."

"That's when you feel fully alive. When you're looking things right in the eye. When you're balanced right on the edge. You hold everything in your own two hands. Hit or miss. Then you bring it off and walk away. Got away with it again."

Coles looked with renewed attention at Brewer. "You've been there too."

"Yes," Brewer said. "I've been there."

"Go on."

"This Gogol," Brewer said. "He never goes near the edge. He uses other people. He's a puppeteer. He's very gifted at it. But he never puts himself on the high wire. Now he's going to have to. For the first time he's going to have to come out in the open and bet the farm on one pass of the dice. He's going to have to put his own butt on the line."

"And you're betting he doesn't have the stomach for it."

Coles sat in thought. Then he asked more questions. One of the waiters hung up his apron and, heavily bundled in a down parka, left the delicatessen. The other waiter looked at his watch. He shrugged at the counterman. Three more inches of snow were on the ground. The waiter put out a bank of lights while the counterman went into the back for his overcoat.

"Okay," Coles said at last. "If we're going to try this, there's one condition, I don't want that idiot Limoges involved. Understood?"

"That's none of my affair. I don't even know why he accepted this idea of mine."

"Don't you know?"

"No."

"He's afraid of you." Coles watched Brewer's face. "Don't turn your back on him. Are we agreed? We'll keep Limoges out as much as possible."

"You tell that to Limoges."

"With pleasure," Coles said. "I just want to know one thing. How sure are you that this Russian will go for this trap? How do you know he'll do what you want him to do?"

"Because I went to great lengths to learn how he thinks. The real Cassandra trap is inside his own mind."

••• Chapter 41

Revin found a parking space on the third deck of the parking building of the Zurich airport. He turned off the engine and looked at Gogol.

"The committee isn't going to give you much time," Revin said. "They want results quickly."

"Results?" Gogol smiled. "That committee is not in a position to demand anything from me. After they failed, I located Cassandra! Me! While that army of idiots was stumbling all over each other. I found it. The only thing that committee is good for is issuing absurd orders."

"If you ask my opinion, Emil, I think your ego is leading you into a blind alley. You want to beat one of the top U.S. agents more than you want to get Cassandra."

"But they're the same thing, Viktor," Gogol said with the wave of a hand.

"Emil, I warn you, if you fail, you are a dead man. All your brilliant work to date won't count. You don't have one friend on the committee. Not one. They're all sitting there just waiting for you to slip once. You've rubbed their noses in the shit too often. If you fail, they won't let you go live on your Swiss mountaintop and spend the rest of your fat capitalist life enjoying all your money. They'll want your head on a pike staff."

"And if I succeed," Gogol said, "when I succeed—I will be the one handing out the pike staffs. It will be the biggest number of heads since Ghengis Khan made his mountain of skulls at Lake Baikal."

"The fly in your ointment, Emil, is Brewer. You will have to kill him. I've warned you. The committee has warned you. Nevans has warned you. He's too dangerous."

Gogol shook his head. "No."

"You should make killing Brewer your first priority," Revin insisted. "Before you do anything else."

"No," Gogol said again. "The time is past for killing Brewer. Now that I've located Cassandra, I need him to get it for me."

Revin looked at him with wonder. "You think you can get Brewer to deliver Cassandra to you?" He shook his head. "This can only end in disaster."

"Wish me luck, Viktor," Gogol said.

"I give you the Spartan mother's salute."

"Which is?" Gogol asked.

"When she handed her son his shield for battle, she said: 'Come back, my son, with it—or on it.'"

Just before Gogol's flight took off, a late passenger boarded his plane. She carried a red umbrella.

Gogol used three different passports. He flew from Zurich to London, checked into an executive suite in the Hotel Bringhurst with a number of pieces of handmade leather luggage, and with great ostentation dispensed excessively large tips. In the morning, after breakfast, he went for a chilly stroll along the rows of expensive shops. Then quickly he descended the steps to the underground and rode it in a aimless pattern, making abrupt changes as he went. Without returning for his baggage, he took a taxi to Heathrow.

In the corridors of the airport he was sure he'd had a glimpse of the woman with the red umbrella.

From London he flew to Amsterdam. He stayed overnight in a small hotel on a side street up from the War Memorial, purchasing a few toilet articles and a change of clothes. He bought an airline ticket for the ten o'clock morning flight to Rome, but at seven A.M., with no baggage, he slipped out of his hotel and took the train from Amsterdam to Brussels. Again, as he boarded his train, he felt he'd glimpsed the woman with the red umbrella. The next morning he flew from Brussels to Paris.

That evening, very late, he walked through the lobby of his hotel and out on the street. Without a glance in any direction, he walked directly to the metro steps and descended. He took the metro to Avenue de Clichy and walked up to street level.

The streets were cold and dark, and he felt his feet growing cold as he stood in a doorway and watched the metro steps. No one had followed him. He decided to make sure. He stepped out of the doorway and walked away from the metro.

The odor of garlic and curry wafted from the fronts of the darkened shops. A woman fed cats in a doorway. A dog had knocked over a garbage bucket, and with his head thrust inside, was noisily chewing a bone.

As he walked, Gogol saw men sitting in darkened cars. Ahead he saw a group of men walking toward him. Five of them. They slowed their pace when they saw him, murmuring to each other. Then they stopped and waited for him.

When he reached them, one of them spoke to him. "Money," he said.

The other four circled him. From his coat pocket Gogol pulled out a pistol and watched the five of them fall back, letting him pass on.

A half block later he turned and looked back. He was astonished to see, beyond the five men, a woman walking the streets. She was carrying an umbrella, and Gogol bet it was red.

He would have liked to have met her, to ask how she had tracked him so brilliantly—so invisibly. He could learn a great deal from her. But now she wouldn't be able to tell him anything. And she wouldn't be able to follow him anymore. He turned the corner and hurried in a circle back to the metro.

Maida Conyers saw the five men ahead of her. And she saw one of them cross the street and hurry past her and behind her. She was trapped.

She continued to walk purposefully toward the four men. When she reached them, one blocked her way and held up his hand. The others murmured to him and laughed. She raised her umbrella and thrust the point of it past his hand and into the base of his throat. As he stumbled back, she felt an arm reach around her neck. She pulled the handle from the umbrella, aimed it at the man's face and squirted mace into his mouth and eyes. She turned and squirted it at another face. The fourth man, trying to seize her by the hair, never saw the thumb she jammed into his eye, never saw the rigid hand that jammed into his gut just below the rib cage into his diaphragm and left him doubled over on the sidewalk.

The fifth man came running up behind her, and she waited until the last possible moment before turning and kicking him. She left him lying on the sidewalk with the others as she walked away, back toward the metro. In her hand, visibly, she carried a small pistol.

As usual, Gogol had gotten others to do his laundry for him while he ducked into a rat's hole and escaped. She knew that she'd lost him.

The next morning, Gogol rented a car and drove back to Brussels. There he took a long evening walk to be sure he'd shaken her, and the next morning he flew to New York.

He stayed overnight in a cut-rate tourist hotel in the Thirties off Lexington, then bought some clothes and luggage at Macy's before taking the Amtrak train from New York to Washington. He rented an economy car at Union Station then drove to Crystal City, just across the river from Washington, where he checked into a housekeeping motel room. He had spent nearly five days in evasive action.

••• Chapter 42

It was Coles who called the meeting. The fake was ready; the trap was set; and to plan the next step, Brewer and Limoges were invited to Mobius, his research laboratories.

When Brewer arrived, Limoges was waiting for him in the parking lot. He stepped from his limousine, waving a cane, and walked with stamping feet and stamping cane in anger up to Brewer.

"You lost him," he said accusingly to Brewer.

"Afraid so," Brewer replied.

"You have no idea how this complicates matters," Limoges said.

"It happens," Brewer said. "All the time. Don't you know that?"

Limoges swayed on his cane irritably. "You have no idea where he is?"

"No."

"What do you do now?"

"Wait."

"Wait."

"Yes. He'll turn up," Brewer said.

"He'll turn up." Limoges stood, leaning on his cane, gazing unhappily into Brewer's eyes. "My. How casual we are. Insouciant. Has it occurred to you that he might just turn up with Cassandra under his arm, heading for the nearest exit? What do you think we should do while waiting for Gogol to"—he flipped a hand in air—"turn up?"

"Put the real Cassandra under lock and key and wait."

Limoges shook his head impatiently. "We can't do that."

"We have no choice," Brewer said.

"That's right," Limoges replied. "We have no choice. We are in one hell of a bind now." He resumed stamping toward the entrance.

"Are you telling me that you're not going to protect the real unit while the top thief in the business is coming to steal it?"

"Let's get inside," Limoges said. "I have some bad news for you."

Mobius Laboratories looked like a toy maker's design center. Computer-operated model tractors were traveling over simulated fields of wheat, working out computer-set patterns for reaping and sowing—ever-reducing squares, ever-reducing circles, and up and down.

Computer-operated model trains traversed complex track patterns, speeding up, slowing, sidetracking, while interactive computers that guided each train negotiated with each other at high speed.

Up and down floor lanes robots prowled, performing a series of complex operations over and over.

Brewer and Limoges were led to a large office, where Coles sat before a computer, watching columns of green numbers parade up the screen.

"Here," Coles said to them. "Sit down." He reached under his desk and pulled out a gray metal case the size of a small valise. He placed it on the desk.

"That's Cassandra?" Brewer asked.

"That's Cassandra," Coles replied. "Everything's inside this one case, ready to travel. All a thief has to do is grab the handle and run. You want to know how it's booby-trapped?"

"Yes," Brewer said.

"It's identical to the real Cassandra in every respect except one. It has one extra command buried deep in its brain. It will do all the tests the Russians run it through. It will perform all the operations as they construct their Star Wars system. Then, when they have the entire network ready to become operational, they will give it the ultimate command, and instead of making their system operational, it will self-destruct. Their screens will go blank and the system will die on the spot. And they will have lost countless man-hours and money. Worse, they

will be light-years behind us." He looked at Brewer. "Revenge," he said. "How sweet it is."

"Where will you keep it?" Brewer asked.

Coles turned and pointed at a vault. "It will be stored in
there."

"And where is the real Cassandra?" Brewer asked.

Coles looked at Limoges. "We have to tell him," he said.

Limoges shrugged and avoided looking at Brewer.

"We are testing the real Cassandra," Coles said to Brewer.
"We couldn't wait any longer."

Brewer looked at Limoges, then at Coles. "You're testing
Cassandra—the real one—while we've lost contact with
Gogol?"

"Precisely," Limoges said. "You've really got us up a creek,
Brewer."

"You've got yourself up a creek," Brewer said. "You've
made an incredible gaffe."

"Steady, boy," Limoges said.

Coles asked Brewer, "Now how do you invite your Russian
playmate to come and steal this fake?"

"He's not going to come himself," Brewer answered.

"You expect him to send someone else?"

"He always does," Brewer answered. "Tell me. Why are you
testing Cassandra now?"

"Mr. Limoges here feels that delay is no longer possible."

"Bravo," Brewer said softly to Limoges.

"That's enough, Brewer," Limoges replied.

"How will you know if Gogol has taken the bait?" Coles
asked.

"Credit checks," Brewer said. "We'll know when a credit
investigation company does a character check on me. That's always Gogol's opening move. He'll be looking for some way to
blackmail me. And probably you two." He looked again at Limoges. "I still can't believe you authorized the testing of the
real unit. I have to say it's wrongheaded to test that unit now."

"Meantime, what do we do about Gogol?" Coles asked.

"We wait," Brewer said. "It's Gogol's move. God help us if
he makes the wrong one." He looked pointedly at Limoges.

Limoges got up and left.

* * *

After he had gone, Brewer asked Coles, "How far along in the testing are you?"

Coles pointed at the computer screen. "It's running now," he said. "We've simulated an SDI network using other computers all over the country. It's big; it's complicated; it took a hell of a lot of planning to set it up. So it's going to go on for quite awhile." He tapped a finger on the screen. "It would be bad news if your Gogol tied into this. Very bad news."

"Well, then, why are you testing now?"

"Limoges. There's something up in the White House. Suddenly everything's urgent."

"How much does Limoges know about the test?" Brewer asked.

"Everything."

Under a faded winter sun, the snow on the ground turned a dirtier gray and developed a frozen crust. The nights remained well below freezing. Every day that passed without a move from Gogol was ominous. Every day Limoges grew more anxious.

Brewer did not realize how short Limoges's patience had become.

One night Brewer heard a slow footstep on the stair. A slow heavy fist rapped on the door. Brewer went and opened it.

Limoges stood in the doorway in his long blue winter coat, leaning on his cane. Behind his heavy glasses his eyes looked very tired.

"Come in," Brewer said.

Limoges shook his head. "I just want you to know that my patience is just about at an end," he said. He gazed around the apartment with his magnified eyes. "I can't conduct any business in my limousine. Every time I see that Nevans, I want to kill him. And I can't keep the charade up much longer." He looked in at the apartment once more, then looked directly at Brewer.

"Then," Brewer said, "stop the test until we find Gogol."

Limoges shook his head. "I'm here to tell you that you have just three more days and it's all over. Clear?"

With a slow, solemn nod—awkward, with his cane—Limoges turned and went heavily down the steps to the front door.

*   *   *

Brewer sat on a stool in a saloon and watched a rerun of a heavyweight-title boxing match from Atlantic City. He went to the movies twice. He played solitaire and did a crossword puzzle and took long, meandering walks through the snow-filled streets of Washington and Georgetown, hearing the wind sough in the branches. He spent afternoons shooting solitary racks of pool.

Each night at three A.M. Brewer watched the gunman pull the trigger and tumble Gogol's car down the mountainside. He watched the car roll over, leap off the road and tumble end over end down down down, shedding doors, spraying glass, losing wheels, and finally bursting into flames.

At three A.M., always at three A.M., Brewer saw the screen in Coles's office pumping frame after frame of test numbers as Gogol worked his way closer to it.

At three A.M. bloodied Defeat, with bent sword and smashed shield, was clearly visible at the foot of his bed.

At three A.M. Brewer cursed the genes that had made him. The truth was, he hadn't wanted to finish his government career with a murder. And that was just what he might have to do to Gogol.

Brewer's luck ran out.

It was three days to the hour when Limoges summoned him to the Jefferson Memorial. They met in the same spot behind it, in the same gray dusk, and walked the same bitter cold path, hearing the forlorn clanking of the chain tolling on the flagstaff while the crows circled silently over their roosts.

Limoges had come this time prepared for the weather. He wore a felt snap-brim hat and a heavy wool scarf and fur-lined gloves. He walked with a heavier cane.

"You could have done this by phone," Brewer said to Limoges.

"I think you'll agree that Gogol should have stepped into your trap by now," Limoges said.

"Of course I don't agree with that," Brewer said.

"If he didn't go for your particular brand of cheese," Limoges said, "he has surely made a move elsewhere. For all we know, he may have tapped into the Cassandra test by now. He may have done a dozen things. Those seven extra days we've given Gogol may cost us frightfully in the end. And this chauffeur of mine, he may not have been working for Gogol at all. He could be working for someone else. Even the South Africans. Or he may be free-lancing. Now I have to decide how to handle that.

"You haven't waited long enough," Brewer said.

"I haven't? Brewer, you're like a Greek bearing gifts—they all exploded at the party."

He paused and tried to work his lighter with gloved fingers. "I must admit, if it hadn't been for you, I would not know about Gogol at all, might not have known about the tape deck in my car." He stood looking at the chain clanging on the flagstaff. "I often wondered why Hell is pictured as a place of fire. To me real Hell is eternal winter. Robert Frost got that right."

He threw down his cigar, turned and walked away.

The meeting was over.

Brewer walked slowly back to his car. He had tried to be mentally prepared for this, but he wasn't. Perhaps it was the weather. It might have all been easier to accept on a pleasant summer twilight. Easier than the dead of winter—a time when the cold darkness made the weather-weary draw their chairs a little closer to each other, to talk in voices a little louder, poke up the fire a little higher, while Loneliness scratched at the windowpane.

It was all over for him. He was out of a job. Out of a career. Out of a paycheck.

And Limoges would order Gogol killed. If he could find him.

Brewer watched Limoges's limousine slowly move away, followed by the escort car. Then both cars stopped. Another car was coming up the park drive. It was halted by Brewer's car, blocking the way, and Sauer got out.

He walked slowly up to Brewer. "Well, it happened," he said. "An outfit in Chicago, Eliott Credit Bureau, is asking all kinds of questions about you."

Chapter 43

L ate in the afternoon, in his motel room, Gogol received the first thick brown envelope from a messenger. He opened it and found two other envelopes inside.

The first, stamped CONFIDENTIAL in thick red letters, was from the Eliott Credit Bureau in Chicago. It was a financial and character report on Brewer.

Gogol snorted when he read Brewer's net worth. Less than thirty thousand. He had few assets—government bonds, primarily—and fewer debts. He rented his apartment, leased most of the furniture, and owned a second-hand automobile. The only other asset was several acres of undeveloped land in Pennsylvania overlooking the Delaware Water Gap.

The report noted that Brewer had been married twice. Once in law school. When he dropped out to enter military intelligence, he and his wife had separated. There was no record of a divorce. Brewer was married a second time, in London, to the proprietress of a profitable pub in Chelsea. It had lasted less than a year. That divorce was still pending.

Under hobbies and pastimes the report listed poker, billiards, and fishing.

Eliott had not obtained much information on Brewer's career in the intelligence field. And it had nothing on his activities as an arms dealer in Europe and the Near East. Gogol wasn't surprised; he hadn't expected to find anything usable in the credit report.

He turned next to the second envelope. Gogol always looked for three characteristics in people—fear, greed, and vengefulness. What he sought was the festering heart. And this second envelope promised to reveal it in abundance. It was Moscow's dossier on Brewer. Thick and thorough, it documented Brewer's life in detail. Gogol skimmed the vital statistics—birth, family, education, early career.

He glanced briefly at Moscow's summary of Brewer's government record—military counterintelligence, then arms control, then out of government as an arms dealer, then back in government as an expert on arms smuggling and high-tech smuggling.

Gogol looked with attention at Brewer's history as an arms dealer working first for Mann, a famous arms seller in Zurich, then another in London. Brewer had had numerous encounters with Russian agents and operations and had won most of them. No wonder the committee called him a bone in the throat.

It was Moscow's account of Brewer's imprisonment that most interested Gogol. This might be the way into Brewer's heart. Brewer had been framed. He'd been framed by a high-ranking government executive using the authority of his public office to commit the crime. Brewer had spent many months in a penitentiary before being pardoned. He emerged bitterly angry.

To compound his anger, the government had inexplicably moved with great slowness in restoring his rights, emoluments, and perquisites, and even then had to be prodded by the determined and unremitting legal moves of Brewer's attorney. Nor was that the end. Limoges had personally intervened to hold up Brewer's next career appointment. The Moscow report surmised that Brewer was working under duress on the Cassandra assignment.

In his habitual quest for the festering heart, Gogol had never encountered a more likely candidate than Brewer. But there was, in Brewer, some key ingredient missing. Gogol reviewed his list: greed, fear, vengefulness.

Greed? How do you bribe a man who doesn't seem interested in money or wealth? Possessions appeared to be an impediment. He had no discernible interests except "poker, billiards, fishing." No lust for an art collection. No hunger for a yacht. No secret dreams for a hunting lodge in the Sierras, a fishing cottage in Ireland. Gogol drew a line through greed. Brewer was not likely to respond to an offer of even a king's ransom.

A greed for power? Brewer shunned power.

Fear. How do you blackmail a man who has nothing to hide, nothing to fear? The report from Moscow contained no secret drinking problem, no hidden sexual gambols, no peculations, no disloyalties or betrayals.

Vengefulness? So far, in spite of ample justification, Brewer did not behave like a man dreaming of vengeance. He handled the Cassandra affair with professionalism and determination. Gogol mentally drew a line through vengefulness.

There was only one thing that seemed to enthrall Brewer. His whole history proclaimed it—the game. The intelligence game. The chase. He'd walked away from a career in law, declined several lucrative opportunities in private industry, and seemingly wrecked two marriages because of his passion for the intelligence game. Gogol guessed that gamesmanship and not promotion was the reason Brewer had accepted Limoges's assignment. So there was the only key to Brewer's heart. Not vengeance or greed or fear. Charlie Brewer was a compulsive gambler and adventurer. He lived for the chase. And he was most excited when the stakes were his own life.

Gogol saw that he and Brewer could not be more opposite. True, both of them lived for the challenge. For the moment of crisis and maximum suspense. But Gogol knew that he himself was a sybarite who loved food and wine and swollen luxury and vast sums and great power. But he did not take chances. Did not risk himself at any time. He worked from behind the scenes.

Conversely, Brewer, who wanted nothing, cared little for food or pomp or circumstance. He was one step away from a fanatic monk in a bare cell. But he loved to take chances. He'd risked himself many times. Anyone who understood percentages would look at Brewer's love of being on the wrong end of long odds and call him a fool.

In this game, a luxury-loving extrovert was confronting an ascetic loner.

Gogol could not understand Brewer. He could not understand a man who was indifferent to the world's largesse. He could not understand any man who didn't put his hand in the goodie jar. Men like that were difficult to suborn, to control, to use.

Gogol knew he was going to particularly enjoy winning this contest. He hated the Brewers of the world heartily.

One thing was quite clear. Both he and Brewer were involved in the Cassandra affair for the same primary reason. Ego. They each wanted to beat the other.

Gogol turned to the Coles report. It had all the bench marks and way stations of a biography of a great scientist. A graduate of MIT summa cum laude, his brilliant college career was preceded by a long list of science awards as a child and teenager. Upon graduation he was eagerly sought after by many different corporations. Almost immediately he was involved in military contracts, and soon there appeared after his name in the Who's Who directories, a long and growing list of credits and breakthroughs. He was a regular contributor to the scientific journals. His specialty became artificial intelligence. In his mid-thirties, at the behest of the military, he started Mobius, his own research think tank. Turned it into a cornucopia of inventions for military application. The list on Gogol's report ran for three pages, and even that wasn't a complete list of all his major developments. Gogol knew. He had stolen much of it.

For a hobby Coles pursued an activity that often had the Pentagon holding its breath. He was passionate about flying. He'd made his first ultra-light in his garage from a lawn-mower engine. Now, at fifty, he eagerly barnstormed in biplanes at air shows all across the country.

The first sign of trouble in his career occurred when he appeared before the Senate investigating committee on illegal acquisitions of U.S. technology to demand that the thefts be stopped. At that hearing he read a long list of names of scientists who were now refusing to work on military assignments. He became a vocal critic of the Pentagon and condemned the Soviet Union as a bandit nation.

His brilliant articles on artificial intelligence which had been appearing in science journals stopped at this point. He felt the Russians were benefiting too much. He wanted his colleagues to stop publishing. Coles had silenced himself.

Why had he resumed working for the military? Because Star

Wars would never work without that central nervous system—
the software that would oversee the whole operation. And only
the most brilliant mind could develop such a unit. It was right on
the frontier of research into artificial intelligence, requiring a
number of new scientific contributions. Gogol would have liked
to have been at the meeting when the Pentagon sought to per-
suade Coles to work on the project. They must have sent their
best salesman to convince him. Developed by a mind like
Coles's, Cassandra must be brilliant. Brilliant. Gogol was eager
to examine it.

Fear. Greed. Vengefulness. Which of the three motivated
Coles?

Fear? He had an exemplary home life. No mistress, no office
affairs. The credit company had included an analysis and summary of his personal checks for two years. It was boringly normal. Coles's private life was a goldfish bowl. Nowhere to hide.
Nothing to hide.

In Mobius, his think tank, there were no business problems.
The company was soundly financed and thriving. Coles had
gathered a number of gifted scientific minds, who were now
working on more projects and assignments than they could
handle.

Clearly, blackmail was out.

Greed. He was worth over five million dollars and had little
time to spend it. A financial advisor was busy with a series of
investments that were earning Coles even more wealth. He collected some pieces of art. If there was anything he was greedy
for, it was more time.

Vengefulness? Against Russia perhaps. There was probably
only one way to control Coles: kidnap his wife or children.
Gogol laid the Coles dossier aside.

The reports on Coles's executive staff began arriving that afternoon—three of them. And they told as much about Coles as
they did about the subjects. In report after report on Mobius
Laboratories, one factor stood out. Coles was an extremely able
and affable administrator who enjoyed the enthusiastic endorse-
ment and loyalty of his staff. He had gathered around himself an
array of brilliant minds that would have made the head of Direc-

torate T salivate. But how had he earned such fierce dedication
for such a group of independent, individual, unpredictable,
quirky, creative personalities?

The first one, Walters, was a marathoner. His scientific specialty was robotization, but if there were a symposium on
robotization scheduled for the same day as a marathon, the symposium lost out. Walters was also an ardent backpacker and
camper, and an amateur astronomer of some standing. His wife
was a math teacher, and their two children were both attending
special schools for gifted students. But it was as a health-food
advocate that Walters drew national attention. He appeared on
lecture platforms everywhere, roundly condemning the American food industry for the chemical additives in prepared foods.
He told young mothers not to buy prepared baby food. In fact
he started a newsletter on the subject. He wrote publicity re-
leases. He frequently went to the local newspapers to badger the
editors. Walters was an obnoxious public scold.

One other common note in his life: he frequently praised his
boss, Coles.

Gogol sensed that he had absolutely nothing to say to this
Walters. He laid the report aside.

One of the first scientists that Coles had ever hired was a
woman named Baines. She was a mathematician who also held a
Ph.D. in Human Biology, and she'd gained an international reputation for her developments in computer software. Her primary
interest was the human mind, and in article after article in scientific journals she had systematically explored the mind's com-
puterlike capabilities. Tolenko on the Directorate T committee
had once said that of all the Western scientists, this was the one
he most wanted to meet and talk with. He said she had a leaping
mind that generated more insights into artificial intelligence in
one day than most scientists developed in a lifetime.

But where was the fretted heart that would make her vulnerable to Gogol's approaches?

Greed? She had a very high income and was worth nearly a
million dollars. In the years ahead, her wealth would easily double or triple. She had no debts to speak of. Rule out money.

Personal history. She was unmarried, sharing a home near
Silver Spring with another woman scientist. They were room-

mates in college and had been living together for fifteen years. A possibility: was she a candidate for blackmail?

Gogol read Baines's list of memberships in professional and political organizations. In addition to membership in the most prestigious science organizations, she was a charter member and president of the Committee of Scientists for Gay Rights. That eliminated that possibility.

Gogol paced. There was nothing here. Nothing in either report that he could use to lever Cassandra free. And he felt the reports on the other dozen scientists in Mobius Laboratories would be just as unpromising. The loyalty that these scientists exhibited toward Coles was like a defensive circle formed by musk ox to protect Coles and his Cassandra.

He picked up the third report.

This one looked more promising—the type of personality Gogol liked to find. A misfit. A social misfit. Gifted—brilliant, even—but neurotically shy and uncommunicative. This man, Jalovac, had been a world-class chess player when he was in college, but had abruptly dropped out of international play after he was falsely accused of violating the rules. Despite the repeated public apologies of the International Chess Federation, Jalovac refused all invitations to enter any future matches. He never played in public again.

Before joining Mobius Jalovac had had several quarrels with colleagues over imagined slights. He felt he was the butt of behind-back office jokes.

He belonged to no scientific or professional groups. He had no friends. He was not married. Lived alone. Had no hobbies or interests other than his vocation. Gogol knew the personality well: brooding, neurotically sensitive, timid and quietly seething with anger at the world that intimidated him.

There was a great deal going on underneath the surface. Possibly Gogol could turn Jalovac into an ideologue, a secret traitor to the society he feared and hated.

Had he time enough, Gogol would have tried to develop Jalovac, but this was a project that would have taken months, and even then, handling quixotic personalities like Jalovac was always dangerous.

Gogol paced some more. He felt an unwonted sense of dread in his stomach. What if he found no one in the Coles organization who could be turned? How would he get Cassandra then?

Another knock on the door, another character report. Like a bettor at the track, Gogol cheered himself on as he tore open the envelope. "Come on, darling, be a winner," he said.

And it was.

From the first sentence, everything clicked. Even his name was right. Perdu: in French, lost. Bewildered. Here Lady Luck had spread a feast for Gogol: greed, fear, vengefulness enough for an army of spies.

At thirty-one Perdu was one of the world's leading experts in microchip design and theory. A product of the public schools of New York City, at sixteen he won a math scholarship to Stanford and became a creative explosion. He was a world-class thinker on microchips before he graduated at twenty. It was said that there were only four other scientists who could discuss his advanced theories on the microchip with him.

Perdu had married four years before. And then his troubles began. His wife gave him a son—autistic, with spinal cord damage that would confine him to a wheelchair, chronically ill, for life. His wife was driven by guilt and dismay into a deep depression that required extensive counseling.

The demands of constantly caring for a child hopelessly autistic and handicapped wore her out. When her son was two, Elena Perdu could conceal her secret no longer: she had become a heroin addict. Now both parents went for counseling while she also entered a drug-rehabilitation program. Perdu went deeply into debt.

Elena Perdu had great difficulty overcoming her heroin addiction, for at bottom she lived in despair. She felt she was chained for the rest of her life to a human tragedy who could never be normal, never be self-sufficient. Every day teams of women came to her home and slowly worked the child's limbs to help develop his nervous system so that he could walk. Patterning every day, day after day, year after year.

Perdu worked hard at helping his wife cope. He was distracted from his career. He took time off to be with her. He took her away on extended vacations and holidays. But always when she returned, the child was there. And the patterning.

Perdu wanted to institutionalize the boy. Elena was overcome with guilt at the thought. She insisted she could handle the child. All she needed was a little more time.

She became pregnant again. At first she was overjoyed. A new child would bring the two of them together, something joyful to share. Then she panicked. What if the baby were another tragedy like the first? Terrified and trapped, she became addicted again to heroin. Perdu struggled greatly to get her back on her feet.

One afternoon he found her unconscious. An overdose. After great effort, the hospital saved her. And Perdu learned that she had had an abortion. Guilt was piled on guilt. She couldn't face Perdu now. She wanted a separation. He agreed reluctantly. The marriage was almost finished.

The IRS audited his income tax return and disallowed many of his medical tax deductions. Coles himself stepped in to provide lawyers and accountants for Perdu to fight his case, but in the end he lost. The tax bill with interest was staggering. Perdu refused to accept financial aid from Coles. He went to a local bank and borrowed the money. Now he was in a constant fury.

He visited his wife regularly, and at last she agreed to put the marriage back together. She'd been off drugs for six months. The night before they were to rejoin each other, she committed suicide with poison.

Perdu threw himself into his work, often remaining seven days a week in his office. He took to talking to himself and flogged his body to produce. He was exhausted, but he had two major projects going that held great promise. Scientists all over the world were feverishly seeking a new supermicrochip that could operate on the new materials with nearly zero electrical resistance. Scientific history would be made. A Nobel prize was a possibility. And Perdu had been considered the leading contender for the invention.

One night he was stopped for speeding, and assaulted a policeman.

Then one of his two key microchip projects failed. The enormous effort and time had come to nothing. Not uncommon in research work, but Perdu was crushed. Not only was it a failure, but it put him two years behind some of the most brilliant scientific minds in the world. He felt his personal problems had been an insuperable distraction.

He became hostile and uncontrollable. He drank. He railed against the government, against the tax gatherers, against the police, against the medical-care facilities of the nation. He pronounced America a failure. He drank more and more. One night he went berserk in a bar and did thousands of dollars in damage.

The next day the mortgage company foreclosed on his home. And the institution caring for the boy sued for six months of unpaid fees. Perdu faced bankruptcy.

The next day Coles paid the sums due on the mortgage and for the child care, then put Perdu on an indefinite leave of absence with pay. Perdu's microchip research project was assigned to others. Perdu had lost his opportunity to make science history. And Gogol had found his way into Coles Laboratories.

Perdu would bring Cassandra to him.

••• Chapter 44

During the evening he rang Perdu's phone repeatedly but there was no answer. Finally, after eleven that night, Perdu answered.

"Mr. Perdu," Gogol began. "I'm sorry to call you so late. I've been trying all evening. I'm the editor and publisher of a new science journal and I'm most interested in talking to you before I return to Europe."

He could barely hear Perdu's answer.

"I want particularly to talk to you about your microchip research."

Perdu murmured that he was no longer doing microchip research.

"I understand that," Gogol said. "All the scientists in Europe that I've talked to say it was a disgrace to remove you. After all, you are the leading scientist on microchips in the world. Coles has done something foolish and shameful."

Perdu's voice was low, listless.

"We need to talk," Gogol said. "I believe I can help you get back into the race. I have some connections in the science world. There's a way you can still create the new microchip—perhaps in Europe—and also pay off a few scores in the process. You know what I am referring to? Yes? Good."

Perdu's voice became stronger. Yes. Yes. He was interested.

"I need to get my work started again," Perdu was saying. "I know how to make that new chip. The people Coles put on the project will never find it. Not in a million years. I've had some personal problems that I hope will soon be behind me."

"How angry are you with Coles?"

"Anger is hardly the word!" Perdu said. "He took away from me the opportunity of a lifetime. I might never again get a shot at anything like this new superchip. I'll never forget this. Never! Someday I'll find a way to pay him back. And so help me God, I'll do it!"

"I might be able to show you a way to get some satisfaction on that score too," Gogol said. "Would you like that?"

"Show me the way," Perdu said.

"Well, first of all, I have connections with several laboratories in Europe that are not now involved in microchip research. I am authorized to speak to you on their behalf. They would like very much for you to come to work right now. You could write your own ticket. How do you feel about that?"

Perdu's voice grew enthusiastic. He would like that very much. When could he talk to them?

"I can arrange that shortly," Gogol said. "First I suggest you make a list of requirements that I can submit to them. They will be delighted to hear that you are definitely interested. You could be back at work in a few days. That would be marvelous. Now about the second part. You are definitely the aggrieved party with Coles. The whole world says so. If you'd like some satisfaction . . . dueling, unfortunately, is no longer in vogue, so you must find another way. Something that would really make Coles wince. You understand?"

"Like what?" Perdu asked.

"Something precious to him. Since he robbed you of your prize, rob him of his. Or at least one of his. Something important to him. What is he working on these days?"

"Classified stuff. Military software."

"Take it from him," Gogol said.

"What do you mean?"

"Take it. Give it to some others to introduce as their own."

"Who? Who would take it?"

"Many people. And Coles would see others get credit for his invention. That's poetic justice, isn't it?"

"Yes," Perdu said thoughtfully. "Yes, it is."

"I tell you, if you could bring that with you to Europe, there's no limit to what could happen to your career. You would have the science world at your feet. Tell me more about the Coles project. Could you really get it?"

"With pleasure," Perdu said. "With pleasure."

Perdu wanted a few hours to write his pro forma for setting his microchip researches in Europe. He also wanted to check into Coles's project. Gogol agreed to call him at six the next evening.

"Oh, by the way," Gogol said. "Does it have a name, Coles's project?"

"Yes. I'm not supposed to mention it. But yes, it has a name. Cassandra."

Gogol was like a dog on a point. Far into the night he paced inside his motel room. To get Cassandra he had to work Perdu carefully, with the help of the three Sisters—Fear, Greed, Vengefulness.

Gogol knew this was going to be his masterpiece—the intelligence equivalent of inventing the supermicrochip. It would be wonderful if there were a Nobel prize for spying. He was surely about to earn it.

The next afternoon, Gogol violated his own self-imposed rule. He went out of the motel room in broad daylight. He had to walk, to burn off the excitement, to calm down. He needed to be collected and alert when he called Perdu. Six o'clock seemed a long way off.

He strode over frozen roadways, past old farms now crowded with new subdivisions. Winter was still emtombing the land, and skies were ladened with more snow. The skiing in the Swiss Alps was superb. Gogol looked forward eagerly to skiing—after getting Cassandra of course. When he got back to his motel, he would do his skiing exercises.

From the machine outside the motel registration office he bought a newspaper and took it back to his room. Then he felt like something had exploded inside his head.

The headline on the front page announced that Perdu had committed suicide.

●●●Part Eight

●●● **Chapter 45**

For a second time Gogol sensed that failure was a possibility. He sat in his motel room going over the reports. Six new ones had arrived, all ranking scientists with Coles Laboratories. He went through them with care then reviewed them a second and third time. But each time he reviewed them, he sensed anew that only Perdu had been a possibility.

He started through the reports once again, starting with Coles himself. Where was the tiny crack in the wall he needed for the thin edge of his wedge? He tried to see through the papers, the paragraphs and sentences, and into the very hearts of Coles's scientists. Which one secretly had a festering heart? Which one could bring him Cassandra? And what was the lure that could bring that about?

Several days had gone by since he'd arrived here, and now, after such great expectations, he was no closer to his prize. What he needed was what he always got when the moment of crisis arrived. He needed a piece of great good luck.

At five P.M. another report arrived. This one from a credit bureau in New York City. "Luck be with me," Gogol said as he tore open the envelope.

The subject of the report was the American agent who had been in Vienna—Sauer, the man he'd sent the ruble to. Cpaceeba, Sauer, Cpaceeba. He remembered listening to the tape with Revin when Sauer first told Brewer about Cassandra. And Sauer had been with Brewer during the rescue attempt of the Chernies in the subways of New York City. Now, as part of the team guarding Cassandra, he was an ideal choice—an agent with access to the unit.

As he read, Gogol's hopes began to rise again. Here was everything he needed. Here was a career in decline. A life in grave crisis. Fear, greed, and vengefulness rampant.

Sauer's personal life was in shambles. His ex-wife had been a promiscuous woman who had put the horns on him in bars and sleazy hotels and motels all across the city—openly, indifferently, with total strangers, with Sauer's fellow agents and friends. Then, after repeated sessions with a marriage counselor, she finally left him.

Sauer is filled with guilt, Gogol reflected. He blames himself, not her. And he blames his job and his career. He blames his superiors. And now he has told many friends and associates that the debacle in Vienna with the empty boxes had put the finish on a dying career.

To rankle the bitterness, he was in debt. His credit rating was in a very shaky condition. Payments to his wife were chronically late. Car payments—slow. His bank loan was overdue and he was paying only the interest and deferring the principle. He was in arrears on his self-imposed payments to his wife. Worse, he was living with a woman and concealing it from ex-wife, children, friends, and superiors. He often got drunk in the evening and for entire weekends.

Gogol picked up the phone. "I want more on this woman Sauer is living with," he said. "And also—I'll bet you a fat penny that Sauer is secretly seeing a psychiatrist. Find out."

Gogol looked thoughtfully once more at the Sauer report. He felt he had found his man. There was more to come.

Dr. Leslie Windbush, psychiatrist, was a man of regular habits. He played racketball three afternoons a week at the Fit As A Fiddle racket courts with a group of other physicians. A new member, therefore—joined the day before—had no difficulty being on hand at the predictable hour and then to open the doctor's flimsy locker lock and remove the doctor's keys, make wax impressions in a john in the men's room, and return the keys to Dr. Windbush's locker, all while the doctor was engaging his cardiovascular system in significant and sustained physical activity.

At two o'clock that morning the new member of the Fit As

A Fiddle Racket Club entered Dr. Windbush's medical offices with copies of his keys, and there in the doctor's own over-stuffed leather chair, comfortably sat for more than an hour reading the files. Using the doctor's copy machine, he made duplicates of the files on his patient Sauer. Using the doctor's audio-tape equipment, he made duplicates of the tapes on Sauer's therapy talks with the doctor. He carefully replaced everything, put the copies in an inside pocket of his jacket, and departed, leaving everything exactly as it was.

"It's that Brewer," Sauer's voice said.

"We agreed to discuss your wife today," the psychiatrist's voice said.

"Brewer's going to push my face into the pie," Sauer's voice said. The voice had the whining quality of a brooding, bitter man, a man who feels he's a victim of other people's chicanery. It was bureaucratic politics. It was bad timing. It was bad luck. It was unfair judgment of his handling of the Vienna job. It was Brewer. He hated Brewer. Brewer is going to be covered with glory on Sauer's ruined reputation. The whine grew more pronounced.

"I wish I were dead," Sauer's voice said.

"We've discussed that before," the doctor's voice said. "A number of times."

"If I go," Sauer said, "there are a few I'd take with me."

Dr. Windbush pointedly cleared his throat.

Gogol, listening to the tapes, looked at his copies of the doctor's notes. The focus of his treatment was on Sauer's depression and suicidal impulses. Recent entries suggested that Sauer's depression was turning violent. Sauer had refused to sign himself in for psychiatric care. Unknown to Sauer, the doctor was considering a court order. And there was another problem.

"Those goddamn pills are costing me my shirt," Sauer complained.

"You are taking too many," Windbush said.

"I can't help it. I need them. They calm me down."

"You're also taking them while you're drinking, and I've already explained that danger to you."

"You said you could find me a cheaper source of the pills," Sauer countered.

"Yes," Dr. Windbush replied. "I'm looking into that."

Gogol looked thoughtfully at the tape deck. What a find. An alcoholic drug addict suffering from severe paranoia and depression with homicidal tendencies and suicidal impulses; filled with bitterness toward the world, his job, his superiors—his own government; just inches away from bankruptcy; and being handled by a doctor who overmedicated and was now thinking of hiding the problem by flinging the drug-dependent patient into a psychiatric hospital.

"Everytime I come here I'm scared to death someone will see me," Sauer said. "If they find out about it, I'll be out on the street in five minutes."

"Let's go back to your marriage," Dr. Windbush said soothingly.

Chapter 46

G ogol had never seen anything like it before: the housekeeping motel complex he was living in was a hive of activity. Most of the units were leased long term by companies to store visiting executives without the staggering costs of downtown Washington hotels.

People arrived and departed around the clock. Luggage paraded in and out of automobile trunks. Airport limousines and buses came and went at all hours. So did the pizza delivery trucks, the liquor-store delivery trucks, the twenty-four-hour cleaners and laundry. So did the furtive men who knocked softly and palmed small white envelopes through the barely opened doors. So did the young women—an ethnic smorgasbord—arriving in cabs and departing an hour later in cabs, leaving only a lingering scent in the frosty air.

It was an atmosphere that would excite the heart of any hustler. The possibilities were limitless. A man with just a clandestine camera could make a fortune. Anyone in the information business could easily phone-tap into a daily tide of sellable information that flowed in and out of the rooms. The thirst for services of all kinds was unslakable. Gogol couldn't stay away from his window blinds.

That evening Gogol rang Sauer's telephone. "A mutual friend of ours," he said, "told me to call you. I understand that you are finding a certain commodity to be very expensive."

"Who's this?"

"Let's just say I have connections with Doctor Windbush. I can offer you a very good deal on that commodity I mentioned at a fraction of what you are now paying. Perhaps you might be interested in this."

Sauer's voice was suspicious and complaining, just as it was on the psychiatrist's tapes. "It's about time," he said. "I've been complaining about this for nearly a year. How much?"

"How about ten percent of current drugstore prices?"

"Ten percent off?"

"No. Ten percent. One tenth of what you are now paying."

"Really? Are you serious?"

"Of course," Gogol said. "You know how outrageously these things are marked up. I'm surprised you haven't found an alternate source a long time ago. I'm going to send you a package—a free sample for you to examine. Then I'll call you back."

"What about a prescription?"

"Unnecessary. Good night, Mr. Sauer."

Gogol waited until the next night then called Sauer again. Sauer was very relaxed and pleasant.

"Marvelous," he said. "Exactly what I need. And I can't believe the price."

Gogol nodded to himself, listening to Sauer's mellow voice. Sauer had taken a quantity of pills and had also been drinking.

"I'm very pleased, Mr. Sauer," Gogol said. "I can arrange to make a delivery at your door on a regular basis. Cash with order of course."

"How can I reach you?" Sauer asked.

"That won't be necessary. I'll contact you every few days. When will you need more?"

"Let's see." Sauer put down the phone then came back. "Tomorrow."

Tomorrow. Sauer must have been popping them like candy. "Is delivery tomorrow evening about right?"

The next evening Sauer was in a chatty mood.

"You sound like a man hard pressed for money, Mr. Sauer," Gogol said.

"You got that right."

"Perhaps we can work something out."

Sauer's voice became suspicious. "What does that mean?"

"I'm sure I don't know myself, Mr. Sauer. I'm a man in

many businesses, and perhaps you might have things to sell that my customers would be interested in. I've made some men rich."

There was a long pause. "I don't know," Sauer said at last. "I have to think about it."

Gogol sent him another package of drugs with a free bonus of extra pills. A few hours later he called Sauer again.

The man was purring like a cat.

"You receive my little gift?" Gogol asked. "Good. Now listen, Sauer. I really insist on doing business with you. I'm talking about a lot of money. A king's ransom. I'm talking about setting you up for life."

"I don't know."

"Yes, you do. You can't conceal your habit much longer. Then you'll be out. For good. Especially if someone with a loose mouth turns you in. It could happen."

"No one knows."

"I do."

There was a long, breathless pause. "What does that mean?"

"If I know, surely others do. I'll talk to you later."

Gogol waited for Sauer's supply to dwindle. He pictured Sauer pacing up and down in his apartment for hours. Finally he dialed.

"You have to give me your telephone number," Sauer complained. "When I need more, I have to be able to call you."

"That won't be necessary," Gogol said. "You sound a little out of it. Did you take too many goodies?"

"I was upset. Bad day at the office."

"You should learn to control yourself. Those things can be dangerous. You take too many and you won't be any good to anybody."

"It's money, goddamn it," Sauer said. "It's driving me crazy. You said you wanted to buy something from me. What is it?"

"Nothing you'll miss. A little information, that's all."

"Lay it out for me. What's the deal?" Sauer demanded.

"How'd you like a big fat package of cash—unmarked and untraceable?"

Long pause.

"Are you there, Sauer?"

Sauer cleared his voice. "Yes. I'm here."

"What do you think?"

"It depends on what I have to do for it."

Gogol sent Sauer a substantial package. Then called him again.

"How's that?"

"Okay. Fine."

"Look, Sauer. There's no sense beating around the bush. It's common knowledge you've been badly treated."

"How do you know about that?"

"Don't worry. I'm very discreet. You've been badly handled by people who don't have half your talent and ability. They've sidetracked you. A man with your skills is a threat. You can get in their way. You know what a dirty, slimy world we live in. So what are you supposed to do? Crawl off into the woodwork and die while these incompetents get all the goodies?"

There was silence. Then Sauer said in a hoarse voice, "Bastards."

"It's something to think about. You should walk away with something to show for your years of service. You're certainly not going to get any more promotions, no more higher G.S. ratings. You have to take care of yourself at this point."

"Enough, enough," Sauer said. "I don't want to talk about it right now."

Gogol called him early in the morning. "I know you're heading for the office," he said. "So I thought I'd leave you with a few thoughts. This whole matter is handled with the utmost discretion. There's absolutely no danger for you. You'd be amazed at the number of prominent people I deal with. And I'm talking about cash deals. Substantial cash."

"How substantial?"

"For a man of your stature? How about a quarter of a million dollars—just for starters?"

That evening Gogol went at Sauer again. Now he added the stick to the carrot.

"I can make you rich, Sauer," he said. "Beyond your dreams. And you deserve it."

"Not now."

"Why wait? This town is never going to do right by you. You should get your goodies when you can. My customers may find another source for the information they want. Then you'll be out a fortune, and maybe there will never be a second chance. It's a simple matter of supply and demand."

"I'll think about it."

"No. You have to do more than that. My offer can be withdrawn quite suddenly. And meantime, if your superiors find out about your drug problem—"

"What drug problem?"

"Oh, come now, Sauer. They can count just as easily as I can. And they'll also be very interested in your psychiatric counseling. So you could be a double loser. Lose a fortune, then lose your job."

"How will they find out?"

"Oh come, Sauer. These things are accomplished. We all live in goldfish bowls. I'm just saying that time is not on your side. You have to move quickly."

"I'll sleep on it."

Gogol called Nevans. "Are you sure there are no taps on his line or mine?"

"The only tap is ours. We've got a complete taping of all your conversations."

"He'd better come around soon," Gogol said.

"I think he's ready to cave in," the chauffeur said.

"I don't."

That evening Gogol sent another package to Sauer—again with a fat bonus. And in the midst of it he tucked in a copy of a tape from the psychiatrist's file.

"Jesus Christ on the cross!" Sauer shouted when Gogol called him. "How did you get that?"

"I warned you, Sauer. You live in a goldfish bowl. The point is, if I got it, your superiors can get it. You said some very damning things to your doctor on that tape. That's all your enemies need. They can ruin you. And you know they would love to do that. I don't think you realize how serious your situation is. You must know that losing your job would be a disaster for you."

Sauer sighed heavily. "Shit."

"You need to be decisive, Sauer."

"What is it you want?"

Gogol hesitated. "Cassandra."

"Cassandra! Are you crazy? Are you out of your mind?"

"No. Of course not. For someone like you it should be a piece of cake. I will pay handsomely for you to tell me how to get it. Just tell me how. That's all."

Sauer hung up.

Gogol paced in his motel room. If he had had more time, he could have developed Sauer first, before springing Cassandra on him. Normally he would have asked for small pieces of insignificant information—material he could verify from other sources. But there was no time. No time for finesse. If need be, he would really strongarm Sauer. He was practically doing that now.

The trouble with the hasty move was, he hadn't really plumbed Sauer. There was always, as a result, the chance that the target would prove to be unexpectedly upright and loyal and report the whole thing to his superiors.

The next phone call to Sauer would be crucial.

Gogol went through all his reports again: Sauer. And Conyers. And Court. And Brewer. And Limoges. He fingered Brewer's. That should have been his prime candidate. But . . . Gogol threw the reports down. And paced again.

The pizza trucks came and went. The long-legged ladies in the cabs came and went. The laundry trucks, the airport limousines, the suitcases, all moved in unison like the parts of a well-oiled old clock.

Gogol paced. He let Sauer soften up, waited until long after Sauer had used up his last pill. Then he waited some more. He waited into the dark hours of the night, when the car doors slammed continuously outside. At three A.M. he picked up the phone.

"Did I wake you up?"

"Wake me up! Christ, I'm halfway up the wall! You've got to give me your phone number. I need a package fast."

"What about our conversation?"

"I can't do that. I mean, I can get my hands on some other stuff maybe. But that's off limits."

"Too bad," Gogol said. "That's really all my customers are interested in. Listen, Sauer, you know my customers are going to get Cassandra. Why should someone else walk off with the money? You can have it all safely tucked away in a Swiss bank account while you sip cool drinks in a tropical paradise."

"Winter," Sauer said.

"Yes, that's it. Winter. No more winter for you, Sauer. Listen. I'm going to send you something that will make you feel better and I'll call you back."

Gogol waited an hour and called.

"Holy God," Sauer exclaimed. "There was fifty thousand dollars in the package."

"I know. It's a small down payment, Sauer. It's yours to keep. It's going to clean up all your financial problems. And the other little package. That's made you feel better already. I can tell by your voice. How do you feel now?"

"Good."

"Wonderful. Tell me a little bit about Cassandra." Gogol held his breath.

Sauer uttered a deep sigh. "Well, what do you want to know?"

Gogol grinned with joy. "What do you know about it? Where is it?"

"Coles has it."

"Coles? You mean the Mobius think tank?"

"Yes. Coles himself developed it."

"Is it operational?"

"Not yet. They're testing it."

"Testing? How testing? In a computer?"

"In a nationwide computer network. It's a simulation of the total system."

"And where's it being tested?"

"In the laboratories. Outside Silver Spring."

"How do I go about getting it, Sauer?"

Sauer hesitated. "You don't want to mess with Cassandra."

"Why?"

"It's booby-trapped, that's why."

"Explain."

"Charlie Brewer rigged a fake and put it in the software vault."

"I see. Then how do I go about getting around it?"

"Beats me."

"Listen, Sauer. I need to access that Cassandra test. What is the access telephone code?"

"I don't know."

"You must get it for me."

"I don't know how. I'm not on the Need to Know list."

"You can get it, Sauer. A quarter of a million dollars says you can. That tropical paradise says you can. A whole new life of comfort and ease says you can. Okay?"

"I'll try."

"No. Listen. I will tell you how to get it."

"How would you know how to get it?"

"Listen, Sauer. The human heart never changes. And neither does the human brain. Someone—maybe more than one—has a bad memory, understand? That means they will write the access code down somewhere. You look for it. Under a chair seat, you see? On the back of a clipboard. The underside of a shelf. Or they may break it up. Part in one place, part in another. You know what I mean. You must think to yourself, 'Where would I write a number like that?'"

"I'll try. Call me tonight."

Gogol had to get out of his motel room. It was too confining and he was getting claustrophobic. It was the ninth inning, bases loaded, and he had to strike the side out. He had to wait more than twelve hours before he could call Sauer again.

•••Part Nine

●●● Chapter 47

T he head of the Eliott Credit Bureau in Chicago had the file on his desk waiting when Brewer arrived.

"It was just a routine check," he protested. "For employment. We weren't probing into the CIA or the guy's intelligence background. Nothing sensitive or illegal."

"Who ordered it?" Brewer asked.

"Trans-Atlantic Bank and Trust in New York. We do a lot of work for them."

"A bank is interested in hiring an intelligence agent?"

"No. The bank does it as a service for their clients—to conceal their identities."

"How do you know it's an employment check?" Brewer asked.

"It says so on the form." The manager pointed at the row of boxes with X's. "See? Purpose: employment. That tells us what kind of information to get."

"It's a character check," Brewer said.

"So? We do thousands of them every year. They're different from a regular credit check but they're perfectly legal. If you were going to hire a guy, you'd want to know all about his past, wouldn't you?"

Brewer shuffled the pages of the report. "You didn't find out much about this guy Brewer," he said.

"We never do when it's intelligence. Government personnel policy. Yes, he's employed here. Since this time. They'll give you his G.S. usually. And that's about it. His record, his performance ratings, none of that."

"How can I find out who the actual client is that ordered the credit check?"

"You have to ask the bank. It's their client."

"You don't show any record about Brewer's divorce from his first wife."

"We didn't find any."

"It was in the same city he was married in. New York. Borough of Brooklyn. Six years ago."

The manager took out a pencil and made a note on the report. "You sure of that?"

"As sure as my name's Brewer."

Brewer sent a telefax to the bank in Los Angeles that Bobby English had used, requesting full data on the deposit of funds into several of the bank's accounts. And he listed two account names that Bobby English had given him: Eureka High-Tech Enterprises and Condor Medical Software Company.

Coles's personnel officer called him. "You asked me to call you about any credit and reference checks on our employees that come in," she said.

"What have you got?"

"We normally don't pay much attention to these," she said. "We don't even keep a record of such requests. We give out just standard information. And very little of that. With the number of employees we have, we get them every day."

"Go on."

"Well, I've been keeping tabs on them, especially for those sixteen of our people you listed. Today we got requests for credit information on two of the sixteen. Do you want them?"

"Yes."

"Okay. One is from a credit bureau in Kansas City. And the other is from San Francisco. The only thing different about them is the cities they're from. Normally, calls come from local Washington credit bureaus or from local banks. Kansas City and San Francisco are pretty far away."

Brewer wrote them down. "Call me when you get others.

She called him later that day. "I have three more," she said. "Shall I read them off to you?"

"Yes."

She called him with two more at the end of the day. "That's a total of seven," she said. One of them was from the Eliott Credit Bureau in Chicago.

Brewer called the Eliott manager. "Where did this request come from?" he asked.

"Let me look it up." The manager put him on hold. "Okay," he said when he came back, "same bank."

"Trans-Atlantic?"

"You got it," the manager said.

Brewer called the bureau in Kansas City.

"The request came from a bank in New York City," he was told.

"Which one?"

"Trans-Atlantic Bank and Trust."

He called San Francisco.

"The request came from Trans-Atlantic Bank and Trust," he was told.

The pattern was pretty conclusive. Gogol was shopping for information. Who in Coles's organization was having problems? Who was desperate for money? An employee with an incurably ill parent or child? A man with five children approaching college age? Who had a prison record? Who had a bad credit rating? Who was divorcing and fighting? Who was bribable? Who black-mailable? To find out, Brewer needed copies of the reports Gogol was getting. And these were flowing to him from all over the country through the Trans-Atlantic Bank and Trust in New York.

Just after five Brewer got another phone call from Coles's personnel officer. "I think you'll be interested in this one," she said. "I just received a request for information from a credit company in Fort Worth, Texas. It's on Mr. Coles himself."

Brewer wrote it down.

"Then," the personnel officer said, "right after that, I got a phone call from Dunn and Bradstreet. They're doing a financial report on the whole corporation."

Gogol was doing a full-court press.

A telefax reply from the Los Angeles bank arrived the next morning. It listed more than a dozen deposits of money into the two Bobby English accounts: Eureka High-Tech Enterprises and Condor Medical Software Company. All deposits had come from one bank: Trans-Atlantic Bank and Trust.

Brewer called Margie at Langley.

"Are we still an item?" she asked. "Are you coming back?"

"I need some information."

"Widowed," she said. "One hundred ten pounds in the bathing-suit season, thirty-four, twenty-four, thirty-five. Good cook. Very agreeable disposition. Excellent family background. Excellent credit references. And you can put your slippers under my bed anytime you say."

"I need information on a bank in New York City."

"We are all business today, are we? Do you miss me?"

"No."

"Did you know that Irish-Catholic girls from Boston make the best wives?"

"That's not what the girls in Brooklyn say."

"Ha. What's the name of the bank?"

"Trans-Atlantic Bank and Trust."

"Sounds like an excellent bank to open a joint checking account in."

"What else?"

"I'll call you back. In fact, why don't you come around tonight and we can discuss it over some hot mulled wine?"

"Call me back," Brewer said.

"Sissy."

Margie called him back an hour later. "You'd better meet me. I don't want to put this on the wire."

"Where?"

"You like the Ambassador Bar?"

"In an hour?"

"I'll be wearing a black suit and a white blouse with a string of pearls. You'll be able to identify me because I'll easily be the prettiest girl there. How will I identify you?"

"I'll be wearing a lonely face," he said.

"You're supposed to look lonely," she said. "Pale. And wan. Underweight. Pining away. Instead you look wonderful."

"You look wonderful," he said.

"That's the best you can do, Brewer? Use your imagination. You need a Cyrano de Bergerac to write some lines for you. How about, 'I'd tell you how lovely you are, except that I'm so blinded by your beauty I can't see you.' Do you kiss girls in public?"

He looked solemnly at her then touched her hand. "Soon. Soon," he said.

"Oh dear," she said, lowering her eyes. "Steady, girl. Switch the conversation to banks." She cleared her throat. "Have you seen any good banks, lately?"

"You look wonderful," he said again.

"The information you want," she said as she leaned closer to him, "is very confidential. Okay?"

"Uh-huh."

"That bank is on the Infected List."

"Oh?"

"It may be owned by fronts for Moscow."

"Why would Moscow want to have a New York bank?"

"My dear sir," she said. "Banks are tremendous sources of financial information. They can examine the deposits and checks of customers and of corporations and reconstruct the most personal and most confidential information. Imagine checks to and from governmental bodies. Payroll information. Taxes and tax exemptions. They can tell what companies are purchasing, what kind of sensitive materials and from whom and for how much. It's just the kind of information Moscow would love to have."

"Go on."

"This bank has been aggressively seeking new accounts. And I mean aggressively. It has been offering terrific deals to companies in sensitive industries—defense and high tech. It has been offering loans to them at less than prime rate, and making across-the-board deals for the personal accounts of the executives of those companies as part of the package. Suddenly, this bank is in possession of very sensitive and detailed information about important companies in key industries and their executives."

"Who are the fronts?" Brewer asked.

"Two slippery pickles. With a background of insider trading.

Hostile takeovers. A couple of all-American boys who were in trouble up to their lips. Suddenly the waters parted, and we have blue skies and sunny days. Soviet money probably did it, coming through the banking systems of Europe."

So that's how Gogol put it to Bobby English and the others. The bank fed him the information list of ready-made vulnerable targets. It was probably a credit check by the Eliott Credit Bureau in Chicago that turned up Bobby English in Gogol's net. Who would he pick this time?

"Did you call her?" Margie asked.

"No."

Limoges called Brewer.

"Got another one for you," he said.

"Who?"

"Personnel has just informed me that someone is very interested in Sauer."

"A retail credit company?"

"How did you know? It's a company in Philadelphia."

"By request of his wife," the Philadelphia office manager said. "Mrs. Margaret Sauer."

"Wife?" Brewer asked.

"Ex-wife."

"What did you find out?"

"That's confidential, sir."

"You'll send me a copy," Brewer said.

"I can't do that, sir."

"Yes, you can."

Chapter 48

Mrs. Margaret Sauer lived outside Washington, near Vienna, Virginia. It was a garden apartment complex that spread over a number of acres. Cars, kids, cats. And mounds of dirty snow with sled tracks and small footprints all over them. Brewer made a private bet that Mrs. Margaret Sauer closely resembled Maida Conyers.

When he rang the bell, a woman opened the door. "Is it spring yet?" she asked. "Christ, I hate the cold weather."

He was right. She had a raspy cigarette voice, a bloated face, and the remnant of what had once been a fine figure. Through the ruins he could see the resemblance to Maida Conyers.

"Oh," she said. "I thought you were the delivery man."

"I need a moment of your time, Mrs. Sauer," he said.

"I got more than a minute, if you want it, honey. What's on your mind?"

"It's about the credit report you ordered on your husband."

"Me? Credit? You got the wrong girl. Are you sure you want me? Margaret Sauer?"

"Somebody ordered it," Brewer said.

"Honey, the last thing I want or need is a credit report on my ex. We are quits, and I have no claim on him or his money."

"What about the alimony?" he asked.

"That's strictly voluntary on his part. I didn't ask for a penny. And I have no beef if he stops it."

"Perhaps it's one of your children."

"Beats me. None of them mentioned it to me."

"Well, thank you." Brewer stepped away.

"How is he?" she asked.

"Who?"

"My ex. What a nerd. You know what happens when someone forgives you?" She stepped back behind her door, drank
from a glass, then put her head back out again. "It destroys you.
That bastard is destroying me. Every month the check comes
like a another note of forgiveness. Wait a minute." She leaned
back in and got a smoking cigarette and an ashtray. "It's my last
one. Do you have any?"

"No."

"You know what would make me happy?"

"No."

"If that nerd would only come around here and wreck the
joint and chew me out and tell me what a bitch I am. You know
what I did to him?"

"No."

"Awful. And he never once criticized me. He'd put things
back together and we'd start off again. And I'd go do it again.
And he'd forgive me again. I diddled him in every car, every
hotel room, every doorway in Washington. And every time he
forgave me, it would make it worse. You know what made me
stop? When he stopped. When we finally broke up. You sure
you don't have any cigarettes until the delivery man comes?"

"No."

"Well, put that in your credit report. He gets credit for being
a nerd. N-E-R-D. Nerd." She shut her door.

Brewer called the credit-check company in Philadelphia.
"You told me that Mrs. Margaret Sauer ordered that character
check on her husband. Will you confirm that please? I'd also
like to know who paid for it."

The office manager had him on hold for a long time. He was
making phone calls, Brewer decided.

"Sir," the manager said at last.

"You just checked my credentials," Brewer said.

"Ah, that's right, I did. And you checked out. So I can tell
you the report on Sauer went to Mrs. Margaret Sauer."

"In Vienna, Virginia?"

"No, sir. In New York City. Care of, let's see, Trans-Atlantic Bank and Trust Company. And they're the ones who paid for
it."

*   *   *

With the persistence of a bill collector, Limoges contacted Brewer. By telephone. Always now by telephone.

"Where's the quarry?" he demanded.

"He hasn't shown his nose."

"Do you know how much pressure there is on me, Brewer?" Brewah.

"As soon as he makes his move—"

"Enough! Enough!" Limoges hung up.

Brewer went out and shot some solitary pool. He was getting no closer to locating Gogol; time was slipping by; Limoges was becoming more insistent; and his own position was becoming more vulnerable each hour. He had to find some way to get past the bank. He had to find some way to find Gogol. At last he had it. As Harry Graybill used to say, "If you want to find a mousetrap, follow a mouse."

Brewer went out and called Margie.

"Do something for me," he said.

"Yes. What?"

"Contact a credit company."

"Okay."

"I want you to tell them about my prison record."

"I don't understand."

"Once Eliott uncovers my prison record they're going to have to send a revised report with that information to Gogol. All we have to do is follow the messenger to Gogol."

"Oh. Okay. When? Now?"

"Yes. How about from a pay phone at the Ambassador Bar?"

"After work?"

"Yes. That'll be fine. There's an hour's difference between here and Chicago."

With Brewer standing beside her, Margie called the Eliott Credit Bureau in Chicago and got the office manager.

"I'm calling about the Brewer character report you did," she said.

"What about it? Who is this?"

"It isn't even half complete. You're going to end up with egg on your face."

"Who is this? I don't understand what you're talking about."

"Brewer has a prison record. And you don't mention it."

"How could he have a record? He's a secret agent of some kind."

"It's a matter of public record."

"Jesus."

"He did a term for selling arms illegally."

"How do you know this? Can you prove it?"

"Why don't you ask around Washington? It's common knowledge. Why don't you start with his old office in the State Department? There's a man there by the name of Borden. Ask him. And you might check into Brewer's record for smuggling contraband into Iran."

"Iran? Jesus."

She hung up then looked at Brewer. "Now what?"

"We wait for some action."

A messenger hunted Brewer down early in the afternoon and handed him a small envelope. "You never saw me and I never saw you and this meeting never took place."

The envelope contained an audio cassette. The first voice he heard he recognized immediately. It was the manager of the Eliott Credit Bureau in Chicago, asking for the credit-report manager of Trans-Atlantic Bank and Trust in New York.

"I'm calling about that report we filed the other day," the Eliott manager said. "The one on Charles Brewer."

"What about it?" The credit-report manager was a woman with an abrupt manner.

"It's incomplete. We have come upon new and very sensitive information about the subject."

"Like what?"

"He had a prison record."

"I see."

"He also smuggled arms into Iran."

"I see."

"There's a lot more," the bank manager said. "The whole

thing was covered up and Brewer was pardoned, but I think your client would want to know all this."

"Yes. I'm sure you're right."

"I'll send it for overnight delivery."

"Better wait until I check. I'll call you back."

Later she did call him back. "I have conferred with certain people here. It has been decided that you should have a special courier carry the new information to Dulles Airport in Washington, where he will be met."

Brewer waited with Sauer at the airport for the courier to arrive from Chicago. A small group of people waited for passengers from that Chicago flight. One of them held a small handwritten cardboard sign. ELIOTT.

When the passengers debarked, the delivery was quickly made. The courier handed a small envelope to the contact, received a signed receipt, and then watched the contact throw the Eliott sign in a trash can and hurry toward the escalators.

By prearrangement Sauer followed the contact and Brewer followed Sauer. They were watching for a handoff.

The contact drove straight back toward the city, traveling fast, weaving in and out of traffic. It was difficult for Sauer to follow him without using the same highly visible maneuvering. Instead Sauer laid back more than a quarter of a mile. He was in danger of losing the contact in traffic.

The contact drove directly from Dulles to Georgetown, and there on M Street made the switch. Sauer was seven cars behind the contact's car and pinned in the two-way traffic when the contact opened his window and extended his arm. A car passing from the opposite direction paused with his window open. The contact extended the envelope to him. Sauer watched the second car speed away right past him.

Brewer, farther back, was ready. He watched the second car turn at the intersection and head north. He turned against the light. There was the squealing of brakes and horns blowing as Brewer got through the intersection and hurried off after the second car.

The second car made a series of turns, crossed the Francis

Scott Key bridge, and hurried back to the Beltway, traveling
clockwise north. He drove fast, like the other driver, then
abruptly dashed down an exit ramp. Brewer lost him, and at the
bottom of the exit ramp paused to scan the streets for the car.
His sense told him the car had not gone far. He continued to the
right and slowly drove past several motels, some gas stations,
and a large restaurant. He cruised by slowly, looking at cars.

Then, in his rearview mirror, he saw it. The car was emerging from a motel driveway. As Brewer made his U-turn, he saw
the car go back up the ramp onto the Beltway.

Brewer drove to the motel and turned in. It was a U-shaped
motel complex, two stories with a balcony around the entire perimeter. The center was filled with cars.

Was Gogol in there somewhere?

"Shit," Brewer said. He went into the registration office and
took a room.

"Four more inches tonight," the deskman said when he gave
Brewer his key. "It's the second Ice Age."

The motel was a hive.

Airport limousines and cars and taxis came and went. Dry-
cleaners trucks, laundries, liquor vans, pizza trucks. Through an
archway in the back was a health club with a swimming pool and
a sauna.

As Brewer watched, he gradually got the rooms sorted out.
He drew a diagram of both floors of the motel on several sheets
of paper. Watching through the blinds, he studied the occupants
of each room. He drew an X through each room on his diagram
that clearly didn't have Gogol in it.

Sauer arrived with Conyers a few hours later and they ordered a pizza and watched the busy motel.

"I'm in the wrong business," Maida Conyers said. "I've seen
that blonde go into three different rooms in the last hour and a
half."

"Those three rooms back there," Sauer said. "I don't think
they're occupied. And these two rooms were just rented to typ-
ical lobby types." He drew X's through the five rooms. "That
still leaves these nine rooms." He looked at Gogol's photo-

graphs. "If he's here, he's not showing himself. Which room you think he's in?" he asked Brewer.

Brewer shrugged. "I just hope he's in one of them."

When Conyers and Sauer left, Brewer sat in the darkened room with the blinds parted, holding a pair of binoculars in his lap. Two more X's had been drawn in his floor plan. That left seven rooms to check out.

In the evening the tempo changed. Not as many new registrants, more call girls, more liquor and pizza deliveries—and a noticeable amount of drug traffic. Young men in sneakers and short zippered jackets, knuckling doors, slipping small envelopes inside, counting the cash that came back out and slipping it inside their jackets. Then a quick dash of the car back into the night.

At seven snow began.

By nine o'clock Brewer had eliminated three more rooms. He drew X's in the appropriate squares. Four to go.

One of the four rooms was eliminated forty-five minutes later. A man and a woman emerged and drove off. Three to go.

Brewer felt his eyes grow heavy, and washed his face in cold water. In the back of his mind was a nagging thought: he was on a wild-goose chase. Gogol wasn't here.

There was some brief activity just before eleven when an airport limousine arrived and the passengers registered then took their rooms. All the rooms in the motel were now occupied. Three of them were still in the unidentified column. If Gogol wasn't in one of the three, Brewer had wasted his time—and lost his quarry.

He must have dozed. He raised his head and looked at his watch. It was quarter after one in the morning. There were several inches of new snow on the ground, and it was snowing thickly. He saw a figure on the second-floor balcony across from him walking toward the stairs. When he got to the head of the stairs, Brewer saw that it was a man, but it was too dark to see his face. The man looked down then raised his head and looked out at the quadrangle into a light.

It was Emil Gogol.

Chapter 49

One night, late, Brewer heard his front door open. He rolled off the bed and onto the floor, reaching under the mattress for his pistol. Then he crawled to the bedroom door and, lying prone, took aim at the front doorway.

A woman stood there, backlit by the hallway light, pulling a key from the door lock. Brewer stood up and turned on the light.

Margie held out an envelope. "Came for you today. I wasn't going to bring it, but I felt so guilty, I couldn't sleep."

Brewer opened it. "I'm invited to a wedding," he said.

"You never called her," she said.

"No. Never did."

"So I don't feel like a poacher anymore."

"You never were."

"Do you miss me?"

"Yes," he said.

She kissed him. "Your kisses still have sadness in them, Charlie."

"Sorry about that."

"Still haven't gotten past prison?"

He shook his head. "No. Still haven't gotten back to the good guys versus the bad guys."

"Nothing's changed," she said.

He looked thoughtfully at her. "Yes, it has. Now I think it's the bad guys versus the bad guys."

She sighed. "Oh, Charlie," she said sadly. "Remember that quotation you told me from Archimedes? Give me a place to stand, and I can move the world. Okay. Let me give you a place to stand. Next to me."

He gazed at her hesitantly.

"Since you won't join me, Charlie, I'm joining you. I even brought my evening attire." She held up a toothbrush. "Entirely in blue." She put her arms around him. "I claim this land for Margie."

"It's not that easy," he said. "I'm still a walking shooting gallery. That could have been anyone coming through that door."

"It's not easy," she replied. "But it is simple."

"After this case is over."

"I can't live that way," Margie said. "There'll always be a case. Everytime a car misfires, you'll send me away until the case is over. I'm all grown-up. I can make my own decisions. And I told you what it is. No promises. No strings. It's now or never for us."

He touched her cheek with his fingers. If he hadn't come to Limoges with that plan, Gogol would be dead and he'd be out of this. Instead— He thought of Margie under a police blanket in the park. For the first time he told himself the truth about himself: the game was the most important thing. It wasn't fun anymore, but it was still the important thing. He was endangering her for the sake of the game. He hadn't changed. He would never change. Could never change.

"You have to decide, Charlie. It has to be here and it has to be now. If I leave, I won't be back. Okay? It's your move."

He sat down, scowling at her.

She watched him then nodded. "I understand." She turned and left the apartment.

Brewer sat, staring at the door. Then he stood and hurried after her. At the bottom of the stairs he took her hand.

"Okay," he said.

Chapter 50

Gogol called Sauer that night.

"How did you make out?"

"I got it. 'Kay? Just like you said

"I told you."

"Someone ought to be shot," Sauer said.

"Where did you find it?"

"I was in the mainframe room, next to the control room. Standing by a panel door. 'Kay?"

"Yes. Go on."

"And the panel door to the memory storage unit is open. And there on the inside of the door someone has put these strips of masking tape, and on them he's written the entire access code, including the challenges and responses."

"It's always the way," Gogol said. It was just as he had seen it so many times before—access-code numbers inside a shoe, on the bottom of a wooden chair, scratched on the back of a wristwatch. "So tell me. What is the access code?"

Sauer hesitated. "Listen. I don't know whether I'm ready for this. See what I'm saying?"

"No."

"This is my Rubicon. Once I cross the river, there's no road back. The die is cast."

"Your Rubicon has already been crossed for you, Sauer. There hasn't been a road back for a long time. You're a ruined man, a victim of office politics and the ambitions of losers. It's the same the world over, Sauer. The unbelievable number of incompetents who have pushed past others and wiggled into high places. Why should you pay for that? Why should you end your days in a back room somewhere, waiting for a pittance of a pension check while these others parade themselves with your feathers?"

"Maybe that's true but—"

"Sauer. You might not get an opportunity like this for the rest of your life."

Sauer hesitated. "It's so damned final."

"What's final, Sauer, is poverty. Being alone and sick and penniless . . . dependent on indifferent clerks in some public program to feed you and care for you. That's what's final. No no, Sauer. If you want to live well and enjoy the rewards of your labors, you have to take them yourself. Reach out and seize it before it flies away."

"Yeah," Sauer said doubtfully.

"Listen, Sauer. You know I can get that number myself. told you where to look for it. So what's the big deal? If I get it, you'll miss your payday. For no reason. You are just saving me some time and effort. And losing a fortune."

He could hear Sauer breathing.

"I ask you, Sauer—if not you, then who? And if not now then when?"

Sauer sighed. Then he said softly the first digit of the number. Then the next. Then a pause.

"Go on, Sauer," Gogol said. "I can hear you."

"Shit," Sauer said.

"Go on. You're almost done."

Sauer murmured another number, then another. Then he read off the challenges and responses. He'd crossed his Rubicon.

"Shit," he said.

Gogol was able to buy all the computer equipment he needed unobtrusively, a piece at a time, from a variety of local computer-supply firms.

Once he connected it all together in his motel room, he set the correct modem configurations. He was ready to dial Coles's computer.

"Don't fail me," he murmured as he dialed the number.

There was a pause, then the computer responded. It asked

for an identity number. Gogol copied it from the sheet of paper. The computer issued a challenge.

Gogol wrote the word Cadiz.

The computer issued the second challenge.

Gogol wrote the word Babble.

The computer issued a third challenge.

Gogol wrote the word Three. Instantly he found himself in the very heart of the computer. In minutes he was scanning columns of test data and recording it on magnetic tape. Then he dialed a number in New York and pumped out his magnetic tape into a computer in New York. A short time later the first of the test data was being transmitted to Moscow. Hour after hour Coles's computer was receiving test responses from mainframe terminals all over the country. It was a simulated Star Wars network.

Late that night Revin called him. There was a tremor of excitement in his voice.

"Our clients are very pleased with the sample you have sent them," he said. "Evidently the product you drew your sample from is much more advanced than they thought. I would even say"—Revin hesitated, then spoke in a lower voice—"they're stunned."

It was the confirmation Gogol had been waiting for. One more step and he could issue his list of heads for the chopping block—the clients. The entire committee. The bone in his throat. He could hear the sharpening of the ax already.

"I have a message from the clients," Revin said. "They want to know when they will get the product itself."

Just one more step. Gogol found the phrase running through his mind over and over. Don't try to rush it, he told himself. Patience. Everything has its own tempo. At night, when he could stand the pacing in his room no longer, he took long walks through the streets. The mantle of snow was like a thick block of dirty-gray ice, smoothed over periodically with another whitewash coating of clean flakes.

Washington was weary of shivering, weary of shoveling, weary of waiting for spring. Yet every few days winter sent another dismaying few inches of white.

He walked sometimes for hours, walked until his mind stopped racing, until his body was tired enough to let him sleep. And as he walked he went over his plan again and again. He rehearsed the next conversation with Sauer again and again. For this would be the most critical conversation of all. He had to maneuver Sauer into stealing Cassandra itself.

Gogol had become addicted to pizzas. He had watched the little pizza delivery truck arrive at all hours, had gotten a whiff of the odor of the pie and, idly, curiously, one night dialed the telephone number on the truck panel and ordered his first pizza. He quickly became a regular customer.

On Sunday evening at dusk he took a long walk, and when he came back, he decided that this was the night he would call Sauer. This was the night he would proposition him. This was the night he would sign Sauer up to steal Cassandra and bring it to him. If he were successful, he promised himself a gift—a pizza with double pepperoni and mushrooms and cheese. And a six-pack of cola. He picked up the phone.

"Ah!" he said to Sauer. "Did you receive the notice from your new banker in Switzerland?"

"Yes," Sauer said. "I did."

"You're a rich man," Gogol said. "A quarter of a million dollars rich. How do you feel?"

"First rate," Sauer said.

"I sent you a little package. Did you receive it?"

"About fifteen minutes ago. Very generous of you."

"Not at all. You deserve much more. Disgraceful the way you have been treated. Frankly, I feel that the quarter of a million is hardly enough compensation. You should be much richer than that."

"Ha," Sauer said. "Sounds like another proposition coming up."

"Seriously, Sauer," Gogol said. "I'd like to see you really well fixed, and I have an idea."

"What's that?"

"It's a half a million dollar deal, on top of what you already have."

"Half a million?"

"You'll be set for life."

"What's the half million for?"

"Steal Cassandra."

Sauer hung up.

Gogol promised himself he would augment the double pizza with vodka if he could sell Sauer. He waited an hour and dialed his number again.

"It's nothing to scoff at," he said. "You may never see another opportunity like this for the rest of your life. Think about it, Sauer. To go with your quarter million, a half million when you bring it out."

"Stop. I don't want to hear any more. If you want it, you go get it."

"I want you to get it, Sauer."

"Don't be ridiculous."

"It should be easy. You told me yourself that Brewer is expecting me to steal the fake. While he waits, you can steal the real thing."

"Impossible. It's booby-trapped."

Gogol hesitated. "Booby-trapped," he said. "How interesting. How good of you to tell me. But you see, since you know that, it ought to be easy for you."

"Nothing is easy for me. 'Kay?"

"Getting the access number was easy—after I showed you how. Suppose I showed you a way to get Cassandra that is absolutely safe, Sauer. No risk at all."

"If there's no risk, why don't you go get it and save the half million?"

"Because you have clearance to be near it and I don't."

"It's still too risky."

"Not if it's done right. Steal a page from Vienna."

"What does that mean?"

"You remember how that equipment was stolen in Vienna, Sauer. It was a shell game. It was all gone long before anyone knew that it was stolen. You can do the same thing."

"No thanks. 'Kay? I have to go to sleep now."

"Yes. That's a good idea, Sauer. Sleep on it."

*   *   *

Gogol had never known such tension before, had never wanted to succeed so badly before, never before feared failure so much. Sauer, loaded with drugs, could collapse. He might turn himself in. Might be a setup. Gogol's own motel phone number might have been traced.

A tap on the door could come at any moment.

Gogol called Sauer an hour later. There was no answer. He waited another hour and tried again. There was no answer. It turned out to be the longest night in Gogol's life.

After six hours of calling Sauer, the suspense and tension had become so great, Gogol decided to leave the premises. To flee to Europe. But his eagerness for revenge in Moscow, his fear of losing face in Moscow, his pride, his thirst for power, his love of money, his great need for adulation, all forced him to stay and brave it out.

It was a nightmare. He packed his bags and put them in the car. He decided that if he didn't get Sauer by four A.M., he would move to another motel. He watched his parking lot for U.S. agents. He watched people come and go in the motel complex. The ladies came and went in their cabs. Young men in sneakers and zippered jackets tapped on doors, passed small white envelopes, and hurried away counting money. At three A.M. pizza trucks were as busy as ever.

At four A.M., with his bags at the door, it was time to go. He decided to try Sauer once more.

"Hullo," Sauer said.

Gogol suppressed an audible sigh. "I've been trying to get you."

"And I've been trying to get some stuff. I'm all out."

"Did you get any?"

"Some. Not much."

"You can't make it without money, Sauer."

"I know, I know. You don't need to tell me."

"Well?"

"Send me a package."

"Tell me your answer first."

"Shit," Sauer said.

Gogol waited.

"Shit," Sauer said. "I mean, man, this is the worst. You see what I'm saying? I'm really not up to this. See what I'm saying?"

"Are you up to the rest of your life the way things now stand?"

"No. I don't want to be sick and old and broke."

"Who does, Sauer? You simply have to put yourself first. I must tell you. If you don't do this, someone else will. And that means that someone else will get the half million."

"Okay," Sauer said. "I'll do it."

"Marvelous."

"For one million dollars."

"A million? One million dollars?"

"Yes."

"Agreed."

"You said it would be easy and safe."

"Guaranteed, Sauer. Guaranteed."

"Send me a package. And hurry."

Gogol hung up his phone. For the first time in his life his hands were trembling.

Gogol ordered his pizza with pepperoni and a bottle of vodka. He had a solitary celebration, eating the pizza, swilling the vodka from the bottle, and crooning softly several Russian lullabies.

He woke in the morning with the sun on his face. His mouth was dry and he had a faint headache. But he woke happy for the first time in a long time. Later he drove to Mobius Laboratories and, for several hours, studied the building and its operations with care. He saw exactly how to get Cassandra out of the building.

Sauer decided to make himself a Bloody Mary for breakfast. He was sitting in the cafeteria waiting for Brewer to arrive. When the waiter brought him a large tomato juice, he poured a stiff shot from his hip flask and stirred it with a knife.

"To all the sunshine in the Riviera," he said softly to himself, and took a long pull on the tomato juice. He signaled the waiter to bring him another.

He'd just managed to pour a shot into the second tomato juice when he saw Brewer come swinging through the front door. And Brewer had no more than seated himself when here came Limoges. He walked along the line of booths aided by a cane and stood before their table.

Limoges asked, "Has Gogol offered you a bribe, Brewer?"

"No. Not yet."

"Has he tried to blackmail you?"

"No."

"Have you found out where he is?"

"No."

"Has Gogol made any sort of a move?"

"No."

"Contacted you in any way?"

"No."

"And he isn't going to." Limoges rapped a knuckle on the table. "We've waited too long. He's made his move elsewhere."

"He'll make his move soon enough," Brewer said.

"No. We're through. I'm scrubbing this operation."

"When?"

"Now."

"Give me five more days."

Limoges hesitated.

"Three more days," Brewer said.

"I'll give you until tomorrow morning. That's it."

"Two days."

"Tomorrow morning the test ends," Limoges said. "We'll put the unit back in the vault and lock it away until I take care of Gogol." He looked pointedly at Brewer. "In the manner I originally planned. And that's it. Tomorrow morning. You've taken too many risks."

Limoges turned and walked away. "That's it," he said over his shoulder.

Sauer drained his glass of spiked tomato juice.

As arranged, Gogol called Sauer at six that evening.

Sauer was not happy. "If you want it, you have to make your move tonight. The test ends in the morning and they're putting Cassandra in a vault."

"Don't panic, Sauer."

"But we can't get it. Once they take the real brain out of the mainframe and store it, you'll never get at it."

"Yes we can."

"It's rigged."

"That's okay," Gogol said. "Listen to me. All you need is an empty carrying case. There must be plenty around there."

"So what?"

"It's Vienna all over again."

"Huh. Don't remind me."

"It's the same shell game. Switch the two Cassandras."

"You mean take the real one out of the mainframe and put the fake in its place?"

"Yes."

"But the fake won't work."

"Oh, yes it will, my friend. You can be sure that it will do almost everything the real one will do. Almost."

"Then what?"

Was Sauer that dense? Gogol wondered. "Then take the Cassandra you got from the mainframe and put it in another carrying case. And leave the empty Cassandra case standing in the vault. Okay so far?"

"Yes."

"Now, you have the fake Cassandra in the mainframe. In the vault you have an empty Cassandra carrying case that's supposed to hold the fake. Right?"

"Okay."

"And you have the real Cassandra in another case with some kind of false identification label on it. Is that not so?"

"Yes."

"Put it in a cardboard carton."

"But I can't walk out of the building with that. They check everything."

"Someone else will carry it out for you."

"Who? What do you mean?"

"Put it in the trash."

"Trash!"

"That's right. The maintenance crew will carry it out of the building for you and throw it in the trash bin."

"Oh, I see . . ."

"Of course you see, Sauer. All you have to do is go back later to the trash bin and retrieve it. Understand?"

"Yes."

"It's absolutely safe, Sauer. You see that, don't you?"

"I guess so."

"It's the easiest million you'll ever make."

"Then what?"

"The rest is as easy as shit through a goose, Sauer. Take it to Dulles Airport and drop it off. I will tell you more about that later."

"When do you want to do it?"

"Tonight," Gogol said. "You said we have to do it tonight."

"Okay. Tonight."

"Now there is just one more matter we have to discuss, Sauer. There must be no slipup. Understand?"

"There won't be."

"I'm not sure you understand. I am delighted to pay you one million dollars into your Swiss bank account. I am delighted that you will be comfortably fixed. But I must warn you, there must be no slipup tonight. I must be absolutely sure that I receive the real Cassandra. Not the fake. The real thing."

"Why would I want to give you a fake? We have a deal."

"I will tell you why you don't want to give me a fake, Sauer. Because if you do, I will first of all expose you and ruin you. And secondly, my clients will personally take vengeance on you and your family. No one will be spared. Your entire family, Sauer. Down to the third generation. Do you understand?"

"Yes."

"Are you sure you understand? If you give me a fake, we will soon enough discover it, and we will find you. You cannot hide from us anywhere. I believe you know how true that is. No place to hide."

"Take it easy," Sauer said. "I want to walk away from this as clean as possible. If I give you a fake, I'm going to have to spend the rest of my life looking over my shoulder. Living on the run. And I don't want my family hurt. See what I'm saying? I'm no fool. I know who I'm dealing with. You'll get the real Cassandra. Don't worry. 'Kay?"

"'Kay," Gogol said.

●●● Chapter 51

Gogol called his contact at the Washington office of the Soviet airline, Aeroflot.

"I will have a package tonight," he said. "It's very important."

"I understand," the contact said.

"You must hold the flight for it, no matter how late it is," Gogol said.

"I understand," the contact said. "Those are my orders."

At ten o'clock Gogol drove to Sauer's apartment and waited in his car. A few minutes later Sauer emerged from his apartment and drove off. His course was obvious and he was easy to follow; he drove directly to Mobius Laboratories. But his driving was erratic.

"The whole world holds its breath," Gogol said to himself, "as we watch History ride on the back of a staggering, over-dosed drunken, drug addict."

Gogol parked on the incline of the service road behind the laboratories and with binoculars watched Sauer moving inside. A night staff was working with a test model of a computerized railroad, and Gogol could see small H.O.-gauge trains running through complicated patterns of trackage as the engineers watched their consoles. They were completely absorbed in their project.

In another room the cleaning staff was at work. Gogol looked at his watch. It was twenty-nine minutes after ten. Abruptly it began to snow.

Sauer's job was quickly done. He entered the vault and a few moments later emerged with a black case which he carried into the computer room. He opened several panels in the mainframe, removed Cassandra, and replaced it with the fake Cassandra.

He placed the real Cassandra in the carrying case and carried it to the shipping room. There he placed it in a shipping carton and taped it shut. He wrote TRASH in large letters on the carton with a felt pen then carried it to a trash barrel and pitched the carton into it.

His work was done. It was, as Gogol had said, the easiest million Sauer would ever earn.

Sauer went back through the security check point at the main entrance, where he opened his attaché case for the guard. He got into his car and drove off.

Gogol waited anxiously. The snow, fine-grained and wind-driven, was accumulating quickly, and soon it could shut down Dulles Airport. He watched two cleaning crews progress from office to office, dusting, vacuuming, and emptying trash. To the impatient Gogol they seemed to move like men underwater.

"Come come," he said. "Hurry it up." The snow seemed to be thicker than ever.

The largest quantities of trash came from the shredding machines. These were dumped into wheeled trash carts, along with all the other debris of the offices and laboratories. As the cleaning crews went from office to office, they pushed the rapidly filling trash carts ahead of them. The two crews were converging on the loading platforms at the rear of the buildings.

Eventually they worked their way to the railroad-model room, where the engineers waved them off. The two cleaning crews then went to the last room, where Cassandra was, and put on all the lights. They stopped for coffee.

Gogol groaned. If anything, it seemed to be snowing harder. He sighed impatiently.

It was after eleven before the cleaning people resumed their cleaning. They dusted the furniture and cleaned the glass partitions. Then they vacuumed the floors. And they emptied the wastebaskets and the shredding machines. Two of them picked up the trash barrel containing Cassandra and dumped it into the trash cart. Another crew dumped the contents of a shredding machine on top of that. The cleaning crews now had four trash carts filled, and they wheeled them out on the loading platform.

They stood looking at the snow fall. Then they went back into the offices, leaving the trash carts on the loading platform, to clean the rest rooms.

The last job they did before they finished for the night was wheeling all the trash units to the huge metal trash bin. They pushed the units up a ramp and tipped them over to spill the contents into the large metal bin. Then they closed the metal flaps on the bin and wheeled the units back inside. Their work was done.

Gogol watched them through the binoculars as they went through the security check and out on the parking lot. They chatted briefly, turned away from the driving fine-grained snow, swept the snow off their windshields, and drove off. It was eleven forty-five.

Out on the highway Gogol could see the flashing yellow lights of a salt truck, sowing the main road. The snow was getting deeper by the minute.

Gogol waited for Sauer to return. He waited until twelve-fifteen. Sauer was ominously late. Gogol drove off, looking for a pay phone. He found one in a gas station and dialed Sauer's phone. There was no answer. Gogol wondered if it were possible to go instantly mad from suspense and frustration. He drove back to the laboratories. Still no Sauer.

He waited until quarter to one. Then, in a rage, he drove off, through more than three inches of new snow, following the route back to Sauer's apartment. There was not much time left; the airport would close down soon.

The interchange ramps of the highways were treacherous, and he skidded down them. When he got to Sauer's apartment, he saw Sauer's car still parked at the curb. He went to a pay phone and called. There was no answer. He drove back to Sauer's apartment and sat looking up at the lighted windows. If Sauer wasn't in there, where was he? And if he was in there, why didn't he answer his phone?

Gogol studied the street—the parked cars and the doorways. This was the first time he had ever been confronted with this problem. The greatest coup of his career was stuffed into a trash bin waiting to be picked up and carried to Dulles Airport by an out-of-control addicted weakling who was—where?

Gogol pulled out the key to Sauer's apartment and considered it. He could either go into Sauer's apartment, find out what had happened to him, and try to push him into completing the job. Or he could himself return to the trash bin, retrieve the case, and carry it to the airport.

Confronting Sauer meant revealing himself. Sauer would see his face, be able to identify him. But retrieving the package from Coles's trash bin meant exposing himself to a possible trap.

Gogol considered both alternatives for a few moments. Then he acted.

For the first time in his career Gogol departed from his iron-clad plan; for the first time he broke his rule of always concealing himself, always making others take the risk. He got out of the car and walked to Sauer's door. He let himself in with the key and mounted the stairs to Sauer's apartment.

He listened, then tapped on the door. He tapped again. Reluctantly, he pushed the key into the lock and turned it. The door swung open.

There was a lamp lying on its side on the floor, and beyond it lay Sauer. Scattered around him on the floor were his pills. Gogol stepped over to him and crouched. Sauer snored. The odor of alcohol was heavy. The man was drunk and high on pills both. He was going to be useless for hours. Gogol looked at Sauer indecisively.

The fine grains of snow tapped on a window: hurry hurry. He was running out of time. Gogol stood, hurried out of the apartment and into the street. He got into his car and drove back through the deepening snow toward Mobius Laboratories.

He was down to two options. He could either run the risk of walking into a trap by trying to recover the carton, or he could get on the Aeroflot flight to Russia empty-handed.

He knew he couldn't go to Russia without the unit. He knew he couldn't try to regroup, find another Sauer, and steal another unit. In a day or so the theft would be discovered and he wouldn't get such a golden opportunity again, wouldn't easily find another Sauer again. It was simply now or never.

*   *   *

For the first time Gogol was exposing himself to the danger of capture. This time there was no telephone to hide behind, no one to be blackmailed or bribed into doing the risky work. Gogol himself had to step forward and do the job. His mouth was dry and his hands shook. For the first time in his life he really knew how a relief pitcher felt with the bases loaded in the ninth and no one out. For the first time he was betting everything on one pitch. On one roll of the dice.

He drove back up on the service road behind the Mobius Laboratories. The tracks of the trash carts that led along the ramp to the trash bin were half filled in. The train-model crew was long gone. The security guards sat at the desk in the lobby reading and looking out at the falling snow. The grains tapping on the roof of his car were like the tickings of many clocks. It might already be too late.

He decided not to touch it. Too dangerous. If he were stopped, his career was over. He would spend years in an American prison. The committee would be overjoyed. Nothing—not even Cassandra—was worth that. He started his car and drove away.

A mile from Mobius Laboratories he stopped his car. He told himself he had to do it. Now. He would not get another opportunity like this. If he ran off and left Cassandra, everyone in Moscow—that cursed committee—would rejoice. His legendary reputation will be tarnished.

"See?" they would say. "Just like his father. A flash, for a moment a diamond, then nothing but glass." His enemies would be quick to crow. He told himself that for once he had to risk it. Had to take a chance. Had to pitch the ball. Gogol turned his car around.

He drove back down the service road and parked. With binoculars he searched all along the perimeter of the site, examining every likely place to hide a surveillance team, to conceal a car or a truck that might be waiting to pounce on him. Then he checked again. He watched one of the security guards making his hourly rounds through the offices. He could find no one lurking anywhere. He sat, unable to leave, unable to go to the trash bin. Then he turned on his engine again.

He drove down the service road and into the rear parking area. With his headlights out he drove diagonally across the area to the trash bin. He got out of the car, and, trying to avoid any sound, opened a top panel and reached into the mounds of shredded paper. He didn't feel the carton. He climbed up on the ramp and groped the full length of his arm. He still found nothing. He stepped into the trash bin and was hip deep in paper and coffee cartons. He tramped up and down trying to feel the carton with his foot.

Then he found it. He crouched and with two hands lifted it, along with great mounds of shredded paper and trash.

Gogol clambered out of the trash bin, carefully, quietly closed the metal flap, and carried the carton to his car. In spite of the biting cold, he was soaked with perspiration.

He drove off in a wide circle around the laboratory buildings and slipped and slid up the access ramp to the main highway. He drove toward Dulles Airport.

Ahead were several snowplows, hulking yellow dump trucks with flashing yellow lights, skiving the snow to one side in great waves. There were few cars on the road, and none following him. He glanced at the carton on the seat next to him. The word TRASH was block printed on it in several places in Sauer's handwriting. He reached out and touched the carton. One of the great intelligence coups of all times was inside there. Was he going to get away with this? Could it all end up being this easy? When he was airborne on the Aeroflot jet, he would believe it.

He felt the snow fighting his tires as he drove. Now he was only a few miles from Dulles. Were the runways still open? He peered through the beating windshield wipers as though trying to see all the way to the airport.

Soon the lights of the Dulles terminal building loomed up as bright smudges in the driving snow. Something had to go wrong. What was waiting for him at the terminal?

He promised himself that if he succeeded in getting Cassandra to Moscow, he would retire.

When he got to the airport parking lot, he drove up and down the aisles looking for the embassy limousine. All the vehicles were covered with snow. Then off in the corner he saw it. His embassy contact got out and signaled him.

"Here," he said to Gogol. "Everything is ready."

Gogol passed the carton to him in the limousine. The contact and another man quickly wrapped the carton and placed the seals and stamps on it. "It's done," the contact said. "This is legally part of the diplomatic pouch. See you on the plane." He handed Gogol an envelope containing his passport and other documents. "This will get you through passport control. Hurry. They'll close the runways any minute. Go."

Gogol parked the car and sat for a moment. It was over. Cassandra was beyond reach of U.S. authorities now. He was beyond arrest. In minutes he would be airborne. He hurried into the terminal.

A short time later the Aeroflot flight left in great haste, the last plane to take off before the control tower shut down the airport due to the heavy snowfall.

Gogol waited until the jet completed its climb and leveled off on its flight to Russia. At last he could relax. With Cassandra in his lap and the nose of the jet aimed at Moscow, he hugged himself with joy. He'd done it. He'd pulled off the intelligence coup of the century. Slowly, mouthing each name with gusto, counting each on his fingers, he began to call the roll of the heads he would demand.

Limoges was the first to arrive at Dulles. "Are you sure?" he demanded, shaking with rage. "It got off the ground?"

"Gone," the man from State said. "It was the last plane to take off before they closed the flight lines."

Limoges turned to the military attaché. "Can we shoot it down?"

"That would be an act of war."

"How about forcing it to land?"

"You're going to have to go to the highest authority for a move like that."

"Well, look who's here," Limoges said.

Brewer came through the entry doors and stepped on the escalator.

"He's gone, Brewer!" Limoges said in a low voice. "He beat you! And we've lost Cassandra!"

"What do you mean?"

"You're too late. The Aeroflot flight took off with Cassandra on board."

"Did it?" Brewer asked.

"What do you mean—did it?" Limoges demanded. "Didn't I just tell you that it did? Sauer put the real one in the trash bin. And Gogol picked it up, and he's flying to Russia with it right now."

"Gogol was conned by his own Viennese shell game," Brewer said. He nodded at Limoges's disbelieving face. "We switched cartons in the trash bin."

Out on the flight line Sauer stood in the blinding snow. He took a dollar bill from his pocket and held it up fluttering in the breeze.

"*Cpaceeba,* you Russian son of a bitch's bastard," he said. *"Cpaceeba."*

Then he let the dollar bill go. Carried by the wind, it blew eastward toward Russia and quickly disappeared in the darkness.